SCENT OF A
KILLER

Also by CHRISTIANE HEGGAN

DEADLY INTENT
MOMENT OF TRUTH
BLIND FAITH
ENEMY WITHIN
TRUST NO ONE
SUSPICION
DECEPTION

CHRISTIANE HEGGAN

SCENT OF A KILLER

MIRA®

ISBN 0-7394-4021-7

SCENT OF A KILLER

Printed in U.S.A.

This book is lovingly dedicated to
Zak, king of the basketball court,
Alek, king of the ice,
and Jeffery, our little king in training

One

In Times Square, where he lived and worked, Pincho Figueras was known as the Brazilian owner of Insomnia, a gourmet coffee shop that provided commuters with some of the best brew in town. To a chosen few, whose names he didn't want to know, he was simply Kravitz. He wasn't sure why he had chosen that alias. He didn't know anyone named Kravitz, and he certainly had no ethnic connection to the name. He just liked the sound of it.

Pincho Figueras was a professional killer. One of the best. In the past ten years, he had accumulated enough money to buy a villa in the south of France, sleep with any woman he wanted and eat in the best restaurants in the world. Not bad for a kid who grew up in the slums of Rio de Janeiro, wondering if he'd ever be anything but a two-bit pickpocket.

Salvation had arrived in the form of a smooth-talking *Norte Americano,* a New Yorker with a booming voice and a pocket full of cash. Through the grapevine, Big Al, as he liked to be called, had learned about Pincho's fast hands and even faster legs. When Big Al offered him five hundred American dollars for stealing a briefcase from a Bolivian salesman, Pincho thought he was dreaming. With that kind of money, he could finally have a place of his own, away from his abusive father and the rest of his miserable family. He might even be able to move to the United States, something he had dreamed of doing all his life.

The job, simple enough, took an unexpected turn. The Bolivian was asleep in his hotel room when Pincho let himself in. As he was about to steal the briefcase, the sleeping man woke up. Frozen in place, Pincho watched him reach under his pillow and pull out a .357 Magnum. Pincho only had a split second to react. And react he did. With remarkable sangfroid and a dexterity he had perfected since the age of nine, he took his knife out of his pants' back pocket, aimed and let it go.

The blade sank into the man's chest, puncturing his heart. He was dead before Pincho reached the door.

Far from being upset by this unexpected development, Big Al complimented his new young friend on his quick thinking and offered him a new assignment—the elimination of another salesman. It didn't take long for Pincho to realize that Big Al was the middleman between a powerful South American cartel and drug lords in the United States, and that the "salesmen" Al ordered killed were competitors who diluted his profits.

Pincho loved his part-time job. Not only because of the money, but because Al respected and appreciated him. At the coffee factory where Pincho worked, he was just another low-paid slob on the assembly line. He deserved more than that. He was gutsy, he was smart and above all, he was creative. He loved tricking the cops, planting clues that led nowhere and watching those morons scratch their heads as they tried to figure out what the hell was going on.

In time, Pincho became proficient in all kinds of weaponry—handguns, knives, ice picks, garottes. He also studied the effects of various poisons and learned how to build bombs. Whatever the situation called for, Pincho had an appropriate scenario and the guts to carry out the assignment to its successful completion. And better yet, he never got caught.

By the time he reached his twenty-first birthday three years later, his little sideline had made him a rich man—at least by Brazilian standards. Aware there was even more money to be made in the United States, where drug traffic had become big business, he applied for an immigrant visa. Three months later, he left his job at the coffee factory and bought himself a one-way ticket to New York.

From the moment Pincho set foot on American soil, he fell in love with the city New Yorkers called the Big Apple. He liked the noise, the crowds, the energy, the bright lights that reminded him of Rio. Unlike Rio, however, there was plenty of work for anyone who wanted it. The problem was, Pincho needed a job where he could come and go as he pleased, and where no one asked any questions. Using the money he had made working for Big Al and what he had learned working at the coffee factory, he opened a coffee shop in Times Square.

Insomnia was an instant success. And thanks to a

referral from his former boss, it wasn't long until the word got around that Kravitz was available for "specialized work."

He was now twenty-nine, spoke English like a native and had elevated his craft to an art form. He wasn't just a killer for hire. He was a thinker who, when necessary, provided the cops with a fall guy—as he was about to do now. The limp, the smeared dirt on his face, the stinky clothes, all were part of tonight's act. Underneath, he was a handsome, clean-cut young man with light brown eyes and a smile that made the ladies cream their panties.

With his money, he could have lived anywhere, but there was the IRS to think of. Sure he would have liked a swanky apartment on the Upper East Side. And a chauffeured limo. And a forty-foot pleasure boat to sail up and down the Long Island Sound, but how would he explain those luxuries to the IRS? Insomnia was doing well, but it hadn't exactly made him a millionaire. So, in order to avoid Big Brother's scrutiny, he continued to live within his means, and reserved his lavish lifestyle for the two months of the year he spent in his villa in Saint-Jean-Cap-Ferrat. There he was known as Rachid Moulaya, a wealthy Egyptian with an affinity for privacy and the finer things in life. The villa, of course, had been paid for in cash and bought under his assumed name. It was amazing how many identities a man could buy when money was no object.

For now, Times Square suited him just fine. Although the area had undergone a certain amount of clean-up in recent years, there was still enough of the old Hell's Kitchen left to keep the neighborhood interesting. He didn't mind the con men who roamed the streets all day, or the prostitutes and their pimps, as long as they kept their noses out of his business. So far they had.

Tonight, Pincho was getting ready for another assignment. Standing in front of his bathroom mirror, he adjusted the gray knit hat over his head and laughed. Although he was a pro when it came to changing appearances, he was amazed at the transformation from successful business owner to street bum. The three-day beard was a nice touch. It made him look even more scruffy. And the stench. He wrinkled his nose. How in hell could anyone live in these clothes for days on end?

His hand moved to his back where the knife was tucked in his waistband, wrapped in a clean cloth to preserve the fingerprints he had already collected. Under the loose, ragged jacket, the weapon was completely invisible.

To make sure he was truly into the skin of the man he was supposed to be, he started walking across the room, dragging his left leg behind him the way he had seen Roy do it. He gave a nod of satisfaction. After only two days of practice, he had the limp down pat. Somebody should give him a fucking Oscar for that performance alone.

With only a few minutes to spare, he checked the address he had written down earlier—Siri's art gallery on Fifth Avenue. A hop and a skip from Central Park.

The location couldn't have been more perfect.

He patted his pockets to make sure his gloves were there. Satisfied he had thought of everything, he turned off the light and left. Once outside the building, he jammed his hands in his pants pockets, hunched his shoulders against the chilly air and started the long walk uptown.

He waited until he was several blocks away before putting the limp into action.

Two

Her throat dry, her palms damp, Jenna Meyerson stood in the still-empty gallery and gazed at the collection of black-and-white photographs artfully displayed on the walls. Not normally emotional about her work, she was suddenly overwhelmed at the sight of her accomplishment and all that it meant. This was her first exhibit—a moment she had dreamed of since she was fifteen years old. Now that the dream had become a reality, though, the excitement she had experienced initially was beginning to wane, giving way to another bout of doubts and anxiety. Was she good enough to be displayed in one of Manhattan's most prestigious galleries? Had she chosen the right photographs to showcase her talent? And the most important question of all, the one that had been nagging her all day: would anyone bother to show up?

That's what she had wondered when Letitia Vaughn, the owner of Siri's Gallery, approached her two months earlier and offered to display her series, *The Faces of New York,* in a three-week exhibit. Flattered and worried at the same time, Jenna had pinched herself, then, assured she wasn't dreaming, she had quickly said yes.

For almost three hours, the two women had sat on the floor of Jenna's studio, sorting through dozens of photographs. By seven o'clock that night, Letitia, whose eye for talent was legendary, had selected thirty photographs that best depicted urban life only as New Yorkers knew it.

The next eight weeks flew by at breakneck speed as Letitia wrote press releases, worked with caterers and sent out dozens of invitations for the opening night.

And now Jenna's big moment was finally here and she was scared to death.

Jenna glanced at her watch, growing more nervous with each passing second. It was a few minutes after eight and there wasn't a single art aficionado in sight. Why in God's name had they chosen a Monday night, the one night of the week when New Yorkers stayed home.

"Stop worrying," a familiar voice whispered in Jenna's ear. "You're going to be a smash."

Jenna turned to look into the smiling face of Letitia Vaughn. At the admitted age of sixty-two, the owner of Siri's looked at least twenty years younger. Her short, pixie-styled black hair, slender figure and fashionable clothes contributed to her youthful appearance. But it was her passion for the work of the artists she sponsored and her bubbly personality that made her the powerhouse she had become in the art world.

Jenna's gaze followed one of the caterers as he walked in, carrying another tray of hors d'oeuvres into the back room. "And I'll owe it all to you, and to what you've done to make tonight a success."

Letitia made a dismissing wave. "Oh, that's just window dressing. Art patrons don't come here to sip champagne or nibble on fancy canapés. They come to meet the artist. New Yorkers love discovering new talent. And this, my sweet,'' Letitia made a sweeping gesture across the room, ''is talent at its finest.''

Her spirits lifted by her mentor's enthusiasm, Jenna once again let her gaze drift along the wall. *The Faces of New York* belonged to men and women Jenna had photographed either doing their jobs, participating in a favorite activity or simply enjoying a moment of total relaxation.

One of the most dramatic shots in the collection was of an exhausted woman firefighter taken at Ground Zero three weeks after the September 11th tragedy. As the woman sat against a pile of rubble for a few minutes' rest, the despair, frustration and weariness etched on her smoke-smeared face had driven straight through Jenna's heart. She'd had a chance to talk to the firefighter briefly and had been moved beyond words by the woman's spirit and her dedication to the job.

There were other equally compelling shots—a Radio City Rockette in a wood soldier costume listening to her choreographer's instruction, a sweaty construction worker driving a jackhammer through the concrete, a business executive running to catch a cab, a uniformed doorman at the Plaza Hotel opening the door of a stretch limo, a harried waitress at Carnegie Deli during the lunch hour, a cop making a bust. Jenna had purposely shunned the rich and famous, the easily recognized faces one could see in the papers on any given day, and concentrated solely on the people she called the backbone of New York.

Letitia leaned toward Jenna and directed her attention toward the door, where a small group had just walked in. ''Smile, darling. It's showtime.''

The next three hours surpassed even Letitia's lofty expectations. More than four hundred people, ranging from art buffs to serious buyers, and even a couple of snooty critics, passed through Siri's doors. Unaccustomed to being the center of attention, Jenna quickly became acclimated to the jostling as people pressed around her, anxious to know all about her and her work. Friends, former college roommates and even distant relatives had come as well, eager to share Jenna's big night. Even Marcie Hollander, Manhattan's busy district attorney and an old friend of the family, had stopped by to congratulate her.

But it was her dad, arriving a few minutes after ten, who made the evening truly special. The moment he entered, all heads turned to look at the tall, attractive widower with the dark green eyes and graying temples. A former district attorney and Manhattan Supreme Court justice, Samuel Meyerson was well-known to New Yorkers. Even now that he was retired, several people greeted him by name. Always gracious, Sam stopped to shake hands with acquaintances and exchange a few pleasantries.

After a few minutes, he was finally able to detach himself from an overly friendly redhead and make his way across the room. "Sorry, honey," he said, kissing Jenna on the cheek. "I couldn't get away."

"So I noticed." Unable to resist a little teasing, she added, "That redhead in the low-cut Bill Blass is throwing me dagger looks. Do you suppose she thinks I'm competition?"

"If she does, she wouldn't be far from the truth, would she?" He wrapped an arm around her shoulders. "You've always been my best girl." Then, turning toward the display on the nearest wall, he gave a slow shake of his head. "I'm so proud of you, Jenna. I know your mother would be, too."

Jenna nodded. Her late mother had been on her mind all day. "She's the one who got me started, remember? When she gave me my first camera?"

"How can I forget? From that moment on, you photographed everything in sight."

"Mostly you and Mom."

They had been so happy in those days—spending long weekends on the Jersey shore, where Jenna's maternal grandparents had a summer home, traveling throughout the U.S. and Europe, or simply spending quiet times in their house in Katonah, New York. Then, four years ago, while Jenna was busy trying to save her own marriage, her parents had fallen out of love. Or rather, her *mother* had fallen out of love. In spite of Jenna's repeated demands for an explanation, Elaine Meyerson had refused to discuss the matter further, and moved out of the house. To this day, the true cause of her parents' breakup still remained a mystery to Jenna.

Aware her somber thoughts were threatening to ruin the evening, she took her father's hand. "Come on, Daddy, I want to introduce you to Letitia."

They spent the next hour moving from group to group, accepting compliments, Jenna with a certain amount of modesty, Sam with a great deal of pride. As the last guests were saying their goodbyes, a latecomer walked in. Startled, Jenna watched as her exhusband, Adam Lear, approached and stood a few feet from her.

He looked just as he had three years ago, when they had left the courtroom together before going their separate ways—handsome, fit and confident.

Except for a phone call after 9/11 to make sure she was all right, they hadn't had any contact with each other, which made tonight's visit all the more surprising.

Excusing herself to Letitia, she walked over to him. Before she could decide on an appropriate greeting, Adam embraced her.

"Jenna." He held her against him for a long second, then released her and held her at arms' length. "You look wonderful. Success becomes you."

"Thank you."

His gaze traveled from one end of the gallery to the other. "You've done it, haven't you? You've made your dream come true."

"I had help."

"Still modest, I see."

Uncomfortable with the compliment, she changed the subject. "How did you find out about the exhibit?"

"From my secretary. She thought I might want to stop by, and she was right."

"You're the last person I expected to see here tonight."

"Why?" He looked genuinely surprised. "Don't you think I'd want to share in your success? Wasn't I always one of your staunchest supporters?"

The answer to both questions was a resounding yes. Even when their marriage had begun to turn sour, Adam had been there for her, encouraging her, supporting her, pushing her beyond what she felt capable of.

He jammed his hands in his pants pockets. "All right if I take a look around?"

"Go ahead." While Letitia was busy writing a

check to the caterers, Jenna played hostess, walking beside Adam and explaining what had drawn her to each subject, the difficulties she had encountered with those who hadn't wanted to be photographed and how she had changed their mind.

"How's your dad?" he asked.

"Great. He just left actually."

"A proud papa, I'm sure."

"Disgustingly so."

His hands now behind his back, Adam resumed his stroll. "This is awesome, Jenna. You've totally captured New York's heart and soul."

"That was the idea."

He turned to her. "You look happy."

"I am happy." Then, because she caught something in his eyes that hadn't been there before, she asked, "And you? Are you happy?" He ought to be. His company, a worldwide provider of computers and related accessories, had recently merged with Small Solutions, the second largest manufacturer of handheld computing devices. The merger, regarded by many as a giant step for Global Access, had been negotiated by Adam, one of the company's most talented attorneys. His success hadn't stopped with his professional accomplishments. A year ago this month, he had married a former beauty queen and although she was almost half his age, they made a dashing couple.

"Oh, you know me," he replied. "I make do."

Jenna laughed. "*Make do?* You have a gorgeous wife, you live in a house that once belonged to the Vanderbilts and you're one of the most successful corporate attorneys in the city. In fact, weren't you made chief counsel for Global Access as a result of the merger with Small Solutions?''

His answer surprised her. ''Success isn't all it's cracked up to be. You bust your ass getting to the top, only to realize that staying at the top is even more difficult than getting there.''

This wasn't the Adam she knew, Jenna reflected. He seemed much more jaded and disillusioned than he used to be.

''Look,'' he said suddenly, ''I know it's late, but...could we go somewhere and talk?''

''Now?''

''That's really why I came,'' he said with disarming honesty. ''To talk to you.'' As she started to ask what about, he shook his head. ''Not here.''

She hesitated. It had been a long day and if she had to make a choice between a conversation with her ex-husband and her comfortable bed, the bed would win, hands down. On the other hand, there was an urgency in Adam's voice she couldn't ignore. Here was a man who had it all—fame, fortune and happiness. So why did he look so troubled? And why had he come to her?

''I guess it wouldn't be rude for me to leave now,'' she said, her mind made up. ''Just give me a minute to say good-night to Letitia.''

Three

She was back a few moments later and found Adam waiting at the door, looking anxious. "Ready?" He opened the door for her.

A cold October breeze blew in from the Hudson River, forcing Jenna to pull her coat collar around her. Just then, a panhandler bumped into them.

"Watch where you're going, will you?" Adam said irritably.

Unfazed, the man rattled a can under Adam's nose. "Hey, brother, can you spare some change?"

His body odor was foul enough to make Jenna recoil. Adam took her arm, shielding her with his body. "Get away from me."

The man mumbled something under his breath, then walked away, limping slightly. Still holding Jenna's arm, Adam led her across Madison Avenue.

The incident forgotten, she asked, "Where are we going?"

"Well, let's see." Adam looked up and down the street. "Do you still like bread pudding?"

The thought alone made her mouth water. "Have you forgotten? Photography is my first passion, bread pudding my second."

"Then you're in luck. I know this place, Just Desserts, that makes the best bread pudding on the planet. They add roasted pineapple to the mixture and the results are incredible.''

''Yum.''

He pointed east. ''It's just a couple of blocks away on Lexington. I'll see you home afterwards. Do you still have the condo on Columbus Circle?''

''I wouldn't want to live anywhere else.''

The walk was brisk and refreshing, a welcome change after the heat of the gallery.

As they headed east toward Lexington Avenue, Adam told her what he had been up to those past three years. He mentioned his wedding, but only briefly.

''I saw a picture in the *Times*,'' Jenna said. ''Your wife is very beautiful.''

''Yes, she is.'' He seemed totally unaffected by the compliment, which Jenna found odd. Most men married to a young, beautiful woman—a beauty queen, no less—would have bragged a little, even to an ex-wife.

Trouble in paradise? So soon?

''Here we are.'' Adam stopped in front of a small shop with a striped yellow and white awning, and pushed the front door open.

He apparently knew the waitress, because although the place was packed, she quickly found them a booth near the window. Before she left, Adam ordered coffee and two bread puddings. ''Heavy on the whipped cream for the lady,'' he added, winking at Jenna.

Once they were alone, Adam watched Jenna shrug off her coat and said, ''I meant what I said earlier. You look wonderful.''

She laughed, feeling suddenly self-conscious.

"Maybe it's the longer hair. After the divorce, I wanted a change, so I decided to let my hair grow."

"It suits you."

The waitress brought their order—two generous helpings of bread pudding, one of them heaped high with whipped cream. Jenna grinned. "I'll have to run twice as far in the morning in order to burn the calories this baby contains." She tried a spoonful and immediately closed her eyes. "But it'll be worth it. This is scrumptious."

"I take it you still run?"

"Every morning, one loop around Heckscher Playground in the park. It gets the cobwebs out of my brain and keeps me in shape." She took another spoonful, glancing at him as he did the same. "All right, Adam. You've kept me in suspense long enough. What do you want to talk to me about?"

He took his time answering, first licking some of the whipped cream from the corner of his mouth, then taking a sip of his coffee. At last he said, "Do you remember that job you did for Faxel just before we split up?"

How could she forget? The CEO of Faxel, a computer conglomerate that happened to be Global Access's only serious competitor, had contracted her to do a brochure that would showcase the company's latest invention—a handheld computer dubbed The Wizard that did everything a PC could do, and then some. Her job had been to photograph Faxel's employees as they went through their daily routines and then put together a brochure. On the night The Wizard was officially unveiled, she had attended the party and taken pictures of some of New York's most influential people. Her fee for the assignment had enabled her to completely refurnish her SoHo studio and re-equip her very antiquated darkroom.

"I remember." She added a spoonful of whipped cream to her coffee.

"Have you done anything for them since then?"

"Another brochure when two new members joined the board."

"When was that?"

"Last year at about this time."

"Nothing since then?"

She was more and more intrigued. "No."

"Did you keep the negatives of the photos you took the night of the unveiling?"

Now she saw where he was going. "I turned them over to J. B. Collins, along with the proof sheets."

Adam's voice was heavy with disappointment. "You have nothing?"

"I wouldn't say that. I kept what I felt were the best shots for my portfolio."

He looked relieved. "How many?"

She shrugged. "I don't remember. Fifteen, maybe twenty."

"How quickly could you make me copies?"

"Why would I want to do that?"

Adam leaned across the table, his expression intense. "Because I need to take a look at the pictures, see who attended the party."

She had already guessed that much. "Why?"

He leaned back in his seat. "I can't tell you."

She didn't try to keep the irritation from her voice. "You are asking me to do something highly unethical, something that could damage my career, but you won't tell me why?"

"How can it damage your career? Faxel wouldn't have to know about it."

"And that makes it even more wrong." She thought of all the corporate scandals that had plagued the financial world in recent years, the insider tradings, the phony profit reports, the arrests of some of the country's most powerful CEOs. "Did Faxel do something illegal?"

Adam pinched his lips together in an all-too-familiar expression that told her he was weighing the pros and cons of giving her a straight answer. "They may have."

"Then you should go to the authorities."

"Without proof, no one will listen."

"Marcie will." During Adam's years as an assistant district attorney, he and Marcie Hollander had become good friends and remained close, even after his move into the corporate world.

"Marcie is swamped right now," Adam said. "It wouldn't be fair to saddle her with my suspicions. On the other hand, if I had sufficient evidence..."

Jenna was still looking for a way out. "Why don't you hire a private investigator?"

Adam hesitated briefly. "I did."

"What did he say?"

Adam wouldn't look at her. "He hasn't turned up anything yet."

"Maybe you need a better investigator."

Adam smiled. "In his own words, there isn't a better investigator in the entire city."

Jenna made a face. "He sounds a little stuck on himself, if you ask me."

"That's what you always thought."

She gave him a quizzical look. "Do I know him?"

This time he did meet her gaze. "It's Frank Renaldi."

Four

Jenna leaned against her chair in stunned silence. Frank Renaldi. The name took her back, way back to her days at NYU, where she had met Adam and Frank. She had been nineteen and studying fine arts. The two men had already graduated and were both in their second year of law school, but were as different from one another as night and day. Frank was unpredictable, unconventional and a bit of a thrill seeker. Adam was steady and focused. Like Jenna, he had his future all mapped out, right down to his final goal—becoming a state senator, maybe even president.

It was an odd trio, bound by a deep friendship. Then six months or so before Frank and Adam were due to graduate from law school, their feelings for Jenna had changed from brotherly love to something much more complicated.

Flattered, Jenna had enjoyed the attention of both men, the harmless flirting, the growing rivalry between the two best friends, even the bets that were being made around campus as to which man would win her heart.

She found herself attracted to both, but was unable to decide which one she'd want to spend the rest of her life with—the disciplined, methodical straight shooter or the rule-breaker.

In the end, she had chosen Adam, perhaps because he had pursued her a little more ardently, as opposed to Frank, who had seemed to grow tired of the game.

Soon after, with no clear goal in mind, Frank had left New York, moved to Richmond, Virginia and was never heard of again. The wedding invitation, sent to the post office box he had given them, had come back with the words "no forwarding address," stamped on the front. Curious, Jenna had called Frank's mother and learned that he was well and working for a prestigious law firm in Richmond. Realizing he no longer wanted anything to do with his two old buddies, they had left him alone.

And now, after a fifteen-year silence, Frank was back in town. Just like that. No phone call, no "hello, I'm back, let's get together." Nothing.

"Frank is a private investigator?" she said at last. "Here in New York?"

"He moved back a little after 9/11 and opened a detective agency in the East Village."

"How did you find out?"

"I ran into a former classmate a few weeks ago. You know him. Mick Falco. He's a criminal attorney now and apparently he's kept in touch with Frank."

"But why did Frank become a private investigator? Why isn't he practicing law?"

Adam shrugged. "You know Frank, always doing the unexpected."

Jenna had a dozen more questions, all regarding Frank, but she didn't voice them. He hadn't been curious about her, why should she be curious about him? "If he's so good at his job," she said a little testily, "why hasn't he come up with the proof you need?"

Once again, Adam averted his eyes. Why did he keep doing that? What wasn't he telling her? "An investigation like that takes time," he replied. "That's why I came to you. You could help me speed things up."

She saw him glance toward the steam-streaked window and turned to do the same. The panhandler who had bumped into them earlier was there, his scruffy face pressed against the glass. She couldn't tell if he was staring at them or their plates. A homeless man looking for food, Jenna thought, feeling suddenly sad. This city was full of them.

She turned back. "Isn't that the man we saw earlier?"

"I think so." He motioned to the waitress for a refill on their coffee. "Don't pay attention to him. He'll go away." When his mug was full again, he came back to the subject at hand. "What about those photos, Jenna? I could drive you to your studio and have you back home by—"

She shook her head. "No, Adam, not tonight. I need to think about this."

"What is there to think about? Either you're going to help me or you're not." He sounded upset.

"I would like to sleep on it, but if you'd prefer an answer right now, then it's no."

He seemed to think about that for a while. It was clear he didn't like the idea of going home empty-handed, but what choice did he have? At last he nodded. "Okay. I guess I can wait until morning."

"Good, because it's been a long day and I'm bushed."

"In that case, let's go." He dropped two twenties on the table. "I'll walk you home."

But after finding out he was parked nearby at the Essex House garage on Central Park South, she wouldn't let him walk any farther than the garage entrance. "I'm perfectly capable of seeing myself home, Adam," she told him when he insisted.

He glanced toward the circle where the towering statue of Christopher Columbus seemed to be standing guard. "Are you sure?"

"Positive. Go home, Adam."

He kissed her on the cheek. "Will you call me at the office first thing in the morning and let me know what you've decided?"

"I will."

As she walked toward the Regent, the twenty-two-story building where she lived, she thought of the ten years she and Adam had spent together as husband and wife. At first, the marriage had seemed made in heaven. She had loved his dedication to his job as assistant district attorney and his determination to serve the people, no matter how small the monetary reward. As a husband, he was caring, supportive and loved to shower her with expensive trinkets she didn't appreciate nearly as much as she did the thought.

Then, somewhere along the way, Adam's ideals changed. He became more ambitious and more obsessed with money, not just his family's fortune or his trust fund, both of which were substantial, but his own. When Global Access offered him a top legal position along with a huge salary, Adam left the district attorney's office and never looked back.

But while Adam's new values and blinding ambition had played an important part in the disintegration of the marriage, it was his adamant refusal to have children that had ended it.

"Children are more a hindrance than an asset," he told her during one of their many discussions on the subject. "Just ask my brother, whose three demons are driving him to an early grave."

That's when they began to drift apart, finding satisfaction in their respective jobs rather than in each other. Then had come the darkest moment of Jenna's life—her mother's death. Divorced from Jenna's father for only one year, Elaine Meyerson was driving back from Connecticut on a dark, rainy December night when she lost control of her car and missed a curve. The Jaguar plunged into a two-hundred-foot ravine, killing Elaine on impact.

Jenna was inconsolable. For weeks, her father and those close to her stood by helplessly while she sank into a deeper and deeper depression. Only Adam was able to reach her and pull her out of her misery until she started living again.

For a while, Jenna and Adam had hoped the tragedy would somehow improve their marriage. Instead, both realized that they were better at being friends than they were at being husband and wife. Six months after Elaine's death, the couple's divorce was finalized.

Having reached her building at the corner of Central Park South and Central Park West, Jenna paused to look back, expecting to see Adam waiting in front of the garage entrance to make sure she got home safely. He was nothing if not the perfect gentleman.

To her surprise, the street was deserted. She had

never been good at figuring out men. Shrugging, Jenna walked into the lobby and headed for the elevator.

Adam was in the forefront of Jenna's mind when she woke up the following morning. Even now, in the clear morning light, she was no closer to making a decision about whether or not to give him the pictures than she had been six hours earlier. No matter what Faxel may have done, she didn't feel she had the right to hand over photographs the company's CEO, J. B. Collins, had paid her to take without his approval. On the other hand, Adam was one of the most respected attorneys in the city and not one to make accusations lightly. If he thought Faxel had done something wrong, then chances were they had. And the public needed to know.

Still mulling over her former husband's request, she dressed for her morning run in Central Park—gray sweats and sturdy sneakers. Maybe the workout would clear her head and help her make a decision. Feeling better already, she walked into the kitchen for that first, much-needed cup of coffee. The room, with its yellow walls and shiny white appliances, was as neat as she had left it the previous morning, which was not surprising. She only used the kitchen to make coffee and to reheat the delicious specialties her neighbor, an old Hungarian woman, brought her a couple of times a week. Before filling the coffee-maker's glass carafe, she turned on the small television set on the counter for a check of the weather.

She had meant what she had told Adam about not wanting to live anywhere else. She loved her apartment, with its small, cozy rooms and spectacular view. Adam, who had bought the penthouse shortly after the building had gone co-op, knew of her fondness for the place. In a typical gesture, he had insisted on signing it over to her at the time of their divorce.

"You have to keep it," he had told her. "You won't take alimony from me, or a cash settlement. At least let me do this."

In the end she had accepted, partly because she loved her home and partly because in spite of her protests, she knew she'd never be able to afford anything as nice as this on her income.

She had furnished the twenty-second floor apartment with flea-market finds, photographic memorabilia and touches of her father's native England for a rustic, turn-of-the-century look. After fourteen years at the Regent, she felt as much at home here as she did in her father's big suburban house.

The coffee was ready. She was about to pour herself a cup when she glanced up at the TV, and almost dropped the carafe.

Adam's photograph was on the screen. Underneath was the caption: Prominent Attorney Found Dead in Central Park.

Five

Jenna slowly sat down as the broadcaster went on.

"The man, found stabbed in Central Park early this morning, has been identified as Adam Lear, chief counsel at Global Access. The computer company's headquarters are in Manhattan. The body was discovered in Heckscher Playground, near the carousel."

Jenna stared at the screen in disbelieving silence. What were they saying? How could Adam be dead? She had been with him only hours ago.

"A preliminary investigation," the morning anchor continued, "indicates that Mr. Lear, who appears to have been robbed, may have fought back, forcing his assailant to kill him. Adam Lear is the oldest son of New York developer Warren Lear and the late Broadway actress and two-time Tony winner, Lorraine Lear. Due to a rash of robberies in Central Park in recent months, authorities believe the stabbing may be the work of a homeless man they have dubbed the Central Park Robber. Stay tuned for further developments on this story. In sports…"

Jenna picked up the remote and frantically clicked through the channels, in search of additional news, but there wasn't any. Still dazed, the coffee and morning run forgotten, she just sat there while the same three words kept swirling around her head. *Adam is dead. Adam is dead.*

The broadcaster had mentioned the Central Park Robber as a possible suspect, but Jenna found it difficult to believe Adam would have gone for a stroll in Central Park at that time of night. He was on his way home. He had told her so.

Her thoughts quickly turned to the foul-smelling panhandler who had bumped into them and later shown up outside the bakery window. Had his presence there been purely coincidental? Or had he followed her and Adam to the pastry shop and then back to the Essex House garage?

On shaky legs, she walked over to the kitchen window with its view of the park. Although she couldn't see the carousel, Heckscher Playground, where she ran every morning, was clearly visible. She had always felt safe there in broad daylight and in the company of dozens of other joggers. Nighttime was different. Anyone with an ounce of common sense knew that it was dangerous to venture into the park after dark. So why had Adam chosen that ungodly hour to do exactly that?

Or had he?

As she kept gazing at the profusion of autumn colors, the golds and the reds and the yellows, her thoughts wandered back to her conversation with Adam and his belief that her photographs were the proof he needed to implicate Faxel in some kind of wrongdoing. What if someone had found out about his investigation and decided to put a stop to it by killing him?

In spite of her faith in Adam's talents as an attorney, she found herself shaking her head. That scenario was all wrong. She knew J. B. Collins personally. He was a respected member of the community, a brilliant businessman and a generous benefactor. How could a man with such credentials be implicated in corporate shenanigans? Or worse, murder?

After a while, she left the window and went to shower and change. If those photographs had been so important to Adam, maybe she should take a look at them and see what she could learn from them.

More than an hour had passed since Jenna had learned of Adam's death, and she still couldn't believe he was gone. Nor could she forget the way he had died, brutally murdered and left there all alone.

As she rode in the back of a cab, heading for lower Manhattan, a fresh tear pooled at the corner of her eye. She caught it with her finger before it rolled down her cheek. The intensity of her grief didn't surprise her. She might no longer love Adam the way she once had, but her affection for him was still intact.

The squeal of tires as her cab stopped in front of the building that housed her studio jolted her back. Giving herself a mental shake, she paid the driver and stepped out into the sights and sounds that made this part of Manhattan so unique.

Jenna had always loved SoHo. When she had attended NYU, most of her free time was spent exploring this upscale enclave of galleries, museums and ethnic shops, never imagining that someday she would be working here.

The Italianate four-story building on the corner of Greene and Broome Streets had been built in the late eighteen hundreds for a wealthy textile merchant who had made news by being the first in the city to install an elevator. A few years ago, a clever entrepreneur had bought and renovated the building, divided it into eight units and put them up for rent. One of them had a shiny brass plate on its door—Jenna Meyerson's Photography.

Even by Manhattan standards, the third-floor studio was tiny—four hundred square feet. Because anything larger would have cost three times what she was paying, she had made the most out of the restricted space. In one corner of the room was her desk and in the opposite corner, her darkroom. A tripod, two umbrellas and several reflectors occupied the center area.

It took her a couple of minutes to locate the portfolio that contained the Faxel photographs. There were fifteen in all, eight-by-ten color shots she had deemed the best of the bunch. The unveiling of The Wizard had been a resounding success, with more than three hundred people in attendance, most of them high ranking politicians, Wall Street gurus, and Fortune 500 CEOs.

Jenna carefully detached the photographs from the book and took them to her desk, where she spread them out. She studied each one, quickly identifying the well-known faces, and studying the others closely, occasionally picking up a magnifying glass for a closer inspection.

At ten-thirty, she fell back against her chair and let out a sigh of disappointment. Except for the guests whose names she knew, she hadn't recognized a single person. Her fingers drummed gently on her desk. Short of going to J.B. himself, which was out of the question, she had no way of finding out who

Adam had been looking for. But she knew someone who might. Marcie Hollander. She and Adam knew the same people, had traveled the same circles and prosecuted the same criminals. Nothing went on in this city without the district attorney knowing about it. But before she gave Marcie the photos, she had to print another set for herself.

Photos in hand, she went into her darkroom and closed the door. At the urging of other photographers she knew, she had tried to make the transition from traditionally made photos to digital images. After a few attempts, she had decided that she missed her darkroom. She couldn't explain it, especially to those who had become pro-digital, but a darkroom was a distinctly personal place, a sanctuary that was hers alone. Without it, she was lost.

She had kept hers simple—a custom-made stainless steel sink, developing tanks, a high-speed dryer, enlargers, a tabletop processor, a clothesline and a shelf to accommodate all her accessories. It wasn't state-of-the-art but it was enough.

She turned on the red light and went to work.

An hour later, a second, much smaller set was ready. She dropped it into her purse and slid the fifteen originals into a manila envelope. If there was a bad apple in that bunch, Marcie would find it.

Pincho sat in the small back room of Insomnia on Tuesday morning, flipping through the pages of the *New York Times.* He found the story he was looking for on page three of the Metro section, with a picture of the victim.

It was all there, just as he had expected. Adam Lear had been found stabbed to death in Central

Park. Although the killer hadn't yet been appre-
hended, the police had the description of a man seen
running from the crime scene, and expected to make
an imminent arrest.

The job had been remarkably easy. After Lear and
his date had parted, Pincho had approached the attorney and told him, in a clear, businesslike tone, that
he worked for Faxel and had information about the
company he was sure Adam would want to hear.
When Pincho had suggested going for a walk so they
wouldn't be seen together, he had expected a flat no,
which would have forced him to kill the attorney
right there. But after a brief hesitation, Lear had nodded and followed him into the park.

The only surprise in Pincho's well-orchestrated
plan had been the woman. No one had told him Lear
would have company, or that he would be heading
for a pastry shop, of all places. Fortunately, Pincho
was nothing if not inventive. Thanks to a little im-
provisation, his plan had gone off without a hitch.
When the police came around to question the
woman, whoever she was, she would remember the
smelly bum with the limp.

"Sorry Roy, old man," Pincho murmured under
his breath. "It's nothing personal. Just business."

A business for which he was handsomely paid.
And why shouldn't he be? His was a risky profes-
sion. One that not only required guts and ingenuity
but a stomach for the unexpected—like those dis-
gusting clothes he'd had to wear for the greater part
of the night. Pincho hated filth. Even more than he
hated poverty. For a moment, he had considered
burning the foul-smelling bundle. Common sense

told him not to. In this business, you never knew when a prop would come in handy again.

His phone rang. That would be his client.

Pincho answered it at the first ring. "Kravitz."

"The usual place," was all the voice said.

Pincho quietly hung up. Leaving the *Times* on the table, he went to tell his manager he had to run an errand and would be back in about an hour. Then, whistling happily, he walked out of the coffee shop and headed for Bryant Park to pick up the rest of his money.

Six

Marcie was on the phone, talking tough as usual, when Jenna walked into her office. The D.A. waved her in, then raised two fingers to signal she'd be finished in two minutes.

Jenna could already see how deeply Adam's death had affected her. Under the expert makeup her face was pale and there were noticeable shadows under her large hazel eyes. While not a raving beauty, Marcie was an attractive woman, even more so now that she had added red highlights to her mousy brown hair and wore more stylish clothes.

At forty-eight she was one of the most influential women in the city and didn't let anyone forget it. Happily married to the chief of cardiology at Roosevelt Hospital and the mother of two handsome teenage boys, she belonged to that rare breed of women whose home and high-level career seemed to be in perfect harmony. Her success as a prosecutor was almost unprecedented. Many attributed it to her ruthless nature and the way she trained her A.D.A.s to go for the jugular. Adam had once called her obsessive. "Almost as much as I am," he had confessed. Which explained why they had gotten along so well.

After a terse, "That's the deal, Raymond. Take it

or leave it,'' Marcie hung up. Then, walking quickly, she rounded her desk and took Jenna in a warm embrace. "I'm so sorry, honey."

Jenna let herself be led to one of the chairs facing Marcie's huge desk. "When did you find out?"

"At four this morning. Detective Stavos called me at home. You know Paul, don't you?"

Jenna vaguely remembered a middle-aged man with tired eyes and a grumpy attitude. "Adam introduced me to him a few years ago."

Marcie took the other chair. "I wish I could have been the one to tell you, but I had to wait until we had notified Adam's family." She paused. "We'll find him, Jenna. I promise you we'll find the bastard who did this."

"That's why I'm here. Adam came to the gallery last night—to congratulate me on the exhibit."

Marcie frowned. "I didn't see him there."

"He came late, just before closing. He wanted to talk to me."

"I didn't know you two kept in touch."

"We didn't. I hadn't seen him since the divorce."

Jenna told her about Adam's visit, trying to relate as much of their conversation as she could remember, including the incident with the panhandler.

When she was finished, Marcie walked back to her desk and picked up the phone again. "Paul," she said quickly, "Jenna Meyerson is in my office. She says Adam's car is parked in the Essex House garage. Send a forensic team there, will you, and let me know what they find. It's a black Cadillac Seville. I believe his wife gave you the license plate number?" She nodded. "Good."

Turning to Jenna, she said, ''Can you describe the man you saw outside the bakery window?''

''Medium height, maybe five-nine or so, not big, but not small either. It was hard to tell under all those clothes.''

''Did you see his face?''

''Yes. It was an ordinary face, smudged, with no particular markings.''

''What about his hair?''

''He wore a knit cap pulled low over his brows. Oh, and he walked with a limp.''

As Marcie wrote down the information, Jenna leaned forward. ''Adam seemed to think that Faxel—''

''Jenna.'' Although Marcie cut her short, her voice remained gentle. ''I understand why you would feel a certain…obligation, shall we say, to find Adam's killer. I'm aware of the history you two shared and how he saw you through a difficult period when your mother died, but whatever he thought he knew about Faxel is probably unrelated to his murder.''

''Why do you say that?''

''Because the person who found the body—a homeless woman who sleeps in Central Park—saw a man running away from the carousel at approximately the time Adam was killed.''

''So?''

''So the man she saw fits the description we have of the Central Park Robber, and of the panhandler who approached you on the street last night.''

At those words, Jenna was momentarily thrown, but not for long. ''If that panhandler wanted to kill Adam, why didn't he do it right there and then?''

Marcie put her pen down. ''Maybe the streets were

too crowded, and he was afraid someone would grab him before he had a chance to get away.''

But Jenna wasn't convinced. ''You're asking me to believe that a common thief, a man who most likely had never heard of Adam Lear, stalked him so he could then lure him to Central Park and rob him?'' She shook her head. ''I don't believe that for a second.''

Marcie folded her arms across her chest. ''What do you believe, Jenna?''

''I told you. Adam knew something damaging about Faxel, maybe something that could have put the company out of business. Surely that's worth checking into.''

''And it will be.'' Marcie spoke with quiet determination. ''Believe me, we'll leave no stone unturned. I can start by taking a look at those photographs you mentioned.''

Jenna took the manila envelope from her purse and dropped it on the D.A.'s desk.

Marcie took out the pictures, studying each one carefully. After a few moments, she repeated the process.

''Well?'' Jenna said a little impatiently. ''Do you recognize anyone?''

''Offhand, I can name at least two dozen people, but none that arouse any suspicion.'' She looked up. ''May I keep these?''

''What are you going to do with them?''

''Circulate them among my staff, and throughout N.Y.P.D. But I wouldn't get my hopes too high. While Adam was a brilliant attorney, he did have a habit of jumping to conclusions before he had all his ducks in a row.''

"Did his instincts ever fail him?" Jenna asked. "Weren't you the first to admit that he was always one step ahead of the rest of your A.D.A.s?"

"We're dealing with facts now, Jenna. Fact number one." She touched the tip of her thumb. "As I said, we have an eyewitness. Her name is Estelle Gold, a Central Park regular. Detective Stavos questioned her intensively, and searched the area where she sleeps. She was clean." Marcie smiled. "In a manner of speaking."

"And she described the panhandler I described to you?"

"Right down to the limp. Fact number two," Marcie continued, "Adam's wallet was empty, except for his driver's license, and there was a red welt on his left wrist where his watch was yanked off. We know from his wife that he left the house that morning wearing a gold Rolex." She tilted her head sideways. "Do you remember seeing such a watch on Adam's wrist last night?"

Jenna nodded, remembering the flash of gold under the cuff of Adam's shirt when he had checked the time. "That still doesn't prove anything. The man who robbed Adam and the one who killed him could be two different people."

"If that's the case, we'll know soon enough. I don't expect the Central Park Robber will be able to stay hidden very long, not with such an intensive search going on." She made one more notation in her spiraled notebook before flipping it shut. "Thank you, Jenna. I'll relay the information you gave me to Detective Stavos, but I expect he'll want to talk to you himself."

"You might also want to talk to Adam's secretary.

They were very close—in a purely professional way, of course. She might know something.''

Marcie seemed amused. ''Are you telling me how to do my job, Jenna?''

Jenna blushed. ''No, of course not.''

''Good.'' Marcie's smile was gentle. ''Because there's nothing worse than a well-meaning citizen to muddle a murder investigation.''

Sam Meyerson found a parking space near Foley Square in downtown Manhattan and walked the short distance to One Hogan Place where the district attorney's office was located.

Before entering, he stood looking at the massive courts building that had been his second home for more years than he could remember. He had begun his law career as a spunky, eager A.D.A., worked his way to the district attorney post and just when he was thinking of retiring, he had been offered a seat on the Manhattan Supreme Court bench.

Because of his twenty-seven years as a prosecutor, no one appreciated the daily difficulties a district attorney faced more than he. With over one hundred and thirty thousand criminal cases to prosecute every year and five hundred and fifty assistant district attorneys to supervise, a D.A. had his or her hands full. But in spite of the long hours, the frustrations and the occasional death threat, Sam didn't regret a single minute of his life as a public servant. The law was in his blood. Even now that he was retired, he still missed the excitement of putting a case together, gathering clues and preparing for the prosecuting phase. Thanks to Marcie, who often called on him for his input, he was still able to use his brains and offer suggestions regarding some of her most puzzling cases.

Her call had come as he was getting out of the shower. She had sounded distraught, and he soon found out why. Adam Lear, her former colleague and Sam's ex-son-in-law, had been found murdered in Central Park. She would give him the details when he got there.

Adam dead. He could hardly believe it. The man was so vibrant, so full of life. Or at least he had been the last time Sam had seen him. That was three years ago, when he and Jenna had called it quits.

His first thought when he saw Marcie was that her friend's death had already taken its toll on her. There were shadows under her eyes and a slump in her shoulders as she walked to meet him.

"Sam." Her smile was strained. "I'm glad you could come. Sit down, please."

"How did it happen, Marcie?"

She answered with a question of her own. "Did you know Adam went to Jenna's opening at Siri's last night?"

That surprised him. "No. I was there. She didn't say anything."

"He came later, apparently." She put her elbows on her desk and rested her chin on her fists. "Afterward they went for coffee. That's when he told her about the real reason for his visit."

"And what was that?"

"A few years ago, when they were still together, Jenna was hired to take pictures of a big bash at Faxel. I'm sure you remember it. You and I were there."

"Of course. The party was to introduce Faxel's new wonder handheld computer to the world."

She nodded. "Adam wanted to take a look at those pictures. At first he wouldn't tell Jenna why, but you know how she is."

Sam smiled. "Stubborn."

"Not unlike a certain former district attorney I know. Anyway, Adam may have come upon some information regarding Faxel and its CEO, J. B. Collins."

"What kind of information?"

"That's where it gets iffy. He wasn't specific. All Jenna could get out of him was that Collins *may* be involved in some kind of wrongdoing and Adam needed Jenna's photographs to prove it." She picked up a stack of eight-by-ten color glossies from the corner of her desk and slid them across to him. "You're welcome to take a look. Maybe you'll recognize someone. I didn't."

Sam studied each picture, recognizing several people, many of whom he had talked to the night of the unveiling. "What are the pictures supposed to prove?"

"We're not sure of that, either. And Jenna never got a chance to talk to Adam again, or show him the photos, which means we don't have anything to support his suspicions." She sighed. "Let's face it, Sam, Al Capone himself could be in those pictures and it still wouldn't prove that J. B. Collins did anything illegal. You remember the crowd. It wouldn't have been too difficult for someone with a little ingenuity to crash the party without J.B. knowing about it."

Sam was beginning to understand why he had

been asked to come here. "Is my daughter giving you a hard time?"

Marcie smiled. "I love your daughter, Sam. She is bright and she is loyal, but she can be a pain in the ass sometimes, especially when she gets an idea in her head."

"What kind of idea?"

"She didn't come right out and say it, but I had the distinct impression that she would like to be actively involved in the hunt for Adam's killer. While I admire her spunk and her loyalty to Adam, I worry about her safety. You and I both know what can happen when ordinary people take the law into their own hands."

"Jenna would never do anything to jeopardize a criminal investigation."

"Maybe not." She glanced at the stack of photos Sam had dropped back on her desk. "But she seemed quite serious about this Faxel matter."

"You don't think there may be some validity to her concerns?"

"Of course I do, and if there is a reason to investigate Faxel, Detective Stavos will do it—*discreetly,*" she added, putting emphasis on the word. "And without a civilian's help. You know how he is about outsiders playing sleuths."

Sam knew Stavos well. He was an old-timer, maybe not the best homicide detective on the force, but he got the job done and had a better than average arrest-conviction record. It was no secret, however, that the detective was not fond of attorneys, which was why he and Adam hadn't gotten along. The last person he would want in his way right now was Adam Lear's ex-wife.

Sam stood up. "I'll talk to Jenna."

Marcie rose as well. "I'd appreciate that, Sam. Thank you."

Seven

"Damn you," Frank Renaldi muttered as his car, a classic 1957 red Thunderbird, shuddered to a stop in the middle of Chinatown. "You picked one hell of a time to die on me."

This latest incident was the crowning touch to what was shaping to be one of the worst mornings of his life. It had begun a couple of hours ago when he had found the girlfriend of his fourteen-year-old son asleep on his living room couch. As he was attempting to get an explanation from Danny, who was upstairs in his bed, the girl's father had showed up and threatened to sue Frank for aiding in the delinquency of a minor.

That problem was barely out of the way when he had learned about Adam Lear's death. The news had hit him hard. He and Adam had met at NYU and had remained friends through college and law school. After graduation, Adam had accepted an A.D.A. position in the district attorney's office, and Frank had moved to Richmond. For reasons he tried not to think about, he had not kept in touch with his old friend, even after his return to New York. Through Mick Falco, Adam had found out Frank was back in town, and a little over a week ago, he had walked into his office, claiming to need a private investigator.

And now Adam was dead and there was so much that had been left unsaid.

Ignoring the cacophony of irate honking behind him, Frank tried to restart the car. Nothing, not even a whimper. Utterly frustrated, he slapped the steering wheel.

A cab driver stuck his head out the window. "Hey, you there!" he shouted. "You gonna move that pile of shit out of the way, or you want me to do it for you?"

"All right, all right," Frank shouted back as he took out his cell phone. "I hear you. Keep your shirt on."

He punched a number and when his cousin Marty answered, Frank didn't give him a chance to say one word. "What's the matter with you, Marty? Have you suddenly gone deaf on me? Didn't I stress that no one but you should work on my car? But did you listen? Of course not. You gave it to that incompetent apprentice of yours and guess what? The car died on me in the middle of rush hour traffic."

"Frankie?"

"Don't Frankie me. Just get your ass down here."

Marty knew better than to argue. "Where you at?"

"Intersection of Bowery and Pell."

"Be there in a jiff, cuz. Don't go anywhere."

"Smart ass."

Frank was trying to sweet talk a cop who was threatening to have the car towed when his cousin's truck pulled up. Marty, looking cool and efficient in his dark blue coveralls, jumped out and started hooking the T-bird to the truck.

"Don't worry, officer," he said, flashing a white

smile. "I'll have that baby out of here before you can say 'book him.'"

Marty laughed at his own joke, but his perpetual good humor failed to warm the officer's heart. "You have two minutes."

Already late for an appointment, Frank slapped the car keys into his cousin's hand. "I want it fixed by five o'clock—no charge. And you can throw in a free wash and wax job."

Marty, totally unfazed by Frank's dark mood, gave one last tug on the chain. "Anything you want, cuz. You know my motto. I aim to please."

Still muttering, Frank nodded to the officer and headed up Bowery, punching his office number on his cell phone as he went. His secretary answered on the first ring.

"Renaldi Investigations."

"Tanya, it's me. Tell Mr. Sanford I've had another delay but I'm on my way. I should be there in—"

"Your client left, Boss."

Frank saw a break in the traffic and sprinted across Hester, barely avoiding an oncoming bus. "What do you mean, he left? When I called from home you said he'd wait."

"That was forty-five minutes ago, Boss. The man got tired of waiting."

Frank let out an oath and hung up. Great. The sum of his business this month amounted to three clients: one who had skipped town without paying his bill, a second who was playing hide and seek in order *not* to pay his bill and a third who was dead.

He wondered what else could possibly go wrong today.

*   *   *

Renaldi Investigations, on Sixth Street in the East Village, wasn't exactly what Jenna had expected. But then, when it came to Frank Renaldi, most people didn't have a clue what to expect. Five businesses, ranging from a physical therapy office to a fortune teller, occupied the three-story building. The detective agency was on the second floor across from a taxidermist whose logo on the front door read: "You bring 'em, we stuff 'em."

The reception room was small, with a single window overlooking the noisy street below and a pretty, mahogany-skinned brunette commandeering the cluttered desk. As Jenna walked in, the girl looked up and smiled, showing perfectly aligned white teeth.

"May I help you?"

"My name is Jenna Meyerson. I'd like to see Mr. Renaldi, please."

"He's on his way. Would you like to wait?" She pointed at one of the three chairs against the wall.

"Thank you."

As the girl returned to her typing, Jenna looked around her. The walls were bare except for several photographs of famous hockey players, each one autographed to Frank. The room reminded her of his off-campus apartment, which had been filled with hockey memorabilia and an impressive collection of trophies he had won over the years. There was nothing else on the walls, no certificate of achievement, no diplomas of any kind, not even a framed license to indicate this was the office of a private investigator.

The sound of fast, hard-hitting footsteps outside the corridor told her Frank had arrived. A second later, her prediction was confirmed as Frank walked in and slammed the door behind him.

Apparently unaware she was there, he banged his briefcase on the desk and picked up a handful of messages. His movements were brusque as he went through each one quickly. "Do me a favor next time I need my car serviced, will you, Tanya? Remind me *not* to go to my cousin for help."

Tanya gave a discreet cough and nodded toward Jenna. "Uh, Boss... You have a client."

Looking startled, Frank spun around, giving Jenna a full view of the man who had once proclaimed he would someday be the father of her children. It was as if the past fifteen years had stood still. His hair was still thick and black and a little mussed, as if he had raked his fingers through it, as was his habit. The deep blue eyes all the girls at NYU had drooled over were still as compelling, if not very friendly at the moment. The only noticeable difference Jenna could see was in the upper body area. Frank's shoulders were broader than she remembered, his chest more powerful, his presence more conspicuous. Suddenly, although he hadn't said a word, the room seemed to vibrate with energy.

"Hello, Frank."

She waited for a smile, a greeting, anything that would break the awkward silence. He just stared at her, his expression blank. He was good at that, keeping his feelings under wrap. Or maybe she was reading him wrong and he was feeling nothing at all.

With a nonchalance that was as familiar as the morning sun, he loosened his tie and said, "What are you doing here?"

So much for a greeting.

Trying not to let his attitude rattle her, she rose from her chair. "I came to talk to you about Adam."

"Why?"

"Because he was killed last night, Frank. Or haven't you heard about that?"

"I heard." Yanking the tie off, he strode toward a door with a simple brass plate that said F. Renaldi on it and pushed it open, not bothering to invite her in.

Okay, so the reunion wasn't promising to be a smooth one. Maybe she should have expected that. Maybe her rejection had hurt him more than she had realized and he still carried a grudge. But they weren't in school anymore. They were all grown-up now, responsible adults who ought to be capable of carrying on a civilized conversation without biting each other's head off.

Taking her own advice, she followed him and calmly closed the door behind her. His office was only marginally larger than the reception room and twice as cluttered. Open folders and crime scene photos were scattered across his desk, law books were crammed into a single bookcase, and one of the two chairs facing his desk was heaped high with newspapers.

Frank dropped his briefcase on top of the folders and turned to face her. "There's nothing to talk about, Jenna. If you had called first you would have saved us both time and trouble."

His chilly tone and even chillier comment ticked her off. "Look, Frank, I realize you're upset with me, but surely you can put your ego aside for one moment and talk to me like an adult."

He tossed his tie on the empty chair and did the

same with his sports jacket. Even in his shirtsleeves, he radiated a quiet strength and a down-to-earth charm that wasn't lost on Jenna. "What does my ego have to do with anything?" he asked casually. "And why would I be upset with you?"

She felt herself grow uncomfortable. This wasn't the direction she had wanted the conversation to take, but she had started it and she would finish it, clear the air once and for all. "You're upset because I chose Adam over you."

The shock on his face brought a rush of heat to her cheeks. "You think I'm still carrying a torch for you? Is that it?"

Jenna's face grew hotter. "I didn't say that!"

"But that's what you're implying." His laugh was short and a little insulting. "Some things never change, do they, Jenna? You're still the same little girl with the high opinion of herself." She started to open her mouth but he didn't give her a chance to speak. "For your information, I got over you long ago. Looking back, I'm not sure why I fell for you in the first place. Maybe it was my competitive side, that insatiable need I had to prove that whatever Adam did, I could do better. It was stupid, childish and didn't get me anywhere. I should have known I couldn't win that battle. You never thought I was good enough for you, well-bred enough, or rich enough."

"That's not true! I never gave a damn about money!"

"But you sure didn't thumb your nose at it."

"I don't believe this. We haven't seen each other in fifteen years and all you can think of doing is to insult me? What's wrong with you?"

Her words seemed to strike a chord. "I had a lousy morning."

"Well, get over it, at least long enough to address my concerns."

"I told you, I have nothing to say about Adam."

She had gained a little ground and she wasn't about to concede it now. "Will you at least admit that he hired you?"

"How do you know that?" He sat on the corner of his desk and folded his arms across his chest.

"He told me. Last night."

Like Marcie, he raised a brow. "Last night?"

"It's not what you think. I'm a photographer and a collection of my work was on display at an uptown gallery. Last night was the grand opening and Adam stopped by to congratulate me."

"Your first exhibit, yes, I read about it somewhere." His gaze remained polite and disinterested.

She waited for his own congratulation. When it was obvious that such civilities were beyond his scope, she forged on. "That's when he told me that he had come to see you, on business."

"Why would Adam confide in you?"

"Because he thought I could help him."

"How?"

"Why don't you tell me what you discussed and—"

"I can't do that."

"Why not?"

"Because what Adam told me and what I've uncovered so far is privileged information—between me and my client."

"Your client is dead!"

"Client privilege still applies."

"Even if there's more to Adam's death than what the police claim?"

She looked for a flicker of interest in his eyes and saw none. Either he knew something and wasn't letting on or the man was made of stone.

"Don't you care just a little?" she pressed when he remained silent. "Your best friend, or ex-best friend, may have died a suspicious death and you won't do anything?"

"Don't stand there and judge me, Jenna. My feelings and how I conduct my job is my business."

"And Adam got me involved, therefore his death is *my* business." She looked down at her hands, which she had folded in front of her to present an appearance of calm and poise. "I owe him that much." Then, meeting his gaze again, she added, "Come on, Frank, we can help each other. You tell me what you know and I'll tell you what I know. Maybe together we can—"

He burst out laughing, an honest, good-natured laugh that reminded her of the old days. "You mean we should form a partnership? You and me?"

"Why is that so funny?"

"Because it is. I don't team up with anyone, Jenna. You want to play detective? Be my guest. Just don't expect me to go along with your little shenanigans. Or to pick up the pieces when you get hurt."

That's it. She wasn't going to take this kind of arrogance one second longer. She yanked her purse from the chair. "You know something, Frank? I always thought of you as one of the good guys. You used to be fun, considerate and loyal to your friends. I don't know what happened to change all that, but somewhere along the way you turned into an asshole.'' She hooked the leather strap across her shoulder. ''Do me a favor, will you? For old time's sake? Forget I was here.''

She stomped out of his office and crossed the reception room, aware that Tanya's round-eyed, bewildered gaze followed her to the door. Jenna mumbled a hasty goodbye and made as graceful an exit as she could muster.

Eight

Frank waited until Jenna had walked out before letting out a long breath. Finding himself face-to-face with her had made him weak in the knees. One look, and all the old feelings had come rushing back in a powerful sweep, as he had known they would. That's why he had broken all contact with her fifteen years ago, and why he hadn't let her, or Adam, know he was back in New York.

He moved to the window and glanced down just in time to see her emerge from the building. She was even more beautiful than he remembered. She had the same honey-brown hair touched with gold here and there, the same big brown eyes that could go from hot to frosty in a microsecond and the same full mouth, the mouth he had kissed, only once, in a moment of sheer lunacy.

He watched her walk toward the bus stop in those easy, long-legged strides, her slender hips swinging lightly. In those snug jeans and black leather jacket, she could still pass for a coed. And she was right. He was still pissed off, pissed off at her for choosing the wrong man and pissed off at Adam for asking her to marry him when he knew damn well it wouldn't last.

And now here she was, back in his life. Fate, disguised in the form of a tragedy, had thrown them together again. Had he fooled her? he wondered. Or had she seen that beneath his seemingly cool indifference he was still crazy about her?

At the bus stop, she stopped and glanced at her watch. For no particular reason, he found himself wondering if she was going home, or to the art gallery where her photographs were being exhibited. He shrugged. What did it matter where she was going? It's not like he intended to see her again. He'd had it with women anyway. First there was Jenna, who had married the wrong man, then his wife, Denise, who had left him for an Italian cyclist and moved to Milan. After Denise, there had been a couple of women, none with whom he cared to have a long-term relationship, although they would have liked nothing better. Maybe it was him. Maybe *he* was the one who had made all the wrong choices.

The reunion between Adam and Frank had been unemotional—two old buddies brought back together by chance. They had made small chitchat, talking about old times, catching up on the past fifteen years, then it was down to the reason for Adam's visit, and his suspicions that his pretty young wife was having an affair.

Frank didn't handle marital cases. He was a criminal investigator, but Adam seemed so down in the dumps that Frank had taken the case anyway, accepting a one thousand dollar retainer and promising to get back to him with his findings.

Tanya, who occasionally doubled as an operative, had volunteered to do the surveillance work. Tailing a philandering wife was boring as hell but for some reason, Tanya liked it. As an ex-police officer, she had the patience of a saint and could sit in a car for hours, as opposed to Frank, who began fidgeting after the first five minutes.

She had tracked Adam's wife not to a love nest, but to a busy snack bar on Sixth Avenue where, twice that week, Amber Lear had met a man Frank had since then identified as Billy Ray Shaeffer, an ex-con who had served two-and-a-half years in prison for involuntary manslaughter. Amber, whose real name had been Teresa Berensky before she changed it, was his girlfriend at the time of the crime and the newly crowned Miss Jersey City. They were driving back from a party when Billy Ray struck a pedestrian and killed him.

Most women would have waited a few weeks, maybe a few months, before writing a Dear John letter. Not Amber. After failing to qualify for the Miss New Jersey pageant two weeks later, she changed her name to Amber North, had her mother deliver a goodbye note to the prison where Billy Ray was serving his sentence and moved to New York City in search of fame and fortune.

Fame had eluded her, but she hadn't made out too badly in the fortune department. Two years after setting foot in the Big Apple, she had met Adam. A year later they were married.

After observing Amber and Billy Ray at the coffee shop, Tanya had concluded they were not lovers. They talked in whispers, she had told Frank, and with a definite undercurrent of hostility. Unfortunately, Ruby's Café was too noisy for Tanya to hear their conversation. The only fact worth mentioning was that at both encounters, Amber had slid a thick envelop across the table. Each time Billy Ray had brought it to his lap, glanced at the contents, and put it away.

"It's got to be money," Tanya had told her boss.

Frank had agreed, but if he was going to find out why the current Mrs. Lear was giving money to an old flame, he needed Adam's approval. On Monday evening, Frank had left a message on Adam's voice mail. Instead of a return phone call the following morning, a 6:00 a.m. news bulletin had informed him of Adam's death.

Now that the first wave of disbelief had passed and he'd had some time to think, he was puzzled. Like most New Yorkers, Adam knew that Central Park was no place to go for a midnight stroll. So why had he? And why hadn't he defended himself? Granted, he was no Schwarzenegger, but he was no weakling either.

What was it Jenna had said earlier? *"Even if there is more to his death than what the police claim?"*

What had she meant by that?

The uptown bus pulled up to the curb. Standing back, Jenna helped an elderly woman get on board. The gesture reminded Frank of the Jenna he used to know—kind and thoughtful, the same Jenna, who, moments earlier, had stood in his office, ready to forgive his fifteen-year silence. If he hadn't been so busy being a jerk, he would have seen that. Now it was too late.

Jenna jumped in, and as the bus disappeared from sight, a feeling of nostalgia stirred inside Frank's gut.

He had spent the rest of the day chasing Ralph Loomis, his hide-and-seek client, finally catching up with him in a seedy bar on MacDougal Street. It wasn't until Frank had threatened to turn the account over to a collection agency that Ralph agreed to pay him half of what he owed him right away and the other half at the end of the week.

At last this crazy day was over and Frank was on his way home, the T-bird purring like a contented cat as he drove through the Battery Tunnel. Marty had returned the car himself at five o'clock sharp, apologizing profusely for letting his apprentice do the tune-up.

"Don't tell my father, okay, Frankie? He'd kill me if he knew I screwed up."

Frank never had any intention of telling Vinnie. Marty was okay. He wasn't the auto mechanic his father had been, but he was learning. Right now, all Frank wanted was to go home, pop open a cold beer and spend a few hours with his son.

Eighteen months ago, when Denise had left him for the Italian biker, Frank hadn't been sure he'd be able to care for a twelve-year-old boy and work for the FBI at the same time. His job as a federal agent was demanding, and required him to travel often and at a moment's notice. Friends and neighbors in Alexandria, Virginia, where he had lived for thirteen years, were quick to pitch in and help, but they were not a replacement for a mother and father.

He was considering hiring a full-time housekeeper when fate intervened. At about the same time Denise left, his uncle Vinnie was coming out of retirement to help his old friend, Johnny Caruso, run his private trash-hauling business. After two heart attacks, Johnny felt he needed someone sharp and vigilant by his side, and Vinnie was just the man for the job.

When a fellow agent Frank despised found out

about Vinnie's new job, he took it upon himself to investigate the hauling company. He found out that when Johnny first started his venture forty years ago, his partner and financial backer was a well-known Mafia figure. Although Johnny had eventually repaid the loan and dissolved the partnership, the fact that Vinnie now ran a business that was once connected to the Mob made the bureau nervous. Frank was told that unless he could convince his uncle to turn down the job, they would have to let him go.

Frank had saved them the trouble. That same day he had handed in his resignation.

He loved his uncle too much to tell him his real reason for leaving the FBI. Instead he had come up with an explanation Vinnie had readily accepted—Frank's desire to spend more time with his son.

Opening a detective agency in his hometown sounded like the perfect career move. The flexible hours allowed him to be there for Danny and do all the things he was never able to do before. The choice of a location for his new business was equally easy. The East Village, with its eclectic mix of artists, students and social advocates, had always been one of his favorite places. And now that scores of businesses had moved away because of 9/11, the price of office space was once again affordable.

After fourteen years of being an absentee grandma, his mother was delighted to have him and Danny close to her. Although proud of Frank's accomplishments as an FBI agent, Mia Renaldi lived by the credo that family came first, careers second. Vinnie went one step further in welcoming his nephew back. He invited him and Danny to move in with him, an offer Frank gratefully accepted. His intention was to stay with his uncle until he found his own place, but, as Vinnie was quick to point out, if he moved out, who would look after Danny? Who would take him to hockey practice after school? Who would cook for him and make sure he did his homework? A stranger?

"Don't make me laugh," Vinnie told Frank with his usual straightforwardness. "You two stay here, where you belong."

Danny couldn't have been happier with the arrangements. As for Frank's initial concerns that a noisy, growing boy would disrupt Vinnie's routine, they were quickly put to rest. The Staten Island house, a three-story Victorian on Sunset Road, had become too big for the widower whose two sons had moved out long ago. Far from annoying Vinnie, the sound of young feet running up and down the stairs, the slamming of doors and the raiding of the refrigerator, had given him a new purpose in life—looking after those he loved.

As always at this time of night, Danny was back from hockey practice and sitting at the kitchen table doing his homework. An apron around his waist, Vinnie was making his famous tomato sauce. At seventy-two, he had a small but muscular built, thick gray hair he claimed made him look like Tony Bennett and a face as weathered as old leather.

"You're going to stir that sauce to death," Frank teased as he tossed his briefcase on one of the deep chairs flanking the large stone fireplace.

Vinnie glanced over his shoulder. "What are you? A cooking expert all of sudden?"

Frank laughed and went to kiss his fourteen-year-old. "Hi, bud." The kid was growing at an alarming speed and looking more like Frank every day, right down to his curly black hair and the dimples in his cheeks.

"Hi, Dad." Danny put his pen down and looked up. His big brown eyes—the only feature he had inherited from his mother—were clouded with worry. "Did you hear from Janice's dad?"

At the mention of Danny's girlfriend, Frank was reminded that his troubles may not be over. He walked over to the refrigerator and took out a Heineken. "Not yet. Maybe he had a change of heart and decided not to press charges."

"Janice told him you had no idea she was even here."

"I told him the same thing, but he didn't believe me."

"He didn't believe Janice either, until..." Danny lowered his eyes. "Until she told him that if he did press charges, she would leave again, and this time he'd never find her."

Vinnie turned around and shook a finger. "Children should not threaten their parents. It's disrespectful."

But Frank knew his son better than the boy knew himself. "Was that her idea?" he asked as he sat across from him. "To tell her father she'd run away again?"

Danny's face turned beet-red. Frank tried not to smile. The kid was such a poor liar. Trapping him that way was almost criminal. "Not exactly."

"Whose idea was it, then?"

"Mine." Danny's dark eyes flared up. "Her father was going to have you thrown in jail, Dad! I had to do *some*thing."

"And I appreciate that, but you should never influence a friend, or anyone, to do something wrong. What if she had run away? And something had happened to her?"

"I'd feel bad." The humble expression lasted only a second. "Her father is so strict, Dad. He doesn't let her do *any*thing. It's like he doesn't remember when *he* was fourteen."

Frank saw Vinnie's shoulders shake with quiet laughter. He was having a hard time trying to keep from laughing himself. "I'm not disagreeing with you, bud, I'm just telling you that bringing her here last night, without telling her family or me, was irresponsible."

"If I had, you would have taken her home."

"Probably. At the very least I would have called her father to let him know where she was."

Danny gave a shrug. "He doesn't care. He didn't even know she was gone until this morning."

"That's where you're wrong. He does care. That's why he was so angry this morning. And that's why this kind of incident can never happen again. Do you understand that?"

"Yes, sir."

"Good. Now that we got that out of the way, how was practice?"

With a resiliency only the very young could pull off, Danny made a complete turnaround. "I was awesome, Dad."

This time Vinnie chuckled out loud. "We're gonna have to work on this kid's lack of confidence, Frankie," he said without turning around. "It's dragging him down."

"How many goals did you score?" Frank asked.

"Four. The coach said that if I play like this on Saturday we'll win for sure. You're coming, aren't you, Dad?"

Frank reached across the table and tousled the black curls. "Would I miss one of your games?"

By nine o'clock, Danny had gone to bed and Frank sat on the porch, gazing at the stars. His thoughts kept drifting back and forth from Jenna to Adam, and back to Jenna again. He was so absorbed, he didn't hear Vinnie until his uncle came to sit beside him, a pipe and a pouch of tobacco in his hand.

"I guess I don't have to ask what's on your mind tonight." Vinnie started packing tobacco into the bowl of his old Meerschaum. "Anything new on your friend's case?"

"Not yet. I called Paul Stavos before I left the office. They're still looking for the Central Park Robber."

Vinnie held his lighter upside down and touched the flame to the bowl, taking quick, short puffs. "Could be a long search."

"He didn't seem to think so."

A minute went by before Vinnie spoke again. "Something else bothering you, kid?"

Vinnie had always had an uncanny, almost spooky sixth sense. "What makes you think something else is bothering me?"

Vinnie laughed. "I've known you since you were two days old. That makes me pretty much of an expert on the subject of Frank Renaldi and his many moods."

Frank debated whether or not to tell his uncle about Jenna, then thought why the hell not. When his father died more than twenty-five years ago, Vinnie was the one Frank had turned to whenever he needed a man's opinion. Over the years, he had become his best friend, his mentor and his confidant. There was no one in the world Frank trusted more than Vinnie Renaldi.

"I ran into someone I used to know today," he said.

"Someone from D.C.?"

"No. From school. Adam's ex-wife—Jenna."

"Ahhh." Vinnie took another puff of his pipe. "The girl you used to have the hots for."

Frank's protest died in his throat. What was the point of lying to Vinnie?

"She came to see me," he continued, "hoping to find out what I knew, if anything, about Adam's death."

"How did that go?"

"Not well. I was rude and insulting."

"And she took it? That doesn't sound like the Jenna I used to know."

"She took it for a while, until she got tired of being polite and let me have it."

Vinnie chuckled. "Ain't love grand?" He gave Frank a sidelong look. "You *do* still love her, right? You wouldn't have pulled such a stupid stunt if you didn't. Only men in love make fools of themselves."

Admitting his feelings for Jenna to his uncle wasn't something he was ready to do just yet. It was hard enough admitting them to himself. "Sorry to disappoint you, Vinnie, but you're wrong. I am not in love with Jenna. What do you take me for? A masochist? The girl made it plain years ago that I was out of her league."

"Uh-huh."

"What? You don't believe me?"

"I didn't say that."

"There are far too many women out there," he pointed out, more for his own benefit than Vinnie's, "for me to pine over one as high-strung as Jenna Meyerson."

"My sentiments exactly." Vinnie was grinning like a fool, as though he knew something no one else did. "But if what you say is true, if you no longer care about this girl, why were you so obnoxious?"

"I don't know. I guess I didn't expect to find her sitting there. In a city of over eight million people, what are the odds you'll run into someone you know?"

Vinnie tilted his face toward the night sky and blew out a perfect smoke ring. "Apparently not as big as you thought."

"Apparently."

"Did seeing her stir old memories?"

"I suppose."

"Spark a few fires?"

More like a blaze. "Absolutely not."

"Want some advice, kid?"

"No," Frank said, knowing Vinnie would give it to him anyway.

"In my days, the only way to make a lady forgive you was with a little romance. A bouquet of roses, a box of expensive chocolates, a Frank Sinatra record to set the mood, and voilà, the girl melted in your arms."

Frank laughed. "It's with that kind of corn that you won Aunt Sylvia's heart?"

"Hell, no. I won her heart by going to her house one night and serenading her."

Frank turned around in his chair. "You didn't."

"Cross my heart, hope to die. I stood on her front lawn and belted out *Enamorada* until she opened her window. Woke up the entire neighborhood, too. Her father, the smart ass, tossed me a ten-cent coin and told me to get lost, but I wouldn't go, and I didn't stop singing until Sylvia came down and said she'd marry me."

"That's very romantic, Vinnie."

"You bet your ass it is. You should try it sometime."

"Not me. I'll never marry again."

A good ten minutes passed before Frank stood up, almost knocking his chair over.

Vinnie, who had finished his pipe and was starting to doze off, jumped. "Where are you going?"

"To call Jenna."

"It's eleven o'clock."

"That's all right, she's a night owl."

Taking a chance she was listed, he checked the Manhattan phone book and found her there, under J. Meyerson.

She answered on the third ring, sounding sleepy. "'Lo?"

"Jenna, it's Frank. Look, I was a complete ass today and I'd like to—"

She slammed the phone down.

Nine

Today was Elaine Meyerson's birthday. Each year on that date, Jenna took her six-year-old Audi out of the garage and drove to Carmel Hill Cemetery in Hartford, Connecticut, where her mother was buried.

As Jenna drove north on I-95, she tried once again to put Frank Renaldi out of her mind, but he kept coming back like a nagging headache. What a jerk. Talking to her as if she were some meddling busybody, embarrassing her until she was left with no recourse but to sink down to his level. That's what had galled her the most, that she had lost her temper and stormed out without learning a thing. Frank was the one person who could have shed a light on the mystery of Adam's death, and she had let him slip through her fingers.

At the cemetery gate, she waved to the guard and drove slowly until she reached Alley G at the top of the hill. Once there, she picked up the bouquet of white roses—her mother's favorites—from the passenger seat, and got out of the car. At this early hour, Carmel Hill was quiet except for the sound of her boots crunching the gravel as she walked up the winding path.

The familiar knot in Jenna's throat was already there when she reached the grave and read the inscription: Elaine Meyerson—Beloved wife and mother—1939-1999. Hunkering down, she propped up the roses against the shiny gray marble stone, the memories of that dreadful night so vivid in her mind that she often wondered why she tortured herself by coming here so often. Yet every time she tried to talk herself out of a trip to Carmel Hill, something invariably pulled her in that direction. She and her mother had been as close as any mother and daughter could be. Even after Jenna had moved out of the house and into the dorm at NYU, the bond between them had remained strong.

Despite that bond, however, Jenna was never able to find out the reason Elaine and Sam had ended their thirty-three-year marriage. Both had cited irreconcilable differences, explaining to Jenna and their friends that they no longer found the same joy in being together. It was a valid reason, one Jenna could easily identify with, but she hadn't bought it. Determined to get to the truth, she had questioned her parents separately, trying to find out if another man, or another woman, was responsible for the breakup. Elaine and Sam had denied any outside involvement and stuck to their story.

"Why did you leave him, Mom?" she murmured as her eyes began to fill. "Why didn't you talk more? Try to make it work? If you had, you'd still be with us."

She stayed there for a full fifteen minutes as resentment built deep within her. She hated feeling this way, but no matter how hard she tried not to, she still blamed her mother for the breakup, for her own death, for leaving Jenna and Sam alone and grieving.

At the sound of footsteps, she turned her head and

saw her father coming up the path, a bouquet of wild-flowers in his hand. A somber expression had replaced last night's proud smile and Jenna knew why. Sam's love for his wife hadn't ended with their divorce or her death, but continued to endure year after year. Considering how much he had cared, Jenna often wondered why he hadn't fought harder to keep her, but that, too, was something Sam wouldn't discuss.

He came to stand beside her and bent to lay his flowers next to Jenna's. "I thought I might find you here."

Jenna wiped a tear from her cheek. "I guess you heard about Adam."

"Marcie called me with the news." He shook his head. "I'll miss him. I didn't always approve of what he did, but I was fond of him. And I was grateful for the way he stood by you when your mother died."

They were silent for a moment, each lost in their own thoughts. He was the first to speak again. "Marcie told me about your visit."

"Did she tell you I was being a big pain in the butt?"

His eyes remained on the grave. "Word for word." He looked down at her. "And for the record, I agree with everything she said. I know you and Adam go back a long way, but this isn't your battle, honey."

"Don't you want to know who killed Adam?"

"Of course I do."

"Then you have to believe me when I tell you that he would never go to Central Park at night. He was much too sensible to do something so stupid."

"He could have been forced there."

"By a partly disabled panhandler?" She let out a brittle laugh. "Come on, Dad."

"There could have been two of them. Or more. Adam could have been hit over the head, or chloroformed and dragged into the park. The possibilities are endless."

"What about his suspicions of Faxel?"

A dark cloud drifted, covering the sun and turning the cemetery a somber shade of gray. "That does raise certain doubts," Sam said cautiously.

"Tell that to Marcie Hollander."

"I didn't have to. She's taking your allegations very seriously."

"That's not the impression she gave me."

"You have to understand her position, Jenna. Even though, technically, the N.Y.P.D. works for her, she can't interfere in a police investigation. Nor can she afford to jump to conclusions every time a well-meaning witness offers to solve a case for her. The only reason she's getting personally involved in this one is because of her friendship with Adam."

Jenna wasn't surprised to hear her father come to Marcie's defense. Their friendship and respect for each other had lasted through more than two decades. In Sam's opinion, there was no one in the district attorney's office more capable of handling the job than Marcie Hollander.

"I wasn't trying to solve her case," Jenna said. "I simply acted as any concerned citizen would. Isn't that what you taught me to be? A concerned citizen?"

Sam smiled. "Yes, it is. And that's fine with me, *if* that's the extent of your role."

"I have no aspiration to be Nancy Drew, if that's what you mean."

"Marcie will be glad to hear that. And if I sound like a pain in the butt myself, it's because I'm your father, and I worry about you."

He put out his hand and she took it, letting him pull her to her feet. After one last look at Elaine's grave, they both turned away and started walking back toward their respective cars.

"Did Marcie show you the photographs I gave her?" Jenna asked.

"Yes. She was hoping I'd recognize someone. I didn't."

"What do you know about Faxel, Dad?" When he looked at her sharply, she raised both hands. "Just being a concerned citizen, nothing more."

She caught the hint of a smile before he answered her question. "Faxel is a solid company, run by a strong management team and headed by the same CEO for the past sixteen years. I've known J. B. Collins for some time, not well, but well enough to know that he is smart, honest and well-liked by his employees. In the mid-nineties, the company suffered a setback due to some serious competition from Global Access. There were large debts, high inventories and dismal sales. Then one of the company's brilliant new engineers came up with an idea for a handheld computer that would revolutionize the industry. In a matter of months, Faxel was back at the top of its game."

They had reached the parking lot. "Do you think J.B. is capable of fraud?"

Sam watched one of the cemetery caretakers come up the drive, pushing a wheelbarrow filled with gravel. "I don't know, Jenna. I've always respected Adam's judgment, but suspecting a man like J. B. Collins of fraud..." He shook his head. "I'm having a hard time believing that."

Jenna opened the Audi door. "That's what everybody said about Enron."

Back home, Jenna looked around her kitchen for a place to hide her set of photographs. She had been carrying them in her purse and it was time to put them somewhere a little more secure.

Her gaze stopped on a recipe box on the yellow-tiled counter. It was a present from her best friend Beckie, who kept hoping to turn Jenna into a master cook.

"It's so simple," she had told her optimistically. "Especially with those recipes they now put on CDs. All you have to do is select a dish, slide the appropriate CD into your laptop and presto, you've got a famous chef by your side, guiding you every step of the way."

Although Jenna had every intention of putting Beckie's words to the test one of these days, she had yet to be brave enough to tackle the task.

Flipping through the colorful plastic envelopes, she pulled out the one marked Coq Au Vin, took the CD out and replaced it with the small stack of photographs. It wasn't a perfect fit, but unless someone looked closely, the envelope's small bulge was undetectable.

As she slid the recipe box back in its place, she let out a nervous laugh. This was a little too cloak-and-dagger for her. What was she afraid of? That someone would break into her apartment in the middle of the night and steal the photos? How would anyone know she had them? Unless some mysterious stalker was watching every move she made, which wasn't the case. She was no Sherlock Holmes, but she would know if she was being followed.

Ten

"What are you all of a sudden, Mike Hammer?"

Sitting at his desk, Frank looked up and saw Tanya standing in the doorway, one hand on her slender hip. "If this is one of your riddles, I'm not in the mood."

His remark didn't seem to faze her. "Does that mean I tell the potential client in the reception room to take a hike?"

Frank was already reaching for his jacket on the back of his chair. "Smart-ass. Who is he?"

"It's a she—a cross between Cindy Crawford and Jennifer Lopez. That's why I made that crack about Mike Hammer. Two beautiful women in that many days. You keep this up and some Hollywood producer is going to want to make a movie about you."

Frank had learned long ago that Tanya wasn't the kind of person you could rush. Although her job didn't require the brains of an Einstein, she was smart, hardworking and easy on the eye. But when she had something to say, she said it her way or not at all.

"This client gave you a name?"

"Amber Lear."

One arm into his jacket, Frank stopped mid-motion. "Adam's wife?"

"Widow. Young, no more than twenty-five or so.

Appropriately dressed in mourning black but not terribly distressed over her husband's passing. Or maybe she's one of those cool dames who doesn't believe in displaying her grief in public, but I don't think so.''

"Is that it?"

"You want more?"

"No, I can assess the rest myself.'' He smoothed down his tie. "Okay, show her in.''

Tanya hadn't exaggerated. Even in her demure black dress and understated black pumps, Amber Lear had an exotic, sultry sensuality she couldn't have hidden under a burlap sack.

She seemed nervous and hesitant, but why shouldn't she be? Coming to the office of a private investigator right after the brutal murder of your husband wasn't something the average citizen did every day.

"Mr. Renaldi?'' Her voice was as soft as crushed velvet.

"Yes.'' He walked around his desk and came to meet her halfway. He shook her hand, which was small and warm. "I'm very sorry about your husband. Please accept my condolences.''

"Thank you.''

He removed the stack of newspapers from one of the chairs. "Won't you sit down?''

She was one of those women who made sitting down an event. One long, shapely leg crossed slowly over the other and as it did, her dress rode up a couple of inches above her knees. Tanya was right. She was right out of a Mike Hammer novel.

Cool green eyes assessed him. "You and Adam were old friends, weren't you?''

"He told you that?"

"He spoke about you often, although he didn't tell me you were a private investigator."

"He didn't know, at least not until a few days ago."

"When he came to see you." She gave him a second to confirm her statement. When he didn't, she gave him a knowing smile. "I know he was here, Mr. Renaldi. I saw your name on his desk calendar at home and I looked you up in the phone book. That's how I found out you were a private investigator."

Pretty *and* smart. "What can I do for you, Mrs. Lear?" The question was just a formality. He already knew why she was here.

"I'd like to know why my husband came to see you."

"We're old friends. Does he need a reason?"

"No, but if his visit was just a casual one, he wouldn't have kept it from me. Since he did, I assume he came here to hire you. Am I right?"

"I can't discuss your husband's visit, Mrs. Lear."

The polite smile disappeared. "I'm going to be very honest with you, Mr. Renaldi, and I hope you'll do me the same courtesy. My father-in-law despises me. And he despises the fact that I stand to inherit several million from Adam's estate even more."

He could believe that. The millions Amber was talking about had been bequeathed to Adam through a trust fund his grandfather had set up when his grandson was just a toddler. At age twenty-one, Adam had taken charge of the trust and, with his father's help, had invested the money wisely.

"I may not have been Adam's wife for very

long,'' Amber continued, "but I know Warren well enough to believe he'll do anything to keep me from getting that money—and that includes spreading lies about me.''

"What kind of lies?''

"According to my father-in-law, Adam thought I was cheating on him and was about to start divorce proceedings.''

"Even if that's true, that's hardly a reason to keep you from getting your inheritance.''

"There's more. He also claims that I had Adam killed. You see, in order to marry Adam, I had to sign a prenuptial agreement that clearly stated that in the event of a divorce, I would have no claim on my husband's money. According to Warren, I cold-bloodedly arranged Adam's death so I could collect the inheritance.''

"Did you?''

Her eyes narrowed and all softness left her face. She no longer seemed so helpless, but appeared quite capable of taking care of herself. "Are you trying to be funny, Mr. Renaldi?''

"No, I'm asking a perfectly legitimate question.''

"And I'll give you a perfectly legitimate answer. No, I did not arrange for my husband's death. I wouldn't know where to begin looking for a hit man. And why would I want Adam dead? I loved him with all my heart.'' She paused long enough to take a white, lacy handkerchief from her purse and dab her eyes, being careful not to smear her mascara.

Frank watched her for a moment, admiring her performance—for he had no doubt that's all it was. Whether or not she had hired someone to kill her husband, however, was another matter.

Amber sniffed. "I'm sorry. I'm not usually so emotional." Looking helpless once again, she raised humid eyes at him. "Someone did kill my husband, but it wasn't me. The truth is, Adam hadn't been himself these past few weeks. He had become short-tempered, and preoccupied. More so than usual."

Frank looked at her with renewed interest. "Did he tell you why?"

"No. He rarely discussed his work with me, but I could tell something was wrong. When I tried to talk to him about it, he told me I was imagining things." Amber put her handkerchief back into her purse. "His problem wasn't with me. Something else was on his mind. Or someone."

Maybe Adam's restless mood was worth looking into. Just in case that nagging feeling Jenna had planted into his head persisted.

From her purse, Amber took out a check and handed it to him.

"What's this?"

"A retainer. I want you to find out who killed my husband so Warren will get off my back."

Frank took the check, read the amount, which was more than generous, and handed it back.

Amber's large green eyes got a little bigger. "Isn't that enough?"

"It's more than enough, but I can't take your money."

"Why not?"

"Because I already have a client."

"Who?"

He smiled. "Me."

She was silent for a moment, her expression speculative. "You are investigating the case?"

"It makes sense, don't you think? Adam was my friend and I happen to be an investigator."

After a long second, she dropped the check back into her purse. "Will you at least tell me what you find out?"

"I only report to my clients."

"I see." She stood up. This time there was no enticing movement of her legs, no subtle attempt at seduction. She was all business. "Goodbye, Mr. Renaldi."

He walked her to the door and watched her walk away, her back rigid. She didn't bother to say goodbye to Tanya as she passed her desk.

His secretary waited until Frank had closed the outer door before saying, "Well?"

"She wanted to hire me."

Tanya leaned back in her chair. "Tell me you said yes."

"I couldn't say yes. I'm already investigating the case, remember?"

"We need the money, Boss."

"No, we don't." He took another check from his pocket, this one signed by the elusive Ralph Loomis, and handed it to her.

She grinned when she saw the amount. "Good work, Boss. I'll deposit this during my lunch hour." Instead of putting the check in her purse, she fanned herself gently with it. "You still didn't give me your impression of the Black Widow."

"She's hiding something. That's why she wanted to hire me. She knows I'm going to investigate Adam's murder and by hiring me, she figured that if I found out something incriminating, I wouldn't be able to use it against her."

"But client privilege only applies to information your client gives you, not information you discover on your own."

"Apparently she doesn't know that."

"So what's your game plan?"

"A trip to Jersey City, for starters. You know how to reach me if you need to."

Before he left, he went back to his office for one more attempt to connect with Jenna, who had already hung up on him twice. This time he got her answering machine.

"Sorry I missed you," the cheery voice said. "Leave a message and I'll call you right back."

Somehow he doubted she would, but he left a message anyway.

Eleven

Situated on the western side of the Hudson River, Jersey City was essentially a blue-collar town with a strong maritime history, a controversial claim on the Statue of Liberty and a spectacular view of the Manhattan skyline.

Amber's mother lived on Washington Street, in a modest two-story house that was in serious need of a fresh coat of paint. The woman who opened the door didn't bear any resemblance to Amber Lear. She was short, painfully thin and wore a flowered housecoat with a tan cardigan over it.

"Mrs. Berenski?" Frank asked.

Suspicious brown eyes inspected him through the torn screen door. "If you're sellin', I ain't buyin'." She started to close the door.

"I'm not a salesman," Frank said quickly. "I'm here about your daughter, Amber."

The frail shoulders seemed to stiffen a little. "She all right?"

"She's fine. I just need to ask you a few questions."

"'Bout what?"

"Her marriage to Adam Lear."

Judging from her bitter expression, Frank concluded she didn't approve of the marriage.

"I don't know nothin' about that."

"Amber doesn't talk to you about her husband?"

"Her name is Teresa."

"I thought she changed it, legally."

"Teresa's her God-given name."

"In that case, that's what I'll call her." He saw that her hold on the door had relaxed and she no longer seemed so hostile. "May I come in, Mrs. Berenski?"

She inspected him again, then glanced at the T-bird parked at the curb. "That your car?"

"Yes."

She stepped out onto the porch. "You'll want to talk out here, then, and keep an eye on it. Car like that won't last long 'round here."

Two white plastic chairs covered with faded green cushions stood against the wall of the house, facing the street. She pointed at them. "You can sit if you want."

"Thank you." He waited for her to sit first before doing the same. "When was the last time you saw Amb...I mean Teresa?"

She started buttoning her cardigan. "I used to see her all the time after she moved to New York. She always needed money or somethin', was always cryin' how she couldn't make ends meet. I told her to forget about that New York nonsense and move back home, but oh no. She didn't want to do that. No siree." Her voice grew bitter again. "Neighborhood wasn't good 'nough for her no more."

Frank looked around him at the crumbling foundation, the rusted gutters, the neglected yard, and wondered what kind of daughter would take money from this woman. "Did you give it to her? The money, I mean."

She shrugged. "I did what I could. I clean houses and don't make much but I'm a good saver—learned that from my mother, who grew up during the Depression."

"When did you see Teresa last?" Frank asked, bringing her back.

Her tongue flicked over thin dry lips. She thought for a moment. "Had to be a couple of years ago. When she met that rich fellow."

"Adam Lear?"

"Yeah. From then on, me and her, we were like strangers."

"Why is that?" But he already knew.

"Girl was ashamed of me, of this place." She waved at the house behind her.

"So after she met Adam Lear, you never saw her again?"

She shook her head.

"No phone calls either?"

"No calls, no letters, not even an invitation to the wedding. Nothin'." She raised a finger. "The only time she called was to tell me she was getting married. You know what she said to me?"

Frank had a pretty good idea, but he shook his head.

"She said I wouldn't fit in with her new crowd, that I wouldn't enjoy myself there. Truth is she was ashamed of me."

"You never met Adam Lear?"

She leaned back against her chair and folded her hands across her flat stomach. "Nope. Man don't even knows I exist. Bet she told him her mamma

was dead. Wouldn't put it past her. Girl can lie like
a rug. Always did.''

She was painting a terrible picture of her daughter,
but one look into those tired old eyes and Frank knew
Jean Berenski wasn't lying. ''What can you tell me
about the accident?''

She frowned. ''What accident?''

''The one she had with Billy Ray.''

''Oh, that.'' She shook her head. ''Terrible thing.
Happened not too far from here. They was coming
back from a party.'' A spark not unlike pride flashed
in her eyes. ''Did you know Teresa was Miss Jersey
City back then?''

''Yes, I know. And I'm not surprised. She's very
beautiful.''

''Takes after her daddy, rest his soul.''

''So your daughter and Billy Ray were coming
back from a party?''

She made a tisk sound with her tongue. ''Still
can't figure out what happened. Billy Ray was a good
driver. Bought that car with the money he made
working at the root beer stand in the summer and the
car wash in the winter. Saved for two long years
before he could finally afford it. And then this happened. I guess it's like he told the cops. He never
saw that poor man until he hit him.''

''The police report says he and Teresa were arguing that night.''

''That night, night before. They always argued,
those two.''

''Why?''

Another shrug. ''Same old thing. Teresa wanted to
move to the big city. Billy Ray wanted to stay here

and work in his father's garage." She sighed. "Then he went to prison and she got her wish."

"Billy Ray couldn't have been very happy when he came out of prison and heard Teresa was gone."

"Kid was fit to be tied. He wanted to go after her, but didn't know where to look. I'd have told him but I didn't know myself. She never told me where she lived. I guess she was afraid I'd show up on her doorstep or somethin'." Her expression turned mournful. "Ain't that something? You raise a daughter, do your damn best for her and that's how she repays you."

"What kind of man was Billy Ray?"

"Okay, I guess. A little wild maybe, but a hard worker."

Wild enough to commit murder for the woman he loved? As Frank asked himself that question, his gaze stopped on a pretty brunette in blue jeans and a black turtleneck leaning against the hood of his car. She was looking at him, arms folded.

"Who is that?" he asked Jean.

Jean Berenski waved at the girl. "That's Angie."

"A friend of your daughter's?"

"You kiddin'? Those two hated each other." She leaned forward, dropping her voice a little. "She was Billy Ray's girl before he fell for Teresa."

Amber's past was getting more intriguing by the minute. Maybe he should talk to the jilted girlfriend and see what else he could learn. Especially since she seemed to be waiting for him.

He stood up. "Thanks for talking to me, Mrs. Berenski."

She remained seated. "Why are you so interested in Teresa?"

"Her husband was murdered on Monday night."

"*Murdered?*" Her mouth opened in shock. "I didn't know. Dear God." A pause. "What about Teresa? How... How is she?"

"She seemed fine when I talked to her. She stands to inherit a lot of money."

The woman gave a nod. "Then she won't be grievin' long. Girl loves money."

After saying goodbye to Amber's mother, Frank walked over to where the brunette stood. She had a flawless olive complexion and very dark, very bright eyes.

She smiled. "Hi, there. I'm Angie Delano."

"Frank Renaldi."

She gave a short nod toward the car. "Nice wheels."

"Thanks."

"Fifty-seven, right?"

"You know your cars."

"I used to have a boyfriend who was nuts about cars." The sun squeezed out from behind a cloud, forcing her to squint. "You're from New York. And you're here to see Jean, so you had to be talking about Teresa."

Frank decided she was too sharp to be given a line. "We were. I'm a private investigator. I'm trying to find out who killed Teresa's husband."

She gave him a wintry smile. "Then this is your lucky day." She glanced toward the porch where Amber's mother still sat, watching them. "And not because of your conversation with Jean."

"You know who killed Adam Lear?"

"I know who *could* have killed him—Teresa. That bitch is capable of anything."

Two for two so far. "You don't like her."

She laughed. "What's to like? The slut stole my guy *and* my crown. I hate her guts. I wish *she* had been the one found stabbed in Central Park instead of her old man."

"You're pretty well-informed."

"My father's a cop here in town. That's how I found out." She jutted her chin toward the house. Amber's mother was still there, watching them. "She knows about Teresa's husband?"

"She does now."

"Poor woman. Teresa dumped her too, the same way she dumped Billy Ray and all her friends. Not that she had many. Teresa always thought she was better than the rest of us."

"What did you mean when you said she stole your crown?"

Angie pushed the tips of her fingers into the front pocket of her tight jeans and gazed down the street. "We were both finalists in the Miss Jersey City pageant. After the talent competition, the odds were in my favor. Teresa knew that, so she seduced Billy Ray, got him to take naked pictures of me and told him to send them to the pageant committee."

Frank thought about the sad, vulnerable young woman who had walked into his office earlier. That woman couldn't have done what Angie accused her of, but the woman who had left his office half an hour later certainly could have.

"I was dismissed from the pageant for improper conduct," she continued. "And Teresa took the crown."

"Did you ever confront her about what she did?"

She stuck her tongue into her cheek, looking smug. "What do you think?"

Frank laughed. "You don't look like the forgiving type."

"You got that right. Unfortunately, there wasn't much I could do about the title. That was lost to me. And I couldn't go after Billy Ray because he's bigger and meaner than I am, and anyway, I felt sorry for him for being such a jerk, for jumping when she said jump, for being putty in that bitch's hands."

She had worked herself into a small frenzy and was smart enough to realize it. She took a deep breath and once again was back in control. "One night, I waited for Teresa to come out of Denny's, where she worked, and I beat the shit out of her skinny ass. Then I told her that if she breathed one word to anyone, I'd come back and cut her up so bad, she'd have to wear a mask, like the Phantom of the Opera." She chuckled. "I never heard a peep out of her again."

Frank smiled. He liked the girl's spunk. "Remind me to never cross you."

Her expression turned sassy as she gave him a quick appraising glance. "You don't look like the type who would."

"Can you tell me anything about that car accident four years ago?"

Angie pursed her lips. "You know about that?"

"Only what I read."

"Yeah, well," her tone turned sarcastic, "don't believe everything you read."

"What do you mean by that?"

"Billy Ray was an excellent driver. So good he

was thinking of turning pro and joining the NASCAR circuit. Then the accident happened and just like that,'' she snapped her fingers, ''his dream was shot to hell.''

She fell silent and Frank didn't rush her.

''I was there that night, at the same party,'' she continued. ''Teresa was drinking, and blabbing about what she would do if she didn't qualify for the Miss New Jersey pageant. Her plans were to move to New York, take acting classes, maybe do some modeling. I could see Billy Ray was getting pissed. After a while, I couldn't stand all that tension, so I went to join some of my friends. Next thing I knew, someone comes running in, screaming there'd been an accident and Billy Ray had killed a man.

''The following morning, after they arrested Billy Ray, I got a chance to talk to him. He told me that he and Teresa had been arguing and he lost control of the car. He never saw that man walking alongside the road until it was too late.''

A little crease appeared between her thick dark brows. ''That's the part I'm not buying. When Billy Ray is behind the wheel of a car or on top of a motorcycle, he gives the road his undivided attention. He couldn't stand it when other motorists got distracted.''

Her lips tightened. ''He spent thirty months in prison and that bitch didn't even have the decency to tell him she was splitting.''

''But Billy Ray found her.''

She gave him another of her long, lazy looks. ''How do you know that?''

''Finding out things is what I do.''

"If you think he killed her old man, forget it. Billy Ray's not a killer."

"You said he was putty in her hands."

"That was back then, before she dumped him like yesterday's garbage. He's smarter now."

"So why did he go look for her?"

"To rattle her cage. He saw the wedding announcement in the papers and once he knew her new name, finding her wasn't all that hard." She laughed as if she had just heard a good joke. "He called her and said he was going to hop on his bike and show up at the church just when the minister said, 'If anyone knows why these two people shouldn't get married, speak now or forever hold your peace.'"

"Did he do it?"

"No. She talked him out of it."

"How did she do that?"

She studied her short fingernails for a moment. "Don't know. Maybe she got him in the sack again. She's good at that."

"I thought you said Billy Ray was smarter now."

"He's also human."

"For an ex-girlfriend, you seem to know an awful lot about Billy Ray. Are the two of you still on friendly terms?"

"We made our peace if that's what you mean. He comes to town a few times a year. When he does, we get together for a beer and we shoot the bull."

"Did he ever try to get you back?"

She laughed. "Every time he's in town."

"Not interested?"

She shrugged. "He's used goods now."

"That doesn't exactly answer my question."

Amusement danced in those sharp brown eyes.

"For a private eye, you're all right, you know that? Pretty smart, too."

"Thank you." He took his keys out of his pocket. "Who could I talk to if I wanted to find out more about the accident?"

"Billy Ray, but you'd be wasting your time. He's sticking to his story."

"One more thing before I go. What do you think really happened that night?"

"Isn't that obvious?"

"I'd like to hear you say it."

She tilted her chin up, looking almost defiant, as though she expected him to shoot her opinion down and didn't give a damn.

"My take is, the bitch was driving. She was pissed at Billy Ray for putting her down in front of their friends, so she snatched his keys from him, got into his car, even though she was drunk out of her mind, and killed that man. Then she got Billy Ray to take the rap."

Twelve

"So?" Tanya watched Frank as he entered the reception room. "What did you learn in Jersey City?"

Frank perched one hip on the corner of her desk. He still had a bad taste in his mouth from the visit. "One thing is for sure—Amber Lear may have won a beauty title, but she'll never take a prize for daughter of the year."

"Bad, huh?"

"Worse than bad. The woman's despicable. I can't understand why Adam fell for her. He must have been one of the few people around to have any kind of feelings for her." He told her about his conversation with Angie Delano.

Tanya brought a stack of mail toward her and started opening it. "The question is, do you think Amber could have had Adam killed?"

He had been asking himself that same question. "Hard to say. From all I heard, she has the stomach to do just about anything as long as there's something in it for her. And if it's true that she killed that motorist and got Billy Ray to take the fall for her, then we know she's cunning enough to pull the whole thing off. But finding a hit man to do the job for her isn't that easy."

"Maybe the boyfriend did it," Tanya said cooly. "Maybe that's what all that money was for."

Frank got up from her desk and headed for his office. "It would be interesting to find out, wouldn't it?"

Jenna had just left Carmel Hill cemetery when her cell phone rang. She glanced at the screen, saw that it was Marcie Hollander and clicked the talk button. "Hello?"

"We've got him, Jenna." The D.A.'s voice, usually so controlled, crackled with excitement.

"Who?"

"The Central Park Robber. His name is Roy Ballard. Detective Stavos took him to the precinct. How soon can you get there?"

"Why do I have to be there?"

"He wants to put Roy in a lineup so you can identify him."

The idea didn't thrill her, but if Marcie and Stavos were right and the man they had arrested was Adam's killer, then she wanted him behind bars just as much as they did. "Where do I go?"

"The Central Park Precinct at 86th Street and Transverse Road. It's right in the park."

She knew exactly where the precinct was. She had passed it many times in the past. "I'm on my way back from the cemetery. Give me about forty-five minutes."

"Take your time," Marcie said as five men, all dressed in dark, scruffy clothes, filed in, holding number cards in front of them. While it was not customary for the district attorney to be present during a lineup, Marcie had made the trip from lower Manhattan to the uptown precinct to offer Jenna moral support. Jenna appreciated the gesture. Stavos was as grumpy as ever and being alone with him would have made her a nervous wreck.

In the next room, the five men turned to face the two-way mirror, their expression solemn. Jenna studied each one, trying to connect their features to those of the man she and Adam had bumped into on Monday night. They looked straight ahead, staring blankly, except for one, number three, whose eyes kept darting from left to right. Under the bright lights, his forehead shone with a thin coat of perspiration.

"Jenna?"

"I don't know, Marcie." Her gaze drifted from one man to another before settling back on the jittery one. "It could be any one of them."

"You said you saw his face, both times."

"I did, but the street was dark. And the bakery window steamy."

"Does one make more of an impression than the others?"

"Maybe number three, but…"

"But what?"

"He doesn't seem quite right."

"Maybe if he came closer?"

"Maybe."

Detective Stavos leaned toward a mike in the wall. "Number three, take two steps forward please."

The sweaty-faced man did as requested, and looked even more skittish. He approached the mirror, dragging his left leg a little. Although the limp was familiar, Jenna still wasn't sure. And he was so jumpy. Would someone who had cold-bloodedly stabbed a man panic so easily?

"How's that?" Marcie asked.

"I don't know. The eyes aren't right," Jenna said after a few seconds.

Less patient than Marcie, Stavos let out an irritated sigh. "What's wrong with the eyes? I thought you said it was dark and you couldn't see him clearly. Now you're telling us you saw his eyes?"

"Something drew me to them at the time."

"What?"

"I don't know!" she snapped back. "I only glanced at him for a second. I never thought I'd have to identify him in a lineup two days later."

"All you have to do—"

Marcie fixed him with a cool, warning look, and lay a hand on Jenna's arm. "Try again, while he's up close."

But Jenna shook her head. "I can't say if it's him or not, Marcie. I'm sorry. He looks like the man I saw, but so do the other four. I'm sorry," she said again.

Marcie removed her hand. "That's all right. A positive ID would have helped in establishing the fact that he stalked Adam, showing premeditation, but it's not absolutely necessary. We have enough evidence to charge him with first degree murder."

Jenna looked from Marcie to Stavos. "What evidence?"

It was Stavos's turn to shoot a warning glance at Marcie. "That's classified," he said in a tone that reminded her why she had never liked him.

The three of them left the room just as two uniformed officers were escorting Roy out of the lineup room. Suddenly, he stopped in front of Stavos, his small, beady eyes shooting from him to Marcie before stopping on Jenna.

"I didn't do it! You hear me, lady? I don't care what you saw. I didn't kill nobody. And I ain't the Central Park Robber neither."

Jenna instinctively backed away from him, just as she had that first night, but he hardly seemed to notice. "I ain't no killer. Ask all my friends. Ask Estelle."

"Get him out of here," Stavos said harshly.

"You ain't sending me to Sing Sing, you hear?"

He was still shouting his innocence when they dragged him out. Her eyes on the disappearing figure, Jenna grabbed Marcie's arm.

The D.A.'s gaze sharpened. "What is it? Are you changing your mind?"

"Yes. I mean, no." Jenna let out a frustrated sigh. "What I mean is, it's not him. I'm sure of that now."

Stavos looked like he was ready to explode. "What do you mean, you're *sure?* Are you jerking us around—"

"Paul!" Marcie exclaimed.

"Dammit, Marcie. She just finished telling us she couldn't make up her mind."

"That's before…" Jenna readied herself for another onslaught of protest. "Before I smelled him."

Marcie and Stavos exchanged glances. Jenna could only imagine what they were thinking. "Before you smelled him?" Stavos repeated. "You are basing the identification of a murder suspect on a *smell?*"

"Yes. The man I saw on Monday night had a different smell. A distinctive smell—like…garbage, you know, sour. This man smells more like...mildew.''

Stavos started to say something Jenna guessed would not be pleasant, but Marcie once again stopped him. ''I'll meet you in my office,'' she told the detective. Then, turning to Jenna, she added, ''Thank you, Jenna. I know you did your best. I appreciate that.''

''You're upset.''

Marcie gave her a weary smile. ''Not with you. Sometimes this job gets to me, that's all.''

Central Park was every weary New Yorker's escape, an eight hundred and forty acre oasis that included a zoo, a theater, an ice rink, a lake, a first-class restaurant and much more. Without Central Park, life in the city would be unbearable.

On this October afternoon, in spite of the chilly air, the park was alive with the sights and sounds that made this area of New York so unique. Cyclists pedaled lazily along the shaded paths; professional dog walkers, with multiple canines in tow, tried to keep control of their herd; while musicians entertained the crowd.

At any other time, Jenna would have jumped at the chance to take a leisurely stroll or sit on a bench to catch the season's last warm rays. Not today. Roy Ballard's outburst a few minutes ago had shaken her badly. What if he was telling the truth? What if the police had the wrong man?

Instead of walking back to the West 86th Street parking lot, where she had left the Audi, she stood outside the precinct for a few seconds. Gazing around her, she wondered where, in all that space, she might find a woman by the name of Estelle Gold. And if she did find her, would the woman talk to her? Homeless people were suspicious by nature, but Roy had seemed so sure his friend would back him up, Jenna had to give it a try. She couldn't let an innocent man go to prison for a crime he didn't commit.

Uncertain as to which way to go, north or south, east or west, she opted for a southerly direction, simply because that's where the carousel was located. It would take a while to get there, but she was in no hurry.

Fifteen minutes later, she found herself at Strawberry Fields, a beautifully landscaped garden designed in memory of the late John Lennon. A man with a long gray beard sat on the grass, watching her. His eyes were bloodshot, his clothes torn. A supermarket shopping cart, piled high with what Jenna assumed were his belongings, stood beside him.

As she approached, his bony fingers wrapped around one of the cart's legs and held it tightly. She smiled, trying to appear unthreatening. "Hi."

He didn't answer.

She sat on the grass, a few feet from him. "I wonder if you could help me. I'm looking for someone. Her name is Estelle Gold."

The man continued to stare at her. To her disappointment, she saw no reaction in his eyes, no sign he had recognized the name. She took five one-dollar bills from her pocket and held them so they were clearly visible. She tried again.

"I'd be willing to pay for information."

He was no longer looking at her. His eyes were now riveted on the bills in her hand.

"Do you know Estelle?" she persisted. "Can you tell me where she lives?"

Slowly, hesitantly, he put out his hand, palm out. Jenna hesitated, aware he could decide to take off with the money; then in a show of good faith, she handed him the five bills. He snatched them up with a speed she hadn't expected. A second later, the money had disappeared.

"Now will you tell me where I can find Estelle?"

He stood up, slowly, his eyes never leaving her face. After a furtive glance around, he started walking away, pushing his cart in front of him.

"Hey, wait a minute!" He kept on walking and Jenna just sat there, feeling stupid. Fortunately, no one seemed to be paying attention to her, except the man with the cart. He turned around from time to time as if to make sure she wasn't following him.

With a sigh, Jenna stood up, brushed her pants off and resumed her walk. In the twenty minutes that followed, she met three more homeless people—two men and one woman. None could tell her where to find Estelle, or if she even lived in the park. By the time Jenna reached the carousel, she was beginning to wonder if she'd ever find her.

"I hear you're looking for me," a gravely voice said behind her.

Thirteen

Jenna spun around. A short, heavy-set woman with close-cropped gray hair and wary brown eyes watched her, not fearfully as had the others, but with curiosity. Her long gray skirt reached all the way to her ankles, stopping short of her scuffed boots. She wore no coat, just a rust-colored cardigan buttoned up to her neck. She, too, had a shopping cart, although the contents were meager—a blanket and two cardboard boxes filled with odds and ends. Cupped between stubby, nicotine-stained fingers was a cigarette butt.

"If you're Estelle, then I'm looking for you."

"I'm Estelle."

"Hi. My name is Jenna."

"What do you want with me?"

"I'd like to talk to you about Roy."

The woman brought the butt to her mouth and took a deep puff, filling her lungs. Her eyes narrowed to slits. "You a cop?"

"No, but I've just come back from the police station." She motioned behind her. "Roy was there."

Estelle gave an angry shake of her head. "Bastard cops. Came to get him while he slept. Hauled him off like an animal."

"They say he killed a man."

"Bullshit! Roy didn't kill nobody! They don't know who did, so they're pinning it on Roy."

"But the description you gave of the man you saw running from the carousel—"

"I *told* 'em it wasn't Roy. It was pitch-black out, except for a streetlight. I never saw the man's face, just his back. In the dark, everybody looks the same to me." She snorted. "But that stupid detective wouldn't listen."

"You said the man limped as he ran away."

Her tone lost some of its conviction. "I never said nothing about a limp. Roy's my friend. I wouldn't rat on him."

"Was the man you saw running away limping or not?"

"No!" Her expression was fierce and defensive, and from the way she averted her eyes, Jenna gathered she was lying in order to protect her friend.

"The police claim to have evidence—proof—that Roy did it. Do you know anything about that?"

Estelle's eyes inspected her from head to toe. "Nice jacket." Her gaze lingered on the black wool peacoat Jenna had bought last week at Barney's. "Must be warm."

Jenna understood the innuendo and removed her coat. The late afternoon chill hit her through the lightweight sweater she wore underneath. "You can have it," she said, holding on to it. "In exchange for information."

But Estelle was still suspicious. "If you ain't a cop, then who are you?"

"Someone who might be able to help Roy."

Estelle's hostile expression softened. She looked at the coat again, then wiped her nose with the back of the hand that held the cigarette butt. "They found money, credit cards and a watch in Roy's stuff, where he sleeps." She looked around her. "And something else."

"What?"

"The knife."

"The murder weapon?"

Estelle nodded. "Roy don't know how it got there."

"Where does Roy sleep?"

Estelle gestured toward a thick cluster of trees north of where they stood.

"Can you take me there?"

"You're really gonna give me the coat?"

"After you show me where Roy sleeps."

Estelle motioned for Jenna to follow her. Cold to the bones now, Jenna threw the coat over her shoulders, and fell into step with the older woman and her cart. Finding those items in Roy's possession was an additional nail in his coffin. But if he was the killer, why would he hide such incriminating evidence where the police could so easily find it?

They walked for about four hundred feet, and entered a densely wooded area. Estelle stopped and pointed at a thick layer of leaves matted down.

"There's nothing here," Jenna said.

"That's because we take everything we own with us during the day. If we don't, it gets stolen."

"Where are Roy's belongings?"

"In here." Estelle pointed at one of the boxes in her cart. "Cops took the blanket away."

Jenna saw a bundle of clothes, wool gloves with the tips torn off, a plastic dish. She bent over the box and sniffed. There was no doubt about it. Roy's clothes were impregnated with that same mildew odor she had smelled earlier at the precinct. Stavos could mock her all he wanted, she wasn't budging from her earlier observation. The two panhandlers smelled differently.

"Tell me about the knife," she said to Estelle.

"That cop found it. I forgot his name."

"Detective Stavos?"

"Yes, that's it. He said he found the knife hidden in the leaves under Roy's blanket. It had blood on it."

"Did you see Roy before the police took him away?"

"Sure did. When he started screaming, we all went to see what was going on. That detective was there, with two other cops. They tried to send us away, but we stayed right there. We don't like it when they rough up one of our own."

"You saw the knife?"

"No, but I know it don't belong to Roy."

If she was telling the truth, then someone had gone to great pain to frame that poor, defenseless man. Someone familiar enough with Roy's habits to know where and when he slept. Once that was determined, all the killer had to do was wait until Roy fell asleep, then slip the incriminating evidence under the blanket. And if the blood on the knife matched Adam's— and Jenna had a sinking feeling it would—Roy's chances of being charged with first degree murder had just increased dramatically.

Estelle eyed her shrewdly. "You said you could help Roy. How you're gonna do that?"

"I don't know yet." Jenna paused. "But I'll find

a way. In the meantime, I need you to do me one more favor.''

''What's that?''

''You can't tell the police I was here.''

''I ain't no snitch.''

''Good.'' Jenna let the coat fall from her shoulders and handed it to her. ''Here you go, Estelle. Wear it in good health.''

Fourteen

Twenty minutes later, the Audi was back in the garage and Jenna was heading for the elevator. Her thoughts kept drifting back to her conversation with Estelle. She wasn't sure if the information the homeless woman had given her was worth a two hundred and fifty dollar Tommy Hilfiger car coat, or if she could fulfill her promise to help Roy, but she had learned long ago to never second-guess her impulses, and she wasn't about to start now.

Going to Marcie or Detective Stavos with her suspicions that Roy may have been framed was pointless. Stavos was already annoyed with her for failing to identify the man he believed was Adam's killer. If he found out she had interfered with a material witness, not to mention bribed her, he would be furious.

She was unlocking her apartment door when Mrs. Szabo, from across the hall, opened hers and walked out carrying a casserole. At seventy-eight, Magdola—Magdi to her friends—was a sweet old lady with a head of curly silky white hair, mischievous blue eyes and a youthful laugh. She and her family had escaped from Hungary in 1971 and moved into the building long before it went co-op. A widow with no children, she devoted her life to her houseplants and her eleven nephews. All lived within a hundred mile radius and four of them were eligible bachelors, with good jobs and their own apartment, three facts Magdi brought up often.

The Hungarian woman had taken a liking to Jenna from the moment she had moved into the Regent, after marrying Adam. With not much to do but watch TV and cook, she had made sure the busy couple had a home-cooked meal at least twice a week.

Jenna's protests had gotten her nowhere. "Cooking for you makes me happy," Magdi had told her in her thick but delightful Hungarian accent. "And you need to eat, no?"

In exchange for her kindness, Jenna set a few hours aside each week to take Magdi shopping, to the beauty parlor where she loved to have her hair tinted blue and to the doctor. Occasionally, she would treat her to a Broadway play and dinner at Seppi's or Da Rosina, two of Magdi's favorite restaurants.

Other residents tended to shy away from Magdi, not because she was nosy, although she was, but because she occasionally claimed to see things that weren't there—flying saucers outside her window, cryptic messages on her TV screen and her late husband, Sándor, who, according to her, visited often. Not too long ago, she had told the tenants that Captain Kirk, of the old TV series *Star Trek,* lived in the building. Everyone thought she was crazy. Her downstairs neighbor was particularly hostile. Angry that the monthly payment for Magdi's rent-controlled apartment was only a fraction of his exorbitant mortgage, he had started a petition to have her committed. Sam Meyerson had immediately put Magdi in touch with an attorney and the petition was thrown out before it even got to court. The truth was, Magdi was lonely and her "visions" brought her the attention she craved.

Looking at Jenna, who was still shivering, she said in a motherly, almost scolding tone. "Why don't you have a coat?"

"It's a long story, Magdi."

As the older woman walked in, Jenna took a whiff of the casserole and knew that tonight's treat was chicken *paprikás,* a delicious combination of fork-tender chicken, onions and sour cream.

"Magdi," she said with only a hint of reproach in her voice. "You've been cooking for me for the past five days. That's far too much."

As always, her protests fell on deaf ears. "You need good food. You run around all day, with no time to eat. You don't eat, you get sick." She put the casserole on the kitchen counter. "I made enough so you have dinner for tomorrow night. Because tomorrow, I won't be here."

Jenna put the casserole in the oven and turned the knob to low to keep the chicken warm. "Where are you going?"

"My nephew's house. It's his birthday." A familiar twinkle lit up her eyes. "You remember Jimmy, don't you? He's the one who works at Bloomingdale's. Did I tell you he was promoted?"

Jenna smiled at Magdi's not-so-subtle attempt at matchmaking. "Several times. He was made head of his department, wasn't he? Men's wear?"

Magdi beamed. "Yes. Such a good boy, my Jimmy. Handsome, too, don't you think? And he cooks."

That alone was worth a special mention, since it was no secret that Jenna's talents in the kitchen were nil.

Before she could find a delicate way to change the subject, Magdi did it for her.

"You look tired, Jenna. Are you tired? You want me to go?"

"No, no, Magdi. It's been a bad couple of days, that's all."

"Bad how?"

There was no way of avoiding the truth. It was a wonder Magdi hadn't already found out with all the gossiping that went on in the building. "It's Adam. He's been killed."

Deeply veined hands went to cover Magdi's mouth. "Such terrible news. How did it happen?"

"Someone tried to rob him on Monday night. According to the police, he put up a fight and that's when he was killed." Jenna saw no reason to go into greater details.

Magdi's eyes misted. "Adam was a good man— a fool to let you go, but a good man." Then, almost in the same breath, she added, "Sándor warned me something terrible was going to happen, but I didn't believe him." She said it with the utmost conviction, as if her husband had actually stopped by a few days ago and delivered some dark premonition.

They talked for a few more minutes, or rather Magdi talked, about Adam and Sándor and her downstairs neighbor who, today, had refused to acknowledge her in the elevator even after she said hello to him, not once but three times.

The cuckoo clock Jenna had brought back from Germany years ago struck six and Magdi stood up to leave. She shook a finger at Jenna. "Don't stay up too late. Eat the chicken, take a warm bath and go to bed. Tomorrow you will feel much better."

Jenna walked her friend to the door and kissed her. "I think you're right, Magdi. And thanks for dinner."

As soon as Magdi was gone, Jenna turned on her answering machine. One message was from her friend Beckie, a hairdresser with her own shop in TriBeCa. She was back from visiting her ailing mother in upstate New York and had just heard the news about Adam.

"Come to the shop tomorrow," she said. "You're due for a trim anyway."

The other two messages were from Frank Renaldi. Both contained some form of apology he apparently thought would win her over. Fat chance. He left her three phone numbers where she could reach him— his office, his home and his cell.

"Don't hold your breath," she muttered as she deleted his messages.

Immersed in a frothy sea of Borghese bath bubbles, Jenna leaned back against the white terry cloth pillow and closed her eyes. Magdi may be old but she was no fool. A warm, scented bath was just what Jenna had needed to soothe her nerves. Little by little the tension left her body as the events of this disjointed day began to recede.

The sound of her front doorbell brought an abrupt end to her peaceful meditation. Magdi again. She had a way of coming back, sometimes several times a night, on one pretext or another. Jenna sank deeper into the bubbles. If she didn't answer, maybe she'd go away.

The bell rang a second time, and a third, sounding a little more impatient each time.

Muttering under her breath, Jenna stepped out of the tub, wrapped herself in a white terry robe and stomped to the front door, barefoot.

Always careful not to hurt Magdi's feelings, however, she took a deep, soothing breath before opening the door.

Frank Renaldi stood on the doorstep. In his right hand was a little white flag made of an eight-by-ten sheet of paper and a swizzle stick. His left hand was behind his back.

He looked at her with a teasing glint in his eyes as he waved the makeshift flag back and forth. ''I come in peace.''

Jenna had to admit the flag was a cute idea, a stunt the old Frank would have pulled a few years ago. But the wounds of their encounter were still too fresh in her mind to be overlooked. ''What do you want, Frank?''

''I thought there might be something wrong with your phone.''

''My phone is working just fine. What do you want?''

''To make amends. You and I started on the wrong foot—''

''Whose fault is that?''

''Mine entirely. That's why I'd like a chance to apologize.''

''You're about thirty-six hours too late.''

''Eating crow isn't something I do well. You know that.''

"You think it was easy for me? I hadn't heard from you in fifteen years, yet I came to see you. I was foolish enough to think that in a moment of mutual grief, we could put our differences aside and form some sort of alliance."

"I wasn't prepared for your visit."

"You weren't prepared for Adam's, either, but you didn't throw him out of your office, did you?"

"I didn't throw you out of my office."

"Damn near."

A shuffle behind the door across the hall warned her that Magdi was peeking through her peephole.

Frank heard it too because he glanced over his shoulder before turning back.

"Are you going to invite me in? Or do we give the neighbors a free show?"

She was no longer as furious as she had been. "Actually I was considering asking you to leave."

He stuck his foot out, preventing her from closing the door. "Don't do that. I drove all the way from Staten Island to see you, got a ticket for speeding and had to circle six blocks twice before I found a parking space. I'm not going anywhere, Jenna. Not until we've talked." When she still didn't move, his left hand came out from behind his back. "Maybe this will change your mind?"

She leaned forward to take a closer look at the box in his hand. "What's in there? A venomous snake?"

"Open it."

After giving him a suspicious look, she lifted the lid and immediately smelled the nearly forgotten aroma of apples and lemon. She looked up. "Are those German apple fritters?"

"Not just any old German apple fritters but the

original Rhineland *apfelküchlein* you were always so crazy about.''

''You remember that?''

''Who can forget? After you came back from that backpacking trip to Bavaria, Adam and I had to listen for hours while you talked about those apple fritters and how Prince Metternich's old recipe was the absolute best.''

''It's true. Unfortunately, they don't make them like that anymore.''

''They do in Staten Island. The problem was getting my friend Hans to make me a fresh batch just when he was ready to close shop. He wasn't thrilled, but he did it anyway. I think he put an old German curse on me before I left.''

Jenna laughed. She couldn't help it. He had always had the knack to make her laugh. ''You're just as crazy as you used to be.''

''Does that mean I can come in?''

She opened the door wide and moved aside.

Fifteen

She led the way into the living room, which was more formal than the kitchen, therefore safer. Safer from what? she wondered as she tugged her bathrobe tighter. Who was she afraid of? Frank or herself?

She left the silent question unanswered. "Why don't you take a seat while I go change."

A light danced in his eyes and he looked as if he was about to say something, then closed his mouth. She didn't even want to know what thought had entered his twisted mind, although she could guess. Pretending she hadn't noticed him, she walked away.

When she came back wearing jeans and an old, baggy flannel shirt, Frank was sniffing the air. "Is that chicken *paprikás* I smell?"

"How would you know that?"

"Don't you remember? My grandmother on my mother's side was Hungarian. I was practically raised on goulash and cucumber and sour cream. And those little pancakes stuffed with apricot jam. What are they called again?"

"*Palacsinta.*"

"That's it, *palacsinta.*" He gave her a questioning look. "Does that mean you finally learned how to cook?"

"Heavens, no. I happen to have this delightful

neighbor across the hall, a Hungarian woman who treats me like a daughter and makes sure I'm properly fed. Tonight it's chicken *paprikás*. Yesterday it was pork roast with chunky mashed potatoes.'' She sat on the pink floral ottoman across from him. "How did you know where to find me?"

"Adam told me you had kept the apartment." He looked around appreciatively. "This is very nice. Different from the bachelor pad I remember."

"I made a few changes, during my marriage to Adam and after."

The photographs on the walls, some of them her own, caught his attention and he studied them for several seconds. She waited for a comment, but all he said was, "Of the three of us, you're the only one who stuck to her original goals."

"Not really. I had to make a few concessions along the way in order to survive, but I'll get there eventually. Hopefully the exhibit at Siri's this month will help."

"What would you really like to do?"

"Photograph ordinary people in their everyday lives."

"Isn't that what you're doing now?"

"Only when I'm not busy earning a living as a commercial photographer."

"And what's that, exactly?"

The conversation was turning a little more personal than she would have liked, considering she was still suffering the aftereffects of his earlier rudeness, but he sounded genuinely curious, so, after a short hesitation, she decided there was no harm in answering his questions.

"I freelance for various cooking and travel magazines. I also do promotional brochures for large companies. It's become a very lucrative business, which is why I'm reluctant to give it up entirely. Maybe I'm being overly cautious.''

"You always were."

She wasn't sure if he meant that as a compliment or a reproach, so she just ignored the remark. "Are you ready to tell me about Adam's visit?"

"I thought we were going to share information."

"We are. You go first."

The hearty laugh that burst out of him reminded her of the old Frank, and of all the moments they had shared, good and bad, sad and hilarious. "All right. I'll let you have your way—this time." His face turned serious again. "Adam wanted me to investigate his wife."

Jenna stared at him. "Amber? Why?"

"He thought she was having an affair."

An affair. That would explain Adam's reluctance to discuss Amber, and his polite brush-off when she had tried to learn more. "Was she? Having an affair?"

"Not exactly."

For the next few minutes, Jenna listened as Frank told her what he had uncovered so far.

"Why would Amber give money to a man she dumped years ago?" she asked when he was finished.

"That's what I hope to find out. But even if Angie is right and Amber *was* driving the night of the accident, it doesn't prove she killed Adam."

"No. And by the way, Amber's infidelity is not the reason Adam came to see me."

"I didn't think so. Not after seeing your reaction just now."

She told him about her conversation with her ex-husband and all that had transpired afterwards, including her inability to identify Roy Ballard and her hunt through Central Park in search of Estelle Gold.

When she was finished, Frank was smiling. "You've been a busy girl."

"I know that questioning Estelle wasn't right. Detective Stavos would have my head if he knew, but I just can't let an innocent man take the fall for something he didn't do."

"You're that sure that Roy is not the killer?"

"If you had seen him at the police station, standing in that lineup and looking like a scared rabbit, you'd be convinced, too. I don't even think he's the Central Park Robber. He just doesn't have the stomach for any kind of violence. He might be down on his luck, but there is something good and decent about him. I can feel it."

"Not to mention the smell."

She gave him a sharp glance to see if he was being sarcastic, the way Stavos had been, but the look in Frank's eyes was only that of a man trying to put the pieces of a puzzle together. "Yes," she said. "An altogether different smell."

"Which means there could be two homeless men out there, both limping and both similar enough in appearance to have fooled you, at least momentarily." There was another brief silence, as if Frank was trying to work through the logic of his own statement.

"Would you like to see the pictures?" Jenna asked.

Frank stopped his musing. "Do you have a set here?"

"I made a copy before I took the originals to Marcie."

She went to the kitchen and was back a few seconds later, carrying the photographs and the magnifying glass. She handed both to Frank before sitting down again, this time on the sofa, beside him. He studied each shot carefully, with the magnifying glass, identifying guests out loud as he went, passing on others.

Jenna found herself drawn to his profile, the straight nose, the strong, firm jawline. One of his female classmates at New York Law School, had once compared his features to those of a Greek god. When her comments had eventually gotten back to Frank, he'd had a good laugh, and promptly dismissed what he thought was a very weird comparison. It was this total disregard for his good looks that made him so utterly attractive.

After several minutes, he straightened and she quickly looked away.

"Except for the obvious," he said. "I don't recognize anyone."

"Neithcr did Marcie, or my dad."

"Wait a minute!" He shook his finger. "Let me see that one over there."

Jenna fanned the photos on the coffee table. "Which one?"

"That one," he said, pointing at a photo of a table filled with food.

"You're interested in the buffet table?"

"Not the table." Frank took the magnifying glass again and held it only an inch or so over the photograph. The long rectangular table held a lavish display of international delicacies the guests had raved about all night. In the center was a large ice sculpture in the shape of a tilted F—Faxel's logo. Also in the shot was a man's hand, reaching for a salmon canapé.

Frank tapped it with his finger. "This is what I'm interested in."

"A man's hand?"

"Look at his wrist."

Jenna took the magnifying glass from him and saw what her naked eye had missed. As the hand reached for the canapé, the cuff of the man's shirtsleeve had pulled up a little, exposing the wrist, and something on it—a tattoo.

"Is that a bear's head?" she asked.

"A bear with his mouth open."

"There's something inside his mouth." She leaned closer. "What is it? A nut?"

Frank's head touched hers as he, too, looked through the magnifying glass. She was quite aware of his proximity, of the clean scent of his cologne, of the fuzzy feeling inside her stomach. Common sense told her to pull away, but she didn't.

"It looks more like a gemstone than a nut." Seemingly unaffected, Frank straightened. "It's green, so my guess is we're talking about an emerald."

Jenna expelled the breath she had been holding. It wasn't easy concentrating, with Frank sitting so close to her. "A bear with an emerald in his mouth. What would be the meaning of that?"

"Maybe the guy has a bear fetish."

She waited for the punch line, but he was dead serious as he continued to look at the tattoo.

"You think that's significant?"

"Only because out of the fifteen photographs, this tattoo is the only thing that's offbeat enough to make me curious. With a little luck, I might be able to trace it to its owner."

"Wouldn't that be like looking for a needle in a haystack?"

"Not if you have connections."

His optimism inspired her to come up with an idea of her own. "In the meantime, I could talk to Claire."

"Claire Peabody? Adam's secretary?"

Jenna nodded. "She knew everything that went on in Adam's professional life. I wouldn't be surprised if he confided in her about his suspicions of Faxel."

"Will she tell you if he did?"

"Claire and I always had a good relationship. I think if I stress how vital the information is, she'll cooperate." She gathered the pictures and tapped the edges against the coffee table to form a neat stack. "There's just one thing that still bothers me."

"What's that?"

"When Adam told me he went to see you, he led me to believe it was about the Faxel case. In fact, he made a point of telling me that you hadn't turned up anything yet, that an investigation as complex as this one took time. Why do you suppose he did that?"

Frank shrugged. "One reason could be that he was embarrassed to admit that his new wife, a woman to whom he had been married less than a year, was cheating on him."

She could believe that. Adam was a proud man. "And the second reason?"

"I'm only guessing, but it's possible that by telling you I hadn't turned up anything, he was hoping to influence you in letting him have the photographs. In legal circles, we call that manipulating a witness. Adam was brilliant in that department.''

She couldn't help bristling at the thought she may have been duped. ''In my circles, we call it lying.''

''Lawyers have been known to play outside the rules on occasion.''

She summoned a smile. ''What about you, Frank? Have you ever played outside the rules?''

He let out a soft chuckle. ''I'll take the Fifth on that, if you don't mind.'' Then, as she lay the photos down, he pointed to the one showing the tattooed wrist. ''Can you make me an enlargement?''

''Sure. How big?''

''Five by seven should do it.''

''I have an early shoot in the morning. I'll stop at your office first. Will someone be there at about eight?''

''Tanya should. If not, slide the photo under the door.'' He stood up as though ready to leave. ''Are we done talking business?''

''I suppose we are.'' She didn't know why, but suddenly she didn't want him to go.

''In that case, why don't we catch up on the past fifteen years?'' He sniffed the air again. ''Maybe over some chicken *paprikás?* If you have enough for two, that is.''

Jenna smiled. ''Magdi never did learn how to cook for just one.''

Sixteen

They sat at the small kitchen table, knees touching because Frank's long legs had nowhere to go. Not a big drinker, Jenna had found a bottle of Saint Emilion someone had given her last Christmas, with a curly red ribbon still tied around it. Moving around the room as if he had lived here all his life, Frank uncorked the bottle, found glasses in a cupboard and did the pouring.

"Shall we make a toast?" He held up his glass.

"All right, but let's keep it simple, nothing mushy."

"Nothing mushy, hmm. Let's see…" He assumed a thoughtful expression. "How about 'Here's to Prince Metternich and his incomparable fritters, without which I'd still be in the doghouse.'"

Jenna laughed. "I don't think that crosses any lines."

They clinked glasses and tasted the wine, which was very good. So was Magdi's chicken, to which Frank did justice by taking thirds. While he ate, Jenna sipped her wine and listened as he told her, in colorful details, about his job, his secretary, who doubled as an operative, and his occasional deadbeat clients. The tête-à-tête reminded her of those long evenings, when they were students and had shared a pizza and a six-pack while discussing world affairs, the state of the economy or studying for their respective exams.

She found that the wine relaxed her, so she refilled her glass. "When did you decide to become a private investigator?" she asked.

There was only the slightest of hesitation before he replied. "A year and a half ago, when I left the FBI."

The shock must have shown on her face because he laughed. "What's the matter? Don't you think I have what it takes to be a federal agent?"

It took her a few seconds to recover from the shock. "On the contrary, I always felt you could do anything you set your mind to. I just never imagined you'd end up working for the government. Somehow the idea of Frank Renaldi in a dark suit and Ray•Ban sunglasses doesn't gel. The last time we talked, you wanted to join the circus."

He helped himself to a slice of Wonder bread, which was all she'd had to offer, and slathered it with butter. "I almost did. I changed my mind when I realized my talents as a trapeze artist were seriously limited."

"And the FBI sounded like a good alternative?"

"As good as any. The bureau was looking for applicants with a law degree at the time and I thought, what the hell, let's give that a try. I liked it, so I made it a career."

"Why did you leave?"

He was silent for a moment and even though his expression remained blank, she sensed turmoil beneath that cool, calm exterior. "I was asked to resign."

That surprised her even more than his decision to join the FBI. Frank was a born perfectionist as well as a high achiever. What could he possibly have done to warrant a dismissal? "What did you do?" She smiled. "And don't tell me you sold secrets to the enemy because I would never believe it."

He speared the last piece of chicken and chewed in silence for a while. "Do you remember my uncle Vinnie?"

Jenna had an instant memory of a small, wiry man with strong hands, a great sense of humor and a passion for Italian food. "The auto mechanic."

"He no longer runs the garage. His son Marty took over."

"I can't imagine Vinnie being retired."

"Neither could he. A couple of years ago, his friend Johnny Caruso became ill and asked Vinnie to help him run his trash-hauling business. My uncle, who by then had realized that retirement wasn't for him, agreed. He's just as happy now as he was when he ran the garage."

"What does that have to do with you being fired from the FBI?"

"Back when Johnny started his business, he had a silent partner, a capo for one of the big mob families. After a couple of years, Johnny's business took off and he was able to buy out Sonny Giordano—"

"Sonny *The Fish* Giordano?" The infamous mafioso had earned his nickname years ago after being fished out of the East River following a dispute with another crime family. The story had captivated America for weeks. Even now that Sonny was old and sick, whenever someone talked about mob icons, his name invariably came up.

"How do you know about Sonny The Fish?"

Frank asked. "You couldn't have been more than nine or ten at the time."

"Little girls have big ears. I was no exception."

"Well, as it turned out, the bureau had big ears, too. When they heard that my uncle was working in a business that was once financed by the mob, they asked for my resignation."

"But why? If Johnny Caruso ended his partnership with Sonny, what was the problem?"

"He ended the partnership, not the friendship."

"Is Vinnie aware of this?" She couldn't imagine that tough little man standing by while a nephew he loved like a son was being treated unfairly.

"I never told him. He would have felt guilty and that's the last thing I wanted."

Jenna watched him take a sip of his wine. She had been wrong about him. He hadn't changed after all. He was still the same considerate, family-loving person she used to know. That he allowed her to see a side of him he usually kept to himself, touched her even more. "And so, you found yourself without a job."

"And with a twelve-year-old boy to raise."

Jenna put her glass down. "You have a son?"

His face split into a huge grin. "Didn't think I was capable of that either, huh?"

"Being a family man was never high on your list of priorities, if I recall."

"People change."

She stared at him as if seeing him for the first time. Frank, a father. It wasn't an easy picture to conjure, but, like he said, people changed. "Tell me about him."

"His name is Danny." His pride shone like a

warm glow. "He's fourteen now, a straight-A student and one hell of a hockey player."

"A true chip off the old block."

"Better than the old block."

"Where is his mother?"

"In Milan with her new husband, an Italian cyclist she met shortly before I left the FBI."

Jenna did a quick calculation. If Danny was fourteen now, then Frank must have met his wife soon after he left New York. How much could he have loved Jenna if he had fallen for another woman so quickly? She couldn't help it, she had to ask. "Did you love her?"

The question seemed to bring him up short, but only for a moment. "I thought so at the time, although I probably wouldn't have married her if she hadn't been pregnant with Danny." He was finally finished with his dinner and pushed his plate aside. "After a year or so, I realized how little we had in common. Not even the arrival of a new baby could help bridge the gap between us. Don't get me wrong," he added. "I have no regrets about Denise and I. If it wasn't for her, I wouldn't have Danny. I'll always be grateful for that."

Jenna wondered what kind of mother would abandon her child for a lover, but refrained from making any comment. "How often does Danny see his mom?" she asked.

"She calls him every couple of weeks, and visits once a year. There's even a possibility he'll spend next summer in Italy."

"How do you feel about that?" She opened the box of apple fritters and bit into one. Frank was right. These *were* the real thing.

"I have reservations, mostly selfish." He

shrugged. "But if Danny wants to go, I won't stand in his way."

"It must have been hard on him. The breakup, I mean."

"At first." She held out the box to him and he helped himself to a fritter. "Coming back here and moving in with Vinnie was a life saver. Danny is surrounded by people who are smothering him with more love than he can handle." He smiled and leaned back in his chair. "How about you? If I recall, you wanted half a dozen children—at least. What happened?"

She wouldn't have thought she could cram fifteen years of her life into a thirty-minute conversation, but that's what she did. The wine helped. She left nothing out, not even the painful events of her mother's death.

"I'm sorry about Elaine," Frank said when she fell silent. "I had no idea she had died."

His hand moved across the table to take hers. She hadn't expected such an intimate gesture, yet it felt right, and immensely comforting.

After a while, he spoke again and surprised her with another unexpected question. "Have there been other men...since Adam?"

It was a question only a very close friend or a new lover had the right to ask, but for some reason, she wasn't offended. "None who amounted to anything. You might say that I've become somewhat of an expert."

A smile tugged the corner of Frank's mouth. "In men?"

"In failed relationships."

Seventeen

Frank left a little after ten-thirty, not too late, Jenna decided, to call Claire Peabody. Only she would know if Adam had had any contact with Faxel in the last couple of weeks. Hoping she still lived on West Fiftieth Street, and had the same phone number, Jenna dialed.

"Claire," she said when the secretary answered. "This is Jenna Meyerson."

"Oh, Jenna." Adam's secretary sounded as if she had been crying, which wasn't surprising. Claire had worshiped Adam. "It's so good to hear from you."

"I should have called sooner," Jenna apologized. "I'm sorry."

"I miss him so much." Jenna heard a strangled sob.

"I know you do, Claire. Have you been assigned to someone else?"

"Dave Black. He'll be assuming the chief counsel position in another week or so. Normally he would have kept his own secretary, but Barbara is going on maternity leave. I'm not sure what will happen to me when she returns."

"You'll always have a place at Global Access, I'm sure of it. You're much too valuable for anyone to let you go."

"Thank you," Claire said, sniffing.

Jenna gave her a few seconds to collect herself. "Claire, I need to ask you a question."

"Of course."

"Did anything out of the ordinary happen at the office these last couple of weeks?"

"I'm not sure what you mean," Claire said in a somewhat cautious tone.

"Did Adam meet with, or talk to, anyone you had never seen before? Did he behave strangely, perhaps? Did he seem preoccupied?"

The line went silent.

Claire's lack of response made Jenna move closer to the edge of her chair. "Your answer could be vitally important, Claire."

"To what?"

"Finding Adam's killer."

"I thought the police already knew who the killer was. Didn't they arrest a panhandler?"

"Let's just say that I'm not convinced they have the right man."

Another silence, then, "I can't help you, Jenna. I'm truly sorry."

"Claire, please. You were his private secretary, his right hand. You knew everything about his daily business."

"I never eavesdropped, Jenna."

"I didn't mean to imply that you did."

The growing silence at the other end of the line was awkward, but it gave Jenna hope. "Don't you want Adam's killer punished?" she asked.

"More than anything."

"Then help me, Claire. Tell me what you know."

There was a brief pause, after which she said in a

dispirited voice, "After we heard Adam had been killed, Mr. Black asked me to make copies of all the files on Adam's computer and give them to him. That's when I came across something disturbing."

Jenna felt a tingle of excitement. "What?"

"It's too complicated to explain over the phone."

"Do you have that information with you? Or is it still on Adam's computer?"

Claire's voice turned to a whisper, as if she expected someone to eavesdrop on their conversation. "I erased it from Adam's computer."

Jenna's hopes dimmed. "Oh, Claire, it could have been important."

"I made a copy. I have it right here with me."

Jenna expelled a long sigh. She stood up and without regard to the time said, "I'll be right over."

If there was such a thing as a prototype for the perfect secretary, Claire Peabody would have taken the top prize. She was efficient, devoted and discreet to a fault. A single parent, she had raised two sons, and still lived in the same modest apartment she had occupied for the past twenty-five years. Jenna had liked the self-effaced woman right away and had never had a reason to change her opinion.

Claire greeted her at the door. She was a small, unremarkable woman with neatly combed brown hair, dark, close-set eyes and, at the moment, a totally defeated look, as if the entire world had turned its back on her.

The two women held each other for a long time. "I'm so glad you're here," Claire said in that same hushed voice. "I've been going out of my mind."

"What's this all about, Claire?"

"I'd better show you."

Jenna followed her into the dining room where a laptop stood open on a polished mahogany table. Next to it was a laser printer and a stack of bills. Without being asked, Claire reached inside her pocket and pulled out a small floppy disk.

"I've been carrying this thing with me for two days," she said. "I just didn't know what to do with it." She bent over the laptop, inserted the disk and entered the password "idiot."

"That was Adam's nickname for a judge he despised," Claire offered. She smiled. "Not your father."

Within seconds, a world map appeared on the screen. Russia and several other countries were colored in red and the United States in blue. The rest of the world was yellow. A straight black line connected New York to Nauru, an island in the South Pacific Jenna had never heard of, continued on to the Cayman Islands and then to London. Another line, this one in green, went from London to Moscow and then to Yemen, where it ended.

According to the legend at the bottom of the screen, the red countries, such as Nauru, Indonesia, Russia, Nigeria and a few others, were most hospitable to money laundering. Under the map was a paragraph explaining the process of getting dirty money out of the United States. Jenna began to read.

"Mr. X, a drug trafficker in the U.S., needs to get dirty money—funds made illegally—out of the country. He opens a bank account in a Nauru bank and deposits the dirty money there. That bank then opens an account with a big London bank. Although that account is in the name of the Nauru facility, Mr. X can use it to write checks, make deposits, withdrawals or transfers, anywhere in the world. Although all banking transactions are done in Great Britain, the money is technically in Nauru. Should anyone try to follow the money trail, he, or she, will get only as far as the Nauru bank account in London before running into Nauru's tough bank secrecy laws.

Jenna looked up at Claire, who stood beside her. "You thought Adam was hiding money offshore?"

Claire looked miserable.

"He would never do that, Claire. Adam was one of the most honest people I knew."

Tears flowed freely from Claire's eyes. "I was too upset to think clearly."

"Did you tell anyone about this?"

Claire shook her head. "A Detective Stavos came to the office to talk to a few of us, but I didn't say anything." She pressed a tissue to her eyes. "I couldn't." She sniffed again and pointed at the screen. "There's more."

Jenna scrolled down and read the last four lines. "Although it has never been proven, not even during an intensive twelve-month FBI investigation, it is suspected that *Bratstvo,* a powerful Russian crime syndicate with branches throughout the world, including the U.S., has been making massive transfers of U.S. funds to al Qaeda training camps based in Yemen."

Jenna was silent, absorbing the implications of Adam's discovery. As an assistant district attorney, he had worked long hours prosecuting suspected members of various organized crime families, including the Russian mafia, and trying to get them convicted. So had her father.

Bratstvo, meaning brotherhood in Russian, consisted of approximately twenty-five thousand members and was broken down into as many as fifty groups dispersed around the world. While its main operation was controlled from Moscow, leaders were appointed at each of the locations. The U.S. branch, the second largest after Southeast Asia, was based in Brighton Beach, a Brooklyn neighborhood so heavily populated with Russian émigrés it was now known as Little Odessa. Over the years, the organization's U.S.-based leaders had managed to remain completely anonymous. Jenna remembered one widely publicized case where her father, then a prosecutor, had offered a Russian-born drug kingpin immunity in exchange for his boss' name. The man had turned down the deal, choosing instead a six-year prison sentence and the restitution of fifty million dollars in assets.

Like other crime syndicates, *Bratstvo* had been successful in hiding its illicit activities behind legitimate businesses. The majority of their revenues came from extortion, gun and drug smuggling, credit card frauds and prostitution. Their infiltration into U.S. e-commerce and banking Web sites had posed enormous economic threats. Equally threatening was the increasing practice on the part of Russian financiers connected to organized crime to invest in American companies, thus creating a perfectly legitimate platform for their criminal activities.

Jenna's gaze remained on the screen. "Adam was onto something," she said. "Or someone, but who?" She looked up at Claire. "Any idea?"

"No." Claire wiped the tears from her face. "Earlier on the phone, you asked if he had been behaving strangely.''

"Yes?''

"A few weeks ago, he told me he was worried about his job. The CEO's son, a Harvard Law School graduate, had just been made partner and the kid was making waves that he'd like to run the legal department, maybe bring some new blood into it. Adam was very upset about that. He called it a classic case of nepotism, even if Andrew, that's the CEO's son, was a bright attorney.''

Jenna leaned back in her chair and was thoughtful. Maybe Adam's concern about his job and his eagerness to prove he was worthy of his position, had prompted him to look into the Faxel matter.

"Claire, did Adam ever mention Faxel to you?''

"Only as it related to Global Access and our company's efforts to catch up with their technology.''

Jenna returned her attention to the map. "You know that he came to the opening of my exhibit on Monday night.''

"Yes. He told me he would be stopping by.''

"During the course of the evening, he told me he suspected Faxel of some kind of fraud, but he wasn't specific.''

"He never said anything to me.''

"You don't remember typing or filing anything?''

"No, but if he had discovered something extremely sensitive, he may have typed it himself.'' Her gaze slid back toward the laptop screen. "As he did with this document.''

"Where would he hide it, Claire?''

"I don't know. It wasn't on his computer.'' She

chewed on her lower lip. "I suppose I could find out."

Her hand still on the mouse, Jenna looked up. "How?"

"I still have his office key, and I haven't copied all the files Mr. Black needs. I could look around at my leisure, go through all the filing cabinets."

The thought of the prim Ms. Peabody playing spy was ludicrous. Not to mention dangerous. "Absolutely not, Claire. It's much too risky."

"How is it risky? I was asked to do a job and that's exactly what I'll be doing. I'll be perfectly safe."

"You could lose your job."

"No one will know what I'm looking for."

There was nothing Jenna wanted more right now than to know the extent of Faxel's involvement in Adam's murder. But she didn't want to do it at Claire's expense. "No, that's out of the question."

"But I *want* to do it." Claire pressed her clenched hands against her chest. "You see, Adam wasn't just the best boss I ever had, he was also my friend. He helped my son Joey get back on his feet last year after he lost his job. And when Jacob applied to the Air Force Academy and needed a letter of recommendation, Adam called a senator he knew. You don't forget kindness like that. And you can never repay it. Now maybe I can."

Jenna was silent for a long time, remembering the many good deeds Adam had done over the years. It was a side of him she had always admired, and one of the reasons she had married him.

"I'll be fine," Claire said again. "I'll call you as

soon as I find what I'm looking for. Maybe we could meet for lunch afterwards?''

One look at the determination in the woman's eyes and Jenna knew that Claire's mind was made up. She was going to do this, with or without Jenna's approval. ''All right,'' she said reluctantly. ''Let's meet at the High Noon Café on Herald Square. It's only a couple of blocks from Global Access. Twelve-thirty?''

''I'll be there, unless I don't find anything. In either case, I'll call you. Do you have a cell phone?''

Jenna wrote down the number. ''Please don't take any chances,'' she said as she handed her the slip of paper. ''If someone is in the office with you, stick to what you're supposed to be doing for Mr. Black.''

''I will.''

Jenna removed the floppy disk. ''I'll need to borrow this for a while,'' she said. ''Is that all right?''

''By all means, take it.'' Claire looked relieved. ''I'll be glad to have it out of my house.''

As soon as Jenna got back home, she went to her own laptop and inserted the disk for another look at the information Adam had gathered.

The name Faxel was nowhere on the document, but what if it was one of the companies *Bratstvo* had targeted and successfully infiltrated? The ramifications could be enormous. From Moscow, the money—*U.S.* money—could be going not only to Yemen as the green line suggested, but to other countries supporting terrorist activities as well, and no one would ever know.

She thought of calling Marcie about this latest piece of information, then changed her mind. She would wait to hear from Claire before saying anything. Once she had incriminating evidence against Faxel, she would turn it over to the authorities and let them do their job.

The cuckoo clock struck midnight, reminding Jenna she had an early morning shoot and needed to get some sleep. Exhausted, she nevertheless managed to brush her teeth and remove her makeup before climbing into her big, four-poster bed with the light-as-a-cloud comforter and fluffy pillows.

Her last thought before she closed her eyes, was of Frank and the rather sisterly kiss he had given her before leaving. It was a far cry from another kiss she remembered, one that had left her breathless and confused. Was she disappointed that tonight's parting had been so tame in comparison? Had she had expected more? Had she *wanted* more?

Mercifully, sleep came before she could find an answer to her questions.

Eighteen

Skin Deep was a tattoo parlor on West 47th Street that had been providing body art for men and women for more than two decades. Its owner and principal artist was Carlos Diaz, a firm believer that in order for an individual to stand above the crowd, he or she had to make a statement. And what better way to do that than by displaying one of Skin Deep's unique designs?

Carlos and Frank had met when they were barely out of their teens. One night, both had found themselves in the same bar and in the middle of a brawl. Within moments, Carlos was facing a man with a ferocious grin on his face and a broken beer bottle in his hand. Before he could do any serious damage, Frank, an expert kick boxer, had quickly disarmed and subdued the man.

Carlos and Frank had been friends ever since, and occasionally got together for a beer and a game of pool.

"Frank, my man!" Carlos exclaimed when Frank walked into the shop on Thursday morning. "It's good to see you." He was a short, stocky man with a black ponytail that hung down his back, and tattoos on eighty percent of his body.

He grinned. "Is this the day you're finally going

to let me do my magic on this fine body of yours?"
He pointed at two colorful drawings displayed on the
counter—one of a curvaceous blonde in full combat
gear, the other of a military plane dropping a cargo
of topless women on the deck of a battleship. "I
came up with two new designs, both of which will
appeal to your patriotic heart."

Frank put up his hands. "Don't even think about
it, Carlos."

Carlos chuckled as he put his artwork down.
"That's right. Tanya told me you're afraid of needles."

"I'm not afraid of needles." Frank glanced at the
open sketchbook on a low table. "And Tanya has a
big mouth."

Carlos leaned his arms on the counter. "So if not
the need for my artistry, what brings you here?"

Frank showed him the enlargement Jenna had
dropped off early this morning. "Ever seen this before?"

Carlos studied the tattoo. "Hmm. Can't say I have.
Not very creative. Definitely not part of my reper-
toire."

"Then whose?"

"Don't know, but I can ask around."

"I'd appreciate that."

Carlos held up the photo. "Can I keep this?"

"Go ahead. I made a copy." He gave Carlos a pat
on the shoulder. "Thanks, pal."

"Hey, anything for a buddy." He winked. "And
a future customer."

From Skin Deep, Frank walked over to a Dunkin'
Donuts shop across the street and bought a dozen of

assorted doughnuts, making sure half of them were the jelly-filled kind—Detective Stavos's favorite.

His purchase under his arm, he took a cab to the Central Park Precinct, wondering if his little bribe would pay off. With Stavos you never knew.

The detective was at his desk, pounding away on his keyboard with two fingers, when Frank walked into the homicide unit.

"Hi, Paul."

Stavos looked up and saw the box Frank set on his desk. He leaned back in his chair. "You've taken up ass-kissing now?"

"What's the matter? Can't I do something nice for one of New York's finest?"

"In exchange for what?"

"You're such a killjoy, Stavos. You take all the pleasure out of a friendly gesture."

"That's because I can smell a bribe from a mile away." He watched Frank sit down. "Don't get too comfortable. It's not like you're staying."

Frank didn't let the detective's grumpy disposition bother him. The two men worked on the same cases occasionally, and while Paul wasn't fond of private investigators in general, he respected Frank and vice versa.

"Have a doughnut, Paul," he said, kicking back. "There's nothing like a sugar high to make a man more agreeable."

"What do you want, Renaldi?"

"A little information."

The detective returned to his typing. "If you're here about your friend's case, forget it."

"Oh, come on, Paul. I'm not stepping on any toes here. I might even be able to help."

"I don't need your help."

"Why are you being so hardheaded? The case is solved, isn't it? You've got your man. I heard you say so at last night's press conference."

"So what are you doing here?"

"I was hoping you'd let me take a look at the police report."

Stavos stopped typing. He laughed. "You feds are all alike, aren't you? Even when you're no longer with the bureau, you think you're the Almighty."

"I never pushed my weight around and you know it."

"Sure you did. You're doing it now. You come waltzing in here, with a box of lousy doughnuts, thinking you can call the shots. Well, Mr. Bureauman, you're not calling the shots here. I am."

"Undermining your authority is the last thing on my mind. Can't you just accept the fact that Adam was my friend and all I want is to find his killer?"

"We have his killer."

"Maybe I don't believe Roy Ballard did it."

"Oh, Christ, not you, too." Stavos sprang out of his chair and planted both fists on his hips as two other detectives looked up from their workstation. "Did you talk to her? She sent you here?"

"Who?" Frank asked innocently.

"Don't give me that shit. You know who. Jenna Meyerson. She was here yesterday when we put Ballard in a lineup. The woman was driving me nuts. One minute, she couldn't ID the guy, the next she was sure it wasn't him. And you know why? Did she tell you the best part?"

"No," Frank lied.

"Because the smell wasn't *right*," he said in a

girlish tone. Frank tried not to laugh. "Did you ever hear such crap? A bum is a bum. They all smell alike."

"I don't know. Maybe she has a point."

Paul waved him away. "Ah, stop wasting my time, Renaldi. Just go."

Frank remained seated. "I mean it, Paul. What if she is right? What if you jumped the gun when you arrested Ballard?"

Stavos almost snarled at him. "I've got twenty-eight years on the force, twenty of them in homicide. Don't tell me I jumped the gun. I know better than to do something so stupid. We have proof Ballard did it. If you had listened carefully to that press conference, you'd know that."

"And if you weren't in such a hurry to pin the murder on the first suspect that came your way, maybe you'd see where you went wrong. Think about it. The man has no alibi, no one to vouch for him, and when you go through his belongings, low and behold, you find not only the gold watch, the money and the credit cards, but the murder weapon as well. How likely is that to happen in a cop's life-time?"

Stavos bristled. "Ballard's fingerprints were on the knife."

Frank pretended to be shocked. "You mean he didn't have the common sense to wipe it clean? He hid it under his blanket and just waited for you guys to come and arrest him?" He shook his head. "You must be living right, Stavos. I'm never that lucky when I investigate a case."

"Maybe you should be in another line of work. Ever thought of that?"

"If I'm so incompetent, then how come I know something you don't? Something that could change the outcome of this case."

They were interrupted by shouting coming from the corridor.

"What the hell?" Stavos walked around his desk and strode toward the commotion, Frank right behind him. "What's going on here?" he demanded.

A uniformed officer held a woman by the arm. She was dressed shabbily, except for a new-looking, stylish black coat. Judging from her red face and angry scowl, she had been doing all the yelling.

"I found her trying to sneak into the jail area, detective," the officer said. "When I told her she had to leave, she kicked me."

"He pinched my ass." The woman raised a defiant chin at Stavos, daring him to contradict her. "Is that any way to treat a lady?"

The officer turned purple. "Detective, I swear, I never—"

Stavos raised a hand. "What are you doing here, Estelle?"

Frank made the connection. Estelle was Stavos's eyewitness. She was also the woman Jenna had talked to in Central Park.

"I came to see my friend Roy," she replied. "The other day you said I could."

"I know I did, but things have changed since then. The only visitors Roy can have are his attorney and members of his family."

"He ain't got no family. I'm all he has."

But Stavos was no longer listening to her. Frowning, he was looking at the jacket with a small American flag pin on the lapel. "Where did you get that coat?"

Estelle crossed her arms protectively over herself, turning to the side, out of Stavos's reach. "I didn't steal it, if that's what you're asking."

"Where did you get it?"

"A friend gave it to me."

Stavos's patience slipped another notch. "Would that friend happen to be Jenna Meyerson?" He almost spat the name.

Frank stepped in, although he already knew the jacket belonged to Jenna. "Why would you think that?"

"Because Jenna was wearing that same jacket when she came here yesterday."

"You can't be sure it's the same one."

"I'm very sure. She had that same pin on the lapel. Am I right, Estelle? Did Jenna Meyerson give you that coat?"

"What if she did?"

He turned away, his mouth set in a tight line as he tried to control his temper. "I don't fucking believe it," he muttered under his breath. Then, turning back to Estelle, he asked, "What did she want?"

But Estelle had said all she was going to say. Looking more defiant than ever, she clamped her mouth and kept her arms crossed. Frank doubted Stavos would get a single word out of her now.

Stavos must have known that, too, because he let out a disgusted groan. "Escort her out," he told the officer. "And make sure she leaves." He strode back to his desk. "You see what I have to put up with?" he told Frank. "Jenna's interfering with an eyewitness, bribing her with clothes and God knows what else.''

''I'm sure bribery was not her intention.''

Stavos's expression turned suspicious. ''Are you two working together on this? Am I dealing with the Nick and Nora Charles of the new century?'' His eyes narrowed. ''Or maybe you're romantically involved with her. That's why you're defending her.''

''Of course not.''

But Stavos was not stupid. ''You tell her to stop undermining my investigation,'' he warned, pointing a threatening finger at Frank. ''Or she's going to find herself sharing a cell with her good friend Roy.'' He sat down. ''Now, what do you know that I don't?''

''Are you going to let me see the report?''

''After you give me the information.''

Frank told Paul about Adam's suspicions that Amber was having an affair, about her secret rendezvous with Billy Ray Shaeffer and the widow's recent visit to Frank's office.

The information seemed to have a soothing effect on the detective. Calmer now, he picked up a pencil and, holding it with both hands, he started to twirl it. ''She really changed on you, huh?''

''Like night and day. One moment she was a helpless damsel in distress, the next she's Count Dracula, out for blood.''

''Doesn't mean she killed her old man.''

''No, but it gives a new spin on the case, don't you think? And surely Angie Delano's suspicions are worth checking out. Just as it wouldn't hurt to requisition Amber's bank statements to see exactly how much cash she withdrew in the last few weeks.'' He paused to see if he still had Paul's attention. He did.

The detective was silent for a moment, digesting all he had heard. After a few seconds, he stood up, pulled out a folder from a stack on his desk and dropped it casually on top of the pile. "I'm going to step out for about ten minutes. When I come back, I want you gone."

Frank got the message. In the doorway, Paul turned around. "And don't touch the doughnuts."

After he left, Frank glanced around to make sure none of the other detectives in the room was paying attention to him before he picked up the file.

Paul had done a thorough job. He had started his investigation by talking to several of Adam's co-workers at Global Access, as well as a few close friends. Members of the Lear household had not escaped his attention, including Adam's widow. However, the latter had been too distraught to question at length. Stavos had made a note to talk to her again after the funeral.

No one interviewed had noticed a change in Adam's behavior. Up to and including that last day, he had been his considerate, cheerful self. His secretary, Claire Peabody, had been subdued, but that was understandable. She had worked for Adam for the past six years and was totally devoted to the man. His car had been retrieved from the Essex House garage, but forensics had found nothing of significance in or out of the Cadillac.

The interview with Roy Ballard was included, along with the panhandler's explanation of how his fingerprints had ended up on the knife.

"This man was sitting on a bench," he had told Stavos, "feeding the pigeons. He looked like one of us, so when he started talking to me, I walked over and sat down. That's when he took out his knife and asked me if I wanted to hold it. When I said yes—''

''Why did you say yes?'' Stavos had wanted to know.

''I dunno. To be friendly, I guess.''

''You didn't think that was a little unusual? Asking a perfect stranger to hold a knife?''

''No.'' In Roy's world stranger things happened every day.

''Tell me about the watch, the money and the credit cards.''

''Already told you. I never saw them before.''

''That's what you said about the knife. Now you're telling me you held it in your hands. Why should I believe you?''

''I was just wakin' up when you came to get me. I didn't know what was happening. I was scared, man.''

''You expect me to believe that?''

''Yes, sir, 'cause it's the God's truth.''

There were three more pages of dialogue, with Ballard continuing to profess his innocence and Stavos trying to get him to confess. Roy had stood his ground and it was obvious from the increased sharpness of Stavos's words that the detective was getting more and more frustrated.

The next page was the lab report. Adam's death had been caused by massive hemorrhaging from a stab wound to the stomach. The murder weapon was an inexpensive combat knife with a four-inch steel blade that had been around since World War II and could be purchased anywhere. Two clean sets of fingerprints, both belonging to Roy, had been lifted from the handle and the blood on the blade and on Roy's bedding matched Adam's blood.

Frank snapped the folder shut, stood up and dropped it back on Paul's desk. Then, with a little grin, he lifted the lid on the pastry box, helped himself to one of the jelly doughnuts and left.

Nineteen

"If you want my opinion," Beckie Hughes said as she snipped Jenna's dead ends, "here it is. Stop playing hard to get with Frank Renaldi and grab that man before someone else does."

At thirty-four, Beckie had the compact, athletic body of a teenager, wide-set green eyes and ginger hair she wore piled on top of her head in a haphazard bun. From the moment the seven-year-old and her family had moved next door to the Meyersons, Jenna had felt an instant liking for the outspoken redhead.

After high school, Jenna had gone to NYU while Beckie chose to pursue a career in hairstyling. A decade later, she had saved enough money to buy Tresses, the TriBeCa salon where she had worked all these years.

"I'm not playing hard to get." Jenna's protest held much less conviction than she would have liked. "And I'm certainly not going to *grab* Frank Renaldi. The two of us are about as compatible as oil and water."

Beckie stopped in midmotion and glanced at Jenna in the mirror. "Excuse me. Didn't you just say you two ate goulash together?"

"Chicken *paprikás,* and sharing a meal is a far cry from having a romance."

"The man remembered your sweet tooth and brought you your favorite apple fritters. It doesn't get much more romantic than that."

"I would agree with you, *if* I was in the market for a man. I'm not, so let's leave it at that."

She gave that last sentence a tone of finality, hoping Beckie would get the hint. The truth was, Jenna had never felt comfortable discussing men, even with her best friend. Maybe because where romance was concerned, she was a total loser. But Beckie was nothing if not persistent.

"Oh, come on. A gorgeous guy like that. Are you telling me you didn't get shivers up and down your spine when you saw him standing on your doorstep?"

"Not even a quiver," she lied.

Her cell phone rang saving her from more questions. She recognized Adam's office number. Keeping her fingers crossed that Claire was calling with good news, Jenna answered with a brisk, "Yes, Claire."

"Jenna, I found it!" Claire could barely get the words out.

"You found the Faxel file?"

"Yes! It was in Adam's safe. He gave me the combination years ago, but I've never had to use it, so frankly, I forgot he even had a safe in the office." She sounded as if she had been running the New York marathon.

"You're wonderful, Claire."

"Thank you." Jenna heard papers being shuffled. "I'll be a little late for our meeting. Mr. Black asked me to stay and type a few letters for him. Could we make it twelve-forty-five instead of twelve-thirty?"

"No problem. I'll see you then."

Jenna yanked the black vinyl cape from her shoulders. "Claire came through for me," she said excitedly. "I've got to go."

"Now?"

"If I wait, I'll never find a cab."

"But I didn't finish doing your hair!"

Jenna bent toward the mirror and gave her damp hair a quick fluff with her fingers. "There. I'm fine."

"You're not. You look like Cruella De Vil."

Jenna grabbed her purse and planted a kiss on her friend's cheek. "Don't worry. I won't tell anyone who my hairdresser is."

Pincho handed the pretty blonde her café mocha and flashed her what he hoped was his most beguiling smile. He knew from past conversations with her that she was an assistant district attorney, single and didn't live far from Insomnia. She stopped in every morning, at different times, depending on the case she was working on, chatted for a few minutes and then left.

The reckless side of him wanted to make a move on her. With that good-time-girl swagger and too-blond hair, he could tell the girl was hot to trot.

An A.D.A. Christ. Was he crazy? What if she wanted to know more about him than he was ready to tell her? What if she got curious and started snooping around? Wasn't that what those people were trained to do? Snoop?

The distinctive ring of his Kravitz line saved him from obsessing further over the blonde. He left Ricardo in charge, and went into the back room. "Kravitz."

"I have an emergency," the voice said.

"I don't do emergencies."

"You'll do this one. It's right up your alley."

"How much time do I have to prepare?"

"Less than an hour. I'll meet you outside your shop for the details. I'm across the street."

For all the hype, Herald Square was nothing more than a small triangle of land where Sixth Avenue, Broadway and Thirty-Fourth Street intersected. The area was made famous a hundred years ago with the arrival of Macy's, the "world's largest department store," and then again with the release of the Christmas movie *Miracle on 34th Street,* several decades later.

The High Noon Café was located directly across from Macy's and two blocks north of Global Access. In spite of her early start, Jenna had been unable to find a cab and had walked the eighteen blocks to Herald Square, arriving at the restaurant a few minutes late.

"May I help you, Miss?"

Jenna smiled at the pretty hostess. "I'm meeting a friend." Her gaze swept over the crowded room. The tables were close together, bistro-style, and all occupied. But no Claire. "I guess she isn't here yet."

"I have a table for two in the back if you'd like." The hostess pointed near the serving station.

"That would be fine, thank you."

When a waitress stopped by, Jenna ordered a club soda and kept her eyes on the entrance. The lunch crowd was still flowing in, some willing to wait, others not. A little after one o'clock, Jenna ordered the chef's salad, and wondered if Claire had changed her mind, although she couldn't imagine why. She had sounded too excited on the phone to cancel the lunch now.

Her salad arrived and she nibbled on it, growing more and more concerned with each passing minute. She checked her cell phone to make sure it was turned on, then, after glancing at her Swiss Army watch and seeing that it was almost one-thirty, she decided to call Global Access.

A woman at the central switchboard answered. "Global Access. This is Ginny. May I help you?"

Jenna thought it best not to identify herself. "Hi. I was supposed to meet Claire Peabody for lunch, but—"

"Oh, didn't you hear?" The woman's voice took on a tragic tone. "Ms. Peabody fell from the seventh floor gallery. She's dead."

"What?" Several heads turned in Jenna's direction. Usually considerate about phone etiquette, she ignored the open stares.

"It happened about half an hour ago," the woman continued. "Claire had just left her office. We're not exactly sure what happened up there, but..." The woman started to cry. "This is too horrible."

Unable to find the words to console her because she was in a state of shock herself, Jenna thanked her and clicked her phone off. She sat there in stunned silence. Aware that some of the diners were still watching her, she dug into her purse for her money, threw a handfull of bills on the table and hurried out.

Global Access's atrium lobby had been cordoned off, but not the reception desk where the daytime security guard who had manned the station for the past twenty years sat, looking grim. Jenna had talked to him many times and had always found him to be polite and helpful.

As she approached him, she glanced beyond the reception desk. The round interior courtyard was framed by balcony corridors that rose from the lobby to the seventh floor, where the legal department occupied all ten offices. Bright sunlight poured in from the dome-shaped skylight and came to rest on the large blood stain that marred the gold-toned marble floor.

"George." Jenna cleared her throat. "I just heard about Claire Peabody."

The guard gave a sad, slow shake of his head. "Terrible thing, Ms. Meyerson. Terrible thing."

"How did it happen?"

"I don't really know. Mr. Black was the last one to see Claire alive. He told the police she was typing some letters for him and was planning on taking a late lunch. I was sitting at my desk when I heard this blood curdling scream. I jumped out of my chair just in time to see Claire hit the floor."

Jenna tried to speak but couldn't form a cohesive sentence.

George lowered his voice. "Some say it was suicide."

Jenna's head snapped around. "Who is saying that?"

He shrugged. "A couple of secretaries from the typing pool. They say Claire had been deeply affected by Mr. Lear's death and wasn't bouncing back the way she should have."

Jenna didn't buy it. Claire had definitely *not* committed suicide. "Were there any witnesses to the fall?" she asked.

"So far the police haven't found any. You know how it is around here at that hour—a ghost town. Most employees leave for lunch at twelve sharp and don't return until one. I spotted a couple of janitors going up the escalator. The police are trying to find out if one of them saw something, but I haven't heard, one way or the other."

Jenna's gaze moved from the bloodstain on the lobby floor all the way to the seventh level. A handful of office workers stood at the wrought iron balustrade, looking down and talking in hushed voices. If Claire had not committed suicide, then how had she died? An accident was out of the question. Claire had worked at Global Access for many years. She must have walked in and out of her office, how many times? Fifteen thousand? Twenty? More? And today, of all days, she had slipped and tumbled over a three-and-a-half foot railing?

Anyone would have to be stupid to believe that. Which left only one possibility.

She had been pushed.

Jenna felt a wave of nausea wash over her. Waiting for the light-headedness to pass, she gripped the edge of the desk for support. George looked at her, concern in his eyes, and quickly came around his station.

"Hey there, take it easy." He held Jenna's arm and led her to a chair against the wall. "You all right, Ms. Meyerson? You want some water?"

She shook her head. "It's just a delayed reaction to the news, that's all. I'll be fine."

"It's been a shock to all of us."

The sudden, implacable heaviness of guilt bore down on her like a hundred-pound weight. She was to blame for Claire's death. If she hadn't let the secretary talk her into searching Adam's office, none of this would have happened.

"Where did they take her?" she asked, barely recognizing her voice.

"Eastern General."

She stood up, waited until her legs could support her, then, working up a shaky smile, she squeezed George's arm. "Thank you, George."

"Are you sure you don't want to sit down a while longer? You don't look too good, if you don't mind my saying so."

"I'll be fine." To prove it to him, as well as to herself, she gave him one last nod and walked out.

It took her a while to realize she was heading south, toward One Hogan Place.

Twenty

Marcie was in a conference room with several of her A.D.A.s when Jenna arrived at One Hogan Place half an hour later.

"I'm sorry, Ms. Meyerson," her secretary said. "Mrs. Hollander left specific instructions not to be disturbed."

"Tell her I have to see her. It's an emergency."

The woman took another look at Jenna, as though quickly assessing the situation. "Wait here."

She came back a minute later, followed by the district attorney, who was clearly not in a pleasant mood. "This had better be good, Jenna."

"Claire is dead," Jenna blurted out.

Marcie pushed her into her office and closed the door. "Who the hell is Claire?"

"Claire Peabody. Adam's secretary. She fell off Global Access's seventh floor gallery."

Marcie frowned as if she couldn't comprehend what was so obvious to Jenna. "Don't you see?" The thread that held Jenna together was coming dangerously close to breaking. "First Adam, then his secretary. This was no accident, Marcie. Claire was murdered."

Marcie glanced at her watch, then at Jenna, as if trying to decide what was more pressing, her meeting or more of Jenna's wild assumptions. "Maybe you'd better start at the beginning."

Jenna talked fast, hardly taking a breath between sentences. She could see Marcie's expression change from puzzled, to concerned, to incensed. The D.A. waited a beat after Jenna was finished, making an obvious effort to collect herself before speaking.

"What is it going to take to get you to back off and let us do our job?" she said at last. "I didn't mind you coming to me with your suspicions regarding Adam. In fact, I was grateful for your input since it helped us apprehend a suspect, but you've gone over the line this time. First by compromising Detective Stavos's investigation—"

"If you mean Estelle—"

"Yes, I mean Estelle. Paul is livid over that, and I can't say I blame him. You had no business questioning that woman. She's confused enough as it is. Your interference only succeeded in confusing her further. And making it more difficult for us to regard her as a credible witness. Now you're telling me that you and Adam's secretary conspired—yes, *conspired*," she repeated when Jenna started to protest, "to search Adam's office? A blunder that may have contributed to her death?"

Somehow, Marcie managed to keep her voice on an even keel, perhaps because her secretary was within earshot, but everything about her demeanor, from her controlled speech to the angry sparks in her eyes, told Jenna that she may, indeed, have crossed the line.

"I tried to stop her." Jenna's words sounded hollow. Who was she kidding? Marcie wasn't telling her anything Jenna hadn't already figured out for herself. She *was* responsible for Claire's death.

Marcie must have sensed Jenna's anguish because her expression suddenly softened, as did her demeanor. "Why don't you sit down," she said, "while I make a couple of calls."

Grateful for the offer, Jenna sat down and kept her eyes on Marcie as she picked up the phone on her desk. After identifying herself, the district attorney told the person at the other end that she was checking on the fatal accident that had occurred at Global Access. For the next couple of minutes, she listened quietly, then asked, "Did you find a briefcase?"

She nodded at Jenna before speaking into the phone again. "There's a possibility that Ms. Peabody's death may be tied to the recent killing of her boss, Adam Lear. I'm sending the lead detective in the Lear case to your precinct to take a look at the accident report. His name is Paul Stavos. I expect you to cooperate with him fully."

She hung up and turned back to Jenna. "Claire's body is still at Eastern General, pending her children's arrival."

"And the briefcase?"

"Also at the hospital, with her purse. Paul will go there first to retrieve both items. If there is such a thing as a Faxel file, we'll soon know. Hopefully, by then the police will have talked to the janitorial staff. Until then, they're calling Claire's death an accident."

"Do you believe her death was an accident, Marcie?"

"Until I have a reason to—"

"I've given you a major reason. Claire called me

a little before noon today to tell me she had found
the Faxel file. At twelve-thirty, as she is coming out
of her office, she falls to her death. Isn't that a little
too convenient?''

''Unfortunately, accidents such as those are an almost daily occurrence in this city.'' But Marcie
looked concerned—more than concerned, Jenna
thought. For the first time since this case began, she
looked doubtful of her own words.

Encouraged, Jenna forged on. ''Do you know
when I'll believe her death is an accident? When
Detective Stavos calls to say he found the Faxel file
in Claire's briefcase. If he doesn't...'' She knew she
didn't have to say anything more. Marcie had understood perfectly.

''You did the right thing by coming to me with
this.'' Marcie came to stand directly in front of
Jenna. ''But don't think for one second that you're
off the hook. I want you to go home, Jenna, or to
your studio, or wherever you need to be as a photographer, and leave the detecting to us. If foul play
was involved in Claire Peabody's death, you could
be in danger as well. Do you understand that? Because I don't know how to make myself any
clearer.''

''Then you believe me.''

''Do you understand?'' Marcie repeated.

''Yes.''

''Good, because if I hear about you interfering
again, I'll lock you up.''

Jenna almost said ''you wouldn't dare,'' but knew
better than to challenge someone like Marcie Hollander. Friend of the family or not, she had her princi-

ples and would do what she had to do to preserve the integrity of her office.

"Will you let me know if you find the file?" she asked.

Marcie sighed. "I'll tell Paul to give you a call."

It wasn't until she had left the district attorney's office that she realized she hadn't told Marcie about the money laundering information Claire had found on Adam's computer.

Once outside the building, Jenna's indecision about where to go next lasted only a second. As a cab with its light on approached, she hailed it.

"The East Village," she told the driver. "Two eleven Sixth Street."

Frank was at his desk, eating what looked like a ham and cheese sandwich, when Tanya let Jenna in. One look at her and he dropped his lunch, coming to his feet. "What's wrong?"

In a voice that was slowly becoming stronger, she took him through the steps of the last two nightmarish hours.

Frank didn't hide his shock. "Jesus." He ran his fingers through his hair and started pacing his office, from the window to his desk and back. "I guess they can't blame that one on Roy. He's still sitting in a jail cell."

"*I'm* the one they should blame. *I* caused Claire's death."

He stopped his pacing and came to crouch in front of her. "No, you didn't." He took her hands in his and held them tight. "You tried to stop her. Or at least to discourage her. She wouldn't listen."

"If I hadn't gone there last night—"

"She is the one who suggested searching Adam's office. Nothing you could have said to her from that moment on would have changed her mind. So stop trying to find blame where there is none. The killer did this, not you."

"How did he know, Frank? How did he know she had found that file?"

Unable to remain still for very long, Frank let go of her hands and stood up. "My guess is that Adam's office or his phone, or both, are bugged. And carefully monitored. That's how the killer also knew that Adam would be at Siri's on Monday night."

"Could Claire's apartment be bugged, too?"

Frank shrugged. "Why should it? She wasn't under suspicion, Adam was. Why do you ask?"

"A day or so after Adam's death, Claire found something else in his office, on his computer to be exact."

"What was it?"

"Information about dirty money and how to move it out of the country. It's rather complicated. You need to see it."

Frank grabbed his jacket from the back of his chair. "Then what are we waiting for? Let's go."

A sax player with his eyes closed stood on the sidewalk when they came out, playing a languorous rendition of *Porgy and Bess*. Next door was a produce stand, and behind the crates of fresh fruits and vegetables, a portly woman with dark hair and a burnished complexion swayed to the music.

Frank waved at her as he tossed a dollar bill into the sax player's hat. "Thanks for the apples, Carlotta. Tanya and I enjoyed them very much."

The woman beamed. "You want more? I'll send you some more."

Frank laughed. "One crate was enough. We can't eat them that fast."

"I'll send some oranges then. I just received a shipment from Florida."

"Friend of yours?" Jenna asked as they started down the street.

"I did some work for her a few months ago and wouldn't take any money, so she keeps supplying me with enough fruit to open my own stand."

"You're a good man, Frank."

In a gesture that brought back more fond memories, he wrapped an arm around her shoulders. "You're just now finding that out?"

"Not really."

As they turned the corner, Jenna saw a bright red car she recognized right away. For a moment, she was able to put the tragedy of Claire's death out of her mind. "You are still driving that old relic?"

"Hey, watch how you talk about my T-bird. She's sensitive."

"How long have you had it now?"

"Since my first year in law school. It cost me everything I made clerking for old Judge Fosse, but it was worth it."

"So you kept saying at the time. What was it you called it? A babe magnet?"

Little laugh lines curved around his mouth. "It got me a few of them. Except the one I really wanted."

She stared at him, taken off guard, then quickly looked away. "Is it still?"

He opened the passenger door. "What?"

"A babe magnet."

He threw her a mocking grin. "You tell me."

Twenty-One

As always at this time of day, the five o'clock Manhattan traffic was brutal. It took Frank more than forty minutes to reach Columbus Circle, and another fifteen to find a parking space.

"I'm going to check your apartment for bugs," Frank told Jenna as they walked out of the elevator. "Once inside, let's keep the conversation casual."

The thought that someone may have come into her home, invading the one place where she had always felt safe, infuriated and frightened Jenna at the same time. Nevertheless, she nodded to signal she understood, and unlocked the door.

"Do you want anything?" Her voice was a little brittle and louder than usual. "Soda? A beer?"

"A beer would be fine. All right if I use your bathroom?"

"Go right ahead."

Jenna went through the motions of opening the refrigerator, taking a Bud Light out and setting it on the counter. Although she knew she could only be heard and not seen, she felt self-conscious and uncomfortable. What if Frank did find a bug? What then? Whoever had put it there would know they were onto him. Would he try to replace it? Or would he do something a little more drastic? As he had done with Claire?

Her heart gave a little lurch as she glanced at the kitchen counter, remembering the photos. The recipe box was where she had left it, looking innocent. She went to open it, flipped through the recipes and let out a sigh of relief. The coq au vin envelope was still there, tightly nestled between thirty other recipes.

She was sipping a glass of water when Frank returned. "I didn't know you also had a view from your bathroom." He motioned for her to remain quiet, walked over to the window and ran his fingers inside the frame.

"That's why I love this place. There's a view from just about every room."

His inspection of the window over, Frank pulled a chair, climbed on it and proceeded to take down the globe light.

"Do you want a glass with that beer?" she asked.

"No. The bottle is fine."

He gave her the thumbs-up sign, snapped the globe back in place and quietly jumped down. He moved with amazing grace and speed, wasting no motion, hardly making a sound as he inspected every nook and cranny—the cabinets, the hutch, the table and chairs, the desk. Not even the refrigerator escaped his scrutiny. When he seemed satisfied the kitchen was clear, he walked into the foyer, subjecting the tiny space through the same rigorous inspection.

"Place is clean." Only then did he take the bottle Jenna held out to him. He took a long swallow. "Okay, let's take a look at that document Claire found."

Jenna booted up the computer and inserted the

disk she had been carrying in her purse since the previous night, and entered the password.

Frank raised a brow. "Idiot?"

"Adam's wry sense of humor." She punched a key and the world map popped up on the screen.

Frank sat down, drew the mouse toward him and began to read the two paragraphs Jenna had practically memorized.

When he was finished he leaned back. "*Bratstvo.* Son of a bitch."

"I thought that name might ring a bell."

"It does a lot more than ring a bell. In 1996, the bureau put me in charge of a special task force. Our mission was to assess *Bratstvo's* strength, both in its homeland and abroad. A week later we left for Russia, where we spent three months in our Moscow office. When we felt we had enough information, we came back home and set up surveillance in Brooklyn, focusing on a handful of wealthy businessmen we had on our radar screen, and two people in particular."

"Who were they?"

"One was Aleksei Chekhov, an ex-KGB known for his brutality and ruthlessness. He owns a hotel and a couple of restaurants in Brighton Beach and leads what seems to be an exemplary life."

"Seems to be?"

"The verdict is still out on Aleksei, at least as far as I'm concerned."

"And the other man?"

"Sergei Chekhov, Aleksei's younger brother and general manager of the Seaside Hotel."

"Also an ex-KGB?"

"No. Sergei was a military man. In 1994, he dis-

tinguished himself in the Chechnyan war and came
home badly wounded. He took an early retirement
and shortly after, immigrated to the United States.
Since then, a third man, an uncle of Aleksei and Sergei, has entered the U.S. on an immigration visa.
Boris Chekhov, another ex-KGB agent, now runs one
of Aleksei's two restaurants. Our investigation turned
out to be a complete waste of time."

He turned to look at her. "Are you familiar with
these people?"

"To a certain extent. *Bratstvo* was my father's
bête noire as well. During his years in the D.A.'s
office, he prosecuted several members of that organization, but was never able to find out who ran it.
Every now and then a name comes across Marcie's
desk and when it does, she comes over to pick my
dad's brain, but it's just as hopeless now as it was
then."

He looked surprised. "Then why didn't you mention this file to Marcie?"

"Because I knew she would have told Stavos."

"As well she should. He's the lead investigator."

"An investigator I don't trust. As far as he's concerned, he caught the killer and he won't waste another second looking elsewhere. If I gave him the
information, he'd probably bury it somewhere and
do nothing with it."

She could tell from Frank's amused expression
that he thought her suspicions were not only unjus-
tified, but silly. "Paul would never compromise an
investigation just to close a case. He's two years
away from retirement. Why would he put his reputation, not to mention his pension, on the line at this
point in his life?"

"You have your opinions of Detective Stavos. I have mine."

"Fair enough." He sat forward and planted his elbows on his knees. "What about me, Jenna? Do you trust me?"

The question caught her off guard, but she didn't hesitate. "Yes, I do."

"And you trust me to do what's best for you?"

"I suppose so."

"Good, because I want to talk to you about this partnership of ours."

Suddenly wary, she contemplated him for a second. "What about it?"

"It's over. From this moment on—"

"What do you mean it's over?" She almost choked on the words. "Since when?"

"Since I found out that *Bratstvo* may be behind Adam's murder. You don't know who you're dealing with, Jenna. Those people are far more ruthless than any criminal organization you know. Next to them the Gambinos and the Gottis are choirboys."

"I'm well aware of that."

"Are you also aware that *Bratstvo* has eyes and ears everywhere, including inside jail cells? Countless witnesses have died accidental deaths while waiting to turn state evidence." He made quotation marks in the air at the word "accidental." "No one is safe from them."

"You wouldn't even know about *Bratstvo* if it wasn't for me. Nor would you have seen the photos of the Faxel party. Or spotted that tattoo."

"You're right, and I'm grateful for all you've done so far, Jenna, but I care too much about you to let you take any more chances. From now on, *I* do the investigating. *I* get to stick my neck out, not you.''

''And if I refuse?''

''You don't have a say in this. I made my decision. I will no longer share any information with you. The less you know, the safer you'll be.''

In other words, he expected her to fade quietly into the background, like a good little girl. He didn't bother to take into consideration her feelings for Adam, how much she owed him, or the guilt she felt, would always feel, about Claire's death. Her safety was all he cared about, and while she appreciated the sentiment, she wasn't particularly flattered at his notion that she was too inept to take care of herself. Who did he think he was dealing with? A six-year-old?

''I don't think you're concerned about my safety at all,'' she said, feeling angry and bitter. ''Nor do I believe that you care about me. All you're interested in is getting all the credit.''

She hadn't meant to say anything quite so harsh. The words had just burst out of her mouth before she could stop them.

She saw his features tighten. ''Is that what you think? That I don't care?''

''That's what you said the other day. Your exact words were 'I got over you long ago. Looking back, I'm not sure why I fell for you in the first place.' ''

Suddenly, with no warning whatsoever, he gripped her shoulders and pulled her to him. For a heartbeat, they stared at each other. Then, he bent his head and took a slow, long mouthful of her.

Blood rushed to her ears as her body came sharply alive. It was a lusty, probing kiss full of passion and urgency. Her anger forgotten, she responded to it without thinking, wrapping her arms around his neck and leaning suggestively against him.

Then, just as abruptly as he had embraced her, he released her. "Do you still think I'm over you, Jenna?"

He swung his jacket over his shoulder and walked out, leaving her standing in the middle of the kitchen, feeling like an idiot.

From her kitchen window, Jenna watched Frank walk with brisk resolve toward his car, parked a few blocks north on Sixty-Fourth Street. She touched her lips, still wet from his kiss. What had that been all about? Except for some harmless flirting, he had given her no indication that his feelings went beyond friendship. But you didn't kiss a woman the way he had just kissed her out of friendship. So what exactly had he been trying to tell her?

She thought of another time when he had kissed her just as passionately. It was the day she and Adam had announced their engagement. Frank had stopped by her dorm later that night to tell her he was moving to Virginia and wanted to wish her well.

At the door, he had turned around, retraced his steps and kissed her with the same hunger as he had tonight, before walking away.

Was there a pattern there? Should she worry she might never see him again?

Before she could drive herself crazy with speculations, the phone rang. Half hoping it would be Frank, she ran to it.

"Ms. Meyerson, this is Detective Stavos."

Jenna hoped he didn't hear her sigh of disappointment.

"The D.A. told me to give you a call and let you know where things stand on the Peabody case."

Jenna gave the detective her full attention. "Did you find the Faxel file?"

"There was nothing in Ms. Peabody's briefcase other than a few inter-office memos, a day planner and the kind of odds and ends you find in most briefcases. Same with her pocket book."

Jenna was disappointed but hardly surprised. Hadn't she more or less predicted to Marcie that Stavos would come back empty-handed? "There's your proof," she said.

"Proof of what?"

She had difficulty curbing her impatience. "That Claire was pushed! Because of what she found."

"Ms. Meyerson—'

"There *was* a file," she said, not giving a damn if she sounded like a broken record. "Claire called me from Adam's office at noon to tell me she had found it and was bringing it to our lunch meeting. Forty minutes later, she was dead and the file is now missing. How do you explain that, Detective?"

"I can't explain it—yet."

"Yet?" She paused. "Does that mean you're reopening Adam's case?"

She thought she heard a mumble at the other end. "If it was up to me, I wouldn't. But in view of what happened today, the D.A. thinks your suspicions deserve to be checked further. So, to answer your question, yes, I'm reopening Adam Lear's case."

Jenna smiled and said a silent thank you to Marcie. To the detective, she simply said, "Thanks for calling, Detective Stavos."

Twenty-Two

Jenna occupied much of Frank's thoughts during the one-hour drive from Columbus Circle to Staten Island. The fact that she had returned his kiss had made it that much harder for him to walk away. So why had he? Why hadn't he simply taken what was being offered? God knows he had wanted to.

Because he was a schmuck. Because he had never been able to take advantage of a woman and never would. Because he wanted Jenna, but he wanted her on his terms, meaning she had to want him just as badly. That was the reason he had given up the chase fifteen years ago. She hadn't been committed enough. She had been more focused on the game the three of them had played than on the depth of Frank's feelings.

Maybe she did want him. The way she had clung to him and leaned into him were signs he couldn't ignore. The problem was, physical desire wasn't enough. He wanted more than lust, more than passion, more than the promise of great sex. He wanted her to love him. The way he loved her. The way he had always loved her.

Vinnie was in the kitchen, reading the evening paper when Frank walked in. His uncle looked up and raised a brow. "What happened now?"

Frank thought about having a beer, then changed his mind. The way he felt, the beer would probably turn sour the moment it hit his stomach. "What do you mean?"

"You look lower than a snake's belly. Women trouble again?"

"Nothing you can help me with."

"Oh, I don't know." Vinnie folded his newspaper. "Why don't you try me? Tell Dr. Love what's bothering you."

Vinnie's remark brought a smile to Frank's lips. He sat down. "*Bratstvo* may be behind Adam Lear's murder."

Vinnie's easygoing expression vanished. "You're kidding me?"

"I wish I was. I found out tonight. Or rather, Jenna found out and relayed the information to me. Bottom line is, now that I know the Russians may be involved, I don't want her within a thousand feet of those people."

"I don't blame you. They're bad news."

"Yeah, well, try telling her that." He stretched his legs out in front of him. "I'm worried about her, Vinnie. I told her that our partnership was over, for her own safety, but I'm afraid she's going to do exactly what she wants."

"Then maybe you should reconsider your position."

"She'll only get hurt. The moment *Bratstvo* hears that she's snooping around, they'll go after her."

"But if you stay close to her, you'll be able to control what she does and where she goes. Come on,

Frank, you're not stupid. All you have to do is give her enough leeway to keep her happy while making sure she stays safe. How hard can that be?''

Frank was silent for a while. Vinnie's suggestion had its merit. By monitoring Jenna's comings and goings, the odds that she would remain out of harm's way were leaning in his favor. There would have to be ground rules, with no guarantee she'd adhere to them, but it was worth a try.

"I think I'll have that beer now," he said.

Vinnie picked up his paper again. "Make that two."

Sam Meyerson stood in front of his refrigerator debating what to have for dinner—leftover pizza or Campbell's cream of mushroom soup. Neither appealed to him, but he was hungry, so he might as well choose one and get the ordeal over with. He decided against the pizza. His stomach was nervous enough as it was. Between Adam's untimely death and his intrepid daughter's determination to help catch his killer, Sam had been popping Tums for the past two days with no hope of relief in sight. Maybe he should have a bowl of corn flakes. That was harmless enough.

A deep sigh escaped from his lips as he took the milk container out of the refrigerator. Would he ever get used to eating alone? Meals had been such a fun adventure when he and Elaine were married. She had been a wonderful cook, surprising him almost every night with something new and exciting. But it wasn't her cooking that had made his coming home so special. It was the time they had shared together, the long evenings spent talking about their respective day, planning weekend outings, birthday celebrations, holidays.

They'd had a good marriage. Or so he had thought. Looking back, he wondered why he hadn't noticed the symptoms of Elaine's discontent sooner. Had he been that blind? That preoccupied with his work that he had neglected the only woman he had ever loved?

Before his spirits could sink any lower, he walked over to the countertop television set, his only dinner companion these days, and turned it on to Channel 4 before taking his cereal bowl to the kitchen table. The evening report was almost over when the words *Breaking News* popped up on the screen.

Curious, Sam picked up the remote and turned up the sound in time to catch part of the broadcaster's sentence.

"...plunged to her death from the seventh floor gallery a little after twelve noon today. The victim was fifty-nine-year-old Claire Peabody, a legal secretary at Global Access."

Sam slowly put his spoon down.

"Ms. Peabody was pronounced dead at the scene. This is the second tragedy to strike the computer company this week. On Tuesday morning, Adam Lear, the chief counsel for Global Access and Ms. Peabody's boss, was found murdered in Central Park. According to co-workers, Ms. Peabody, who had been working at Global Access for the past ten years, was despondent about Lear's death, and they were concerned about her. While the police are not ruling out suicide, they are still calling the death an accident."

Sam didn't wait for the bulletin to be over. His cereal forgotten, he picked up the phone and dialed

Jenna's number. "Jenna, I just heard about Claire," he said when she answered. "What is this about her plunging to her death? Where was she?"

"At Global Access. Oh, Dad, it's so awful. She and I were supposed to meet for lunch and..."

"You and Claire?" To his knowledge the two women hadn't seen each other since Jenna's divorce. "Why?"

"Marcie didn't tell you?"

He didn't like the sound of that question. "I haven't talked to Marcie today. Why do you ask? What have you done now?"

He listened while she told him. After the first few words he sat down and reached for the roll of Tums on the lazy Susan.

"I know what you're going to say, Dad," Jenna said as he popped the tablet in his mouth. "But before you do, listen to me. Claire called me shortly before she died to tell me she had found a file in Adam's safe with incriminating evidence against Faxel."

"I thought we agreed—"

"Let me finish, please. It's true that Claire was upset over Adam's death, maybe even more so at work, because of all the memories, but she was not suicidal, Dad. In fact, she was excited at the prospect of looking for that file. And even more excited when she called to say she had found it."

"What are you saying?"

"Claire was killed, Dad! Marcie didn't want to believe it at first. She didn't know who I was talking about, but after I mentioned the file—which, by the way, is missing—she had to admit that Claire's death sounded suspicious."

Her voice suddenly broke. "I feel so guilty, Dad. Frank keeps telling me I shouldn't, that I'm not to blame, but deep down I know I am."

Sam ran a hand down his face. He couldn't bring himself to scold her when she was feeling so low. "You didn't cause her death, honey."

"Maybe not directly, but if I had stopped her—"

"You tried."

"I should have tried harder."

"Jenna, stop it! You can't take the blame for this. Claire was a grown woman. And she was devoted to Adam. If her mind was made up to search his office, I doubt you could have done anything to stop her."

He thought of his daughter all alone in that apartment while a maniac was running around loose. "Look, honey," he said gently. "You're upset right now. Why don't you come spend the night here, where you'll be safe."

"I'm safe where I am."

"Don't tell me you're safe! Two people have already been killed and you could be next." Sam admonished himself for the outburst. He didn't normally give in to fits of temper, but few things in this world could still make him snap, and the possibility that his daughter was in danger was one of them. "I'm sorry, honey. I didn't mean to yell at you."

"I know. Please don't worry, okay? The killer has what he wanted—the Faxel file. He doesn't need to come after me."

Sam prayed she was right. "Just know that this is your home. You're always welcome here."

"Thanks, Dad." He heard her sniff and his heart ached for her. For all her fearlessness, deep down, Jenna was a gentle, sensitive soul, and the thought she could have caused anyone harm, let alone fatal harm, had to weigh heavily on her shoulders.

In a husky voice, he said, "I'll see you at the funeral tomorrow morning?"

"At 11:00 a.m. I'll be there. Good night, Dad."

Twenty-Three

Located at Brooklyn's southern-most end, Brighton Beach had once been an affluent seaside resort complete with a casino, a racetrack and a major hotel. By the end of World War II, the area had taken a downturn due to a declining economy and an aging local population. The arrival of the Russian community in the seventies and eighties had changed all that. New businesses such as specialty food shops and restaurants began to flourish and employment rose as the neighborhood underwent a long overdue spruce up.

As a boy growing up in Manhattan's Little Italy, Frank was familiar with Brooklyn, and especially Brighton Beach, where his mother liked to go occasionally for homemade *pelmeni,* meat-stuffed dumplings and *borscht,* a beet soup he had tried to avoid like the plague.

It wasn't until the mid-eighties, when a powerful organization known as *Bratstvo* was rumored to have made its stateside headquarters in Brighton Beach that the seaside resort had caught the attention of the FBI.

Years later, during his own investigation, Frank had set his sights on one man—Aleksei Chekhov. A former KGB agent, Chekhov had immigrated to the

U.S. after the fall of the Soviet regime, and opened a restaurant in Brighton Beach. Over the next few years, as his business flourished, he began expanding, first by purchasing a second restaurant, then a hotel, a dilapidated building he had restored to its former Victorian splendor.

On the surface, all seemed on the up-and-up. It was true Chekhov had turned to organized crime after the KGB was dismantled, but like many Russians with similar criminal backgrounds, he had started a new chapter in his life upon arriving in the U.S.

On the surface.

Despite Frank's beliefs that there was more to the man that met the eye, he hadn't found a damn thing to justify his suspicions. For more than a year, the two men had played a game of cat and mouse, with the mouse proving much more difficult to catch than Frank had expected. With a candid, self-assured manner, Chekhov had cooperated fully and introduced Frank to his key people, including his younger brother Sergei. Although Sergei hadn't been pleased with his brother's open door policy, Chekhov had remained firm. Frank had carte blanche to come and go as he pleased and could inspect the books *and* the computers whenever he wished.

"I have nothing to hide," Chekhov had said in his deep, accented voice. "I love this country and I will do whatever it takes to keep it safe, even if it means having the FBI intrude on my privacy."

Frank's search had been futile. Not that he was surprised. What fool would invite the FBI to go through their books and then leave incriminating evidence behind? Whatever proof existed that Chekhov was *Bratstvo's* leader wasn't where it could be found.

And now here he was again, standing outside the Seaside Hotel on Brighton Beach Avenue, reminiscing about old times and hoping Aleksei hadn't heard about Frank's dismissal from the FBI.

The six-story building, with its intricately carved dormers and red awnings, was not only an eye-catcher but a moneymaker as well, judging from the number of cars in the adjacent parking lot. Inside the hotel, the pace was brisk, due mostly to an unusual amount of shrieking toddlers running up and down the lobby. Frank soon saw the reason for their excitement. A large sign directed young guests to a children's theater. The program, scheduled to open in half an hour, promised old Russian tales, a magic show and a puppet salute to the American flag.

Nice touch, Frank thought as he crossed the lobby to the reception desk. Since 9/11, foreigners living in this country had made a point of pledging their allegiance to the U.S. in a number of ways. This one certainly struck a chord.

Moments after Frank gave his name to the clerk, Aleksei Chekhov walked out of his office onto the first floor balcony overlooking the lobby. There was a broad smile on his face as he ran down the red-carpeted staircase, as though he was actually glad to see him.

To show that he, too, could play the diplomatic game, Frank smiled back. Except for an extra ten or fifteen pounds that hadn't been there the last time, and a touch of gray throughout his thick black hair, Chekhov hadn't changed much. He was a big man, with a broad torso and a look of confidence about him that most people found intimidating. Frank merely found it challenging.

"Agent Renaldi!" he exclaimed, right hand extended. "What brings you to our lovely town?" If the Russian was surprised or concerned by the visit, he didn't show it.

Frank took the offered hand and shook it. "Business, what else?"

Chekhov assumed a chagrined expression. "With me? I thought I had finally convinced you that I am nothing but a honest, hardworking man."

"I'm here for another reason." He looked around him. "Could we go somewhere to talk?"

Chekhov motioned toward the staircase. "My office?"

Once they were comfortably settled in front of a window overlooking the Atlantic Ocean, Frank eased into small talk.

"Your hotel seems to be doing well."

"It's getting better. After 9/11, business slowed down to a point where I thought we would have to close. Sergei said it was just a phase and we should not worry. I'm glad I listened to him." He smiled. "What about you, Agent Renaldi? Are you still with the district's field office? Or have they moved you somewhere else?"

"You know the bureau's motto," Frank said with as much casualness as he could manage. "If it ain't broken, don't fix it."

Chekhov laughed, a booming, good-natured laugh that sounded sincere enough, but then again, knowing the man as well as Frank did, it was quite possible that he had seen through his adversary's little lie and wasn't letting on.

"So," he said, "how can I help you?"

"I'm hoping you can give me some information."

Chekhov spread his arms wide. "Anything."

"There's a rumor circulating around Washington these days that *Bratstvo* has a new leader."

"Really? Who is he?"

Frank laughed. "I was hoping *you* could tell me that."

Chekhov put his elbows on the chair's armrests and steepled his fingers. "I wish I could, really I do. But I'm too busy these days to pay attention to rumors. And if you remember, I never agreed with you that *Bratstvo* had settled in Brighton Beach. I don't deny there are some bad elements here, but the way most of us approach that problem is by ignoring it."

Frank had to admire the man. Even with his guard down, he was quick on his feet. "Still, in your line of work, you can't help hearing rumors."

"Unless you make a point of avoiding them, which I do. You see, Agent Renaldi, the people I work with know that I value my privacy. Of course, they expect me to respect theirs."

Frank couldn't have come up with a better answer, but all this dancing around wasn't getting him anywhere. He had to start asking the tough questions. "Have you ever heard any of your customers, or acquaintances, mention the name Adam Lear?"

Chekhov tapped a well-manicured finger on his chin. "Isn't he the attorney who was found murdered a few days ago?"

"You know about that?"

"I read about it in the papers." He frowned. "Do you think that someone in our community is involved in the killing?"

"It's a possibility."

"But what would be the connection?"

Frank decided it was time to rattle that seemingly unshakable poise. "Faxel."

The Russian's reaction surprised him. "Now *that's* a name I know well."

Frank raised a brow. "You do?"

"I'm a gadget freak, Agent Renaldi. Show me an electronic device and I must have it." He reached inside the breast pocket of his brown tweed jacket and took out a hand-size computer, looking as proud as a little boy showing off his new trains on Christmas morning. "This is the latest in electronic gadgetry. It shows my schedule at a glance, connects me to the Internet, and gives me GPS positions." He turned it around so Frank could see the two-by-two-inch screen. "It's also a video phone. I bought a dozen of them and sent them to all my friends in Russia so we could talk and make faces at each other."

Frank gave a tolerant smile. "That's not what I meant."

"Then what did you mean, Agent Renaldi?"

"I'm looking for one or more wealthy, well-connected Russian businessmen who may have secretly invested in the company."

The flicker in the man's eyes was so slight, so quick, that if Frank wasn't such a keen observer, he would have missed it. "Is that another of those rumors?"

"You could say that."

"You really have to stop listening to idle gossip, Agent Renaldi." The affable smile tightened a notch. "It's not healthy." Then, before those words could be misconstrued, he added, "You seem stressed enough as it is."

"All part of the job, I'm afraid."

"True, but to answer your question, no, I don't know of anyone who may have invested in Faxel. Personally, I invest my money the way millions of other people do, by buying stocks and bonds, annuities, even a little gold every now and then. I suspect that's what most of my comrades in Brighton Beach do as well."

Frank continued to play along. "But if you should learn something to the contrary..." He left his sentence unfinished.

"I'll keep you informed." The thought that he was volunteering to help the FBI, an organization that had been a thorn in his side for the better part of a year, seemed to please him immensely. "Can you still be reached at the same number?"

"I move around a lot these days. Why don't I call you instead?"

"Very well."

They walked out together and stopped at the balcony overlooking the lobby. Sergei, dressed in black slacks and a cream-colored sweater, stood in the center of a group of squealing little children ranging in ages from two to four. Five years younger than his brother, and with hair as blond as Aleksei's was black, Sergei Chekhov had the kind of movie star good looks that seemed to appeal to children as well as their mothers.

"Your idea of starting a children's theater seems to be paying off," Frank commented.

"My brother gets all the credit for that. At first, I didn't like the idea of little boys and girls running loose in my hotel, but Sergei can be very persuasive. And as it turned out, he was right. Again."

Frank observed the younger brother for a while, admiring the way he seemed to relate to the youngsters. Because the younger Chekhov was a former military commander with exceptional leadership capabilities, he had been high on Frank's list of suspects as well. After talking to him, however, and putting him under surveillance, Frank had changed his mind. While Sergei was good at his job, he didn't have the sophistication, the personality or even the ruthlessness to lead an organization like *Bratstvo*. The one that bore watching, however, was the Chekhovs' uncle, whose arrival in the U.S. three years ago happened to coincide with the appointment of *Bratstvo's* new boss.

Chekhov leaned over the railing. "Sergei," he called out. *"Smotri kto prishol."*

Frank, who spoke fluent Russian, translated to himself. *Sergei, look who's here.*

Sergei looked up, saw Frank and waved. *"Podozhdi minutu. Ya seichas podoidu."* *Wait a minute, I'll be right there.*

Sergei waited until a hotel employee had led the children safely inside the theater before walking across the lobby and up the stairs. He wasn't as affable as his brother, but was no less polite. His handshake was firm and his gaze direct.

"It's been a while, Agent Renaldi." He glanced at Aleksei, not quite as skilled as his brother in hiding his concern. "There is no problem, I hope."

"Agent Renaldi was hoping I could help him with a little matter," Aleksei explained. Then, as Sergei obviously expected more, he added, "He thought I might know the identity of *Bratstvo's* new leader."

"Ah." Sergei's voice held a trace of irritation as if he had meant to say, "That again."

"I don't suppose *you* would know," Frank said.

Sergei smiled. "If I did, I wouldn't tell you, Agent Renaldi. Even in a civilized country like the United States, that kind of indiscretion could earn you a one-way trip to the bottom of the bay. If you know what I mean."

The three men laughed, and to anyone looking up, they could have been old friends sharing a joke.

"In that case, I won't take any more of your time. You're both busy and I have a funeral to attend." As they started down the stairs, Frank turned to Aleksei and said casually, "How is your uncle?"

"Very well, thank you. He runs one of my restaurants. You must stop by one evening, as my guest, and try some of our specialties. Unless you have to return to Washington right away."

Frank, too, was quick on his feet. "My plans vary from day to day, but I appreciate the offer."

When Frank reached the T-bird in the parking lot, he turned around. Sergei had gone back inside, but Aleksei stood at the side entrance, watching him. He raised his hand in a salute, and Frank did the same before getting into his car and driving away.

Twenty-Four

More than three hundred people attended Adam's funeral. The high turnout wasn't unusual considering Warren Lear's popularity as a developer and generous community benefactor. From the Church of the Trinity in Great Neck, Long Island, the procession had made its way to Crestwood Cemetery five miles away for the burial.

Jenna stood beside her father and gazed at the familiar faces she had glimpsed earlier at the church— Warren and his youngest son, Richard, also an attorney; the CEO of Global Access as well as several company employees; Marcie Hollander and three senior A.D.A.s. Jenna even recognized a couple of judges she had met years ago.

Amber stood on the other side of the freshly dug grave, across from the Lear family. She was beautiful and trim in a dark suit and pillbox hat that lent her just the right amount of quiet dignity. From time to time she would glance at the Lears, but their gazes remained focused on Reverend Clayburn as he spoke of redemption and eternal peace.

Jenna leaned toward her father. "Warren and Richard are acting as if Amber wasn't even here."

Sam followed her gaze. "Warren is a great guy,

but he can be pretty obnoxious when he puts his mind to it."

"Have you had a chance to talk to him?"

"I stopped by his apartment yesterday."

"Does he really believe that Amber hired someone to kill Adam, or is he just trying to intimidate her?"

"He's not only convinced she had Adam killed, he's going to great pain trying to convince everyone else—including Detective Stavos."

"What do you think?"

"I don't know her so I can't form an opinion. But I do know that Warren didn't approve of the marriage. He was always emphatic about his conviction that Amber married Adam for his money and was determined to get her hands on every cent one way or another."

"And now she's going to inherit not only Adam's fortune, but Warren's house as well. He must be fuming about that."

"There might not be much he can do about the money, but the house still belongs to Warren. He only let Adam and Amber live in it after he moved to the city. My guess is that she'll have to vacate the premises very soon."

Or sooner, Jenna thought, if Warren found out she was supplying a former boyfriend with Lear money.

Sam looked at her. "What about you, honey? How are you doing?"

She knew he was referring to the events of the previous day. "Better. I still can't believe Claire is dead."

"Will there be a service?"

"For family members only. Her older son told me she will be cremated, as per her wishes, and her ashes scattered somewhere in her hometown of Joliet, Illinois.''

Even though a cemetery seemed like the appropriate place to discuss such matters, Jenna couldn't help feeling uneasy about the conversation, perhaps because any reference to Claire dredged up feelings of sadness and guilt.

Always perceptive, Sam found her hand and squeezed it. ''Where's Frank?'' he asked. ''I thought he'd be here by now.''

''Me, too.'' She glanced toward the road, anxious to set things straight between them regarding her role in the investigation of Adam's murder. Yesterday, she had been too shaken by his kiss to have any kind of reaction about the decision he, and he alone, had made. Now that she had recovered, more or less, her determination not to be pushed aside was stronger than before.

At last, the red Thunderbird appeared and went to take its place behind a long line of dark sedans. ''Speak of the devil.'' She waved as Frank approached. To show him there were no hard feelings, she squeezed against her father to make room for him. ''What happened to you?'' she whispered.

''My meeting ran late.'' His hands folded in front of him, he stared at the minister.

''Sleep well?''

She'd had a terrible night. ''Of course,'' she lied, matching his cool tone. ''You?''

''Like a baby.'' A smile pulled at the corner of his mouth as he spoke. He hadn't slept well either, Jenna guessed. Good.

When the services were over and the mourners began to disperse, Jenna said goodbye to her father, promising him once again to be careful, then turned to Frank. "Do you have a minute?"

"Sure."

She waited until a small group passed by before speaking again. "I wanted a chance to tell you how much I appreciate your concern. In fact, I think it's rather sweet of you to want to protect me, but contrary to what you may think, I'm not some foolhardy female looking for a few thrills. All I want is to see Adam's and Claire's killer brought to justice. I didn't ask to be thrown into this mess, but I'm in it now, neck-deep, and I owe it to two people who are dead to find out why."

He started to speak but she raised a hand. "Obviously, I would prefer to work with you, but if you'd rather handle this matter alone, I'll understand. Just don't expect me to stand by and do nothing. I'll be conducting my own research and asking my own questions. I may not be a top-notch detective or an ex-FBI agent, but I know how to talk to people and I know how to get answers."

Frank rubbed the back of his neck for a while, then gave a bow of his head. "All right."

Jenna stared at him. "Excuse me?"

"I said all right. The partnership is reinstated."

"Just like that."

"Isn't that what you wanted?"

"It's what I wanted, but not what I expected."

"What did you expect?"

"A down and dirty fight. At the very least, a strong argument." She regarded him thoughtfully. "You already thought it over, didn't you? You realized how unfair that decision of yours was and you had a change of heart before I even said a word."

He smiled. "Something like that."

"And here I was thinking I'd have to borrow a page from your own book and kiss you senseless until you changed your mind."

A wicked light danced in his eyes. "Don't let me stop you."

Caught in the pleasant banter, she was trying to come up with an appropriate reply when she saw Warren head toward another group of mourners. "We'll have to finish that conversation later," she told Frank. "Right now, I need to talk to Warren."

"Hey, wait a minute! We need to seal our new partnership. Establish a few rules."

She waved as she walked away. "Later."

The rapid clatter of her heels against the walkway made Warren turn around.

"Jenna!" He came to her, arms extended. "I'm so glad to see you. You're just what an old man needs on a day like this."

Old man, my foot, Jenna thought. At sixty-six, Warren Lear had the physique of a forty-year-old and the stamina of a teenager. Semiretired, he spent his free time sailing, playing golf and even managed to squeeze in a game of tennis every now and then. He was a silver-haired replica of Adam, with the same strong, angular features and piercing hazel eyes. Today, however, his demeanor was subdued and it was obvious from his red eyes that Adam's death had affected him profoundly.

She kissed his cheek. "How are you holding up?"

Warren shrugged. "Well enough, I suppose. Richard arrived from Chicago on Tuesday and hasn't left my side. We've been busy with funeral arrangements, returning phone calls, greeting visitors. I don't know what it's going to be like after today, when the reality of what happened hits me." He removed his glasses, which had misted, and started to wipe them with a handkerchief he had taken from his pants pocket. "The prospect of never seeing my son again is terrifying." His eyes glittered with fresh tears.

Jenna felt helpless in front of such grief. In all the years she had known Warren, she had never heard him sound so defeated. "Give yourself time," was about all she could manage to say.

"I'm glad you were the last friendly person Adam spoke to," he said unexpectedly.

"I wish I could have done more—like prevent his death."

He put his glasses back on. "You and Adam should never have separated."

The mildly reproachful tone reminded Jenna that he still held her responsible for the breakup. "It was a mutual decision, Warren, one we didn't make lightly."

He waved his hand. "I know, I know. Please forgive me. I didn't mean to sound as if you alone should bear the guilt of what happened. It's just that I miss you. You were good for him, and for the rest of us."

Jenna felt a wave of guilt. Now that his wife of almost fifty years was gone and Richard lived a thousand miles away, she should be making an effort to see Warren more often.

"How long will Richard be staying?" she asked.

"A few more days to help me get Adam's affairs in order. And get Amber out of the house," he added in a bitter tone.

Jenna let that last part slide. "Why don't we plan on having lunch in a couple of weeks? You can take me somewhere outrageously expensive."

As intended, the statement made him smile. "I'd like that, Jenna." He pointed a finger at her. "And I'll hold you to that promise."

"I expect you to."

He glanced at his watch. "I don't mean to be rude, but I have to get back to the apartment and make sure the caterers have everything under control. You'll stop by for something to eat, won't you?"

"I wish I could, Warren. Unfortunately I have a two o'clock shoot. But my dad is coming. And as far as I know, so is Frank."

"Make sure he does," Warren said. "I need to talk to him about the case."

She waited until Warren had walked away before turning around, but just as she started heading back toward Frank to relay Warren's message, she saw Amber marching in the same direction, looking indignant.

Jenna stopped short. Although she didn't want to eavesdrop, Amber's sharp tone was loud enough for her to hear every word.

"I hcar you've been checking up on me, Mr. Renaldi."

Her tone didn't seem to affect Frank. "Who told you that?"

"I have my sources."

"Maybe this isn't the place to—"

She ignored him. "I'm the wife of your best friend. Doesn't that mean anything to you? Do you think Adam would approve if he knew you were trying to dig up dirt about me?"

"What is it exactly you object to, Mrs. Lear?"

"You interrogated my mother."

"I didn't *interrogate* her. We talked...Teresa."

At the sound of her birth name, Amber's face turned red. "You smug son of a bitch," she said in a low growl. "I came to you in good faith, confided in you. I even asked you to find my husband's killer and how do you thank me? By stabbing me in the back. Because of you, Detective Stavos paid me another visit. Except that this time he wasn't so friendly. He treated me like a criminal."

"I'm sure that's an exaggeration."

"It's not. He wanted to know if I had an alibi for the night my husband was murdered. Can you imagine that? Suspecting *me* of stabbing Adam?"

"That's standard procedure. Frankly, I'm surprised he didn't think of it sooner."

"He didn't think of it sooner because he had no reason to, but after talking to you, he had second thoughts." Her voice was barely audible now and Jenna found herself straining to hear her next question. "Just what did you hope to find in Jersey City?"

"Depends." Frank looked as though he was enjoying the confrontation. "What are you hiding?"

"I'm not hiding anything."

"Then you have nothing to fear."

A nasty smile tugged at the corner of her red mouth. "Stay the hell out of my affairs, Mr. Renaldi."

"That sounds ominously like a threat."

Her smile sent a chill down Jenna's back. "Let's just call it a friendly warning. You being such a good friend of Adam's and all."

She walked away, a striking figure, alone, but from what Jenna had just witnessed, by no means defenseless.

"What was that all about?" she asked when Frank finally spotted her and came over.

"I thought you'd left."

"Warren wanted to make sure you remembered to stop at his apartment. He wants to discuss the case with you."

She watched Amber drive away in a sleek, silver Jaguar. "How did she find out you went to Jersey City?"

They started walking toward the Audi. "From Stavos, I suppose. Or her mother. Or possibly even Angie Delano. The girl would derive a lot of satisfaction in rattling Amber's cage."

"Watch out for Amber, Frank. I felt some sympathy toward her earlier, but after what I've just heard..." Jenna shook her head. "I believe that woman is capable of anything."

Frank threw her an amused glance. "Worried about me, Jenna?"

"I wouldn't want to lose my new partner to a vengeful widow."

"Which brings us to the subject of those rules I mentioned a moment ago."

"I hate rules."

"You'll have to follow these, Jenna. Or we don't have a deal."

She saw that he was serious, and nodded. "Okay. Let's hear them."

"I need your promise that you will not do anything reckless."

"Define reckless."

"You will not question anyone, go anywhere, snoop around or do anything remotely secretive without running it by me first."

"How am I supposed to remember all that?"

"Make a list. Do we have a deal?"

Relieved, because she had expected a much harder sell on her part, she extended her hand. "Deal. But on one condition. It's share and share alike."

He shook her hand. "I wouldn't have it any other way."

Twenty-Five

Warren's apartment on Park Avenue was only a fraction of the size of his old house but no less luxurious, a fitting tribute to a man New York had dubbed the builder of the rich and famous.

Frank's late arrival had been carefully planned. He hated those postfuneral functions where the guests either spoke in hushed tones or overcompensated the grim atmosphere by talking too loud and recounting amusing stories of the dearly departed.

He found Adam's father in a corner of the living room, surrounded by a half-dozen men wearing dark suits and even darker expressions. Warren, who had been watching the door, waved at Frank when he saw him and quickly came over.

"Let's go in the library." He wrapped an arm around Frank's shoulders and led him toward a small, richly-paneled room filled with books and the kind of marine memorabilia Warren loved. The crackling of red and orange flames in the brick fireplace added warmth to the rather formal surroundings.

Direct as always, Warren sat down and came straight to the point. "I understand you don't believe Roy Ballard killed Adam."

"Who told you that?"

"Detective Stavos."

"Well, for once Stavos quoted me correctly."

"So it's true."

"If I had doubts before, I don't now."

"Because of what happened to Claire."

"Certainly that, but also because of Jenna's beliefs that the panhandler she saw on Monday night and the one she was asked to identify at the lineup are not the same man."

"What about the evidence? The bloody knife, Adam's watch, the credit cards, the money. All were found under Roy Ballard's blanket."

"They could have easily been planted there by the real killer, someone who may have been impersonating a homeless man."

"A homeless man with a different smell."

Frank saw the skeptical look in Warren's eyes. "You heard about that, too, huh?"

"Oh, yes. Stavos made a point of telling me about Jenna's rather unusual observation." He sighed. "And to be completely honest, Frank, I'm not sure what to make of it. Don't get me wrong. I love the girl, and I love her for caring so much, but this smell thing..." He shook his head.

"I know it sounds a little over the top, but I wouldn't be too quick to dismiss Jenna's instincts. They've been pretty much on the mark so far."

Shrewd eyes studied him. "You were in love with her once, weren't you? Before she married my son? Adam told me," he added when Frank remained silent. "And he never held it against you, by the way. His only regret was that the two of you couldn't get past the conflict and stay friends."

"I'm the one who closed that door, and I'm not proud of it."

"Are you still in love with Jenna?"

Frank had no desire to get into that subject with Warren. "I thought you wanted to talk to me about the case."

Warren nodded. "You're right, let's stick to the business at hand. I know I'm not your client, and therefore you can't go into any details. I just want you to know that I'm glad you're investigating Adam's death. Stavos is competent enough, but not at all open to suggestions."

Frank had an immediate image of the overbearing Warren Lear and the crusty, uncooperative detective going head to head. "Stavos works alone," he said in the detective's defense. "And he makes no exception. Once you accept that, the two of you will get along much better."

Far from resenting Frank for speaking honestly, Warren gave a slight nod. "Point taken, but I'd like to help in some way, do something constructive. Stavos can't grasp that, because he never had children, but you do, don't you, Frank? You're a father. You see where I'm coming from. My son is dead. I have all this money and where is it getting me? Nowhere."

Frank thought of Roy sitting in a jail cell. Chances were his court-appointed attorney was someone from legal aid, a well-intended but inexperienced lawyer who would most certainly botch the job.

"I know how you can help," he said.

Warren raised his chin and waited.

"You could hire an attorney for Roy Ballard."

"Doesn't he already have one?"

"He needs one experienced in criminal matters. One who will fight for him, one who knows his way around the Manhattan court system."

"You have someone in mind?"

"As a matter of fact." Frank reached inside his briefcase, searched through the mess until he found a business card. He handed it to Warren. "Mick Falco and I went to law school together. Adam knew him. He's a good man, and good at what he does."

"Did you say she was a friend of yours?" Danny stopped in front of one of Jenna's photographs and studied it closely.

After leaving Warren's apartment, Frank had driven to Staten Island to pick up Danny from school, then, on impulse, had dragged the reluctant fourteen-year-old back to the city to Siri's, for a look at the more than thirty photographs Jenna Meyerson had on exhibit there. From the boy's reaction so far, Frank could tell he was not impressed.

"We still are," he said in answer to his son's question. "We met when she was in college and I was in law school."

They moved to the next photograph—that of a window washer halfway up the Empire State Building. "Why aren't they in color?"

What else would a fourteen-year-old ask? "I suppose because black-and-whites are more artsy, more dramatic."

"Are you going to buy one?"

"Actually," a soft voice behind them said, "Ms. Meyerson's photographs are not for sale."

Frank turned around and found himself looking down at an older, attractive woman in a sleek black suit. "Hi, I'm Letitia Vaughn," she said looking from Frank to Danny.

Frank offered his hand. "Frank Renaldi. I'm a friend of the artist. And this is my son, Danny."

"Hello, Danny." And to Frank, "I don't recall seeing you here the night of the reception."

"I couldn't make it," he lied.

"So, what do you think?"

He looked at the photograph in front of him—two cabbies with their head sticking out the window, yelling at each other. "I'm no expert, but they're all very good, very... I'm not sure how to put it...true?"

His answer seemed to please her. "And what about you, young man?" She turned to Danny. "What do you think?"

The boy shrugged. "They're all right, I guess."

"But you would have preferred to see a few sports photographs, right? Let me guess. Football? Or maybe soccer?"

Danny gave signs of warming up to her. "Hockey."

Letitia gave him an appraising look. "Of course, hockey. I should have known. You have the build for it." She waved a finger. "You know, I think I saw a few shots of the New York Rangers while we were going through Jenna's collection. Maybe you could ask her to show them to you sometime."

Danny didn't seem particularly excited at the prospect. "Why doesn't she want to sell the pictures?"

Letitia laughed. "Is he always this inquisitive?"

"It's a family curse, I'm afraid."

"Actually, Danny, that's a very good question, one a lot of people asked the other night. The answer is simple. Jenna wants to include the photographs you see here in a book some day. Displaying the work of an artist is an excellent way of generating public interest. The more interest Jenna generates now, the more people will buy her book later.''

She spent the next twenty minutes walking with them from photograph to photograph, explaining how the artist had tried to capture the spirit of her subjects, their hopes and fears, even their despair. To Frank's surprise, Danny listened attentively, asking an occasional question. It was much more than he had expected from the fourteen-year-old, and Frank told him so as they left the gallery.

Danny shrugged. ''I just saved myself a lot of time on next week's English assignment.''

''What assignment is that?''

''We have to do a paper on careers and why people choose them.'' He held up the two flyers Letitia gave him before they left. ''Now I don't have to do any research. I'll pick photography as the career and use the information I have here.''

Frank laughed. ''I should have known you had an ulterior motive.''

''That's not cheating, is it, Dad?''

''No, bud, it's not cheating. In fact, you might be able to write a better paper if you talked to the artist herself. What do you think of that? Would you like to meet Jenna?''

Danny's shrug was noncommittal, so Frank didn't push it.

Twenty-Six

The dinner hour at the Renaldis was just over when the front doorbell rang. Vinnie stood up. "I'll get it. You and Danny take care of the dishes."

He was back seconds later. "The guy says he's an old friend of yours, but the name didn't ring a bell, so I told him to wait out on the porch." At Frank's questioning look, he added, "Name's Carl Badger."

Frank's blood did a one-eighty. Few names could get him that riled up. Even now, after almost two years, he needed all his willpower to keep his anger under control. FBI agent Carl Badger had deeply resented Frank being named head of the *Bratstvo* task force. Taking into account his seniority and many years in intelligence, he had expected the position to go to him. That's why it had come as no surprise to Frank when he found out that the person who had told the bureau about Vinnie's new association with Johnny Caruso was none other than Carl Badger. Three weeks after Frank's dismissal, the agent had assumed command of the *Bratstvo* task force.

What brought him here tonight was anyone's guess. Frank draped the dish towel over Danny's shoulder. "Looks like you're in charge, bud."

"Hey, that's not fair," Danny protested. "I did the dishes last night."

"I'll owe you one."

Carl Badger loved to look like a fed, right down to his shiny black oxfords. The body was still lean, the buzz cut fresh and laced with a little more gray, but the eyes, little black pinpoints in a too pale face, were still as probing.

He stood against the railing, framed against the night sky, that same obnoxious smile on his lips. "Hello, Frank."

Frank sat down in one of the chairs without inviting Carl to do the same, and propped one foot over his knee. "Why, Carl, I didn't know you missed me so much."

"I don't."

"You've come a long way to see someone you can't stand."

"Every job comes with its price."

Frank stifled a fake yawn. "What do you want?"

"I hear you've been impersonating a federal agent."

Frank kept his face blank. So Chekhov hadn't bought his act after all. Or if he had, he had been smart enough to check it out. "Chekhov called you?"

"Are you surprised?"

"Nothing that man does surprises me anymore. And for the record, I never claimed to be a fed. He just assumed."

"And you let him."

"Wouldn't you have?"

"That wasn't smart, Frank. You can't harass hardworking, tax-paying people, especially when you no longer have any credentials."

"What are you going to do? Have me fired?"

Badger ignored the dig. "Lucky for you I took the call, or you would have been in serious trouble." He threw a casual glance around him and dropped his voice. "Maybe we can make a deal. My silence for a little information."

Frank laughed. The man's arrogance never ceased to amaze him. "That'll be the day that I make a deal with you, Carl, although I admit, I'm curious. What do I have that you want so badly you'd come crawling to me?"

"Tell me why you're suddenly interested in *Bratstvo*."

Meaning the new head honcho hadn't made any headway over the past two years and could use a little help. "You're pathetic, you know that? You actually expect me to play ball with you? To forgive and forget what a backstabbing rat you are?"

Badger's oily smile vanished. "If this is a matter of national security, it's your duty to help your government."

Frank leaned forward. "You want information? Get it the old-fashioned way—by digging for it."

"I can have you hauled down to Washington with one phone call."

Frank stood up. He'd had enough of this shit. "Give it your best shot, Carl."

He walked back inside the house and let the screen door slam shut behind him.

When Frank returned to the kitchen, the place was spotless and the dishwasher humming softly. An old Italian espresso pot and two miniature cups and saucers were already on the table.

"Where's Danny?" he asked.

"I sent him to bed. He has a game tomorrow."
Vinnie motioned toward the chair across from him.
"Sit down, have some coffee."

Frank was too pissed to be social. "I'll pass tonight, Vinnie."

"Sit down, Frankie. I want to talk to you."

Surprised at his uncle's mild but commanding
tone, Frank did as he was told. He had learned long
ago that with a man like Vinnie, you learned to pick
your battles. This clearly wasn't one of them.

He let Vinnie pour him a cup of his famous espresso, a brew so strong, it had sustained Frank
through many pre-exam nights during his law school
days. "What's up?"

After he had filled his own cup, Vinnie put the pot
down. "Would it kill you to ask for my help every
once in a while?"

Frank assumed an innocent expression. "I don't
know what you're talking about."

"Then let me spell it out for you. I've been waiting for almost two years for you to tell me what
really happened in D.C. Why didn't you?"

"Because you already know what happened."

"I know what you told your mother and your sister, but did you really expect me to believe that you'd
voluntarily leave the bureau? When I know damn
well how much that job meant to you?"

"You forget that I had Danny to take care of."

"I didn't forget. Just as I didn't forget that you're
one of the most resourceful men on this planet. You
would have found a way to be the father you wanted
to be without compromising your career. *If* you had
wanted to."

Frank slowly put his cup down and held his uncle's calm gaze. Nothing in Vinnie's comments at the time of Frank's dismissal had led him to suspect the old man hadn't bought his story. "What brought that up?" he asked.

"Seeing that fed outside."

"How do you know he's a fed."

Vinnie laughed. "Well, it ain't Halloween, so I figured anyone who looks like that has to be a fed." He was serious again. "He's no friend of yours, is he?"

Frank laughed. "Hardly."

"Is he the one who got you fired?"

That old fox. He had known all along. "Yes."

"Say the word and I'll break his knees."

Knowing that Vinnie wouldn't need much encouragement, Frank gave a firm shake of his head. "No, Vinnie. No rough stuff."

"Why the hell not? The guy screwed you, didn't he? Somebody's got to teach him a lesson."

"Not that way."

"Drastic situations call for drastic measures. Haven't I taught you anything?"

"How did you find out, anyway?"

Vinnie leaned back in his chair, cup in hand. In that big paw of his, the demi-tasse all but disappeared. "After Johnny Caruso had his first heart attack, he had a visit from another private hauler, a guy from Brooklyn, looking to expand. He made Johnny one hell of an offer, but when Johnny found out the business was run by the Russian mafia, he said no, thanks."

Frank's antenna went up. "I never knew that."

"Johnny didn't want the offer to become public knowledge. A lot of his business was, and still is, generated by the Staten Island municipality, and he didn't want to jeopardize that relationship. A few months after I came aboard, I found out that some creep had tipped the feds about my job, and as a result, you got fired.''

"Why didn't you say something sooner?''

"What for? It was too late to save your job. You were already here, working as a P.I. Danny was happy. I figured someday, when you felt like it, you'd tell me.''

"I never wanted you to find out.''

"I know that, kid.'' Vinnie took a sip of his coffee. "Tell me about this Carl Badger.''

"I was his boss. He thought it should be the other way around, so when the opportunity to stick it to me presented itself, he jumped at it.''

"You should have told me right away, Frankie. I could have turned down Johnny's offer.''

"That's exactly what I didn't want you to do. I knew how much you cared about Johnny, and how much you wanted to help him. I wasn't going to screw that up.''

"This Badger guy, why did he come here to-night?''

Frank knew that whatever he told Vinnie would never go any further. "To find out why I was suddenly interested in *Bratstvo*.''

"You think *Bratstvo* is connected to your friend's murder?''

"Maybe,'' Frank said cautiously.

Vinnie leaned across the table, his dark eyes bright. "Then maybe it's time you asked for my help, kid.''

Frank thought about that for a moment. Vinnie had

tons of connections—good and bad. And he wasn't stupid. He would know exactly where to go and what questions to ask and do it in a way that would not attract attention. Frank picked up his cup. "How's your Russian?"

Vinnie grinned.

Twenty-Seven

On Saturday morning, the Staten Island Black Hawks' spectacular four-week-winning streak came to a sad end when the Yonkers Flyers beat them nine to six. Nothing Frank and Vinnie could say during the ride home, no amount of praise for Danny's three goals, could get the boy out of his funk.

"How about we stop at IHOP for some of those pancakes you like?" Vinnie suggested.

"I'd rather *die* than be seen in public," Danny replied.

Frank and Vinnie exchanged a glance. Frank shrugged. "Then I guess we go home."

He had just swung into the driveway when his phone rang. The name Falco, M. appeared on the screen. "You two go ahead," he told Vinnie. "I'll take this here."

"Hey, Frank," Mick Falco said when Frank answered. "Know a good P.I.?"

"I happen to be tight with the best P.I. in town. Too bad you can't afford him."

"Oh, I don't know about that. Thanks to a buddy of mine, I've been retained to work on the hottest case in town."

"I take it you and Warren Lear hit it off?"

Mick laughed. "Hit it off is a bit of as stretch. The

man is one huge pain in the ass, but I'm learning to tolerate him.'' His tone turned serious. ''Thanks, Frank. I appreciate the recommendation.''

''No need to thank me. I chose you because I knew you were the best man for the job, but I have to be honest. My intentions were not entirely pure.''

''No!'' Mick said with feigned shock. ''And what exactly were your intentions?''

''I want to be on the case.''

''Well you're in luck, old buddy, because I need your services.'' Mick was all business now. ''I talked to my client. Roy was able to give me a fairly good description of the man he met in the park the day before the murder—the man with the knife?''

''Go on.''

''Apparently Detective Stavos dismissed Roy's claims because they sounded phony. When you hear the description he gave him, you'll know why.''

''What does the guy look like? Godzilla?''

''Better than that. According to Roy, the man bears a striking resemblance to Columbo.''

''You mean Columbus? As in Christopher?''

Mick laughed. ''No, Frank, I mean Columbo as in that rumpled TV detective. Don't tell me you never heard of the show.''

''Sorry. Except for the NHL and Monday Night football, I don't watch much TV.''

''Unruly hair, a raincoat that looks like it's gone through two wars, a Peugeot that's about to expire its last breath. Doesn't any of that ring a bell?''

''Sorry.''

''All right then, just listen. That description I gave you, the hair, the raincoat, the messy appearance is what led Roy to believe the man was another street bum, like him. So after a minute or so, he sat down to chat. Then, out of the blue, this Columbo look-alike pulls out a knife and asks Roy if he wants to hold it.''

"I know, I read the police report."

"You're kidding me? How did you manage that?"

"My boyish charm, of course, what else? Go on, Mick. This is interesting."

"It gets better. The man was carrying a paper cup from one of those fancy coffee houses you see all over town these days."

"You mean like Starbucks?"

"Yes, but not Starbucks. Their cups are brown. The cup Roy's pseudo buddy was carrying was or-ange with a tree on the side of the cup as a logo. Could be a coffee tree."

"Did it have the name of the coffee house on it?"

"If it did, Roy didn't notice." He paused. "I need you to get on this right away, Frank."

"You want me to find where your Columbo guy bought his coffee?"

"I know it's a lot of leg work. Do you still want to do it?"

"You know I do. I was hoping for a little more to go on."

"You'll have it. A friend of mine is an artist. He's working on the two sketches as we speak. Now, about your fee, feel free to—"

"This one's on me," Frank cut in.

"Frank, no. Warren gave me a very generous re-tainer. Believe me, I can afford to pay you what-ever—"

"I'm not taking any money. Is that all right with you, Counselor?"

There was a short silence, then, as though Mick knew it would be useless to argue, he sighed. "If that's the way you want it."

"It is."

"My secretary will drop the sketches at your office first thing Monday morning."

"Good. Give my love to Gloria."

Jenna and the crew from *Today's Cuisine* magazine had spent the past two hours putting the finishing touches to Jenna's roof garden. Now that everyone had left, at her request, she was alone and finally able to go on with the shoot.

The roof garden, a dozen steps above her apartment, was one of her favorite places in the entire city. It was her own private oasis, a restful area overlooking Central Park, where she came to read, find solace or occasionally, to entertain. Twenty-two floors above the city, the view was breathtaking, especially now that the leaves had changed and a hint of winter was in the air.

Twenty-four hours ago, the magazine's "Christmas at the Met" story had to be scrapped for legal reasons, leaving the editors pulling out their hair. When Lou Frankel, the very gay, very flamboyant editor-in-chief of *Today's Cuisine* had found out that Jenna had a roof garden, he had come up with the idea of replacing the defunct piece with a "Christmas al fresco" story. One look at Jenna's special place, with its profusion of shrubs, vines and trees, and he had been like a child in a candy store.

"This is fabulous," he had declared, walking excitedly from one end of the garden to the other, touching everything and practically drooling in anticipation. "We'll put poinsettias and holly every-where, string golden miniature lights through the trees and put the dinner table right here."

He had pointed two fingers down in the center of the garden. "It'll be dynamite, darling. You'll see." Always professional, he had added, "And we'll tack another five grand to your fee for the use of the garden."

Not particularly thrilled with Lou's brainstorm at first, Jenna had slowly warmed up to the idea. Looking at her surroundings now, she had to admit, the project had turned into a spectacular feast for the eyes. Dozens of red and white poinsettias were scattered across the twenty-by-twelve-foot space, a Christmas tree decorated with Victorian ornaments stood in one corner, and garlands dotted with tiny lights had been wrapped around the doorway and along the two-foot wall encircling the rooftop. In the center stood the pièce de résistance—a table set for eight and gleaming with holiday china on gold chargers, sparkling glassware from France and antique silverware from Tiffany's. Short, stubby candles in shades of green and red ran the entire length of the table. On each plate was a small, foil-wrapped present strung with a gold ribbon and topped with a tiny gold bow.

After one last look at the sun, which was now in perfect position, Jenna took her Leica off the tripod. Camera in hand, she started clicking away, lining up the shots, circling the table, capturing it in every possible angle she could think of. Earlier, she had brought the ladder out of the shed. She stepped on it now, climbing as high as she dared, and continued shooting.

She was totally absorbed by the task when a voice behind her said, "Hello, Jenna."

Startled, she turned toward the sound of the familiar voice. And almost tripped. "J.B."

The CEO stood only a few feet away and she wondered why she hadn't heard him. In his late fifties, he was a tall, lanky man with a slow, almost lazy manner about him, until you looked into his eyes and saw the energy there, the strength, the power.

"I startled you," he said. "I'm sorry. I rang the bell, but no one answered. Then I saw that your front door was unlocked and I let myself in. I hope you don't mind."

Of course she minded. Didn't most people turn around and leave when no one answered the door?

"No, of course not." She came down the ladder, feeling a little shaky and awkward. J.B. had never come to her home before and there was only one reason he was here now. He had heard about Adam's accusations and had come to confront her.

As if to dispel her anxieties, he glanced around the roof garden, taking in the festive table, the Christmas tree, the profusion of poinsettias. He smiled. "Christmas in October?"

"I'm working on the December issue of *Today's Cuisine*. A last-minute assignment."

"That explains it." His gaze swept toward the edge of the roof, protected only by that small wall, then came back to her. He waited until she had snapped the ladder shut before saying, "A Detective Stavos came to see me yesterday. He said your ex-husband had some suspicions about my company, and me in particular, and that he had expressed those suspicions to you. Is that true, Jenna?"

So Marcie had told her the truth, and Stavos, happy or not about it, had followed through with the D.A.'s instructions to question J.B. "Yes, it's true." Glad to have something to do with her hands, she started folding the tripod.

"Why didn't you come to me, Jenna?" He sounded pained and disappointed, which made her feel worse.

"It would have been a little awkward, don't you think?"

"So instead you went to the police."

"I'm not the one who made the accusations, J.B." She was beginning to regain some of her lost composure. "I simply relayed the information I had."

Hands in his pockets, he walked toward her. "Information you believe may point to a killer other than Roy Ballard."

Stavos hadn't pulled any punches. Maybe she had been wrong about him. "Roy didn't kill Adam."

He stood close enough now for her to see the little flecks in his hazel eyes. She willed herself not to take a step back. She had nothing to fear from this man, she reasoned. She knew him, had worked with him, had seen a humorous, almost zany side of him that few people knew existed.

"You're making a terrible mistake, Jenna." His tone had changed, turned sharper. "I don't know what Adam told you to make you feel this way about me, but whatever it is, he wanted only one thing— to discredit me. It wouldn't be the first time a rival company tried to muddy our reputation. Or spy on a new product. I'm not blaming them, mind you. We're all guilty of unethical behavior every now and then. But for you to think I would commit fraud, or worse, that I would kill a man, is preposterous."

"I never accused you of fraud, or of killing Adam," she protested. "I only suggested to Detective Stavos that he should be looking for another suspect because in my opinion, Roy did not do it."

Once again, his gaze flicked to the low wall behind Jenna. Why did he keep doing that? "Then who do you think killed Adam?"

Not even the relative warmth of the sun above could dispel the sudden chill Jenna felt at that moment. It seemed to get right through her skin, down to her very bones. She moistened her lips. "I don't know." She wanted to move toward safer ground, but didn't know how to do that without being obvious.

His face took on that same pained look. "You're afraid of me, Jenna. Why?"

"No, I'm not."

"What did Adam tell you?"

"He thought the photos I took the night of the Wizard's unveiling would implicate someone at Faxel."

"Ah, yes, the photos. Detective Stavos showed them to me, hoping I'd be able to identify some of the guests. Fortunately, I did, and I assure you, Jenna, there was no mysterious, sinister figure lurking among the crowd." He spread his arms out wide. "So, you see, whatever Adam told you, whatever he thought he knew, or saw, or heard, was either a lie or a figment of his imagination."

Jenna had always been a believer of the doctrine, "when faced with incoming disaster, retreat." It wasn't the bravest quote she could think of, but at this moment, it worked for her. "I suppose he could have been mistaken." She took a step back.

J.B.'s smile turned frosty. "You know, Jenna, I had a chance to get to know you pretty well when we worked on the Wizard project together. And one thing I learned about you is that you tell the truth. Always."

Another step back. "Yes, I do."

"You're not telling the truth now, Jenna. You don't believe for one second that Adam was mistaken. I look into your eyes and what I see is the absolute conviction that I am guilty of some unspeakable crime."

"You're wrong." Half a step back. Another and her heel would hit the wall.

"What are you hiding, Jenna?"

"Nothing."

"How can I defend myself if I don't know the accusations I'm facing?"

"I told you I don't know anything. I'm sorry if I'm giving you the impression that I'm—"

"Do you have another set of photographs?"

The question took her aback. She hadn't been prepared for it. "Excuse me?" The words, meant to buy her a little time, only succeeded in making her sound more guilty.

"I asked if you had another set of photographs. I thought that if you did, maybe I could take another look at them, you know, in case I missed something."

Her heart began to pound in her chest. Could he hear it? Could he tell she was terrified? "No, I don't." She wasn't sure how she managed to hold his gaze, but was glad she did. "I gave the only set I had to the district attorney."

Something flashed in his eyes, but before she could decide what it was, it was gone.

Jenna stepped aside, determined to get away from him. In her haste, she bumped into the ladder and would have lost her footing if it hadn't been for J.B.

His arms shot out, taking hold of her elbows and squeezing them tightly. "Careful, Jenna." He glanced beyond her shoulder. "It's a long way down from here."

Twenty-Eight

Her back pressed against her front door, Jenna didn't exhale until she heard the hiss of the elevator as it started its descent. When she was sure J.B. was gone and her door was securely locked, she went back to the kitchen and poured herself some of the wine left over from the other night. She took a sip, and a second, waiting for the liquor to soothe her nerves. It didn't.

Usually decisive about any matter, she had no idea what to make of J.B.'s visit. If she listened to her instincts, the answer was simple. He had come to find out what she knew and when that had failed, he had threatened her. But had he? Only a few days ago, Marcie had accused her of having an overactive imagination. She didn't deny that, but that imagination was balanced with a strong dose of common sense. And right now, her common sense told her she had grounds to worry. J.B.'s behavior had been odd at best. Why hadn't he moved out of her way when he knew perfectly well that she wanted him to? Why had he said *it's a long way down from here*, knowing those words would frighten her?

When Adam had first mentioned his suspicions of Faxel, she hadn't wanted to believe that a man like J.B., a man the *Wall Street Journal* mentioned weekly, a devoted father and husband who was often photographed with his family outside his beautiful Long Island home, could stoop to something as sordid as corporate fraud. Then Adam was murdered, and everything changed.

J.B.'s visit had done little to erase her doubts about the man. He may have kept her from falling a moment ago, but the expression in his eyes had told her that if he had wanted to he could have just as well pushed her over the edge.

She put the glass down and went to check the lock a second time. Worrying about what might have happened wasn't helping her. She should keep busy, do something that would end the morbid maze of speculation that swirled inside her head.

Remembering the decorations and expensive table settings that were still up on the roof, she ran up the spiraled staircase, took the empty boxes out of the shed and began putting things away, starting with the china.

By the time she was ready to take the last box down, the sun had disappeared and the temperature had dropped several degrees. She was about to call the magazine to arrange for a pickup, when she heard the sound of a rapid, insistent knocking on her door.

Jenna crossed the foyer and peered into her peephole. Magdi's frightened face was staring back at her.

Jenna opened the door. "Magdi, what's wrong?"

The Hungarian woman held up a rose—a *black* rose. "This was on your doorstep," she said in a muffled voice.

Jenna took the rose and instinctively glanced around her. "On my doorstep?"

Magdi nodded, then with the tone of one who knows, she said, "A black rose is bad luck, Jenna."

Jenna had been around criminal attorneys long enough to know that a black rose was much more than bad luck. It was a symbol of death, a warning to the recipient that unless instructions were strictly followed, tragedy would follow.

"Who would send you something like that?" Magdi's face was creased with worry.

"Oh, Magdi, it's just a silly prank." Jenna forced a laugh. "You know how kids are when they have nothing to do." As she spoke, she glanced at the elevator shaft, empty at the moment. The rose hadn't been there when she had walked J.B. to the door. Was it from him? Had he come back with another threat? Something she would take a little more seriously?

The long-stemmed flower felt as if it was burning a hole in her skin. "Did you want something, Magdi?"

The older woman didn't seem able to take her eyes away from the ominous flower. "I made some of that green tea you like. I thought maybe you could come over for a cup?"

But Jenna's wasn't in the mood for a tea party. She needed to get out of here, go where she would feel safe, where she could think what her next step should be. Or if she should do nothing at all. After all, wasn't that the rose's message? To do nothing?

"That sounds lovely, Magdi, but I can't come over tonight." She started to tell her where she was going, then stopped. Magdi had a loose tongue, although there was nothing malicious about it. She just couldn't help herself. "Maybe another time?"

"Okay." She cast another glance at the black rose. "Please, Jenna, be careful?"

"I will."

The rural, picturesque village of Katomah, an hour north of Manhattan, was country living at its best. With its busy downtown district, historic homes and easy commute to Manhattan, this charming enclave had become one of the most sought after communities in the area.

The big white Colonial, so empty now that her mother was gone, still felt like home to Jenna, making it easy for her to visit often.

Her father had been delighted to hear that she was taking him up on his offer to spend a few days with him. She hadn't told him why. In fact, she had managed to conceal the anxiety in her voice quite well, explaining that she'd had a difficult week and needed to unwind.

By the time she arrived, a local Chinese restaurant had delivered all her favorite dishes—Kung Pao chicken, Hunan roast pork, Mu Shu vegetables and double orders of fortune cookies. She and her father ate in front of the TV while watching a *Happy Days* marathon and laughing like children.

She had gone to bed early and slept remarkably well, partly because she was exhausted, but mostly because her old room was one of the most peaceful places she knew. There, lulled by happy memories and the rumble of the old furnace, she had fallen into a deep, restful sleep and hadn't awakened until she heard the clatter of pots and pans coming from the kitchen below.

"How would you like to take a walk through your

mother's garden?'' Sam asked when they were finished with breakfast. ''The maples are brilliant at this time of year.''

''I'd love that.''

Arms entwined, they walked slowly through the garden Elaine Meyerson had so lovingly tended to for more than thirty years.

''You're taking good care of her roses.'' Jenna bent to smell an American beauty, still in bloom.

''It's all I have of her that's alive.'' Sam squeezed Jenna against him. ''Except for you, of course.'' He stopped to look at her. ''Are you all right, honey? You're quiet this morning. Did you have enough to eat?''

Jenna laughed and pressed a hand to her stomach. ''Dad, please. Two pancakes, two strips of bacon and two eggs? That's a week's worth of food. I can't believe I ate it all.''

''Maybe you're still a growing girl.''

She nudged him in the ribs. ''Bite your tongue.''

She loved spending time with her father, laughing with him the way they used to. Here she felt renewed and unafraid, as if J.B. and the black rose were nothing but a distant memory.

''So,'' Sam said as they reached the pond. ''How are things between you and Frank?''

Now that was something she hadn't been prepared for. ''Things?''

''You know. How is the relationship progressing?''

Her laugh felt just a tad forced. ''Dad, there is no relationship.''

He stopped again. This time his scrutiny was much

more thorough. "That's not the impression I had at the cemetery on Friday."

"We were just talking."

"If you say so."

A full minute went by before she asked, "Was I awful to him, Dad? When we were in school?"

Sam laughed. "Oh, honey, you were so young."

"That's a yes, isn't it?"

"Why worry about it now? Frank doesn't seem to be."

"I'm not so sure about that."

"What do you mean?"

"That first day I went to see him? After Adam died? Frank was pretty nasty to me, *purposely* nasty."

Her father turned to look at her. "Frank? I find that hard to believe. The man doesn't have a nasty bone in his body."

"That's exactly my point. He *wanted* to be mean. He wanted to hurt me."

Sam nodded, as though he understood. "That was probably his defenses reacting."

"Defenses against what?"

"You, sweetheart." He gave her a knowing look before bending to pick up a rose that had broken off. "Oh, come on, Jenna. Don't tell me you haven't noticed. The man is in love with you, and this time it's much more serious than it was fifteen years ago."

"You mean he's attracted to me."

"No, I mean he's in love with you. No man looks at a woman the way Frank looked at you on Friday without having strong feelings about her. And those feelings could be the reason his defenses went up when you went to see him. He didn't want a repeat of what happened fifteen years ago, when you rejected him.''

''I didn't reject him. He stopped fighting for me.''

''Did you ever ask yourself why?''

''He stopped caring.''

There was a lively twinkle in Sam's eyes. ''You could be wrong about that.''

Jenna felt suddenly uncomfortable with the conversation, as though it might reveal something about herself she didn't want to hear. But she had started it and she would finish it. ''How do you know so much? Did you talk to him?''

''I didn't have to. I'm a man. I'm well aware of the games women play to get men's attention.''

''You make me sound so shallow.''

''Like I said, you were very young—nineteen.'' He brushed her nose with the rose's dried-up petals. ''And only a little bit shallow.'' When he failed to make her smile, he asked, ''Do you have feelings for Frank, honey? Is that what this conversation is all about?''

She let out a nervous laugh. ''Is it that obvious?''

''Only to a father.''

She remained silent for a while, remembering those crazy days when she had been courted by the two smartest, most handsome men in the entire school. The fact that she hadn't meant to hurt anyone was of little comfort. No wonder Frank was pissed. She had played with his emotions like a cat played with a mouse and thought nothing of it. Then fifteen years later, she had reappeared into his life, expecting him to greet her with open arms.

How could she have been so damned insensitive?

She kicked a small stone out of the way and watched it settle into a flower bed. Maybe it was time for Frank to realize that the brat he had once loved had turned into a woman worth loving again.

Twenty-Nine

Sunday dinner at the Renaldis' was always an event. At noon, sharp, Frank picked up his mother, Mia, who still lived in the same Little Italy apartment where he and his sister grew up. He loaded the trunk of the T-bird with her lasagna, her ricotta pie and her handmade rolls, and drove back to Staten Island for a feast that began at two o'clock and didn't end until five.

Occasionally, his sister Lydia joined them, adding even more color and excitement to the day. But most of the time, "The Actress," as Mia called her twenty-four-year-old daughter, was too busy dividing her time between her sales job at Banana Republic and her acting classes to be part of the weekly ritual.

This Sunday, the family was halfway through Vinnie's potato gnocchi when the roar of a powerful engine outside the house brought the conversation to a halt.

Danny was the first one out of his chair. He raced to the dining room window, sliding the last few steps on the polished hardwood floor. "Holy cow! Dad! Uncle Vinnie! Come and see this."

Judging from the kid's excitement, the object of his attention could only be a motorcycle. After hockey, motorcycles were his second passion. And now that he subscribed to *Motor Bike* magazine, he knew every machine manufactured, whether it was domestic or foreign.

"Finish your dinner first, before it gets cold." Frank's mother said. She was a plump, petite woman with dark good looks and an easygoing personality, except when it came to Sunday dinners. Those were sacred, and nothing short of a national disaster was allowed to disrupt them.

Vinnie gave her a playful tap on the arm. "The kid says to come see, we go see. He can eat later."

Mia started to object, then as Frank motioned for her to follow, she muttered something unintelligible and walked over to the window.

"It's a hog, Dad," Danny said excitedly as Frank came to stand beside him and took in the black and chrome Harley Davidson parked outside their window. "A late model Fat Boy. And it's loaded."

While Danny pointed out the bike's various accessories, Frank watched the rider, as he dismounted the machine. He was a young, slender man, about five eight or five nine, dressed in black leather. The back seat rider was a young woman, also dressed in black leather. Frank had never seen either one of them before.

Danny's attention suddenly shifted from the machine to the girl. Still straddling the Harley, she had removed her helmet and was shaking her long black hair loose. "Wow!" Danny said the word with such reverence that Frank almost laughed out loud. He stopped himself in time, remembering that fourteen was an age when the heart was vulnerable and egos bruised easily.

"She's a looker, all right," Vinnie volunteered.

"Who are they?" Mia asked. "What do they want?"

"Maybe they're lost," Danny suggested. "If they are, can we invite them in?" He addressed the question to his grandmother, as if knowing she would not be able to resist feeding one more mouth—or two.

Frank decided it was time to take charge of the situation before it got out of hand. "No one comes in until I find out who those people are and what they want. You all go back to your dinner. I'll join you shortly."

Danny was still protesting when Frank closed the door behind him and stepped out on the porch. "Hi, there." He looked from the man to the woman. "Can I help you?"

The man stood with his legs about a foot apart, his fists on his hips. He was in his late twenties or maybe early thirties, with dark blond hair cropped short and a cocky expression. "You Frank Renaldi?"

Frank leaned against the support beam. "I am."

"I'm Billy Ray Shaeffer."

Frank looked at the man with renewed interest. Now *that* was a surprise.

"What can I do for you, Billy Ray?"

"I hear that Angie Delano is badmouthing my friend Teresa, so I came to set the record straight."

"How is Angie badmouthing Teresa?"

"She's saying things that aren't true, like Teresa was driving my car the night we had the accident."

"Are you here to dispute Angie's allegations?"

"I'm here to deny them." He took a couple of steps forward. He was about six inches shorter than Frank, and at least fifty pounds lighter, but that disparity didn't seem to bother him. He had tough guy written all over him.

"No one ever drove my car but me," he continued. "So whatever Angie told you, it's a lie. She's still pissed because I dumped her for Teresa."

A feeling Frank could definitely relate to. "Since you came here to set the record straight, you don't mind answering a few questions, do you?"

Billy Ray shrugged, which Frank took as a green light to proceed. "I understand you and Teresa were arguing that night. Is that true?"

"We argued every night. What's your point?"

"My point is this... Taking into consideration your turbulent relationship with Teresa, Angie's scenario doesn't sound so far-fetched."

"And what scenario is that?"

"You and Teresa had been arguing. She was pissed off and wanted to get back at you, so she snatched your keys and got into your car, giving you just enough time to jump in the passenger seat."

Billy Ray shook his head. "You've got it all wrong. First of all, nobody snatches anything from me, and second, even if Teresa had managed to do that, I'd have caught up with her before she was halfway to the car."

His version was plausible enough, but the fact that he had come all the way to Staten Island to "set the record straight" proved he was concerned enough to want to see who he was dealing with. Frank glanced at the girl. She had dismounted the bike and stood a few paces behind Billy Ray, looking bored. If she was his girlfriend, how did she feel about Billy Ray defending a former love?

"Have you been in contact with Teresa since you came out of prison?"

"What is it to you if I have?"

"Look, Billy Ray, you're the one who came looking for me, so what the hell is your problem? Did you think I'd take everything you told me at face value and not ask any questions?"

Billy Ray didn't even blink. He just stood there, looking like he'd like nothing better than to take him on. After a moment, he shrugged. "Yeah, I've been in touch with her. So what?"

"I find it strange, that's all. In my days, when a girl dumped a guy, that was pretty much the end of it. But the way Teresa did it, leaving town while you were in prison and then changing her name so you wouldn't find her," Frank shook his head, "man, that's low."

"Maybe I'm not the type who carries a grudge."

Frank glanced at the gleaming hog. Or maybe he had found the golden goose and wanted to make sure it kept on laying those valuable eggs. He shifted his attention to the girl. "Is that your girlfriend?"

"Yeah."

"How does she feel about your renewed friendship with Teresa?"

"She's cool with it."

Frank walked over to the motorcycle and started circling it, much as a prospective buyer would do. "Nice bike. Looks expensive."

Billy Ray didn't answer.

"What do you do for a living, Billy Ray? If you don't mind my asking."

"I sell electronics in a midtown shop."

"Make a lot of money?"

"Why don't you just tell me what's on your mind?"

"Okay, I'm not going to play games with you. I know Teresa gave you money. I don't know how much, but it was probably enough to buy this bike. Am I getting warm?"

Billy Ray's mouth tightened. "Teresa was right about you. You've been a busy little shit, haven't you?"

"You can either talk to me or talk to Detective Stavos. He's already taken steps to requisition Teresa's bank records. The truth will be out soon enough."

Billy Ray shrugged. "Okay, so Teresa's been helping me out."

"Why is that?"

"Because she felt bad for dumping me."

"Are you sure you didn't put a little pressure on her? You know what I'm talking about."

"No, I don't."

"The word is blackmail, Billy Ray."

The biker threw his head back and laughed. "Man, you're a real nutcase, you know that? Why would I blackmail Teresa? *I* was driving that night, not her. You can stand here and bang on your drum all day and all night, it won't change a damn thing."

Frank took another long look at the man. With a little makeup, the right clothes and a limp, he could easily pass for the panhandler. And in spite of his smallish size, he looked strong enough to overpower Adam, especially with the element of surprise in his favor.

"Where were you last Monday night, Billy Ray? Say between 11:00 p.m. and 1:00 a.m."

Billy Ray stared at him for a moment, not grasping the meaning of Frank's question. When he did, his eyes flared with anger. "What the fuck? You think I'm the one who killed her old man? Just because I did time you think I turned into a murderer?"

"It wouldn't be the first time."

Without taking his eyes off Frank, Billy Ray snapped his fingers. "Josie, come here."

The girl walked over in a slow, swinging walk that must have had Danny drooling, if he was still watching. The girl was a babe, all right, street-smart and tough. She came to stand beside Billy Ray, wrapped an arm around his waist and leaned against him. "Yeah?"

"Tell Mr. Renaldi here where I was on Monday night between 11:00 and 1:00 a.m."

She pressed herself a little closer to Billy Ray. "We were in bed, fucking." She flipped her hair over one shoulder. "Want to hear the play-by-play?"

Frank could see from her sassy expression that she was dying to tell him. Before he could think of an answer, Billy Ray slapped Josie's butt. "Come on, babe, let's go. We're done here."

Thirty

Bright and early on Monday morning, Vinnie came down while Frank was making coffee. "I'm glad I caught you," he said, taking a lumberman jacket from the closet and putting it on. "I just finished talking to a friend of mine who works at the Brooklyn Marine Terminal."

Frank handed him a cup of coffee. "I thought all the dock workers were on strike this week."

"They are. Joe was home, working on a picketing sign."

Vinnie took a sip and nodded approvingly. "You've finally learned how to make good coffee. I'm proud of you, kid." He added a scant quarter spoon of sugar to the cup. "I found out something I know will please you. Or piss you off, depending on the mood you're in. The person who made that anonymous call to the bureau about my job was Mikhail Fetisov, an important member of the *Bratstvo* crime family, but not high enough on the pecking order to know who runs it."

Frank nodded. "I know the guy."

Fetisov was one of the businessmen who had caught Frank's attention while he was in charge of the task force. A wealthy banker, he had possessed the right profile to head *Bratstvo*. Like Sergei, however, he hadn't passed a second, closer examination and Frank had dismissed him, concentrating his efforts elsewhere.

"I have one more juicy bit for you, then I'm off to work. According to my same source, there's a leak in the N.Y.P.D. I don't know at what level, or in which precinct, but there's a leak, so be careful, okay?"

"If you mean Stavos—"

"Now, don't go nuts on me. I didn't say it was Stavos. It could be anybody." He glanced at the clock on the wall and drained the rest of his coffee. "Remember. Watch your back."

When Frank arrived at his office an hour later, Mick Falco's two sketches, one of the pseudo panhandler, the other of the coffee cup, were waiting for him on Tanya's desk.

"His secretary dropped them off a few minutes ago." Tanya pointed at the charcoal drawing of the man. "Interesting looking character. Not someone I'd want to meet in a dark alley."

Frank studied the unshaven face and unruly hair. "Mick says he looks like Columbo. What do you think?"

She gave him a blank stare. "Who's Columbo?"

Frank chuckled. "A TV detective I'd never heard of either." He flipped through the rest of his messages. "Jenna Meyerson didn't call?"

He didn't miss the twinkle in Tanya's eyes. "Not yet. You want me to get her for you?"

He wanted to say yes. She had been in such a hurry to get to her shoot on Friday, she had left him without a clear understanding of when he would see her again. He had been itching to call her all weekend, going as far as to pick up the phone several times, only to put it back a few seconds later because he couldn't think of a valid excuse for the call.

"Maybe later," he said, not meeting his secretary's amused gaze. "In the meantime, do me a favor and call Detective Stavos. Tell him Billy Ray Shaeffer came to see me yesterday and admitted to receiving money from Amber Lear. I don't know how much. Possibly enough to pay for a Harley Davidson worth about twenty grand."

"Trying to get on the detective's good side, Boss?"

"It can't hurt." Vinnie's warning about the N.Y.P.D. leak had not changed his mind about Stavos. He simply refused to believe Paul was a dirty cop.

From his office, he took the subway to Fifty-Ninth Street. Because the murder had taken place in the southern section of Central Park, he decided to use that as a starting point and work his way down Fifth Avenue. For the next nine blocks, he checked every coffee shop on his route. Everywhere he went, the answer was the same. Neither the coffee cup nor the man on the drawing were familiar.

It wasn't until he reached a shop called Java on Rockefeller Center that he hit pay dirt.

"Sure, I know that cup," the kid behind the counter said. "I drank gallons of that stuff before I came to work here. The place is called Insomnia. It's on Times Square."

Frank vaguely remembered having stopped there once or twice. It was one of those upscale coffee boutiques where the blackboard of specialty coffees read like a table of contents and the prices were not for the faint of pocketbook. The coffee was better than most, however, and the look of the place, when he walked in, fifteen minutes later, as enticing as the aroma. A map of Brazil hung on the wall behind the counter.

He waited a few minutes, until the rush was over, before approaching the server, whose name tag read "Ricardo—Manager." Frank showed him the sketch. Ricardo studied the drawing, then shook his head. "Sorry. We get a lot of people in here. I just don't remember him."

"It was a Sunday."

Ricardo shook his head. "Then I definitely wouldn't have seen him. I don't open the shop on Sundays. My boss does."

"Is your boss in?"

"He's in the back, roasting coffee beans. Do you want me go get him for you?"

"I'd appreciate that."

A handsome man no older than Ricardo walked out a few moments later, smiling broadly and drying his hands on a cloth towel. With his neatly creased gray trousers, conservative blue shirt and matching tie, he was the perfect image of today's young, successful business owner.

"I'm Pincho Figueras. Please excuse the smell. The oils from the beans have a way of clinging to you, no matter what you do."

Despite the fact that he spoke without a trace of an accent, the name and the map on the wall told Frank that Pincho Figueras was Brazilian. He took the offered hand and shook it. "Don't worry about it. Actually, it's quite pleasant. I didn't realize you did your roasting on the premises.''

"That's the only way I can be sure it will be done properly.'' He draped the towel over his right shoulder and looked at the sketch in Frank's hand. "Is that the man you're looking for?''

"Yes. I was hoping you'd remember him. He bought a large cup of coffee from your shop on the morning of October fifth. Last Sunday.''

Figueras didn't spend nearly as much time studying the sketch as Ricardo had. "I do remember him,'' he said, nodding. "He was one of my first customers, and looked as if he had been up all night.''

"Did he say anything to you?''

"No. He ordered a cappuccino, the sixteen-ounce size, paid me and walked out.''

"Have you seen him since?''

"No.''

"Who else works here beside you and your manager?''

"No one. There are times when we could use an extra hand, but for the most part, we manage.''

Frank was disappointed. What had sounded like a hot tip at first had turned out to be of little use. Pincho Figueras had only confirmed what Frank already knew. The Columbo look-alike had purchased a cup of coffee before heading for Central Park and vanishing into thin air. Unless someone else could come up with additional information, Frank had reached a dead end.

He handed Figueras his card. "Would you let me know if he comes back? I wrote down my cell phone number.''

"Sure." Figueras read the card. "Can I ask what he's done?"

Frank met the man inquisitive gaze. "He may have murdered two people."

Holding the private detective's card, Pincho walked into his office, cursing himself for his stupidity. Usually so obsessive about not leaving any clues behind, he had come close to being identified through a stupid coffee cup. His own, no less. Just the thought that a private investigator had traced it to his shop made him edgy. What if the guy found out he had closed the shop for a couple of hours that morning, and he came back with more questions? What if he decided to put a surveillance team on the shop? As far as Pincho knew, unauthorized surveillance was illegal, but would that stop a private investigator?

On the other hand, Pincho's disguise as the unkempt TV detective had worked like a charm. And his performance just now as a mildly curious, eager-to-help shop owner had been no less than brilliant. What reason would anyone have to be suspicious?

He put the business card in a drawer, and told himself there was nothing to fear. He had handled the situation well, considering he had been caught off guard. In fact, he had rather enjoyed taking the extra risk, watching the interest in the investigator's eyes grow as Pincho provided just enough information to peak his interest. The experience had given him a rush similar to the one he experienced when he prepared for a job.

Nevertheless, the P.I.'s visit was not something he could ignore. From now on he would have to be more careful. Something about that private eye told him he was no two-bit gumshoe. This one was different. He was smarter, more observant, not easily fooled.

Would it hurt to report the visit to his client, just to see if there was any cause to worry?

After a few more seconds of reflection, he picked up the phone.

Outside Insomnia, Frank looked around him, at the profusion of multicolored neon signs that advertised anything from Broadway shows to men's underwear and tried to decide where to start his search for Columbo. He had thought of asking Tanya to do the legwork, but since he was here and didn't have anywhere else to go for the next couple of hours, he might as well put the time to good use.

The fact that the man had bought his coffee in Times Square raised the possibility that he lived or worked in the area. Finding the man in this part of Manhattan, however, where the concentration of people was heavier than anywhere else in the city, wouldn't be easy. But Frank was an optimist.

An hour and a half later he was still at it, and about to give up for the day when a hooker in a black miniskirt and a fake fur jacket in bright purple, handed the sketch back and said, "I know that dude."

"Do you know his name?"

She shook her head and made noisy sounds with her gum. "I don't know him *personally,* but I've seen him." Calculating, turquoise-lidded blue eyes looked him over. "What's the information worth to you?"

Frank pulled out a twenty and held it just out of her reach.

The blonde sashayed a little closer. "You make that fifty and I'll throw in the best fuck you've ever had."

Frank didn't want to make an enemy out of her by being insulting, so he put just enough regret in his voice to tone down the rejection. "Look, sugar, not that I don't appreciate the offer, but I'm kind of in a hurry."

She looked disappointed. "It's still fifty. With or without the fuck."

Frank took another thirty dollars out of his pocket. "Tell me about the man."

She plucked the bills out of his hand and tucked them between her ample breasts. "Not much to tell. I saw him one day last week, can't remember which."

"Sunday?"

"Yeah, it could have been Sunday." She winked. "I make out like a bandit on Sundays, with all of them churchgoers on their way to confession."

"About the man?" Frank prompted.

"What exactly do you want to know?"

"Did you talk to him? Did you notice the direction he was coming from? Where was he going? Did anyone in the neighborhood seem to know him?"

She watched the traffic, her keen gaze alert for any slowing cars, ready to pounce the moment one came to a stop. "No to all your questions." She snapped her gum again. "But I can tell you this. The man is one rude son of a bitch. I approached him, friendly like, you know, and the bastard almost knocked me to the sidewalk. No apologies, nothing. He just kept on going.''

"Which way?"

She pointed north. "Uptown."

Frank's gaze swept up and down the busy street with its constant flow of misfits as well as legitimate workers. If the hooker had told him the truth, there was a chance the Columbo look-alike was no stranger to this area. And if that was the case, Tanya would have better luck in finding him than Frank had. As a cop, she had walked this beat every day for two years. Hookers knew her. Some even liked her. For someone looking for information, a friendly hooker was worth her weight in gold.

After thanking the blonde, Frank started walking back toward Forty-Second Street. As he crossed Broadway, he spotted an Indian restaurant sandwiched between a Radio Shack and a sex shop. On impulse, he took out his cell phone and called Jenna. She answered from Siri's, where Letitia had introduced her to a book publisher she knew.

"If memory serves, you used to love Indian food," he said.

She actually sounded happy to hear from him. "I still do."

"In that case, why don't you meet me at the Bombay Palace on Broadway? You can't miss it. It's right across from the Fox theater and an oversized photograph of Antonio Banderas above the marquis."

Jenna laughed. "What makes you think I'd even notice a photograph of Antonio Banderas?"

"You'll notice that one."

Frank was on his third cup of jasmine tea when Jenna walked through the restaurant's door, drawing looks from women as well as men. He could hardly blame them. In that long camel skirt, a matching turtle neck, black boots and the same black leather jacket she had worn in his office that first day, she looked as if she had just stepped out of the pages of *Vogue.*

She stood at the entrance for a moment, eyes scanning the crowd. When she saw him, she waved and quickly came over.

"Hi." She slid gracefully into the booth, bringing with her the smell of the crisp autumn air.

"Hi, yourself." He couldn't take his eyes off of her and didn't try to.

"Did you order yet?"

"Only the appetizer." He pointed at a plate of lentil fritters the waiter had brought earlier, along with a small bowl of fiery Thai chili sauce and a cup of yogurt to cool the heat. "Careful," he warned. "They're hot."

She popped a fritter into her mouth. "Just the way I like them."

He watched her face, waiting for her eyes to glaze.

She laughed. "What's the matter? Didn't you think I could take the heat?"

"Are you referring to the fritters?"

She gave him a teasing look. "What else?"

She took another, and this time she dunked it into the potent chili concoction, bypassing the yogurt. She chewed without as much as a blink. "What are you doing in this part of town?"

True to his promise, he told her about his conversation with Warren Lear, then went on to explain about the work he was doing for Mick Falco, which had eventually led to his talk with Pincho Figueras and the hooker.

"Can I take a look at that sketch?"

Frank took the now well-worn drawing out of his pocket and handed it to her.

"Hmm. I see what Mick means. He does look like Columbo. And I can see why Roy would mistake him for a homeless compadre. He looks pretty scruffy."

"Any resemblance to the man you and Adam bumped into last Monday night?"

Jenna only took a second or two to answer. "No. It's definitely not the same face." She looked up, her intelligent brown eyes suddenly bright with new interest. "Or are we dealing with someone who changes his appearances at will?"

"That's a strong possibility."

"Hmm." Her gaze returned to the sketch. "You think this possible master of disguises lives in this area?"

"Two people claim to have seen him. I'm hopeful."

"How will you find him?"

"Tanya used to be in vice when she was a cop. She knows this area, knows the people. She'll have better luck at getting the information than I did."

Jenna's smile was wicked, her words full of innuendos. "Oh, I don't know. Judging from that offer you told me about, I'd say you're doing very well on your own." The waiter had come to take their orders, the vegetable curry for Jenna and the grilled tuna for Frank.

"What's that?" Jenna asked when they were alone again. She pointed at a cocktail napkin on which he had been doodling to pass the time while he waited for her.

He pushed it toward her, turning it around so she could read it. "I was making a list of suspects and motives. It helps sort things out."

She read out loud. "Number one—Aleksei Chekhov. Motive—possible involvement with Faxel, possible money laundering, possible financial support of al Quaeda. Number two—Billy Ray Shaeffer and/ or Amber Lear. Motive—Money, blackmail, possible cover-up of an earlier crime. Number three— J. B. Collins. Motive—money. His company wasn't doing well, then miraculously recovered and went on to become a major force in the computer industry."

Jenna tapped a slender finger on J.B.'s name. "You may want to put him ahead of the pack."

"Why?"

Frank felt a stirring of alarm as he listened to Jenna's account of J.B.'s visit and the black rose she had found on her doorstep. Although she didn't appear afraid, he was glad to hear that she had moved in with her father for a few days.

"I'm not sure that was such a good idea," she said with a short laugh. "The man guards me like a rottweiler. This morning he insisted on driving me into the city and said he'd pick me up when I was ready to come home. He's turned into a one-man car service and it's driving me crazy."

"Let him take care of you, Jenna. It's what fathers do."

She raised a finger. "Just don't expect me to stay cloistered in that house like a nun. I have a life, I have responsibilities, people who depend on me."

"Did I ask you to stay cloistered?"

"You didn't have to. I'm starting to know how your twisted mind works."

"Oh, so now you're a mind reader. Another talent I wasn't aware of."

"Laugh all you want, but my intuitions have served me well in the past."

"All right, I'll bite." He leaned forward. "What do you see in your crystal ball, Madame Cleo?"

"Now?"

"This very second."

Playing along, Jenna pressed two fingers to her temples, pretending to concentrate. "I'm getting a message about the other night at my apartment. Ah, yes, here it comes. You wish you hadn't run like a scared rabbit."

He burst out laughing. "I didn't run. I walked out of a potentially dangerous situation because I knew you wouldn't be able to handle it."

"You've got it in reverse, don't you, Renaldi? *You're* the one who can't handle sticky situations."

Frank had never been able to turn down a challenge. Especially one as enticing as this one. He reached into his pocket, found a twenty dollar bill and slapped it on the table. "Twenty bucks says you're wrong."

"You realize that the only way of proving who is wrong and who is right is by having a replay of what happened the other night."

"Does that scare you?"

She opened her purse, rummaged through it. Another twenty went over his. "Name the time and the place."

He laughed again. "Oh, no, that's much too clinical. Why don't we just play it by ear and see what happens?''

''And give you the clear advantage of knowing where and when? That doesn't seem fair.'' After a short pause, she shrugged. ''Oh, why not? I can be a good sport. You're on.''

Thirty-One

As it turned out, Tanya didn't have any more luck in finding the Columbo look-alike than Frank had the previous day. Two hours and a dozen hookers later, she was back at the office, with nothing more than the promise from one pimp she knew to call if he spotted the man in the drawing. Either the people questioned were afraid to talk, or the gum-smacking hooker had taken Frank for a ride.

"I'm sorry," Frank told Mick on Tuesday morning. "The man exists but we can't seem to find him."

"That's all right. Finding that coffee shop was a big help. I'll subpoena Pincho Figueras to testify at Roy's preliminary hearing. At least he'll be able to establish the fact that the man does exists."

"How is Roy holding up?"

"He's scared. He doesn't understand the concept of a preliminary hearing. He thinks he's going to prison."

"Will you put him on the stand?"

"I'd like to. There's a sweet, honest side to him I think will appeal to a judge, but he's unpredictable, so to answer your question, I don't know yet. I have another week to decide. How reliable is that hooker of yours?"

Frank laughed. "Why? Are you thinking of putting *her* on the stand?"

"I might. Where exactly does she hang out?"

"The corner of Forty-Second and Sixth Avenue." He described her.

"I'll check her out. In the meantime, why don't you send me your report. I'll need it to prepare my witness list."

"I'll do better than that. I'll deliver it in person. That way we can talk about the case in greater detail. Half an hour?"

"I'll be here."

Five minutes later, Frank was unlocking the Thunderbird, parked a block away, when a gray Ford Taurus pulled up and a man in the back seat stuck his head out the window. "Hey, Chief," he called out. "How do I get to Astor Place?"

Frank pointed east. "Take Bowery. Go through two lights, then make a left on—"

The man cupped his ear. "What d'you say?"

Frank approached the Taurus. "I said take Bowery—"

The back door sprung open, slamming against his knees and knocking him to the ground. "Hey!" He started scrambling to his feet. "What the hell—"

Two strong hands grabbed him by the collar and pulled him inside. Then, before he could react, something hard hit him in the back of the skull and blackness enveloped him.

When he woke up, he found himself sprawled on a cold cement floor, staring at a single lightbulb hanging from a low ceiling. Without moving his head, he looked right, then left. From what he could tell, the place looked like an abandoned warehouse, and if the train whistle he heard in the distance was any indication, he wasn't far from railroad tracks.

He lay perfectly still, his senses alert as he tried to pick out other sounds. After another few seconds, he tried to sit up and as he did, his right foot hit something that felt like a bucket. In the cavernous silence, the sound it made as it toppled over had the effect of an atomic blast. Great work, Renaldi.

"Hey, Slim, our guest is waking up."

"So he is," a rough voice replied. Two very large snakeskin boots stopped beside Frank's head. "Had a nice nap, Renaldi?"

Frank sat up and felt the back of his head. There was a bump there the size of an egg, but he wasn't seeing double and he didn't feel sick to his stomach, so, hopefully, there was no concussion. The man who had addressed him was built like a mountain. Six foot six or taller, he weighed close to three hundred pounds, all muscle.

"Who the hell are you?" He could have come up with something a little more intelligent, but with that throb in his head, his brain wasn't exactly in peak working condition.

Laughter erupted again. "Guy's curious. And rude, too, don't you think, Raul?"

Raul was no slouch in the build department either. Younger than his partner in crime, he was just as tall, although not as heavy.

The man Raul had called Slim laughed. "You think we should teach him a lesson?" he asked. "So he shows a little respect in the future?"

Frank sprang to his feet, but the other man was quicker. A fist that felt like a wrecking ball sank in his stomach. Frank folded over and almost simultaneously, that same hard fist smashed into his face, not as hard as he had expected, but hard enough to split his lip and send him crashing against a wall.

The room started to tilt then steadied as he took a couple of ragged breaths. Hands braced against the wall, he gave himself a second or two to contemplate his options. Considering his clear disadvantage, his chances against these two bulls were grim. But they had made one major mistake. They had pissed him off.

With his head low and his shoulders loose, he let out a grunt and charged his attacker. His satisfaction as he made contact with the man's midsection was short-lived. Eager for a piece of the action, Raul whipped him around and clipped him with an uppercut that should have broken his jaw, but didn't.

Come on, Frank, you've been in situations worse than this. Do something.

Ignoring the fiery pain in his gut, he summoned every ounce of strength he had left and kicked, aiming at Raul's face. The point of his shoe caught Raul on the chin. It wasn't much of a blow, but it was enough to draw a grunt from the man and encourage Frank to do an encore. This time Raul was ready for him. He sidestepped in time to avoid the kick, then in one smooth motion, he picked up a baseball that stood nearby, and hit him in the stomach.

The blow brought Frank to his knees.

"Had enough?" Raul asked.

"Let's find out." His partner grabbed a handful of Frank's hair and yanked his head back. "Raul wants to know if you got enough?"

"Get...your...dog breath...out of my face."

Another vicious pull of his hair made him regret the insult. "Got any more wise cracks, smart mouth?"

Frank had a bag full of them, but now didn't seem like the right time to impress his aggressors. Instead, he shook his head from left to right, slowly, so it wouldn't suddenly fall off his shoulders.

Slim bent over until his lips touched Frank's ear. "You listen to me good, pretty boy. You've been asking too many questions. It ain't healthy, if you get my drift." He gave Frank's head another yank. "You get my drift, pretty boy?"

Frank didn't think he could get as much as a sound out of his throat, but somehow, he managed a feeble, "Yeah."

"Okay. So here's how it's going down. Let Adam Lear rest in peace. There ain't nothing you can do for your buddy now. So be smart. Don't ask no questions, don't talk to nobody. Got it?"

This time Frank only nodded. Talking, even in one syllable words, was too much of an effort.

"I hope you mean it," the man continued. "'Cause if you don't, if I hear you've been sticking your nose where it don't belong, me and Raul, we'll be back. And next time it won't be you we'll take for a ride, but your kid and your mama." He snickered. "And your little sister, too, for good measure." With his free hand, he cupped his balls. "Can't wait to get me a piece of that sweet, young thing."

Enraged, Frank tried to get up. He'd make that son of a bitch eat his own words if that was the last thing he did. But something happened when his brain tried to transmit the message. His battered body didn't respond. He slumped back.

The big man released his grip. "Aw, hell, he ain't no fun no more, Raul. Let's load him up."

Frank sat in the passenger seat, curled up, his head pressed against the window.

The ride back was short, no more than fifteen or twenty minutes, and painful. Every bump in the road, every turn of the wheel, every jam of the brakes, felt like another assault on his body. Frank just gritted his teeth and didn't make a sound. He wouldn't give them the satisfaction.

The car eventually stopped. From the driver's seat, Slim opened the door and unceremoniously rolled Frank out onto the sidewalk.

Carlotta, who was at her post behind her produce stand, let out a piercing scream, then shouted something in Puerto Rican before switching back to English. "Frank? Is that you? *Madre de Dios!*" Instead of giving him a hand, which he could have used, she ran inside the building. "Tanya, come down quick!"

The commotion around him was enough to make him want to tell them all to shut up. Christ, these people were loud, louder than his own family, if that was possible. As he started to pull himself to his knees, someone grabbed him under the armpits and helped him up.

"What happened to you, man?" The voice was young and male. "You look like you ran into a bull-dozer."

Frank couldn't have said it better himself. And didn't try. He took a painful step and was considering taking another when Tanya came running out of the building.

Much less emotional than Carlotta, she quickly assessed the situation and didn't ask any stupid questions. "Okay, folks, show's over." She took Frank's left arm and wrapped it gently around her neck. "You," she said to the kid who was still standing by. "Take the other side and be careful. Boss, can you hear me?"

"The whole neighborhood can hear you, Tanya."

"If he's ornery, he's all right," she told the kid. And to Frank. "Can you put some weight on your feet?"

"I think so."

He had no idea how long it took for the three of them to reach the second floor. Once they had, Tanya and the boy took him straight to the couch in his office. It wasn't long enough to accommodate his height, so they draped his feet over the armrest.

"What's your name?" Tanya asked the kid.

"Jerome."

"Okay, Jerome. You stay with him while I make a couple of calls."

Thirty-Two

Jenna had taken Frank's advice and stopped fighting her father on the subject of her safety. Sure, he was overprotective and a tad too doting, but wasn't that one of the reasons she had moved back with him in the first place? To be coddled and protected?

She was at her studio, deep into the layout of a promotional brochure for a soft drink company when Tanya called.

"Frank was beaten up," the secretary told her with remarkable calm. "It's pretty bad. I thought you'd want to know." She filled her in with a few more details.

Once the initial shock had passed, Jenna didn't waste a second. She told Tanya she'd be there as soon as possible, then called her father.

"Don't bother to pick me up," she said when he answered. "Frank's been hurt—"

"Hurt how?"

"He was beaten up. I don't know much more than that." Her cell phone pressed to her ear, she walked out of her studio and hit the elevator button. "A cousin of his, a doctor, is with him now, patching him up."

"You're not going there alone, Jenna."

She could hear the panic in his voice and did her

best to reassure him. "I won't be alone, Dad. There's a building full of people."

"Have the police been called?"

"Frank doesn't want the police."

"Jenna—"

She walked out of the elevator and into the street. Though it wasn't the rush hour yet, there wasn't a free cab in sight. "Got to run, Dad. Stop worrying, okay? I'll call you with a report on his condition."

At the risk of being run over, she stepped out into the street and raised her hand, waving it frantically as cars sped by, horns blaring. At last, a yellow cab screeched to a stop in front of her, and she jumped in it.

The ride to the East Village seemed to take forever. When the cab finally stopped in front of Frank's building, she paid the driver, jumped out and ran up the two flights.

At the sight of Frank sitting on the couch, with his shirt off, she felt a wrenching pang. Tanya hadn't exaggerated. He looked awful. Although his mouth seemed to have been cleaned, his lower lip was still bleeding. His right eye was swollen shut and an ugly red scrape ran from his left cheekbone to his chin.

A slender man in round, rimless glasses stood over him, ready to wrap a wide bandage around Frank's chest.

Frank glared at him with his good eye. "You're not rolling me up like a mummy."

"Either I tape your ribs or I'm taking you to the hospital. I'm not even sure I shouldn't be doing that anyway. You're not in the greatest of shape, cousin."

"I told you, no hospital. I'm fine."

"You won't be fine if I don't tape your ribs."

The argument seemed to have exhausted Frank. "All right, all right, do what you have to do."

Standing in the doorway, Jenna pressed a fist over her mouth, trying to keep control of her emotions. They could have killed him, she thought as her eyes filled with tears she struggled to hold back. I could have lost him.

A small whimper escaped her throat, and two pairs of eyes turned in her direction.

"What are you doing here?" Frank didn't sound happy.

Tanya walked in from the other room. "I called her."

"Why?"

"Because Vinnie is in Atlantic City and I couldn't very well call your mother, could I? She would have freaked out."

"But why her, for God's sake?"

"I thought she should know, all right? It's a woman thing. Now, stop yelling at me before you crack another rib."

Jenna pasted on a phony smile and walked over to the sofa. "Yes, stop yelling at her." She sat beside Frank so her eyes were level with his. "You weren't thinking of keeping this from me by any chance, were you?"

Frank's cousin glanced briefly in her direction. "Do you have any influence on this man?" he asked.

"Don't answer that," Frank mumbled. "It's a trick question."

When the doctor was finished, he extended his hand to Jenna. "Hi. I'm Stan Cooper, Frank's cousin."

Jenna shook his hand. "Jenna Meyerson. How badly is he hurt?"

"Seriously enough to warrant bed rest for at least forty-eight hours, which of course, Frankie here refuses to do. That's why I asked if you had any influence on him."

"He'll do as—"

Frank looked from one to the other. "Will you two stop talking as if I wasn't here?"

Jenna ignored him. "As I was about to say, he'll do as I tell him to. What choice does he have?"

Stan grinned. "I like her already, Frank." He dropped a pair of surgical scissors into his medical bag. "What do you say, cousin? Will you cooperate, or do I have to get my big bad needle out and pump you full of sedative?"

"You're a barrel of laughs, Stan, you know that?"

"So you keep telling me. Now give me your word you'll go home without a fuss."

"I will, right after I pick up Danny from hockey practice."

"You're not going anywhere but to bed. Tanya can pick up Danny. I'd do it myself but I have hospital rounds and I'm already late."

"Tanya can't go. She has a child of her own to take care of."

Stan turned to Jenna, a brow up.

"Oh." She looked from one man to the other. "You want *me* to pick him up?"

"That's one of the reasons I called you," Tanya said. "With Vinnie in Atlantic City, there's no one else."

"Then it's all set," Stan said crisply. "But first, you take Frank home and put him to bed." He shook two tablets into his palm and handed them to her. "Give him these in four hours. Call me if there's a problem. I'll stop by in the morning to see how he's doing."

After instructing Tanya to take his report to Mick Falco on her way home, Frank waited until she and Stan had left before letting out a thin sigh. He hated being fussed over or medicated, or feeling incapacitated. Fortunately, Jenna on her own would be much easier to handle.

He told her what he needed to take with him—his laptop, a couple of case files, the morning paper and his cell phone. He watched her gather the items one by one, moving efficiently and looking up from time to time to make sure he was still sitting. Once or twice, he thought he saw something more than concern in her eyes, an almost tender expression that hadn't been there before.

Or maybe the pills Stan had given him were making him delusional.

When the briefcase was full, Jenna walked over to the sofa and put her hand out.

Frank shook his head. "If you give me a minute, I'll stand on my own."

"I was asking for your car keys."

His car? She wanted to drive the Thunderbird? The thought gave him chills. "That's all right. We'll take a cab."

"Why should we take a cab when the Thunderbird is downstairs? And how am I supposed to pick up Danny if…" Then, as she realized the truth, she gave a startled laugh. "You don't want me to drive your car? Is that it?" For a moment he thought she was going to hit him with the briefcase. "For your information, I'm an excellent driver."

"You never drive. You travel by bus or by cab."

"Because they get me where I want to go faster than driving." She shook an impatient hand. "Come on, we're wasting time. Hand over the keys."

He did so, slowly and reluctantly. Maybe he was being silly. She had dropped what she was doing to be by his side, and had not only agreed to take him home but to pick up Danny as well. The least he could do was to trust her with his car.

By the time they walked out of the building, Stan's little pink pill had performed its magic. Frank could shuffle by himself with a minimum of pain. Not even that damn wrap around his midsection bothered him much anymore.

Jenna's eagle eye watched his every step. "Are you all right?"

"Never been better," he deadpaned. Jenna was already jiggling the car keys as though she was itching to get behind the wheel. Somehow he didn't find that reassuring. "The bird handles differently from other cars," he warned. "For starters, it's a clutch."

Jenna opened the passenger's door for him. "I know how to drive, Frank."

"A clutch?"

"Yes, a clutch."

He lowered himself into the passenger's seat and watched her run around the front of the car, slide behind the wheel and turn the ignition on. Glancing over his shoulder to check the traffic took some doing, but he managed it. "You're clear."

Jenna kept the car where it was and turned around in her seat. "Are you going to be one of those irritating back seat drivers? You know, the kind that tells the driver what to do, when to do it and how to do it? Because I'm warning you right now, I hate that.''

"Great." He let out a frustrated sigh. "While you were busy yapping, the light changed. Now we'll never get out of here.''

"Watch me.''

He wished he hadn't. She rolled down the window, stuck her arm out and waved it up and down as if she actually expected the stream of cars and trucks and buses to stop just for her. In typical fashion, New York motorists ignored her, so she yelled something Frank couldn't quite make out, yanked the wheel to the left and hit the gas. The T-bird shot forward, forcing an oncoming van to come to a screeching halt. The driver hurled out an insult, but either Jenna didn't hear it or she had heard worse.

"Are you crazy?" Frank yelled. "What the hell was that all about? When was the last time you were behind the wheel of a car?''

"Relax, will you?" She eased into traffic. "I know what I'm doing.''

"You could have gotten us killed.''

"Are you dead, Frank? Do you see a scratch on your precious car?''

He didn't want to agitate her further so he shut his mouth and leaned back against the seat. Once they were on Bowery, the ride got smoother, due mostly to the bumper-to-bumper traffic. "Do you need directions to Vinnie's house?" he asked after a while.

"I think I remember. Let's see, I take the Battery Tunnel into South Brooklyn, go across the Verrazano-Narrows Bridge, then east on the Staten Island

Expressway. I stay on the SIE until I get to the exit for Sunset Road.'' She gave him a smug look. "How did I do?''

"Not bad.''

"Not bad, my ass. If there was a better way to get there, you would have made a point to tell me.'' As they approached a construction crew, she merged into one lane. "Now will you tell me what happened to you?''

"Isn't it obvious?''

"You know what I mean. I want details. Who, when, why.'' When he remained silent, she shot him a quick look. "Talk to me, Frank, or I might forget to use the clutch when I change gears.''

Knowing she was crazy enough to do it, he waited until she had safely entered the tunnel before telling her the events of the past two hours.

Her expression grew more horrified with each word. "They could have killed you!''

"Believe me, if that's what they wanted to do, they would have.''

"Who are they? Or more important, who are they working for?''

"My guess is *Bratstvo*. They're worried about all the attention they've been getting from me lately and decided to do something about it.''

"But why not kill you?''

"Because the FBI now knows that I'm investigating *Bratstvo*. If I was suddenly found dead in some dark alley, that would be a definite tip-off that our boys in Brighton Beach have something to hide. The warning they gave me was much more effective.''

"Aren't they worried you'll go to the authorities?''

"And tell them what? That two thugs took me for a ride and worked me over? What would that prove? I have nothing to give the police other than a description of the two men and the make of the car. Big deal."

Jenna remained silent until she pulled up to the curb in front of Vinnie's big Victorian house. "Here we are." She came around to open his door. "Let's get you inside."

Whatever reasons he'd had to believe that Jenna would be easier to handle quickly vanished as they walked into the house.

"Where is your bedroom?" she asked.

"Upstairs but—"

"Lean on me. We'll take the stairs one at a time."

"There's no need for that. The sofa in the family room will be fine."

"Stan said to put you to bed and that's where you're going."

"Beds are for invalids."

"Don't make me fight you on this, Frank. Right now, I'm a lot stronger than you are. So stop trying to be a macho hero and do as I say."

Frank winced. "Christ, you're turning into Nurse Ratched."

"Thank you."

"It wasn't a compliment."

He could have stood his ground, but it didn't seem worth the effort. Besides, the pills were beginning to make him sleepy, and the thought of his bed right now was infinitely more appealing that the downstairs sofa.

Following Jenna's instructions, he sat on the bed

while she took off his shoes, then his socks, then very carefully removed his pants.

In spite of his discomfort, the touch of her hands against his skin almost made him forget the pain. Suddenly, his head was swimming with visions of he and Jenna in bed together. Her naked body felt soft and pliant, her mouth hot as it devoured his.

"Okay," she said. "Down you go."

He grinned like a fool. "My pleasure."

She was too caught up in her nursing duties to have heard him. Her face serious, she lifted his legs and stretched them out on the bed. Then, holding his shoulders, she eased him down onto the pillows.

He didn't want her to leave.

"Jenna..." His tongue felt thick, his mind fuzzy, but he got the words out somehow. "Comnherwzme."

She bent over, her hair brushing against his cheek. She smelled of honeysuckle. He loved honeysuckle. "What did you say?"

Concentrating hard, he tried to tell her she shouldn't go, that he wanted her to slide under the covers with him, but this time, the words wouldn't come. A pleasant cottony feeling began to envelop him. He closed his eyes.

Thirty-Three

Standing behind the glass, Jenna watched the action on the ice as she tried to pick out Danny. It wasn't easy. The players skated across the rink at dizzying speed, making it difficult for her to read the back of their jerseys. Then she spotted him—number fifty-five—as he broke away from the rest of the players, scored and raised his stick up in the air.

Ten minutes later, the final buzzer sounded, announcing the end of the practice game. Both teams exchanged high fives and skated back toward the bench.

Another ten minutes went by before four boys, each carrying an equipment bag in one hand and their hockey sticks in the other, walked out. Now that his helmet was off, she would have recognized Danny Renaldi anywhere. His eyes were brown, but he had his father's dark good looks and nonchalant walk, and his gaze as he studied her from afar, was as penetrating as Frank's.

"Danny?"

The other three boys elbowed each other.

Danny gave them a dirty look. "Cut it out, will you?" Then turning back, he said, "Yeah, I'm Danny."

"I'm Jenna. Your dad called your coach to say I'd be picking you up?"

Danny nodded before addressing his friends. "I'll see you tomorrow, okay?"

A freckled-face boy with a mischievous gleam in his eyes and a voice that had begun to crack, tossed a parting shot. "So long, *lover*boy."

But Danny had already dismissed his buddies' teasing. "What's wrong with my dad?" he asked when the threesome was out of earshot. "Why couldn't he pick me up?"

"He ran into some trouble, but he's all right now. He's resting."

"What kind of trouble?"

Frank had anticipated his son's questions and had instructed Jenna to tell him as much as she felt the boy could handle. He'd fill in the rest later. "He got a little roughed up, Danny."

"You mean...somebody beat him up?"

The boy was as direct as his father. "Yes."

His expression went from concerned to alarmed and she felt sorry for him. The poor kid had already been abandoned by one parent. The thought he could lose the other must be terrifying.

"Are you sure he's all right?" He was watching her, trying to be strong.

"Very sure. Your cousin Stan came over, bandaged him and sent him home. Your dad will have to stay in bed for a couple of days, but that's about it."

"Is he hurting?"

"He was earlier. Stan gave him something for the pain and he feels a lot better."

"Who did this to him? Why?"

They had reached the parking lot. Jenna opened the trunk of Frank's car and let Danny swing his equipment bag into it, along with the stick. "I think he'll want to tell you that himself."

Danny didn't say anything more. After a while, he looked at her, not a passing glance, but a thorough study. She could feel his eyes on her as she drove, and made a conscious effort not to fidget. As much as she would have loved to have a child of her own, she felt inadequate around them.

She took her eyes off the road for a moment. "Something wrong, Danny?"

"I was just wondering how come my dad let you drive his car. No one drives his T-bird. Not even my uncle Vinnie."

"There was no other way to come and get you. Stan had rounds to make and Tanya had to go home to her child." She smiled. "So I was elected."

An awkward silence fell between them. She broke it by steering the conversation toward something she knew he loved. "Your father played hockey when I met him."

"I know. Center, like me." He glanced at her again. "You play?"

Jenna laughed. "Heavens, no. The closest I ever came to contact sports was basketball."

She thought she heard him snicker. "That's not a contact sport."

"To me it was. I always seemed to be trampled on by the bigger girls." She gave him an apologetic smile. "I'm afraid I'm not the athletic type. I never seemed to excel in anything except when I had a camera in my hand."

Another silence, then, "My dad took me to see your photographs the other day."

That took her by surprise. Frank hadn't said anything about going to Siri's. "He did?"

"Yeah." His eyes on the road, he offered no other comment.

"So...what did you think?"

He shrugged. "It was all right. For black-and-white pictures. We met a lady there."

"Letitia Vaughn."

"Yeah. She was kind of cool. She said you had taken pictures of the New York Rangers but didn't include them in the exhibit."

A major omission apparently. "They didn't turn out as well as I had expected." She gave him a quick glance. "I could show them to you sometime, if you'd like."

He couldn't have thought much of her offer because he didn't answer. Just when she had given up any hope of forming some sort of bond with him, he asked, "Do you use a digital camera?"

She hadn't done very well in the hockey department, but now she was on familiar territory. Now was her chance to dazzle him. "I'm old-fashioned," she said. "I shoot only on film—Tri-X."

He didn't seem impressed so she continued. "I use different cameras for different jobs. Most of the time I shoot with a Leica M6 and a couple of lenses—28 or 35 mm. Even with my Canon SLR, I never use a lens larger than 100 mm."

Was he listening? she wondered. Was she boring him to death with all that technical stuff? "I don't like filters," she added, feeling brave. "I prefer to capture what's out there without any artificial props.''

Not a moment too soon, the sign for Sunset Road came into view. The kid probably couldn't wait to get out of the car and away from her. She tried to help him with his equipment bag, but he beat her to it.

''I've got it,'' he said.

Vinnie's house had been a haven of quiet and tranquility when Jenna left an hour earlier. Not so now. Vinnie and Frank's mother had arrived and Jenna could hear them talking above each other all the way from the street.

''My grandmother is here,'' Danny said as he opened the door. ''She's going to try to feed you. It's easier if you let her.''

Jenna choked back a laugh. If there was one thing she remembered about the Renaldi family, it was their fondness for food and their belief that the entire New York population was underfed, a problem they did their best to rectify every chance they got.

Mia and Vinnie stood in front of the sofa, each dispensing medical advice and stopping only long enough to argue about which one was right. Somehow between the time Jenna had left and now, Frank had moved from his bed to the family room sofa. Judging from his ineffective attempts to keep his mother and uncle quiet, she guessed he was already regretting the decision.

Amused, Jenna glanced at Vinnie. His dark hair had turned a rich pewter color and although he had aged in the past fifteen years, he still looked strong and healthy. Mia on the other hand, hadn't changed much. She was still the same plump petite woman with hair as dark and thick as her son's and a voice that demanded to be heard.

"Dad!" Danny rushed to his father's side. "You're okay, Dad? Are you sore?"

Frank tousled the mop of hair, still damp from the exerting game. "I'm fine, bud. Don't get spooked by what you see, okay? It looks worse than it is."

While Danny bombarded Frank with questions, Mia turned to greet Jenna, opening her arms. "*Bella.* Come here."

Jenna let herself be swallowed by the chubby arms. "How are you, Mia?"

Mia released her and let out a dramatic sigh. "Not good, Jenna. When Frankie resigned from the FBI, I thought all my worries were over. I don't know if he told you, but I never liked the idea of him chasing master criminals and serial killers." She raised her arms and let them drop at her side in a gesture of total helplessness. "Look at him now. Look at what they've done to my boy."

"Stan said he'll be fine."

"Stan lies." She shook a finger under Jenna's nose. "And what about you? How come you never come to see me anymore?"

"I'm sorry, Mia. I should have."

Mia gave her a quick up and down glance, patting Jenna's hips. "You look thin. Did you lose weight? Vinnie, you think she lost weight?"

"Leave the girl alone," Vinnie said. "She looks terrific. If I was twenty years younger, I'd marry her." He waved her over. "Come here, you. Give Uncle Vinnie a big kiss." His arms closed around her in one of his bear hugs. "Thanks for picking up Danny."

"You're welcome. He's quite a handsome boy."

"Takes after his grand-uncle." Vinnie assumed a Caesar-like pose, chin raised, one foot forward and one fist on his hip. "Don't you think so?"

Jenna laughed, remembering how easily he could turn her mood around. "You're still the most handsome man in all New York, Vinnie." Then more seriously, she added, "When I left, Frank was in bed. What happened?"

"He said he took a short nap and started feeling better, so he came down."

"He's feeling better because he's under the effect of the painkiller Stan gave him. He still has to take it easy."

"I'll make sure he rests." Vinnie tweaked her nose. "And don't look so worried, okay? The kid's tough. It's going to take a lot more than two thugs to get him down."

"Did he tell you what happened?"

"He told us he was mugged." He lowered his voice. "But that was for his mother's benefit. She's an old worrywart. Drives me up the wall sometimes."

Mia, who had ears like sonar, walked over to them. "What are you two whispering about?"

Vinnie waved toward the sofa. "We were talking about Frank."

"He should be in bed."

"The bed, the sofa. What's the difference? The important thing is that he's laying down."

Mia didn't look convinced. "He looks terrible."

"He was just beaten up," Vinnie reminded her. "How do you expect him to look?"

"Maybe if he ate something?" she asked of no one in particular. "Frankie? Are you ready for some of my manicotti?"

"Not yet, Ma."

"You have to eat. How will you get your strength back if you don't eat?"

"I'll eat when I'm hungry."

She looked disappointed, then remembered her guest. "You'll eat some manicotti, won't you, Jenna? I made it fresh today. And there's plenty."

Of that, Jenna was certain. Remembering Danny's warning at the door, she nodded. "I'd love some, Mia. Thank you."

Half an hour later, they were all assembled around the sofa, holding vigil on Frank and eating manicotti from little tray tables. Frank had asked them to have dinner in the kitchen but Mia wouldn't hear of it.

"We're eating in here, where we can keep an eye on you."

A few minutes after eight, the front door opened and then banged shut. They all turned around as a young woman Jenna guessed was Frank's sister, Lydia, blew in like a gust of wind.

She could have been Britney Spear's twin sister. She was short and curvaceous, with blond hair brushing her shoulders and a sexy rosy mouth. Heavy makeup made her look ten years older than her twenty-four years, but the Renaldi blue eyes, splattered with punk rock mascara, still looked innocent. She wore a black leather newsboy cap, black leather pants, a turtleneck that stopped just below the rib cage and a black leather vest. A profusion of silver chains were strung around her neck and large silver hoops hung from her ears.

She put her fists on her hips and assumed a sassy pose. "Well, Frankie, who did you piss off now?"

Thirty-Four

After dinner, Jenna insisted on helping out with the dishes, in spite of Mia's protests. Lydia sat at the kitchen table, playing with a sliver of tiramisu Mia had also "made fresh today," and talked nonstop.

"I don't mind being a salesgirl," she told Jenna. "Banana Republic is a great store. I love the clothes, and I get an employee's discount. Plus the money goes toward my acting classes. Did you know I was in three plays?"

Without much prompting, Jenna learned that Lydia had already appeared in three off-off Broadway plays—one that was shut down by the vice squad after the first performance, one so bad, the audience walked out and demanded a refund, and a third in which she had played a down-in-her-luck hooker.

But for all her stage misfortunes, Lydia was an optimist. "I have two auditions this week alone," she told Jenna. "One could be the break I've been waiting for. Do you watch the *Guiding Light?*"

"I'm afraid not. Is that a soap opera?"

"It's a *fabulous* soap opera, with lots of intriguing storylines, and big name stars joining the cast every week. I know the girl who plays Marina. She used to be in my acting class."

"All right, Lydia," Mia said after a while.

"You're making me dizzy with all that talk. Go see how your brother is doing. Maybe he wants something to eat."

"I don't want anything to eat," Frank said behind them.

They all turned around to find him standing in the doorway, looking pale but steady on his feet.

"What I would like, however," he continued, "is to talk to all of you. You too, Jenna."

Whether his take-charge attitude was due to the painkillers or not, it had the desired effect on the rest of the family. Without a word, they all filed into the next room and took the same seats they had occupied earlier.

Danny was the first to speak. "What's up, Dad?"

Frank surveyed his audience for a few seconds before speaking. "I know you're all curious to hear what happened to me—"

"We already know what happened to you," Mia said. "You were mugged. By two thugs—two *cowardly* thugs."

"That's not exactly true." His gaze traveled slowly from his mother, to Danny, then to Lydia. Not Vinnie.

Curious, Jenna glanced at Frank's uncle and knew by the way he was studying the knobby pine floor that he already knew why Frank had called this little family meeting.

"What happened to me earlier," Frank began, "was not the work of muggers. It was an intentional attack, a warning for me to back off from the case I'm currently investigating—the murder of my friend, Adam Lear."

Mia sucked in a quick breath.

"I'm sorry if I'm frightening you." His gaze stayed on his mother. "I just want to make you all understand how serious the situation is and why I have to take certain measures—measures you're not going to like."

"What measures, Dad?" Danny seemed more curious than worried.

Frank leaned forward, his features tightening imperceptibly as he tried to get comfortable. "Before those two men brought me back, they gave me a warning. If I didn't stop my investigation, they would come back, not after me, but after my family."

Mia leaned back in her chair, one hand over her heart. "Who are those people, Frankie?"

"Were they bluffing?" Danny asked.

Lydia rolled her eyes. "Just look at him. Is that the work of men who bluff?"

"Well." Mia had already recovered from the shock. "It doesn't matter if they were bluffing or not. The warning was enough. Frankie, you do as they say. You stop that investigation at once."

Frank's expression didn't change. Jenna guessed he had already anticipated his mother's reaction and was prepared for it. "That's not the answer, Ma."

"It's the only answer." She turned to her brother-in-law, who hadn't said a word. "Vinnie, tell him I'm right."

Before Vinnie could get in trouble, Frank reached over and took Mia's hands in his. "Ma, do you remember the day I decided to become a private investigator?"

She nodded.

"You remember that I told you the job would have its pitfalls, like any other job?"

"You didn't tell me you would be left for dead on a sidewalk."

"I wasn't left for dead. Those men had no intention of killing me."

"But if you knew the job would be so dangerous, why didn't you tell me?"

Frank smiled. Jenna found herself smiling, too. He was so gentle with her, so considerate. "If I had," he said, "you would have insisted I go into the priesthood."

Laughter rippled across the room.

"That's not such a bad job." Mia was dead serious. "Look at your cousin Ernie. He's never been happier."

"I'm not Ernie, Ma. And what happened to me today is just one of the pitfalls I was talking about."

"I hate what they did to you."

"I'm not so crazy about it myself. But what kind of criminal investigator would I be if I walked away from a job every time some two-bit thug told me to?"

Frank's gaze encompassed the entire room but no one seemed to have an answer to his question. After a while, Lydia spoke up, perhaps echoing the thought on everyone else's mind. "What's going to happen to us?"

Frank let go of his mother's hand. "Nothing is going to happen to you, because I'm going to make sure you all stay safe." His gaze stopped on Jenna, but only briefly. Had he included her in that statement? Or was she imagining things again?

"But, Dad, you're in no shape to fight those guys off, are you?" Danny asked.

Frank kept his tone light. "Not right this minute, bud. That's why I'm going to send you all away."

Chaos erupted, a cacophony of cries and protests that, if the situation hadn't been so serious, would have been comical.

Frank didn't interrupt them. He remained calmly seated, waiting for the furor to die down. When it appeared it had, he said, "It will only be for a little while, until the case is solved and all danger has passed. You'll be in a safe, secure location I can't disclose just yet. A friend of Johnny Caruso's will drive you there and stay with you the entire time."

Lydia sprang out of her chair, looking indignant. "That is so not going to happen, Frank. I'm auditioning for a part on *Guiding Light* day after tomorrow and I'm not going to miss it."

"And I have a big game on Saturday," Danny chipped in. "We're playing last year's champions."

"The team will have to play without you, Danny. You, too, Lydia. There will be other auditions."

"Not like that one! You can't spoil this for me. I won't let you!"

"You don't have any choice." This time, his voice had an edge to it. "I'm not doing this because I enjoy upsetting your plans. I'm doing it to keep you all alive."

His gaze stopped on Jenna and she realized, with some dismay, that he was including her in his little getaway plan.

Confirming her thoughts, Frank added, "The four of you will leave tomorrow morning—early, so I suggest you pack tonight. Take enough to last you a week. We'll make arrangements if your stay has to be extended."

"What about school?" Danny asked.

"I've already spoken with your teacher. She stopped by earlier and dropped off a week's worth of assignments."

Danny seemed to have accepted his fate, but not Lydia, whose eyes were filled with youthful rebellion. "I'm twenty-four years old, Frank. You can't boss me around anymore like you used to. I'm not going and that's that."

Wincing a little, Frank stood up. The room went silent as he walked over to his sister. "Look at me, Lydia. Go ahead, don't be afraid, take a good, long look. You think what you see is bad? It's nothing compared to what those guys will do to you if I give them the chance. Is that what you want? To be beaten to a pulp? Or worse, killed? Because, believe me, next time, that's exactly what they'll do."

Tears ran down Lydia's cheeks. She shook her head.

"Then stop fighting me. Ever since Dad died, you've trusted me to do what's best for this family. Trust me now."

Lydia's shoulders slumped. The fight had drained out of her. "Okay," she said in a small voice.

Mia quickly went to her. Handkerchief in hand, she murmured comforting words and wiped her daughter's eyes, smearing mascara over her face. For a moment, Jenna thought she was going to offer her something to eat, but she turned to Vinnie instead.

"You were in on this, weren't you? That's why you've been so quiet."

Vinnie shrugged. "It's Frank's show."

"You should have told me."

"It wasn't my place to tell you."

As though he had played referee before, Danny placed himself between his uncle and his grandmother. "Uncle Vinnie, aren't you going with us?"

"No," Frank interjected. "I need him here." Before anyone had a chance to ask any more questions, he stopped them. "That's all I'm going to say on the subject, except that Vinnie will take your grandmother home to pack and then bring her back here."

"What about Jenna?" Mia asked.

"She'll take the Thunderbird, go home and pack and then come back here. You don't mind sharing a room with my mother, do you, Jenna?"

What was she going to say? One negative word on her part and Lydia and Danny would start arguing again. She shook her head.

Just then, she saw Danny walk away, not toward the staircase leading to the upstairs bedrooms, but out the front door. Worried he might do something drastic, like run away, she looked around her. When she saw that Frank was occupied with the others, Jenna followed the boy out.

He sat on the porch step, his elbows on his knees, his chin resting on his fists. It was a relatively mild night and the stars were out. Jenna sat down beside him and gazed at the sky for a moment, watching some of the stars blink on and off.

After a minute or two, she began to talk. She wasn't sure why she chose this young stranger to share memories she seldom discussed with anyone, but all of a sudden, she was talking, even though she wasn't sure he was listening.

"When I was growing up, my friends used to envy the fact that I was an only child. They kept telling me how lucky I was not to have to share a room with a bratty sister, or be forced to baby-sit a little brother. In some ways, I guess I was lucky, and in others, I wasn't. My parents were overprotective and much too strict for my liking. They didn't have a houseful of children to focus their attention on, so they focused it on me. I can't tell you what a pain in the neck that was. There were so many things I wanted to do and couldn't, either because it was too dangerous, or inappropriate, or simply because my parents didn't approve of it."

She glanced sideways, but Danny was still staring into the darkness. "One day," she went on. "They told me I couldn't go to a party I had been looking forward to for weeks. I was furious. I couldn't understand why they were being so unfair. They knew the girl who was giving the party, they knew her parents, and they knew they could trust me not to do anything wrong, so what was the big deal? They wouldn't tell me. I accused them of being tyrants. At some point, I even said something to the effect of 'I wish I were someone else's daughter.' I know I hurt them when I said that, but they wouldn't change their mind.

"The following morning, I heard that the police had been called to the party and several of the kids were taken to jail."

That seemed to get Danny's attention. He broke his silence with just one word. "Why?"

"Two of the boys had brought drugs and booze with them. Within an hour, the place was in shambles. A fire, caused by a cigarette, broke out and one girl was badly burned. I found out later that my parents suspected there would be drugs at the party and made the decision to keep me away. The girl who was burned never took a drink or a hit of grass. She just happened to be at the wrong place at the wrong time. It could just as easily have been me. That day was the day I finally got it.''

"Got what?''

"That parents do know best. Their decision may make us angry at times, but in the end, they do what they do because they love us.''

Danny looked at her with renewed interest. "You still live with your parents?''

Jenna smiled. "No. I have my own apartment.'' She paused. "My mother passed away four years ago. I miss her more than I can say. I wish she were still here, still worrying about me, still trying to protect me.''

"You don't mind dropping everything you're doing and going into hiding?''

She didn't have the heart to tell him she wasn't going anywhere. He'd find out soon enough. "It won't be for long, Danny.''

A moment later, the front door opened. She turned around. Frank stood in the doorway, his broad shoulders blocking the light inside. "What are you two doing here?''

Danny rose. "Nothing. Just talking.''

"Time to go to bed, bud. Revelry is at 4:00 a.m. tomorrow.''

"Okay.'' Danny looked down. "Good night, Jenna.''

In the shadows, Jenna caught the hint of a smile. "Good night, Danny.''

Thirty-Five

It was no easy feat, but Frank had finally convinced his family to go to bed. While he was upstairs helping Danny pack, Jenna had called her father to give him an update on Frank and to let him know she would be home shortly.

Alone in the family room, she listened to the hum of voices coming from the bedrooms, and thought of the people who had disrupted the lives of this wonderful family, and nearly killed Frank. What was it about *Bratstvo* that made that organization so powerful, so difficult to catch and therefore so feared? Money? Connections? Ruthlessness? A combination of all three?

Like other mafias, they felt they were untouchable, and to a certain extent, that was true. But there were ways of punishing the guilty. There were informants, men and women willing to talk, and even sacrifice themselves, as some had, in order to protect others.

Jenna's father had known such informants. He had never revealed their names, except to his closest associates, but the data they had provided from time to time had enabled him to prosecute some very shady characters. Most of those informants now lived under the witness protection program, enjoying a new identity and a new life. A few had chosen to stay and were still considered "active" informants. As far as she knew, they could be helping Marcie, as they had helped Sam, although Jenna hadn't heard about any arrest of *Bratstvo* members in recent years.

Would any of those informants know who was threatening Frank and his family? And if they did, could they be persuaded to talk?

Jenna knew that her father kept files at home, old cases he had prosecuted and lost, psychological profiles of criminals he had hunted down and never found. Even now, four years after his retirement, he still enjoyed getting his dusty folders out from time to time to see what he had missed, or what he could have done differently in order to win a conviction. If she could get her hands on the *Bratstvo* file, she might find the names of those active informants.

"Hey." Two hands pressed on her shoulders.

She turned to see Frank standing behind her. "I didn't hear you coming down."

"You were deep in thoughts."

"Just relaxing." She watched him come around the sofa, walking somewhat gingerly. "All is well on the western front?"

A smile brought a little brightness to that handsome but battered face. "It did look like a war zone in here for a while, didn't it?"

"Yes, but if it's any consolation, you were a superb commanding officer."

He laughed. "We'll see how things are in the morning." He motioned toward the kitchen. "Vinnie made a fresh pot of coffee. Would you like a cup before you go home to pack?"

"Not right now." Jenna patted the cushion next to her. "Sit down, Frank. I need to talk to you."

"Uh-oh. I'm not sure I like the sound of that." He sank into the sofa. "All right, I'm all ears."

"First take these." She handed him the two pain killers she had brought from the kitchen earlier, along with a glass of water.

He made a face. "Can't that wait?"

"You've waited long enough. There's no need for you to suffer when you don't have to. So, come on, stop being so difficult and take the damn pills."

"Did anybody ever tell you that you're the most stubborn, diabolical woman I know?"

"And you thought I'd be a pushover." She laughed at his expression. "Don't look so surprised. I told you I'm learning to read you."

He tossed the pills into his mouth and washed them down with the water. "Satisfied?"

"Completely." Noticing he was favoring his right side, she gently pushed a pillow behind his back. "Better?"

"Much."

She glanced toward the staircase to make sure they were no curious ears listening. "I didn't want to undermine your efforts in front of your family earlier, but now that we're alone, there's no reason to continue this little charade, is there?"

"What charade?"

"That little country outing you've arranged for all of us. Sending your family away is a terrific idea and I agree with you wholeheartedly on that, but don't count on me joining the expedition because I'm not going anywhere. I'm staying right here—not in this house exactly, but in New York, where I can keep an eye on you."

"You can't stay in New York. It isn't safe."

"It's a lot safer for me than it is for you. You're the one they came after, remember? You're the one they beat up, and threatened." She folded her arms. "I'm going to make sure that doesn't happen again."

"How do you plan on doing that?"

"You're the one who's going to do it." She gave him a long look, gaging his reaction. "The situation has become much too dangerous for one man to handle alone. Drop the case, Frank. Let's call Stavos in the morning and tell him all we know. Once he takes a look at Adam's document on money laundering, hears about the tattoo, realizes that the Columbo look-alike really exists and sees what those two men did to you, he won't doubt us anymore."

"I thought you couldn't stand the man."

"I was wrong about him."

His mouth quirked. "You're serious about this, aren't you?"

"Very."

"Why is it so important for you that I drop the case?"

Afraid her eyes would give her away, she focused her attention on a General Patton biography on the coffee table. "Your mother already explained that. We don't want to see you get hurt again."

"Yes, but why don't you, *you* in particular, want to see me hurt?"

"Oh, for God's sake, what is this? Are we playing Twenty Questions now?"

"It's just one question. Why do you care so much?"

"You just said it. I care. I'm a caring person."

"Say it, Jenna."

Her pulse quickened. "Say what?"

"I'm not going to put words in your mouth."

This time he wouldn't let her look away. He took her chin between two fingers, making it impossible for her to look anywhere else but into those deep blue eyes. "Say it," he said softly.

"All right! I love you!" she blurted out. "Is that what you wanted to hear?"

Now that she had finally said the words out loud, a huge weight seemed to have lifted off her chest. She felt buoyant, light as a cloud, almost giddy.

Frank looked at her with an unblinking gaze. "I've been waiting a long time to hear you say those three little words. You don't mind repeating them, do you?"

"I love you." She spoke quietly now, with a voice that shook with emotion. "A part of me has always loved you, and I think a part of you has always known it."

Before she could say another word, she was in his arms and his mouth had claimed hers. This time there was no hesitation, no startled moment of surprise on her part, or feeling of guilt. She took his face between her hands and kissed him hotly, the way she had wanted to kiss him the other night.

Suddenly she drew back. "Your lip. Did I hurt you?"

"Pain was never sweeter."

"I did hurt you." She touched his lip where the cut still looked raw and was relieved not to see it bleeding. "I practically mauled you. I'm sorry."

"I like that kind of passion in a woman."

"I could have reopened the wound."

"You don't see me running, do you?" His eyes twinkled. "This time?"

It took her a second or two to realize he was referring to their recent conversation at the Bombay Palace, and the bet they had made. "How much of what just happened was a setup?" she teased. "To insure you'd win?"

"Would I trick you, Jenna?"

"Absolutely. You've always been a sore loser."

"If you're worried about your twenty bucks, relax. I never take money from a woman. Unless she's a client." He kissed her again, a gentle, feathery kiss that trailed from her mouth, to her cheeks, and to her eyes. "Oh, Jenna. If we were anywhere else right now, I'd already have your clothes off."

Aware someone could come down at any moment, she gently disentangled herself from his arms. "In your condition?"

"Never underestimate the power of love and lust."

"Then perhaps I'd better go. I wouldn't want to be responsible for another sprained rib."

They walked to the door, arms around each other. "You never answered my question," she reminded him.

"I must be having a memory lapse. What question was that?"

"Do you agree to talk to Detective Stavos in the morning and let him, and only him, handle the case from now on?"

"No," he said flatly. "I don't agree and I'm not going to do it. I've already explained why, but if you weren't listening, I'll be glad to go over my reasons again with you in the morning. Why don't you come for breakfast, right here at Casa Renaldi? I'll dazzle you with my cooking." He leaned toward her for one last kiss. "And you can dazzle me with...everything else."

Thirty-Six

Jenna had hoped her father would be in bed by the time she arrived, leaving her free to search his study, but Sam Meyerson stood at the stove, making hot chocolate when she walked through the back door.

He grinned, the relief on his face evident. "Perfect timing," he said, nodding at the pan of steaming hot cocoa. "How's Frank?"

"Mending." She came to lean against the refrigerator. "He's sending his family away in the morning. To a safehouse."

Sam stopped stirring. "Why? Have they been threatened?"

"Yes. Raul and Slim—the two men who abducted him—told him that if he didn't back out of the case, they would go after his family."

"He has to go to the police, Jenna. He can't possibly be thinking of going after those people all by himself."

"That's exactly what he intends to do."

"Why won't he go to the authorities? He trusts Detective Stavos, doesn't he?"

"Stavos, yes, but not the others. He thinks there's a leak in the department."

Sam slowly nodded. "It wouldn't be the first time. And all that's needed to jeopardize an operation is one bad apple.'' He took two mugs from the cabinet and set them on the counter next to a jar of marsh-mallows. ''Are you worried that if Frank strikes out on his own, he might do something unconventional?''

Wasn't that the reason he had kept Vinnie with him? And sent one of Johnny Caruso's men to accompany his family to their destination? ''Yes.'' She looked at her father. ''But you can't say anything, Dad. Frank's life is on the line.''

''I would never divulge a confidence. You know that.''

He filled the two mugs, added a fat marshmallow to each, and took them to the table where he and Jenna sat down. ''There's only one thing that bothers me,'' he said, looking preoccupied. ''Why didn't he ask you to leave town with his family?''

She poked the marshamallow with her fingertip, trying to submerge it. ''He did. I wouldn't go.''

''Why not?''

''Because I won't leave him.''

Sam shook his head. ''You two make a good pair. One more stubborn than the other.'' Then more seriously, ''I want you to be extra careful, Jenna. Don't go anywhere without letting me or Frank know. I want your word on this.''

''You have it.''

They talked for a while, about love, the fear of commitment, the many pleasures of married life. It felt good to share her feelings about Frank with her father, to lay them bare at last, and to know that she had been brave enough to admit them to the man she loved.

A little before midnight, Sam stifled a yawn. ''I

guess that does it for me.'' He stood. "You're coming up?''

She averted her eyes. "In a bit. I think I'll have a little more hot chocolate.''

"Very well.'' He kissed the top of her head. "Sleep well, honey. I'll see you in the morning.''

She waited until she heard his bedroom door close before rising from her chair. The thought that she was about to sneak into her father's sanctuary, and go through his files, made her feel like a thief. She had hoped she wouldn't have to do that, but now that Frank had flatly refused to drop the case, what choice did she have?

Walking quietly down the long hallway, she listened for any sounds coming from the upstairs area. Satisfied her father was asleep, she pushed the study door open. With its dark wood shelves, well-read books and the smell of that special soap the cleaning lady used on the leather furniture, the room felt as though it was a hundred years old.

The familiarity of it brought another pang of guilt. This was where she had spent hours with her coloring books while her father worked, where her mother had joined them, late in the day, carrying a tray of hot chocolate and oatmeal cookies, their special nightly treat. If it hadn't been for the fact that she was trying to save Frank's life, she would have left immediately.

Instead, she headed for the first obvious place where one would store important papers—Sam's desk, an antique piece he had bought in England. The top drawer contained office supplies, the second, larger and heavier, was filled with road maps. The credenza behind the desk was equally disappointing.

It yielded nothing more than financial documents, wills, mortgage papers and her parents' divorce decree.

Fifteen minutes later, she was still searching. This time, she went through the contents of the large bookcase where Sam kept his law books, biographies of famous politicians, and various mementos. The two bottom drawers had become home to several photo albums Jenna had leafed through over and over as a child. There were old photographs—her parents on their wedding day, their Hawaiian honeymoon, three-year-old Jenna on the backyard swing.

Jenna's eyes filled. What was the matter with her lately? Any little thing seemed to set her off.

As she reached deeper into the drawer, her fingertips brushed against something that did not feel like a photo album. She pulled it out. It was a manilla envelope, held closed with only a metal clasp.

She opened it, and took a shallow breath. Inside the envelope were four pages documenting *Bratstvo's* early activities in Brighton Beach, and the people Sam had prosecuted over the years— names like Mikhail Krychkov, Yuri Shokhin, Lev Mogilny. All were well-known criminals who had faced charges ranging from racketeering to drug trafficking and even murder.

At the bottom of the third page, were two names: A. Plushenko and V. Orloff. There were no other identification, no address or phone number, no mention of how those two men—or women—had figured in any of the cases her father had prosecuted. They could be the informants she was looking for, but she had no way of knowing for sure.

After committing the two names to memory, she

snapped the file shut. As she did, something slipped out—a photograph.

Jenna bent to pick it up and then turned it around. She went still.

One of the two persons in the photograph was her father. The other was a beautiful young woman with long, lustrous black hair and a lazy smile. She and Sam were in bed, in each other's arms.

Thirty-Seven

Jenna stared at the photograph with a kind of morbid fascination, her feelings wavering between shock and disbelief. Her father, in bed with another woman. It couldn't be true. It had to be trick photography. Someone with a twisted sense of humor had played a joke on Sam, maybe at one of those silly bachelor parties, or at a college reunion where attendees tried to outdo each other with one absurd prank after another.

Anxious to put her theory to the test, she took the snapshot to the floor lamp next to her father's La-Z-Boy, and held it to the light. She studied it closely, looking for the faint telltale sign that the photograph was really a composite of two. There was none.

She wasn't sure how long she remained standing there, with her heart racing, before she thought of turning the photo over again. Something was written on the back. *"Dear Judge Meyerson. Even the mighty fall. Let's talk."*

No signature, no date, no way of knowing if the picture was taken before or after her parents' divorce.

A memory broke through the fog in her head. It was the evening her parents had announced they were separating. She could still hear her mother's voice, cold and dispassionate, a sharp contrast with the sorrowful expression in her father's eyes.

Her stomach felt suddenly queasy, her skin clammy. Instinctively, she reached for the chair, hit the lamp instead and sent it crashing to the floor.

"Damn."

Upstairs, a door opened. "Jenna?" her father called. "Was that you? Are you all right?"

She didn't answer. She didn't want him here, didn't want to confront him when her emotions were so raw. That choice was taken from her when she heard the sound of footsteps hurrying down the stairs, coming toward the study.

And then he was standing in the doorway, wearing blue-striped pajamas and a puzzled expression. "Jenna, what in the world are you doing in here?" Concern gave way to panic as his gaze fell on the photograph in Jenna's hand. His face went gray with shock.

Jenna's shoulders slumped. Whatever hope she'd clung to that the picture was a fake vanished. Her father couldn't have looked more guilty. She waited for him to say something, even something as ridiculous as "It's not what you think," or "I can explain." He just stood there, as motionless as a statue. This man who had made a career out of words had been rendered speechless.

The cold fist that had lodged itself in her stomach began to spread, sending a chill through her entire body, down to her very bones. When she was finally able to talk, her voice sounded as though it belonged to someone else. "When was this taken?"

"Jenna, don't."

It wasn't what she wanted to hear. "It's a simple

question, Dad. Give me a simple answer—like a date. Was it taken last week? Last month? Last year?'' Her tone turned scathing as she slapped the photograph with the back of her hand. ''Surely this isn't something you'd easily forget.''

''April fifth.''

''April fifth...of what year?''

Sam closed his eyes. ''Nineteen ninety-nine.''

Jenna felt as if the roof had crashed down on her. Her mother had moved out of the house on April eighth of that year. On December twenty-first, Elaine Meyerson had crashed her car on a winding, rain-slicked Connecticut road.

''You cheated on Mom.'' The words sounded unreal, the truth incomprehensible.

''No! I mean...'' Sam ran shaky fingers through his hair. ''It wasn't like that.''

''It wasn't like that?'' she repeated with all the sarcasm she could muster. ''Are you saying you didn't sleep with that woman? What do you take me for?''

''What I meant...'' He cast a quick glance at the photo before looking away. ''There was no affair. She meant nothing to me—''

''Oh, please, spare me the clichés. And don't insult my intelligence. Apparently she meant enough for you to risk everything.''

''I never thought it would come to that. She was just a...''

He let the sentence dangle so she finished it for him, drawing a perverse pleasure in seeing the anguished look on his face. ''A one-night stand? You threw away thirty-three years of marriage, a woman

who loved and respected you, for a cheap piece of ass?''

The crude language coming from Jenna's mouth made him wince. "I know what I lost, Jenna. Not a day goes by without that thought coming back to haunt me, without being reminded of the wonderful life your mother and I had.''

"Not wonderful enough, or you wouldn't have needed to look elsewhere for sexual gratification.'' She turned the picture over and skimmed the short message again. "So your one-night stand decided to blackmail you? Is that it?''

"There was a blackmail attempt, yes.''

"Attempt?''

"I didn't go along with their demands.''

Jenna blinked. "Who are you talking about?''

Sam walked over to the bookcase and stood in front of a framed photograph of Elaine in happier days. "A Russian businessman suspected of having ties with *Bratstvo* had just been found guilty of extortion. He was coming up for sentencing. Rumor had it, correctly, that I was about to throw the book at him.''

He took Elaine's photograph in his hand and gazed at it for a few seconds before putting it back. "A few days before sentencing, I received the photo. I never knew it had been taken. Along with it was the sentence I was expected to hand out to the defendant—a stern lecture and a hundred hours of community service. If I didn't comply, a copy of the photograph would be sent to your mother.''

Jenna remembered the case, which had been widely publicized. "But you didn't comply. You sentenced the man to four years in prison.''

"That's right. They tried to set me up and found out they picked the wrong judge—one who wouldn't play ball."

"The woman was a plant?"

Sam nodded.

The moment of compassion she had experienced passed quickly. "I suppose someone held a gun to your head? Forced you to have sex with her?"

"No. Your mother and I were going through a difficult time. I had just been asked to run for mayor. I was excited about the offer. Your mother wanted me to turn it down. She was afraid the job would mean longer hours at the office, countless events to attend. She said we would have to live in a fishbowl, that our private life would never be private again."

"So you jumped in bed with the first woman that came along," Jenna said sarcastically. "Was she more understanding than Mom? Did she stroke your ego? Tell you how wonderful you were? What a fine mayor you'd make?"

Sam looked miserable and she was glad. She wanted to hurt him.

"I'm not sure I remember what happened exactly. It was a vulnerable time of my life and those people knew it. They have ways of finding out a man's most intimate secrets."

"How did they learn yours?"

He hesitated, then, his step slow and heavy, he walked over to the window. He spoke with his back to her. "I started falling into the habit of going for a drink at The Plaza Oak Bar every evening on my way home. The woman seemed to be a regular, too. We started talking. One evening, I drank a little more than I should have and was worried about the drive home. When she told me she had a suite in the hotel where I could rest for a while, I took her offer.''

Jenna made a derisive sound.

"Once we got upstairs, everything changed.''

"She seduced you.''

He nodded.

"And you, a brilliant attorney, one of the smartest, most level-headed judges in New York, never saw it coming? You never realized you were being conned?''

"The liquor—''

"Ah, yes, the liquor.'' She touched her forehead with her fingers. "I forgot.'' She waited until she was sure he had caught the sarcasm in her voice before adding, "So you called your blackmailers' bluff, stepped down from the bench and that was the end of it?''

Sam gave a mirthless laugh and turned around. "Don't I wish.''

She waited, not sure of what she was about to hear, but fearing it all the same.

"In order for my unexpected resignation to be accepted,'' Sam continued, "I had to tell the chief judge the truth. And then I had to go one step further.''

Jenna held her breath.

"I had to tell your mother.''

The words hit her hard. The photograph slipped out of her hand. "Mom knew?''

"She would have found out. Those people don't accept defeat lightly. Even though their scheme failed, they would have wanted to punish me. By telling your mother, I took their power away.''

The image of her parents telling her about their

separation flashed through her mind again. Now she understood why her mother had sounded so cold that night. She had been numb with shock, as numb as Jenna was now.

"I always thought..." She swallowed, pushing back the sobs that were threatening to erupt. "That Mom was the one who had betrayed her marriage vows. Every time I tried to talk to her, to get her to open up to me, she told me the same thing. There was no one else."

"She didn't want you to—"

"She was protecting you!" Jenna cried. "After all the pain and humiliation you put her through, she still protected you." A sob caught in her throat and died there. "She must have known I was suspecting her of infidelity, but she never said a word, never tried to turn me against you."

"I never meant to hurt her."

"And that's supposed to make me feel better? You actually thought you could screw someone—a stranger—and no one would be hurt? No one would suffer any consequences?" She came to stand in front of him. "You hurt her, Dad. You hurt her so much, she didn't want to live anymore."

"Don't say that!"

"It's the truth!" she spat. "You only had to look at her that last year to know she no longer gave a damn. She started drinking, and going to parties— the kind of parties she loathed. I begged her to stop, but she wouldn't listen."

She felt the venom rise in her throat, could almost taste it. "You killed her, Dad! You know that, don't you? You killed her as surely as if you had pushed her off that road yourself."

Sam bowed his head, looking utterly defeated.

"Why didn't you tell me the truth?" she yelled. "Why did you let me believe that Mom was having an affair when it was you all along?"

At any other time, the pain in his eyes would have broken her heart. Tonight it left her indifferent. "Because I was afraid of losing you. I was afraid you'd look at me the way you're looking at me now—with disgust and contempt."

As if drawn by a magnet, Jenna bent to pick up the photograph. She held it up. "Why did you keep this here?"

"To remind myself of what my stupidity cost me."

She held his gaze, trying to remember the man she had always thought to be strong and honorable. A man whose integrity she had always admired. A man she had been proud of and had wanted to emulate. A man who, in the end, was nothing more than a liar and a cheat.

Sam took a step toward her. "I know you're upset—"

Jenna put up her hand. She had heard enough. After one last look at the picture, she dropped it on her father's desk. Then, after a long, painful silence, she said quietly, "I will never forgive you for what you did. Do you hear me? Never."

Before he could see the hot tears streaming down her face, she strode out.

Thirty-Eight

Sam didn't try to stop her. It would have been pointless. She was angry and hurt and needed time to heal. He tried to tell himself that it wasn't the first time she had stormed out of this house. As a teenager, Jenna had been a handful, always challenging him and Elaine and then walking out, slamming the door behind her and swearing she'd never come back. She always did. And if she didn't, Sam would take the initiative and go looking for her. Fortunately for the three of them, Jenna never carried a grudge for very long.

It wouldn't be so easy this time. The look in her eyes as she had uttered those chilling last words had taken all the starch out of him. What if she had meant them? What if he had lost his daughter forever?

His gaze was drawn to the file on the floor, in front of the bookcase. Recognizing his *Bratstvo* folder, he walked over and picked it up. It didn't hold any great secrets, just the names of some of the better-known Russian criminals he had prosecuted. His gaze skimmed the list. Why the sudden interest in *Bratstvo?* he wondered. And if she had been looking for something specific, why hadn't she asked him?

As he kept reading, he caught the name of two of his informants, and stiffened. Was that what she had

---

been after? Was she planning to look for Plushenko and Orloff and question them?

Oblivious of the late hour, he walked back to his desk and searched through the phone book for Frank's number.

Frank answered on the third ring. He sounded groggy. "Hello?"

"Frank, it's Sam. I'm sorry if I woke you, but I need to know something. Did you ask Jenna to look into my *Bratstvo* file?"

Frank was suddenly wide awake. "What are you talking about? What *Bratstvo* file?" The surprise in Frank's voice was genuine. "Where is Jenna?"

"She left."

"Left?" Sam heard the sound of something being knocked over, followed by an oath. "At this time of night?" he bellowed. "Why did you let her go, Sam? The only reason I agreed not to send her away with the rest of my family was because I thought she was staying with you."

"Calm down, Frank, will you? I'm sure she's all right." But the doubt in his voice betrayed him. "Why don't you call her?" he said in a low voice. "She'll talk to you."

"And not to you?"

"I doubt it."

"Why? What happened?"

"We had a falling out. Nothing I can talk about."

"That's great, Sam. Just great." The phone slammed in his ear.

Feeling utterly defeated, Sam put the phone back in its cradle and sat down. Then, as if the events of the last few minutes had finally caught up with him, he took his head between his hands and wept.

* * *

Jenna had been traveling on I-95 for about twenty minutes when the headlights that had disappeared from her rearview mirror some time ago suddenly reappeared. She had noticed them shortly after leaving her father's house because one light was higher than the other and had made her squint.

She glanced through the rearview mirror. The car, an SUV, kept its distance. Was she being followed? She began pressing on the accelerator, and watched the speedometer needle climb to seventy, then seventy-five, then eighty. The SUV stayed with her. When she slowed down, the truck did the same. No doubt about it. She was being followed.

She thought of dialing 9-1-1, then changed her mind. Whoever was behind her didn't seem to have any intention other than to stay close to the Thunderbird. At this time of night, the road was practically empty. If the driver wanted to hurt her in some way, he would have had plenty of opportunities to do so. It wasn't until she left the highway and took the exit for East River Drive that the headlights disappeared again. Almost immediately, her cell phone rang. She fished it out of her bag and recognized Frank's number on the screen. What was he doing up at this time of night? He should have been in bed, sound asleep.

"Hello?"

"What are you doing?" he asked angrily. "You told me you were staying with your father."

He knew. Her father must have called him. "There's been a change of plans," she said flatly.

"We had an agreement, Jenna."

"I know we did. This couldn't be helped."

"What happened? Why did you leave your father's house?"

"I can't talk about it."

"Then tell me this. What were you doing reading his *Bratstvo* file?"

"I was looking for information." She hesitated before plunging into the lie. "I didn't find anything."

"Didn't we have an agreement about that, too? No snooping without running it past me first? Do you remember that agreement, Jenna?"

"Are you through?"

"Not by a long shot. Where are you?"

"On my way home."

"I want you to come back here."

Even in her lousy mood, she found the offer tempting. The thought of being at home, alone, while the events of the past couple of hours replaying in her head, was depressing at best. But the last thing Frank needed right now was a neurotic female crying on his shoulder.

"I need some space, Frank," she said. "I need to be alone. Just for tonight. Can you understand that?"

"Do I have a choice?"

"No."

His voice softened. "Bolt your door. Don't open it under any circumstances. Is that understood?"

She glanced in her rearview mirror again. The headlights hadn't returned. Maybe she had been wrong after all. "Understood," she repeated.

"I'll call you in the morning. I love you."

She smiled. "That's more like it." A pause, then, knowing he was waiting, she added, "I love you, too."

Pincho was not a patient man. And what patience he did have had left him long ago. He had searched the woman's entire apartment, not once but twice. He had opened every cabinet, poked under every sink, checked the toilet tanks and gone through every drawer he could find. The photos his client had asked him to find weren't there. Or at Jenna Meyerson's downtown studio.

Frustrated, he pulled down the lid of a toaster oven, peeked into it and let it swing shut. He shouldn't have taken this stupid assignment. He was a professional killer, damn it. His days as a two-bit burglar were over. But this client was special, and never complained about the fee. You learned to make exceptions for people like that.

He let his gaze sweep around the small kitchen one more time. A stack of fifteen eight-by-ten photographs weren't that easy to hide. Was it possible that Jenna Meyerson just didn't have them? That his client had been given false information?

His cell phone rang. Shit, what now?

He flicked it on. "Kravitz."

"Get out of there."

"What?"

"You heard me. Get the hell out. She's coming back."

Pincho spun around, feeling trapped. "You said the place would be empty."

"Did you hear me? Get the fuck out of there!"

The line went dead.

Neither the call from Frank nor the one-hour ride from her father's house had helped to loosen the knot of anger in Jenna's stomach. Anger toward her father for having been so incredibly stupid, and anger toward the unscrupulous people who had trapped him.

Bratstvo. How ironic that the very people Frank suspected were after him, and who may have killed Adam, had turned out to be the same people who had caused her mother's death.

Her resolve to see the guilty punished was stronger now than ever. First thing in the morning, she would start looking for A. Plushenko and V. Orloff. She didn't know how, and didn't want to figure it out now. She was still too shaken, too overwhelmed by what she had seen and heard to think rationally.

She had just stepped into the Regent's lobby when the elevator doors hissed open and a man dressed in black ran out. When he saw her, their eyes locked and he stopped short, looking transfixed, like a deer caught in the headlights of a car.

Jenna took in the startled face, the dark hair and long sideburns, the handsome features, the eyes that seemed vaguely familiar. She tried to remember if he was a new tenant or if he might be a late night visitor. Looking closer, she was certain she had never seen him before. "Good evening."

He didn't return the greeting, but hurried past her, his head down. As he went by, she was conscious of his light, citrus cologne, and another smell, masked by the cologne, that she couldn't identify.

Anxious to be alone, she stepped into the elevator, where that same odor lingered, and pressed the button for the twenty-second floor.

To her surprise, Magdi was waiting for her when the elevator doors opened. No wonder they called New York the city that never sleeps. "Magdi, what are you doing up at this hour?"

"Elvis was here." Magdi's voice was a mixture of reverence and dread. "Elvis is alive!"

Thirty-Nine

Jenna held back a sigh of impatience. Under different circumstances, she would have played along with her friend, but not tonight, not in her frame of mind. "It's late, Magdi, and I'm very tired."

"You don't believe me, but it's true!" Magdi's tone had turned urgent. "Elvis was here. I saw him." She looked around her as if she expected the late pop icon to jump out of the shadows. "He went into your apartment."

Jenna tensed. "What did you say?"

"Elvis went into your apartment."

"How do you know?"

"I watched him through my peephole."

The man Jenna had seen rushing out of the elevator had looked a little like Elvis, but why would he go into her apartment? No one had ever had a reason to break in before. She had nothing of great value in there. She kept no cash on hand, and except for that one day when she had done the "Christmas al Fresco" shoot, her cameras and photo equipment stayed at the studio.

The photos! Of course. Why hadn't she thought of it before? She started fumbling for her keys, praying her hiding place, which she had thought so clever a few days ago, had stood up to the search of a burglar.

At last, she found her house key and inserted it into the lock. It turned easily, showing no sign of forced entry. Was it possible that Magdi had imagined the whole thing?

"Are you going to call the police?" Magdi followed her inside.

"Not unless something is missing."

Jenna's nostrils twitched again as she picked up that same cloying scent. Magdi had not imagined it. Someone had definitely been inside her apartment. And that someone could only be the man she had seen in the lobby.

In a few quick steps, she reached the kitchen counter. The recipe box didn't seem to have been disturbed, but then, neither did the rest of the room. As she had a few days earlier, she flipped through the cards, found the coq au vin recipe and verified that the photos were still there.

Magdi watched her every move. "Did he take your money, Jenna?"

Remembering that Magdi kept cash in a cookie jar, Jenna smiled. "No, Magdi, everything is here and accounted for."

The older woman followed her from room to room. "What did he want? Why was Elvis in your apartment?"

"I don't know." She tried to give her friend a reassuring smile, but her heart wasn't in it. Even though nothing had been taken or was out of place, she felt violated and more vulnerable than ever before. Her home, her sanctuary, was no longer safe. "Thanks for being so vigilant, Magdi."

Gently, she took her neighbor's arm and led her toward the front door. "Maybe it would be best if

you didn't tell anyone about…about Elvis's visit.
Can you do that for me?''

The old woman was thoughtful for a moment.
"Can I tell Sándor?"

"Yes, you can tell Sándor, but absolutely no one
else, okay?"

"Okay."

Once Jenna was alone in the silent apartment, the
man's presence seemed as strong as his smell. Who
was he? she wondered. Was he working alone or was
he just a hired hand? And what was it about his eyes
that had reminded her of someone?

When her question remained unanswered, she
turned her attention to another pressing matter—getting that smell out of her apartment. Walking
quickly, she went from room to room, opening every
window. Then, because she felt as though she was
herself impregnated with the smell, she undressed
and stepped into the shower. Tilting her face to the
hot, powerful spray, she closed her eyes and stayed
under the waterfall for a long time, letting the steam
wash away the fear, the helplessness, the anger.
When the water went from hot to lukewarm and then
to cold, she dried off and slipped into a clean pair of
pajamas.

One by one, she closed the windows, then, afraid
the intruder might return, she took a kitchen chair to
the front door, tilted it backwards, and tucked it
snugly under the knob.

Only then was she able to go to bed.

Pincho stood at his window, watching a neon ad-
vertisement for a Japanese watch flash on and off, a

psychedelic succession of red, blue, green and yellow that had become as familiar as his own skin.

The bitch had seen him. Not only she had seen him, but she had taken a good, long look at him. Just as she had the night he had bumped into her and Adam Lear. What if she made the connection? And was able to ID him?

After a few more minutes, he came to the conclusion that Jenna Meyerson was a liability he had to eliminate.

He picked up his cell phone from the table and dialed a number. "What was Jenna Meyerson driving when she came home?" he asked when his client answered.

"Why?"

"Just answer the question. What was she driving?"

"Her boyfriend's red Thunderbird. Kravitz, I demand to know—"

Pincho hung up and went into the bedroom, opened his closet and unlocked the built-in safe he had installed when he had first moved in.

The tools of his trade were all in there—knives, handguns, ice picks, poisons, a coil of strong nylon rope. Way in the back was a soft, doughlike material that could be formed into practically any shape and squeezed into odd spaces, such as under a driver's seat.

He picked up the high-energy plastic explosive and fingered it almost lovingly. It had been a while since he had put together a bomb. The thought he was about to do it again lifted his spirits.

Jenna's cell phone had been ringing for some time when she finally decided to answer it. If it was her father, she would simply hang up, and continue to do so until he got the message that she did not want to talk to him.

"Hello?"

"Ouch."

"Frank?" She bolted to a sitting position. "What's wrong? Are you all right?"

"I'm fine. I was referring to your tone. It feels like the edge of a razor."

"Sorry." She ran a hand through her hair. The events of the previous night were still fresh in her mind, acutely painful. "I thought it was someone else." She glanced at the clock—8:00 a.m. "I suppose you want your car back."

"I want *you* back. How soon can you be here?"

She kicked the covers and stood up. "In about an hour, if I hurry. Are you strong enough to make a pot of coffee? Because I'm going to need it."

"Get your ass over here, woman, and I'll show you just how strong I am."

She dressed in record time. Before she left, she took the photos out of their hiding place and dropped them into her bag. She had been lucky once, but why tempt fate?

Last night's light rain had ended, leaving the skies bright and the air smelling of wet earth. She walked north on Central Park West, trying not to think about her father, his lies and about her own guilt for having suspected her mother of betrayal.

As she reached Sixty-Second Street, she drew a sharp breath. A man stood on the driver's side of the Thunderbird, his hand on the door handle. "Oh, no!"

She started to run, unable to remember if she had locked the car last night.

"Hey, you! Get away from that car!"

A jogger, a small, slender man about to enter Central Park, stopped and turned around. "Stop that man!" Jenna screamed. "He's stealing my car!"

As the jogger hesitated, the thief threw a panicked look around. For a moment, Jenna thought he had lost his nerve, then he opened the door wide.

She hadn't locked the car. Frank was going to kill her.

Jenna started to run. How long did it take a thief to hot-wire a car? Would she have time to stop him? "Get away from that car!" she shouted again.

His only reply was to jump behind the wheel.

"I'm calling the poli—"

The explosion knocked her to the ground.

Forty

Jenna lay face-down and remained perfectly still, not sure how badly she was hurt, or if she could move at all. She was aware of debris falling all around her, of windows shattering and people screaming.

Careful to avoid any sudden motion, she tested her arms and legs, then slowly got up on all fours. The motion caused the ground to tilt, and just when she thought she might pass out, two strong arms got hold of her.

"Here, let me help you." A man eased her down to a sitting position. "Miss? Can you hear me?"

She nodded. "What happened?"

He looked up the street. "A car exploded."

She followed his gaze and watched in horror as roaring flames engulfed the Thunderbird. "That's my car," she mumbled.

"Your car?"

With the man's help, she pulled herself to her feet. "Not exactly. I mean… It belongs to a friend. I was returning it to him." She began to shake. "Oh, my God, there's a man inside! He was stealing the car!"

"I'll call 9-1-1. Can you stand on your own?"

"I think so."

He let go of her and took out his cell phone. "My name is Jackson Biddle," he said crisply after punching the three numbers. "I'm at the intersection of Central Park West and Sixty-Second Street. A car exploded. I think it was a car bomb. Yes, it just happened. The owner of the car is here with me." He glanced at Jenna. "I only see a few facial scratches." He gave a short nod. "I will."

He flipped the phone shut and tucked it back into his pocket. "The police are on the way. So are the fire trucks and ambulances." His gaze went back to the burning vehicle. "But I'm afraid it's too late for him."

Jenna kept staring at the blaze. Dozens of people had come out of several apartment buildings and were watching from a distance, looks of shock and disbelief on their faces.

Jackson Biddle's gaze came back to her. "You're one lucky young lady. A few seconds sooner and *you* would have been inside that car."

The words, with all their implications, sank in slowly, almost reluctantly. Jenna's first impulse had been to think the explosion was a fluke, one of those inexplicable mishaps older cars occasionally fell victim to. Jackson Biddle's chilling statement about a car bomb had quickly dispelled that notion. But why would anyone want to kill her? What she knew was completely circumstantial, or she would have gone to the police long ago.

Then she thought of J. B. Collins's terrifying visit a few days ago, of the SUV that may or may not have been following her last night, of the man who had rushed out of the building as though he couldn't wait to get away from her. All those strange incidents were beginning to add up to one frightening possibility. Someone wanted her out of the way.

Her eyes searched the crowd. The bomber could still be out there, cursing the fact that the wrong victim had been killed. He may even be trying to think of a way to rectify his mistake.

A yellow cab with its roof light on, slowed to a crawl. Then, as the driver realized the street was blocked and he couldn't go any farther, he started to turn around.

Jenna made a run for it.

"Hey, lady!" Jackson Biddle called out. "Wait! The police want to—"

Jenna was already inside the cab. "The Freemont Hotel," she told the bewildered driver. "Make it quick." She glanced over her shoulder. Two fire trucks, lights blazing, had arrived on the scene, followed by three police cruisers and an ambulance. Then the cab driver whipped around Columbus Circle and the inferno disappeared from sight.

The smell of bacon sizzling in the frying pan gave the Renaldi kitchen an illusion of normalcy. An ordinary family preparing to have breakfast together. What could be more normal than that? Frank thought as he spooned coffee into the filter. But, like it or not, there was nothing normal about today. Not with three members of his family on the run from the Russian mob, and the remaining two plotting to crack the organization.

Two hours ago, the house had been a beehive of activity, with everyone running in different directions, talking over each other, searching for one more item to take with them.

Lydia had insisted on borrowing Vinnie's portable TV, because, in her own words, she wasn't going to be stuck in the middle of nowhere being forced to watch stupid hockey games and boring cooking shows. She needed to study her soaps, especially *Guiding Light,* so she could observe the actors with whom she would be auditioning. Provided she was back in time for the audition.

"If I don't make it, I'm through as an actress," she had said in a tone worthy of an Academy Award. "The word will get out that I'm unreliable and I'll never get another chance."

Frank had wrapped an arm around her shoulders. "If you don't make it, I'll personally go to Warren Lear and ask him to use his connections to get you another audition. His late wife was a well-known Broadway actress. He knows everyone in show business."

The promise had restored some of Lydia's spirit. Even Danny's attitude had improved greatly since the previous evening, although Frank had no idea why. That big game meant a lot to him and if he missed it there wasn't anything Frank could do about it. The only promise he was able to make was to explain to Janice that a family emergency had come up and Danny would call her at the first opportunity.

But it wasn't hockey, or even his girlfriend, that Danny had on his mind as he was about to leave. In a voice he tried to keep strong, he'd asked, "You're sure you'll be okay, Dad?"

Jokingly, Frank had put up his fists, like a boxer ready for action. "You just watch me."

"I'm not kidding, Dad."

"I know you're not, bud." Frank had held him close. "I'll be careful. I promise. But you have to do your part, too, and that means doing as Ricco says and looking after your aunt and your grandmother.''

"I will." Then came the question Frank had been waiting for. "Why did you let Jenna stay? Aren't you worried about her, too?''

"Of course, I am. But Jenna is not my sister, or my mother. I can't force her to do something she doesn't want to do. Much as I'd like to. The best I can do is to make sure she stays out of trouble.''

A few minutes later, Ricco Benini, Johnny's friend, had showed up at the door and helped them load up the black Lincoln Navigator. So far, only he, Johnny, Frank and Vinnie knew their destination— Johnny's hunting cabin in upstate New York.

Two other men, also on loan from Johnny, were already at the cabin, which by now would be stocked with food, firewood and enough ammunition to qualify as an arsenal.

Johnny had assured Frank there would be no need for firearms. He had bought the Catskills cabin five years ago and no one except the realtor in Prattsville and a handful of close friends knew about it. As for the muscle he had provided, that, too, was for added insurance. In the event trouble did arise, the two men were highly qualified to handle any emergency situation.

"You won't get better credentials anywhere," Johnny had said proudly. "They used to work for my good friend, Sonny the Fish."

Frank chuckled as he took the bacon out of the pan and laid each strip on paper towels. What would the bureau say if they knew Frank was relying on the mob to protect his family? He could already hear the conversations around the water cooler, see the heads shake in disbelief. Well, screw them. It was no longer his problem what the bureau thought. His family was what mattered now. Anyone not happy with the steps he had taken to insure their safety could just take a flying leap.

He checked his watch. Nine-thirty. What the hell was keeping Jenna?

The phone rang. He pounced on it, oblivious of the lingering pain in his gut.

"Hello?" It was Carlos, his buddy at the tattoo parlor.

"You're going to be pleased, my man," Carlos said. "I located the artist who did that tattoo."

A tingle of excitement worked its way through Frank's aching body. "Good work, Carlos. Where can I find him?"

"He works out of his home in the Bronx. His name is Rudy Seigel." Carlos gave him the number, told him not to be a stranger and hung up.

The man who answered the phone greeted him with a friendly hello. "Normally I don't give out that kind of information," he told him. "But you come highly recommended, so I'll make an exception." Frank heard the click of computer keys. "I have what you're looking for right here. My client was very specific about what he wanted. In fact, he brought me a drawing and went as far as giving me his own interpretation of it. The bear for strength, the emerald for wealth. Together they spell power."

"Interesting logic. Who was your client?"

"A man by the name of Sergei Chekhov."

Frank could barely get a thank-you out before he hung up. Sergei. The poster boy. Son of a gun.

Vinnie walked in, dressed in his favorite dockers and lumberman jacket. "Who was on the phone?"

"The man who did that tattoo I showed you the other day."

Vinnie poured himself a cup of coffee. "From the look on your face, I'm guessing he had good news. Are you going to tell me what it is, or are you going to keep me in suspense?"

"The man in the picture was Sergei Chekhov."

It was Vinnie's turn to be astonished. "Aleksei's brother? He was the one who attended the Faxel party that night?"

"No one else has a tattoo like that. It's a one-of-a-kind, designed by Sergei himself." He repeated what Rudy had told him. "The bastard was under my nose all the time, but I dismissed him. How could I have been so stupid?"

"You weren't stupid. He was just a little more cunning than you expected, that's all. The important thing is that you've got him now."

"I'm not so sure about that."

"What are you talking about? He was at the party. How is he going to explain that?"

"Why should he have to? He's a respected member of the business community. Why wouldn't he be on the guest list?"

"So you're not going to do anything?"

"I didn't say that. I'm going to check Sergei Chekhov from the top of his impeccable blond hair to the tip of his shiny Bruno Maglis. By the time I'm finished, I'll have enough to hang that slick bastard, but it's going to take time." He took Vinnie's empty cup and put it in the sink. "Where are you off to?"

"Brooklyn, to talk to some of my dockworker

buddies. They're still striking, and bitching, and willing to talk. Somebody is bound to have seen Raul and Slim at one time or another. Men that size don't go unnoticed.'' He started buttoning his jacket. ''No news from Jenna yet?''

''No. And she's not answering her phone.''

''She's caught in traffic. She'll be here soon.''

Frank walked out with Vinnie and watched him drive off in his old but reliable GMC. His uncle hadn't been gone more than a minute when Stavos's gray Buick pulled up at the curb. The detective got out of the car and stood at the bottom of the steps, looking up.

''What the hell happened to you?'' he asked. ''You look like you went six rounds with Mike Tyson.''

''I walked into a door, what else?''

''That door have a name?''

''Didn't think of asking.'' Frank watched Paul come up the steps. ''What are you doing here? You run out of doughnuts?''

''Just paying you a courtesy call.'' Stavos followed Frank's gaze. ''Are you waiting for someone?''

''Jenna.'' He returned his attention to the detective. ''What's up?''

''I thought you'd want to know that the information you gave me the other day paid off.''

''And you came here empty-handed? No doughnuts? Some friend you are.'' Then, more seriously. ''What did you find out?''

''Plenty. The detective who arrested Billy Ray four years ago decided to reopen the case based on the new information. It so happens he was never satisfied with the outcome of his investigation and smelled a rat from the beginning.''

"Then why did he arrest Billy Ray?''

"Because the guy signed a confession, and there wasn't much he could do about that. It didn't help that he hated Billy Ray's guts and wanted to see him behind bars.''

"How come?''

"Oh, didn't I tell you? The detective is Anthony Delano—Angie's father. He was pissed at Billy Ray for taking those naked pictures of his daughter and causing her to lose the Miss Jersey City crown.''

"And now all of a sudden, Delano wants to nail Amber and clear Billy Ray's name? That doesn't make sense.''

"It does if your daughter is putting pressure on you. It seems that in spite of what Angie told you about not wanting Billy Ray back, she's still in love with the guy and wants him exonerated.''

"There's only one problem with that. Billy Ray doesn't want to be exonerated.''

"Yeah, well, I'm not sure how long he'll stick to his story once Delano starts grilling him. Or Amber Lear, for that matter. The man has a reputation for being relentless.''

"What about Amber's bank statements?''

"She made four withdrawals within a two-month period, each in the amount of ten thousand dollars. I'll bet a month's pay that by the time Delano is finished with the two of them, they'll be ready to sing the blues.''

"Does Amber know Delano is reopening the case?''

"I had the pleasure of delivering the news myself

just before I came here." He chuckled. "You ought
to know that she holds you personally responsible. If
I were you, I'd take cover. If you think you look bad
now, wait until she catches up with you."

"If I need police protection, I'll let you know."
Frank's gaze flicked back toward the intersection.
There was still no sign of Jenna and the Thunderbird
and he was beginning to experience some major anxiety.

"What's the matter with you this morn—" Paul
was interrupted by the ring of a cell phone. He patted
his pockets until he found the instrument. "Stavos."

Except for a slight tightening of his jaw, Paul's
expression didn't change as he listened. "Thanks,
Val. Yeah, I'm on it."

When the brief, one-sided conversation was over,
the detective folded his phone with a snap of his
wrist. Frank didn't like the look on his face.

"What's wrong?" he asked.

"There's been an accident. A car bomb."

Frank's back went rigid. "Where? Whose car?"

"The explosion occurred at Columbus Circle. The
car was a red Thunderbird."

Forty-One

Jenna leaned back against her seat and took a few calming breaths. She had never run away from a killer before. Nor had she ever come so close to death. Until now, she had led a relatively sheltered life, free of violence and bloodshed. Then, a little over a week ago, everything changed. Overnight, her priorities had shifted from job, home and family to something much more primal—the hunt for a killer.

Today, the tables had been turned.

The hunter had become the hunted.

So what happened now? she wondered. Did she go to the police? Seek help elsewhere? Or seek no help at all?

Frank's warning about *Bratstvo's* long arms echoed in her mind, forcing her to consider the third option. Twenty-four hours ago, she had been willing to walk into the Central Park Precinct and tell Stavos all she knew, in exchange for his promise to keep Frank safe. But after one attempt on her life and possibly a second waiting in the wings, she couldn't afford to go to the police. They wouldn't be able to protect her from an organization like *Bratstvo*. Or from whomever in the department was leaking information to them.

For the time being, she was safe. How safe she remained in the hours and days that followed would depend on how well she could outsmart the killer.

That thought nearly made her laugh. What did she know about outsmarting a killer? Just because she had escaped an attempt on her life once was no guarantee she would again.

"Miss?" The Middle Eastern taxi driver had turned around and was looking at her curiously. "Freemont Hotel."

"Oh." Quickly, she shoved a twenty dollar bill in his hand and told him to keep the change. A group of noisy Japanese tourists stood by the revolving door, blocking the entrance, but a friendly doorman in full regalia opened the side door for her. "Here you go, Miss."

"Thank you."

Trying to appear as casual as possible, she approached the reception desk. She had chosen the Freemont because it was big, busy and rather impersonal. An attentive staff was the last thing she wanted right now.

"Good morning." She gave the man behind the counter a smile she hoped didn't look as if it belonged to an escaped convict. "I'd like a room, please."

"Certainly." The clerk lowered his gaze and started to punch a few keys. "Smoking or non?"

"Non. Preferably on a lower floor." At the last moment, she added, "Close to the elevator." In case she had to make a quick getaway.

"We have a non-smoking room on the fourth floor, king-size bed, two doors from the elevator. Would that be all right?"

"Perfect." She handed him her Visa card.

"Do you have any luggage, Ms. Meyerson?"

"Not with me," she lied. "A colleague will be bringing it by later."

Once in her room, she locked the door and secured it with the night latch. Feeling relatively safe, she went into the bathroom, poured herself a glass of water and gulped it down. Only then did the shaking inside her seem to subside.

Glass in hand, she walked over to the window overlooking Fifth Avenue. There were no balconies, no ledges, just a straight glass-and-concrete facade that would make it hazardous, if not impossible, for even for the most agile of climbers to get to her room.

Emotionally drained, she closed her eyes and pressed her forehead against the cool glass.

Sitting in the Buick beside Stavos, Frank held on to the dashboard as the detective maneuvered through the streets of Manhattan with a master's touch, his siren clearing the way as much as was possible in a city like New York. An earlier call had brought good news. The body inside the Thunderbird was not that of a woman, but of a man, an individual who had apparently been attempting to steal the car. Further reports from the police scanner had informed them that Jenna Meyerson had fled the scene of the accident.

"Now why would she do a dumb thing like that?" Stavos muttered.

Frank, who had been unsuccessfully trying to reach Jenna on her cell phone for the last twenty minutes, hung up in frustration. "Wouldn't you get the hell out of there if you thought someone was trying to kill you?''

"We can't protect her if she's roaming the streets."

Frank prayed she wasn't.

When they arrived at the intersection of Central Park West and Sixty-Second Street, the blaze had been extinguished and the area was crawling with police, firemen, paramedics, television crews and on-lookers.

A bomb squad had been dispatched to the scene and was gathered around the Thunderbird, or rather what was left of it, trying to collect whatever evidence they could from the burned-out hulk. The scene brought a sigh of regret from Frank's mouth. He'd miss the car, but Jenna was safe and that's all that mattered.

Contrary to department policy, Paul allowed Frank to tag along when he walked over to the police officers who had first arrived on the scene.

"Three people are confirmed dead," one officer told them. "The thief inside the car, a jogger who had just entered Heckscher Playground and a passerby. Both were within twenty-five feet of the explosion. They didn't stand a chance."

"Miss Meyerson wasn't hurt?" Frank asked.

The officer shook his head and glanced at his notes. "According to an eyewitness by the name of Jackson Biddle, she only had minor facial injuries, nothing serious."

"Is he the one who saw her get into the cab?"

"Yes. He's also the only person who spoke to her. That's how he knew the car wasn't hers. She was returning it to a friend."

Stavos thumb pointed at Frank. "That's the friend."

"Oh." The officer glanced back at the blackened wreckage. "Sorry about that."

As much as Frank had loved his car, the Thunderbird was the last thing on his mind right now. "Is the eyewitness still around?" he asked.

McCay pointed at a rescue van. A man in a suit, with his tie off, sat on the tailgate being attended to by a paramedic.

"What's wrong with him?" Stavos asked.

"Just a few cuts."

A talk with Jackson Biddle confirmed what the officer had already told them. After talking to a 9-1-1 operator, Biddle had tried to keep Jenna from leaving, to no avail. He had been too shaken to think of looking at the name of the cab company, which was usually written on the doors.

When Paul was finished questioning Biddle, he headed for the charred Thunderbird. "Let's go have a chat with the bomb-squad people. The head honcho is Ted Brunnel. He and I worked a few crime scenes together over the years. He knows his stuff."

Brunnel was a big man with watchful eyes and a face black with smoke. "We're still gathering bomb fragments," he explained after Paul had made the introductions. "Off hand, I'd say our man used C-4. It's readily available, safe to store and easy to work with. Add a few wires, an ordinary blasting cap and you're in business." He gave an apologetic look to Frank. "Sorry, I didn't mean to sound so callous."

Frank waved the apology away. "Will you be able to tell us anything about the bomber after you've analyzed the fragments?"

"Every bomber leaves a signature of some type when he constructs a bomb, but unless he uses the same method again and again, identification is difficult. Our database might help." He glanced behind him. "I've got to go back to my men."

"Sure," Paul said. "Thanks for your help."

The three men shook hands. As soon as Brunnel was gone, Frank surveyed the crowd. Dozens of people were still hanging around, gawking at the car, probably thanking God they hadn't been in the vicinity at the time of the explosion.

He searched each face, aware that one of them could be the face of the killer. Like arsonists, bombers took special pride in their work and often lingered at the scene of a crime to admire their handywork.

Fortunately for Jenna, the bastard had missed his intended target.

Would he miss next time?

After only a slight hesitation, Jenna turned on her cell phone and dialed Frank's number.

When he answered, his voice was filled with such relief that she wished she had called him sooner.

"Jenna! Thank God! Are you all right? Are you hurt? Do you need medical attention?"

"I'm fine. A little shaken. I'm sorry about the car—"

"I don't give a damn about the car! Just tell me where you are and I'll come and get you."

"Where are you?"

"At the scene of the explosion, with Stavos—"

"What are you doing out? You should be home in bed."

"Stop beating around the bush and tell me where you are."

"I can't. I don't want you hurt any more than you already are."

"You're the one who was almost killed! You're not safe out there on your own. No matter where you go, they'll find you."

A reminder she didn't need to hear right now, even if it was true. "I didn't call to fight with you, Frank. I just wanted to let you know that I was safe so you wouldn't worry."

"You only *think* you're safe. You don't know the resources *Bratstvo* has at its disposal. They'll find you. Are you listening?"

Jenna quietly hung up.

Forty-Two

Sitting on the edge of her hotel bed, Jenna pointed the remote control at the television set and clicked the power button. Within moments she was listening to an on-the-scene reporter give the latest information on the car explosion that had taken place earlier near Columbus Circle. Before the fire could be contained, it had spread inside Heckscher Playground, causing the destruction of more than a dozen trees. Four other vehicles had also caught fire and three people had died, including the unlucky car thief.

The Thunderbird was still at the scene, a black, twisted carcass that was a stark reminder of the horror she had witnessed.

Jenna's picture suddenly appeared on the screen.

"Authorities are still looking for Jenna Meyerson," the reporter went on. "Ms. Meyerson was last seen getting into a yellow cab. Anyone who knows her whereabouts, or took down the name of the cab company or the license number, is asked to contact the New York City Police Department at the number below—"

Jenna groaned. How long would it be before the police—and the killer—located the cab? And found the hotel where she had sought refuge?

She rubbed her right temple where a headache had

begun to throb. The thought of leaving her room didn't thrill her, but she had to do it. She had to find another hotel, one that didn't ask any questions and took cash, now that her credit cards were no longer safe to use.

Maybe her search didn't have to be so risky. All she had to do was change her appearance a little, cover her hair with a wig, slip on a pair of sunglasses, and no one would be the wiser.

After muting the TV, she picked up the phone again and this time, she dialed Tresses. Beckie's assistant answered. She, too, sounded relieved to hear from her. "Beckie's in the back," Lori said. "I'll get her for you. She's going to be so happy you called. We thought—"

Beckie's voice interrupted the chatter. "Jen! Is that really you?" Beckie was half-crying and half-laughing. "I've been frantic. When Channel Four showed pictures of the Thunderbird, I thought it was you who had died in the explosion. Then Frank called and told me about the car thief. I was so relieved. Are you really all right, Jen? Did you hear from Frank? He's out of his mind with worry."

"I talked to him a little while ago. And I'm fine, Beck. Still in one piece. Still kicking."

"How can you joke at a time like this?"

Yes, what was wrong with her? Maybe she was losing her mind. Maybe all that cloak-and-dagger had finally fried her brain. Or it could just be nerves.

"Everyone is looking for you," Beckie said reproachfully. "Your father, Marcie, your Hungarian friend."

"I'll call Magdi."

"Not your father?"

"No."

"But Jen—"

"Look, Beckie, I don't have time to explain right now. I need your help. Are you with me or not?"

"Yes, sure." She sounded a little put off by Jenna's sharp tone.

Jenna immediately felt guilty. "I'm sorry, Beckie. I shouldn't have snapped at you."

"It's all right." Beckie's voice softened. "You've gone through a lot. What do you need?"

"Clothes, slacks and sweaters and a warm jacket. Nothing I would normally wear. Find something a couple of sizes larger—a twelve, maybe, or a fourteen. Yes, make it a fourteen. Dark shades, browns and charcoals."

"A size fourteen in dark shades." Beckie's tone was quietly cautious. "What else?"

"Sunglasses—large ones. And I'll need a wig, something short and black, or maybe red. Oh, and add some underwear, pajamas, toiletries, makeup and a tote bag large enough to carry everything. I'll pay you as soon as I get some money from the ATM."

"I don't care about that. I care about you. What's going on, Jen? What are you doing?"

New footage of the explosion scene showed the wreakage being loaded on a flat bed. "Just be a pal and don't ask any questions, okay, Beckie?"

"You're scaring me."

"There's nothing to be scared about. I told you I was fine."

"Does Frank know about…about whatever it is you're planning to do?"

"No, and you can't tell him. You can't tell anyone. This conversation is between you and me."

"I don't like this."

"If you think for one moment that I'm enjoying running from a killer, you're wrong. I'm scared. I've never been so scared in my entire life. If there was another way out of this mess, a *safe* way, believe me, I would take it."

"If I help you and something happens to you, I'll never forgive myself."

"Beckie, listen to me. By now the killer knows I survived the explosion, and that I'm on the run. Unless I change my appearance, he'll find me. And he'll kill me. How will you feel then, Beckie?"

Beckie started to cry, sounding as pitiful now as she used to when she was a kid and cried to get what she wanted. "Beckie, don't cry. Please. And don't force me to go out there and buy the things I need myself."

Her friend sniffed. "When do you need them?"

"As soon as possible." She gave her the name of the hotel and her room number, then hung up to call Magdi.

Jenna was anxiously pacing her hotel room when she heard the faint rasping at the door.

"Jenna?" a voice whispered.

She flung the door open. Beckie stood in the hallway, holding two large shopping bags by their handles. Jenna grabbed her arm and pulled her in.

"I thought you'd never get here."

"It took me a while to get everything you wanted." She looked at her friend and saw the scratches. "Oh, my God, you're hurt."

"It's nothing, just a couple of scratches. Makeup will cover them up."

"This is crazy, Jenna. I know you don't want to hear it, but I've had time to think on the subway. You have to go to the police. They'll protect you."

"They can't. Not from *Bratstvo.*"

"And what makes you think you can?"

"I know what I have to do to keep myself safe." She opened the bag and pulled out a pair of baggy brown cords, a black sweatshirt and a dark gray jacket with a quilted lining inside. The second bag held toiletries, underwear, a pair of pajamas and two wigs—one short and black, the other a little longer, in a subtle auburn shade.

"I'll try this one first." Jenna held the red wig in front of her. "I've always wanted to be a redhead."

"Where is Jenna Meyerson? What have you done to her?"

Pincho made a face and held the phone away from his ear. He hated to be talked to as if he was some incompetent amateur. It wasn't his fault the job had gone sour. "I don't know where she is. And what the fuck is it to you, anyway?"

"You idiot, you could have killed her."

"That was the idea."

"Are you insane? Do you realize the trouble you've caused me?"

"You have only yourself to blame. If you had given me enough warning, I would have been out of the building sooner. As it turned out, I ran right into her. Do you know what that means? She can identify me."

The voice at the other end had changed to a thin whisper. "Listen to me, Kravitz. Until we have the photos, I need her alive, do you hear me? You find her. And when you find her, you bring her to me unharmed.''

The line went dead.

Feeling completely anonymous in her new clothes, her red wig and her dark glasses, Jenna stepped out of the elevator, crossed the lobby of the Freemont and walked through the revolving doors, hardly drawing a glance from the doorman who had greeted her with a friendly smile less than two hours ago.

After withdrawing three hundred dollars from an ATM, she went in search of a new hotel. Ten minutes later, she had found exactly what she wanted, a shabby establishment she suspected was rented to hookers by the hour. The interior was even more depressing than the outside, but the clerk took her thirty dollars in advance, and asked no questions. He didn't even look at her when he slid the key across the counter.

Her new room was no larger than her kitchen at home and didn't look as if it had been cleaned in weeks, but until she found something more acceptable, this would have to do. Right now, all she wanted was a strong cup of coffee and a little time to figure out what to do next.

After one last look in the mirror and a quick adjustment of her wig, she left.

She spotted a Starbucks just down the block, its wonderful aroma wafting toward her like a lifesaving elixir. She was about to cross the street, when she stopped, feeling the hair on the back of her neck rise.

The rich coffee smell had triggered a series of images and sensations—''Elvis'' coming out of the elevator, the smell of his cologne masking another odor she hadn't been able to identify, then smelling it again, in her apartment.

Suddenly, she knew. The smell she hadn't been able to identify was the smell of coffee.

But how could someone carry the smell of coffee with them? Even if her intruder had been drinking it at the time, his clothing wouldn't have been impregnated with the smell. His breath, maybe, but not his entire person. It wasn't like tobacco, which clung to every fiber.

Still trying to sort out her thoughts, she crossed the street and entered the busy shop. More than a dozen people stood in line, waiting to be served, while three young women worked the machines. On the counter were several stacks of paper cups with the familiar Starbucks logo on the side.

Jenna froze. *Paper cups with the logo on the side.*

Frank had been looking for a coffee cup with a logo on the side. And he had found it—at Insomnia, the coffee shop owned by an eager-to-please Brazilian. Hadn't Pincho Figueras apologized to Frank about the smell on his hands, explaining he had been roasting coffee beans and the oils had a way of clinging to one's person?

Her thoughts raced in her head. When she had looked into her intruder's eyes last night, he had seemed vaguely familiar. Now she knew why. She had seen those eyes before. Up close. They belonged to the panhandler she and Adam had bumped into on Fifth Avenue.

"Miss? Are you in line?"

At the question from the woman behind her, Jenna

realized she hadn't moved forward with the rest of the crowd. "Uh... No. No, I'm not."

Her morning coffee forgotten, Jenna hurried out. Frank had told her Insomnia was on Forty-Second Street, in the heart of Times Square and a short distance from here. She walked quickly, slowing down only when she had reached her destination.

Insomnia was as attractive as Frank had described it. And the aroma of freshly roasted coffee was much more prevalent here than it had been at Starbucks.

When her turn came, she ordered a medium size cappuccino from the man behind the counter. A name tag told her he was the manager—Ricardo. There was no sign of the owner. Several customers had made themselves comfortable in one of the many chairs scattered throughout the shop. After selecting a newspaper from a rack, Jenna walked over to a table and chair and sat down.

She had been sipping her coffee and pretending to read for about ten minutes, when another man came out of the back area and started taking orders from the growing crowd of customers. He was of medium height and weight, and when he turned around and Jenna was able to see him full-face, she almost spilled her coffee.

Pincho Figueras was the man she had seen coming out of the elevator last night. He had the same large hazel eyes, the same well-defined mouth, the same strong, square jaw. She didn't need to imagine him in a black wig and long sideburns. She didn't even need to smell him to see if she recognized his cologne. It was him. She was as sure of that as she was of her own name.

Forty-Three

Hands in his pockets, Stavos peered inside the window of Tresses. "She has customers. Maybe I should go in there alone. One look at that ugly mug of yours and the women are gonna freak."

"And if you think that your badge and your attitude will get you anywhere with Beckie, you're sorely mistaken, my friend. I'm not only coming in, I'm doing all the talking."

Before Stavos could protest, Frank pushed open the door to the beauty shop and walked in. At the tinkle of the bell, two women sitting under hair dryers looked up, their expression registering instant alarm.

One of them spoke, her voice trembling slightly. "Beckie?"

Beckie, who had been standing at the sink, mixing chemicals, turned around. Startled at first, she quickly recognized Frank. "It's okay, Mrs. Savich." She walked over to where the two men stood and gave only a passing glance at Paul. "What are you trying to do, Frank? Chase away my customers?"

"Do I look that bad?"

"Only when you smile."

Thirty minutes ago, on the phone, Beckie had been

near hysteria. Now she was cracking jokes. Clearly the situation had changed.

She removed her black plastic gloves and tossed them in a nearby sink before she glanced at Paul again. "Who are you?"

Paul started to take out his badge, but Frank stopped him. "That's Detective Paul Stavos. He's helping me look for Jenna."

"Have you seen her?" Paul asked.

"No."

Aware the two women were watching them with growing interest, Frank nodded toward a door in the back. "Could we talk in there?"

Beckie shrugged. "Sure." She led them to a back room that had become home to a ladder and several cans of paint, a mop and broom, an ancient vacuum cleaner, a table and a microwave. She closed the door and kept her gaze on Frank. "Aren't you hurting? Shouldn't you be home in bed?"

Now he was certain something was wrong. The Beckie he knew wouldn't have given a damn how badly he was hurting as long as he found Jenna and brought her home safe and sound. "When did you talk to her last?"

"Yesterday."

"Not since then?"

She looked at a fingernail, painted a bright purple. "No."

She was lying, and not very well. "Beckie, listen to me." He took her by the shoulders and watched her expression turn mildly apprehensive. "You're Jenna's best friend and probably the first person she would turn to for help. I think you know where she is, but you've given her your word that you wouldn't tell anyone. Am I right?''

"Is this an interrogation?" She was trying to act tough, but under his grip, he could feel the tension building in her shoulders.

As usual, Paul had no clue how to question a frightened, reluctant witness. "Would you like it to be?" he asked. "Because I can arrange it."

Frank gave him a dirty look. "It's not an interrogation. Jenna is in serious danger. That's why I have to find her."

"She's not stupid. Why don't you just trust her to do what's right?"

"Because she has no idea the kind of people she's up against. And I don't think you do either. Someone tried to kill her today, Beckie. I don't know why, but I know this—they'll try again, and this time, they'll succeed."

"Who are you talking about? Who is after her?"

During his career as an FBI agent, Frank had learned that in order to get the cooperation of a witness, it was sometimes necessary to answer a question or two. This was one of those times. "The Russian mafia," he said, letting go of her shoulders.

Paul looked at him sharply, but Frank paid no attention to him. His gaze remained on Beckie, who looked torn as she tried to decide what to do. Finally, her shoulders slumped. "I took some stuff to her," she said in a small voice.

Paul started to say something, then must have thought better of it, because he snapped his mouth shut.

"What kind of stuff?" Frank asked.

"Clothes, wigs."

"Where to?"

"A midtown hotel. The Freemont."

"When was that?"

"Maybe an hour ago." She spoke fast. "I told her to call you, Frank, I swear I did, but she wouldn't listen. She was afraid you'd get hurt again." She made a valiant effort not to cry. "I'm so scared."

"I know you are."

"I don't know if I did the right thing."

"You did what any good friend would do in the same circumstances." He gave her a reassuring smile. "Now, dry your tears and tell me what she's supposed to look like."

"So what's this about the Russian mafia being after Jenna?" Paul asked as they drove toward the Freemont.

Frank had expected the question and was fully prepared to answer it. How could he expect the detective to help him without complete honesty? And anyway, if his instincts were right, Stavos was *not* the leak Vinnie had warned him against. If he was, well, he'd know soon enough.

Paul listened, his face blank as he kept his eyes on the traffic. He didn't berate Frank for not telling him sooner. His only input was to offer a few comments every now and then.

"You're right about one thing," he said after Frank was finished. "Placing Sergei at the Faxel party doesn't prove a thing other than he and J.B. may know each other."

"It's still a hell of a break."

"A break I intend to take full advantage of." He

glanced at Frank. "Did you catch that, Frank? I said *I*—not you, not us, just I."

"You'll need all the help you can get."

"I agree, but it won't be your help. Not after seeing what those men did to you. P.I. license or not, you're still a civilian, Frank. And civilians need to stay out of police business."

Frank's reply would have to wait. Paul had just pulled up under the Freemont portico. "Police," he said, flashing his badge as a valet ran up to him. "Keep the car here."

"Yes, sir."

At the reception desk, Paul and his badge once again received instant cooperation. "Yes," the clerk said, his eyes on his monitor. "We have a Ms. Meyerson registered. She checked in at nine forty-seven."

"Room number?"

"Four thirteen on the fourth floor."

"We'll need someone with a pass key to come with us."

"Certainly."

A moment later, Frank was knocking at the door of room four thirteen, but he had a sinking feeling they were too late. As Beckie had pointed out, Jenna wasn't stupid. She knew that in order to stay alive, she had to keep moving.

He knocked anyway. "Jenna, it's Frank. Open the door."

Paul didn't waste any time. One nod from him and the maintenance man had the door unlocked. As Frank had expected, the room was empty. The paper bags Beckie had described were in the bathroom, also empty.

Frank stood in the middle of the room. He had never felt so helpless. "Where are you, Jenna?" he asked under his breath.

Sitting in a luncheonette across from Insomnia, Jenna had prepared for a long wait. Lucky enough to have found a table by the window, she had ordered a turkey club and a cup of coffee and told the waitress there would be a handsome tip for her if she let her keep the table indefinitely.

As it turned out, Pincho Figueras walked out of the coffee shop a little before two in the afternoon. Jenna almost knocked her chair over reaching for her jacket. True to her word, she fished into her new tote bag, took out fifty dollars from a zippered pocket and dropped the bills on the table before hurrying after Pincho.

He walked briskly down Forty-Second Street. Just before Bryant Park, he turned right on Sixth Avenue, then made a left on Fortieth Street. As he neared a five-story apartment building, he stopped in front of a grocery store and shook hands with a large man whose apron bore the name of the store—Armando's.

After a brief chat, Pincho disappeared into the building. Jenna waited several seconds, then followed him. She found herself inside a foyer that was no bigger than a closet, but surprisingly clean and well lit. The elevator was already moving, its gears grinding loudly. Jenna waited until it stopped before looking up the shaft, but because of the circular staircase, she couldn't tell if it had stopped at the fourth floor or the fifth.

Frustrated, she looked around her. One wall held a row of fifteen mail boxes, all bearing name cards instead of apartment numbers. Pincho's was the third box from the left. Fifteen boxes and five floors meant there were three apartments per floor. And no way of knowing which one belonged to the Brazilian.

She walked back outside, grateful that no one seemed to be giving her a second look. No big surprise there. In those drab clothes she wasn't exactly an attention grabber, even with her red wig.

With no clear plan in mind, she posted herself in a doorway across the street, her eyes drifting up to the fourth floor window, then the fifth. If Pincho had gone home for the day, she was out of luck and would have to return early tomorrow morning, before he went to work.

She was trying to decide how long she'd be willing to wait when Pincho came out. He had changed into jeans, a brown leather jacket and sneakers. Slung over his shoulder was a gym bag with the words "Body by Jake" written on the side.

This time, Jenna did not follow him, but watched him disappear down Fortieth Street. As a UPS van pulled up and its driver jumped out, she approached him. "Excuse me, is there a gym nearby? A place called Body By Jake?"

The man pointed in the direction Pincho had taken. "Three blocks down. You can't miss it."

Three blocks wasn't very far, but hopefully, Pincho would be gone at least an hour, maybe longer. Now, if only she could find out his apartment number....

Across the street, a woman pushing a baby stroller entered the grocery store. Just then, Jenna's heart did a somersault. There might be a way for her to find out after all. The stunt she was thinking of pulling wasn't something she did every day, but even if she failed, what harm was there in trying? The worse that could happen was that she'd have to make a hasty retreat and come up with a better plan.

With that thought in mind, she rubbed her clammy palms against her corduroy pants and ran across the street. At the store entrance, she paused long enough to take a hand basket before proceeding toward a row of shelves. The woman and her baby were at the counter where Armando was slicing cheese and listening to his customer's woes about her older daughter's impending wedding.

Minding her own business, Jenna went from shelf to shelf, picking out items and dropping them in her basket. When she was finished and the chatty woman was gone, she walked over to the counter and started to unload.

"Hi," she said, smiling brightly. "I'm Marie Figueras."

The man arched a brow. "Any relation to my friend Pincho?"

She set a six-pack of strawberry yogurt on the counter. "I'm his sister, visiting from Atlanta for a couple of days." She talked fast, not giving him time to wonder if his friend had told him about a sister living in Atlanta. "And of course, he's out of all the things I like." She took a handful of bills from her bag. "You wouldn't mind delivering this to his apartment, would you? Pincho is at the gym and I still need to run to the liquor store. You can just leave everything outside his door. I won't be long."

"Be glad to." Armando tallied up her purchases. "That comes to thirty-three dollars even."

Jenna paid him, adding a five dollar tip to cover the delivery. "Thanks a lot."

"Thank *you*. And welcome to New York, Marie."

Her heart was still pounding when she walked out, pretending to be hurrying toward a liquor store half a block down the street. Once there, she stopped, realized she was on the verge of hyperventilating and forced herself to take a few shallow breaths. She had gone too far and done too well to fall apart now.

No more than a minute later, a teenage boy carrying a brown bag came out of the grocery store and went into Pincho's building. Jenna was impatiently stomping the sidewalk when he finally came back out. The delivery had been made.

Quickly, she retraced her steps and took the elevator to the fourth floor. No bags. She ran to the next level. "Bingo," she said under her breath. The brown bag stood in front of Apartment 5-C.

With two other apartments on the landing, and two very large peepholes on each side of her, she couldn't quite keep her hands from shaking when she took her Visa card out of her bag. What would happen if one of those doors suddenly opened? How would she explain what she was doing?

Rather than dwell on that possibility, she slid her Visa card between the doorjamb and the lock and tried to push it through. She had watched her locksmith do the exact same thing a few months ago when she had found herself locked out of her apartment. The trick had worked like a charm. But it wasn't working now. She kept pushing, actually forcing the plastic card through the thin opening, aware her Visa would probably be ruined, but so what?

Maybe Pincho had installed a dead lock, in which case she'd never get that door open.

Just when she was ready to try with another card, the bolt gave in and the door swung open. She dropped her mutilated Visa in the tote bag and closed the door.

Pincho's apartment was a surprise, definitely not what she had expected in a place like Times Square. Her gaze swept over contemporary brown suede sofas and chairs, the teak tables and the reproductions of impressionist paintings on the walls. An entertainment center with a large-screen TV built into it stood along one wall. The hardwood floor, buffed to a high shine, was partially covered by an oriental rug in rich cranberry tones.

The rest of the space consisted of a galley kitchen, a bedroom and an adjoining bathroom. She decided to search the bedroom first. There, too, luxury prevailed, from the king-size brass bed with its navy comforter and matching drapes to the plush white carpet. The closet held an impressive collection of slacks, shirts and jackets, all bearing designer names—Ralph Lauren, Armani, Bill Blass. Either the coffee business was a lot more lucrative than she realized, or Señor Figueras was independently wealthy.

The single shelf up above was packed tight with sealed boxes, six of them, none labelled. Stretching herself as far as her five feet six inches allowed, she reached for the box on the extreme left, pulled it toward her and brought it down on the floor.

Pincho was in a foul mood. For the first time in his twelve-year career as a hit man, a job had taken a wrong turn and a client had lost faith in him. His instructions had been to look for Jenna Meyerson, but how the hell was he going to do that in a metropolis like New York City?

Uncharacteristically jumpy, he had left Insomnia early and gone home to pick up his gym bag. Today wasn't his regular day at Body By Jake, but he was in serious need of a work-out. Maybe taking his frustration out on the machines was just what he needed to come up with a new plan.

One look at the place when he arrived however, and he knew today was definitely not his lucky day. More than two dozen men and women of all sizes and shapes seemed to have chosen this very day to get back in shape. As a result, there wasn't a free machine in sight.

Disappointed, Pincho walked out and started back toward his apartment, already thinking of another way to occupy the afternoon. Going back to work was out of the question. So was the prospect of spending several hours looking for Jenna Meyerson. Maybe he'd call that dancer he had met at Insomnia last week and invite her over. The thought of those long, chorus-line legs wrapped around his back had been haunting him for days. Now was as good a time as any to make his fantasy come true.

Armando stood outside his store, people watching as usual. Pincho wouldn't have bothered to stop for another chat, but the grocer called out his name.

"Hey, Pincho. You didn't tell me you had such a good-looking sister."

Pincho stopped dead in his tracks. "What are you talking about?"

"Your sister Marie from Atlanta. She was here a

little while ago, buying groceries.'' He laughed. ''What's the matter? You keeping her a secret?''

Still puzzled, Pincho played along. ''I've got eight sisters, Armando. I can't remember them all.'' He looked up and down the street. ''Where is she?''

''At your place, I guess. She asked me to deliver the groceries while she ran to the liquor store. Looks like she was planning on cooking you dinner.''

Pincho tried to think of the handful of women who knew where he lived, and which one of those would play a prank like this. There were a couple. One in particular, Cheryl, knew he liked surprises, and was always coming up with new ways to please him. She was also the only woman with a key to his place.

He smiled. Maybe an evening with the Broadway dancer wasn't in the cards after all.

Another surprise was waiting for him when he came out of the elevator. The bag Armando's nephew had delivered was still there, braced against the wall. Had Cheryl changed her mind about coming over? Now that he had worked up a monumental erection just thinking about her?

He unlocked the door and grinned when he heard sounds coming from the bedroom. So the little wench was here after all, and her mind was not on cooking dinner. He started removing his jacket as he walked soundlessly down the hall.

A woman, but definitely not Cheryl, sat on the floor, three open boxes in front of her.

He slammed the bedroom door shut. ''Who the fuck are you?''

Forty-Four

Vinnie called a little before noon, as Frank and Paul were leaving the concierge desk of the Crowne Plaza, a hotel close enough to the Freemont to qualify as a possibility. "I just heard about the explosion." Vinnie was talking over loud background noise. "Is Jenna all right? They say she's missing."

Paul's car was waiting for them in front of the revolving doors. Frank tipped the valet and slid into the passenger seat. "She's not exactly missing, Vinnie. I talked to her several hours ago. She had booked a room at the Freemont and was fine, just scared, but wouldn't tell me where she was. She moved out of the Freemont a couple of hours ago. Paul and I are checking all the hotels within a five-mile radius, so I could use some good news just about now."

"And I'm about to give it to you. The two goons who beat you up are dockworkers at the Red Hook Marine Terminal. Raul's full name is Raul Santana and Slim is Doug Crowley. Now that they're on strike, they hang out at a pub called Indigo, on the Brooklyn waterfront."

"Are they there now?"

"Drinking and carrying on like fools."

"That's about to change. What's the address?"

"If you're planning to take them on, you'll need

help. Johnny already said we can have a couple of his truckers—big strapping guys who scare the shit out of you with just one look.''

Frank laughed. ''Believe me, Vinnie, I'd like nothing better than to take them on, and thank Johnny for me. But Paul is with me and you know what a stickler he is for doing things by the book.'' In the driver's seat, Paul gave him one of his rare, lukewarm smiles.

Using a scrap of paper he found in the Buick's messy glove compartment, Frank jotted down the address, repeating it out loud for Paul's benefit. Stavos was already on the radio, requesting backup to proceed, quietly, to the Brooklyn waterfront.

The pub was crowded and the juke box was playing *Stand By Your Man* when Paul and Frank walked into the smoke-filled room. Four police officers, who had arrived at approximately the same time, were posted outside, two covering the back door, two in front as they waited for a sign from Paul.

Vinnie and Johnny were at the bar, nursing a beer and chewing on pretzels. When Vinnie saw them, he nodded discreetly at a large table in the back. The six men sitting around it had already done major damage to several pitchers of beer, when a waitress stopped by their table and put down two more refills.

Raul wrapped an arm around her waist and pulled her down on his lap. Frank couldn't hear what he was saying, but the others must have found it funny because they broke into uproarious laughter.

Paul turned to Frank. ''Well?''

''It's them,'' Frank said in a tight voice.

"Are you sure? You've got to be sure, Frank. I don't have an arrest warrant. I need probable cause."

"It doesn't get much more probable than this. It's them. The one with the scar on his chin is Raul, the big one is Slim. If you don't believe me, watch this."

"Dammit, Frank, where are you going? Come back here." He tried to stop him, but Frank shook him off, and made his way around the crowded room until he reached Slim's table.

Slim was the first one to look up. The expression on his face when he saw Frank was worth all the pain Frank had endured since Tuesday. Raul reacted a second later, and looked just as shocked to see Frank standing there.

"What the fuck?"

"Hello to you, too, Raul." Frank looked from one to the other and grinned. "How have you guys been?"

They rose slowly, as if expecting trouble. Perhaps sensing the same, the waitress scurried away. "What's the matter with you, boy?" Slim spoke in a low growl. "You got a death wish or something?"

The man on Frank's right stood up. He wasn't as big as Slim or Raul, but he looked just as tough. "Watch it, *gringo,*" he said, his tone menacing. "You got a beef with my friend here and you got to deal with me, too. *Comprende?*"

Slim held him back. "That's all right, Luis, he ain't staying. Are you, Renaldi?"

As the big man spoke his name, Frank laughed. "Oh, Slim, you're making this way too easy."

"Huh?"

While Slim was still trying to figure out what Frank had meant with that remark, Paul, who had been standing behind him, motioned to the two officers. "All right, guys, cuff them." Then in the same breath, he added, "Raul Santana and Douglas Crowley, you're both under arrest for the kidnapping and aggravated assault of Frank Renaldi." He turned to Luis. "And you, sit down." The man obeyed.

Slim recovered quickly. "What kidnapping are you talking about?" He actually did a decent job of sounding outraged. "And who the fuck is Frank Renaldi?"

"Nice try, Crowley, but we heard everything." Paul nodded to the officers. "Make sure to read them their rights before you take them to the Central Park precinct. I'll be right behind you."

Paul turned out to be a much better strategist than Frank had suspected. He began by locking the two men in separate rooms and letting them stew for twenty minutes while he ran a background check on them. Then, after talking to Frank about some of the FBI's well-documented cases, he agreed that because of their low intellect, Slim and Raul were the perfect candidates for one of Frank's old tried and true methods of interrogating—divide and conquer. The problem was trying to convince Paul's boss, Lieutenant O'Dell, to go along with it.

Rumored to be next in line for the job of deputy chief of police, O'Dell was a solidly built man for whom the word tough seemed to have been invented. After Paul explained what he wanted to do, the lieutenant looked skeptical.

"I don't know, Stavos. What you're proposing is deep into the gray area."

"Standard interrogating techniques won't get you

far with those two," Frank said. "They're too damned tough. Fortunately for us, they're not too bright."

"What if it doesn't work?"

"It'll work. How do you think we caught the Dougherty brothers?"

This time the lieutenant was impressed. "You're the one who interrogated them?"

"I was part of the team."

"Frank's being modest, Lieutenant," Paul put in. "He's the one who got them to crack."

O'Dell looked from Frank to Paul. "Which of the two is going to be the sucker?"

"Slim."

Frank smiled. Paul had made the right choice.

O'Dell took another few seconds to think it over before giving a nod. "Okay, let's do it."

From the adjoining room, Frank, O'Dell and a detective by the name of Leroy Washington watched through a two-way mirror as Stavos began his interrogation by asking Slim if he wanted to consult with an attorney. Slim shook his head.

"Speak up, please, Mr. Crowley. I'm recording this conversation."

"No, I don't want a fucking attorney. I can take care of myself."

"Very well." Stavos leaned back in his chair. "Who ordered the beating of Frank Renaldi?"

For the next ten minutes, Slim remained consistent, insisting he didn't know a Frank Renaldi and that whatever Stavos had heard at Indigo had been misunderstood. "My friends will vouch for me," he said confidently.

At the end of those ten minutes, Stavos turned toward the mirror and touched his nose. O'Dell turned to Washington. "All right, Sergeant. That's the signal. Go."

Leroy entered the interrogation room and whispered something in Stavos's ear while Slim watched them. As the hushed conversation went on, the big man began to fidget.

Stavos grinned as if he had just been given the best news in the world. "Well, well." He waited for Sergeant Washington to leave the room before turning back to Slim. "It looks like your friend Raul turned chatty all of a sudden."

Slim snickered. "I ain't falling for that crap."

"That crap is going to get you about twenty-five years in the slammer, my friend, give or take a few."

Slim was actually amused. "How d'you figure?"

"Well, let's see, there is the kidnapping charge. As you know that's a federal offense and carries a stiff sentence all by itself. To that you add the aggravated assault on Frank Renaldi, the threat on his family, and you're in shitville, man."

"I told you I don't know any Frank Renaldi."

"Now you see," Paul said mildly. "That's where you and Raul differ. He says the two of you kidnapped Renaldi, took him to an abandoned building and beat the shit out of him."

The abandoned building part triggered a flicker of interest, but he wasn't ready to concede just yet. Far from it.

"What d'you do to get Raul to lie like that? Beat him with a hose?"

"We don't beat people here, Crowley. We make deals. And the one we offered Raul must have sounded very attractive because he took it."

This time the bluff worked. "What the hell you're talking about? What deal?"

"I thought a smart man like you would have figured it out by now. Raul is walking, Slim. In exchange for his signed confession, and the goods on you, we've agreed to drop all charges against him."

"I don't fucking believe you."

"Then I'll prove it to you." After checking his watch, Stavos walked over to an intercom near the door and pressed a button.

The baritone voice of Leroy Washington came on, loud and clear. In the room were Frank and O'Dell watching and listening, Frank heard every word.

"Sign here, please."

There was the rustle of papers, the scratch of a pen, then Sergeant Washington spoke again. "Here are your personal belongings. Check the envelope, please, Mr. Santana. We wouldn't want to be accused of stealing anything."

More rustling, the jingling of car keys. "It's all here," Raul said. He sounded slightly bewildered, which was understandable since he had no idea of what was going on and only thought he was being released. "I'm really free to go?"

"A deal is a deal, Raul. We'll let you know when we need you to testify. Crowley's preliminary hearing will take place sometime next week. In the meantime, thanks for all your help. We couldn't have nailed Slim without you."

As Paul shut off the intercom before Raul had a chance to say anything more, the shackled man lunged, dragging his chair behind him. His face was white with rage.

The two uniformed officers standing by the door grabbed him and held him down.

"You miserable, backstabbing son of a bitch!" Slim shouted at the intercom. "I'll kill you, you hear? I'll crush your double-crossing skull with my bare hands!"

"You might as well save your breath," Stavos said calmly. "He can't hear you."

Slim slumped back in his chair, let his head fall backward and closed his eyes.

With nerves of steel, Stavos turned to one of the officers. "Tell the lieutenant that we're ready to book him."

The officer was halfway through the door when Slim stopped him. "Wait a minute!"

Stavos just raised a brow.

Slim gave him a dark look. "What do you want from me?"

"Nothing. Like I said, Raul gave us everything we needed to put you away for a very long time."

"I mean—" Slim twisted in his chair "—what do I have to do to get a deal like Raul got?"

"I can't make a deal with you."

Next to Frank, O'Dell was getting nervous. "He's overdoing it."

"No, he's not. He's playing it just right. Wait and see."

"Why the hell not?" Slim asked.

"Because you already said you won't give us what we want—the name of your boss."

"Why didn't you ask Raul?"

"He said he didn't know, that he took his orders from you."

"What if I change my mind and tell you?"

"I'd be willing to listen." Paul walked back toward him. "Let's hear it."

Slim shook his head. "Uh-uh. First you put your deal on the table."

"I can't. Not until I hear what you have to say."

"I don't trust you."

"Raul did. And he walked."

"What about me? I'm gonna walk, too?"

Paul gave a noncommittal shrug. "As I said, that depends on you, Slim. I can't be more specific than that."

The big man glanced toward the two-way mirror. "Who's behind there?"

"My boss, Lieutenant O'Dell, and Frank Renaldi."

"I want protection," he said to the mirror. Then to Paul, "I ain't gonna say a word until you say I'll have protection."

"We always protect our informants," Paul said.

There was a long silence while Slim thought things over. Then, as he seemed to make up his mind, he shifted in his seat again. "I work for *Bratstvo*," he said at last.

"I suspected that much. What I want is your boss's name."

"I take my orders from Alexander Ivankov, but he's not the big boss. Nobody knows who that is."

"Ivankov is the one who ordered the beating on Frank Renaldi?"

"Yeah."

"What else can you tell us?"

"Nothing. That's all I know."

Paul gave a regretful shake of his head. "I'm

sorry, Slim, but that piece of information won't get you a walk. We need the name of the big guy.''

''I told you I don't know his name! Nobody does!''

O'Dell turned to Frank. ''What do you think?''

Frank didn't hide his disappointment. ''He's telling the truth.''

''We could pick up Ivankov.''

''He won't know the name either. Those people work in levels. Like in the FBI and the CIA, everyone has a different security clearance. The higher the clearance, the more important the job. I know Ivankov. He's just a low clearance guy, a dispatcher. He doesn't know anything.''

In the interrogation room, Slim leaned over the table, looking directly into Stavos's eyes.

''What if I told you something else? Not the boss's name, since I don't know it, but something you'd really like to know.''

''I'm listening.''

''That broad you're looking for? Jenna Meyerson?''

Every muscle in Frank's body went rigid.

''What about her?'' Stavos asked.

''I know where she is.''

Paul did a masterful job of remaining cool. ''Where?''

''They're holding her prisoner aboard the *Arzamas*.''

Forty-Five

Marcie's phone rang incessantly, making it difficult for Sam to hold her attention for more than a few minutes at a time. The frequent interruptions made him even more restless than he had been when he first walked into her office. Why was she taking all those calls? What could be more important right now than finding Jenna?

"I'm sorry," Marcie said again as she hung up. "I don't mean to seem insensitive. I know how worried you are about Jenna. I am, too, Sam. If I could do more—"

"Exactly what *is* being done to find my daughter?" he demanded. "I don't think you've made that clear."

"Didn't you talk to Paul?"

"I've been in constant touch with Paul. He and Frank are combing every hotel in Manhattan, trying to find Jenna, but that's not enough, Marcie. We need more people out there, in the streets. We need to find her before *Bratstvo* does." He'd had no choice but to tell her that Jenna had gone through his files and could be looking for the two informants who had worked for the D.A.'s office—Anton Plushenko and Viktor Orloff.

"What you are suggesting is impossible," Marcie

replied. "The N.Y.P.D. doesn't have enough man-power as it is. It can't afford to mobilize a hundred men and women just to find your daughter. And it would be irresponsible for me to pressure them to do so."

"So you're going to let Jenna be killed."

"You're not giving her enough credit, Sam. She is smart and she is resourceful. If Paul and Frank haven't found her, it's because she has checked into a safe, comfortable hotel."

"If she had, she would have called Frank, or Beckie. She wouldn't let the people who love her worry unnecessarily. She hasn't made one single call since she talked to Frank at a little after ten this morning." He looked at his watch. "It's now five in the afternoon, and there's no sign of her anywhere."

"Calm down, Sam. You're not accomplishing anything by—"

"Would *you* calm down?" he asked, his voice ris-ing. "If Wayne or Matt were missing? Running from the mob?"

"No," she said quietly. "I would be every bit as distraught as you are."

He leaned back in his chair, angry at himself for having so little control of his emotions. "Only our children can get us into such a state. I'm sorry."

"I understand." She observed him for a moment before saying, "You never did tell me why she left your house last night."

"We had a disagreement."

She raised both brows. "It must have been seri-ous."

"It was."

"And you don't want to talk about it?"

"No."

She didn't press him any further. "All right, let's get back to the hunt for Jenna. Are you keeping in contact with her friends? One of them may know something by now."

"She's only spoken to Beckie."

Marcie nodded. "Beckie, who took fat clothes to her." She leaned forward, her voice soothing. "You see, Sam, this proves that she is thinking—"

Her phone rang again. Calmer now, because Marcie had that effect on people, Sam watched her answer with that crisp, authoritative voice that had intimidated more than one defense attorney in the past, even when she was a new A.D.A. In the space of three seconds, however, her face had turned a sick shade of gray.

"I'm on my way," she said in a faltering voice.

Fear grabbed Sam in the gut and squeezed. "What is it?" He already knew the news would not be good.

"That was Paul. Jenna is at the Red Hook Container Terminal on the Brooklyn waterfront. She's being held prisoner on a Russian ship."

Sam was already out of his chair.

"You're not coming with me," Marcie warned.

"Try to stop me."

Jenna came to slowly, awakened by a gentle rocking that almost lulled her back to sleep. Then, as the haze in her head lifted and she started to remember, she bolted to a sitting position. The room she was in was small, dank and smelled of fuel. The furnishings consisted of a stripped bed where she had been sleeping, a desk and, on a far wall, a double row of shelves.

Where was she? What was that noise she kept hearing?

It wasn't until she recognized the sound as the lapping of water against a hull, and saw the porthole, that she realized she was on a boat.

Her mouth tasted of blood, and there was a dull ache to her jaw, where Pincho had backhanded her. He had come back early from the gym, and had caught her going through his boxes, one of which contained the soiled clothes he had worn the night of Adam's murder, confirming her suspicions. He was the panhandler who had accosted them. She could still see his face, white with fury, as he stared at her, not knowing who she was—at least, not right away. The vicious backhand had come with the recognition, a blow that was so hard, she had passed out. When she had come to, the Brazilian was bending over her, holding a cloth soaked with chloroform.

She had no recollection of anything after that. Nor did she have any idea of how long she had been asleep. She glanced at her wrist, half expecting to find her watch gone, but it was still there, still working, its illuminated green dial glowing softly—six o'clock.

She stood up, holding on to the bed for support, glad that there seemed to be no residual effects from the chloroform, no light-headedness, or wobbly legs. Hopeful she could get out of this hole of a room, she walked over to the door and tried it, knowing that the odds of finding it unlocked were slim. It was bolted solid.

Her gaze swung back to the porthole. It was about sixteen to eighteen inches in diameter, big enough for her slender frame to fit through. Maybe. The problem were the three heavy brass wing nuts that held it closed. How long had it been since they were last unscrewed? What if the salted sea air had corroded them, making them impossible to open?

There was only one way to find out.

Gripping the first bolt with both hands, she twisted hard, grunting with the effort, repeating the process over and over, until she could no longer feel her hands and had to let go.

She tried again, this time using the corner of her jacket as padding, but the thick cloth prevented her from getting a firm grip, making the effort useless.

She took a step back and examined the porthole. Maybe the problem was its position. It was set high on the bulkhead, offering little in the way of leverage. If she could stand on something, maybe the desk, she would have a better chance.

Her hopes renewed, she pushed the piece of furniture under the porthole and climbed onto it. This time, she was able to brace her elbows on her knees and apply more pressure as she attempted to turn the knob. She almost let out a cry of victory when she felt it give. A few more turns and the first bolt was completely unscrewed. The second and third were just as tightly closed, but at the end of five minutes that felt more like an hour, she gave a final tug and the heavy glass swung inward.

Now that the porthole was open, she could hear voices coming from the deck—men speaking in a language she couldn't understand but recognized as Russian. She poked her head through the opening and realized she was not on a boat but a ship—a cargo ship, judging from the row after row of giant steel containers that stretched the entire length of the deck.

She searched the dock for activity, but except for

a dozen or so containers, waiting to be loaded, and a huge crane, the place was deserted.

Ignoring the freezing wind that blew in, she removed her bulky clothing, working as fast as her cold hands allowed. In nothing but her bra and panties, she rolled the pants and sweatshirt into the jacket and dropped the bundle onto the deck.

"Here goes nothing." After taking a deep breath, she hoisted herself through the opening, one arm and shoulder at a time, praying she wouldn't get stuck halfway, as she had seen happen in a notable Marilyn Monroe late night movie.

She wiggled through the opening easily enough until she felt the first resistance. Her hips. Another wiggle brought her an inch farther. Another, and her hips had cleared through. Her hands braced against the cold steel deck, she let herself slide down to a crouching position, glancing both ways before standing. The containers were even larger now that she stood near them, almost twice her height and several feet long. A person could get lost in that maze.

She dressed quickly, conscious that the voices were closer now. She could hear laughter, and the clink of glasses. Drinking sailors weren't exactly a novelty, but weren't they worried about her?

She moved forward, looking for a gangway, or a ladder, anything that would connect the ship to the dock and lead her to safety. She spotted the stairs on the forward deck, directly under the bridge. She was about to sprint toward them when she saw the two guards. They stood at a short distance from the gangway, a machine gun hanging casually over their forearms. Now she knew why no one seemed concerned about her. Even if she managed to get out of her cabin, she had no way of escaping from this ship.

"Damn." Up on the bridge, the drinking sailors were getting rowdy, shouting jokes at the two men below. That was the only time the guards took their eyes off the dock, when they looked up to shout something back. If Jenna had been wearing sneakers, she would have taken a chance and made a run for the gangway. But in those boots, the sound of her footsteps against the iron deck would immediately alert them.

Instead, she decided to play it safe and investigate other options. The containers provided excellent protection from onlookers and offered a passageway between the first row on her right, and the edge of the ship on her left. She walked along that passageway now, glancing over the railing and wondering if one of her options might be to jump from the deck. She was a strong swimmer, but the forty-foot drop would make the plunge into the murky, icy waters risky.

A shout from the bridge brought her to a standstill. Had they spotted her?

She flattened herself against a container, holding her breath as a series of exclamations broke all around her, followed by the clatter of feet running down metal stairs, getting closer. She raced deep into the sea of containers, turning and turning until she no longer had any sense of direction. Was she still going forward, toward the gangway? Or was she running around in circles?

A scream broke out of her throat as she turned a corner and found herself eye to eye with the muzzle of a machine gun.

Forty-Six

Located on the Brooklyn waterfront, the Red Hook Container Terminal was a multifaceted cargo-handling facility capable of loading and unloading more than sixty-five thousand containers annually. On a normal day, the place would have been teeming with dockworkers and stevedores working around the clock. Today, because of the strike that had paralyzed the entire New York/New Jersey port complex, the cranes were standing still and there was no telling how long the cargo that sat on the dock would remain there.

By the time Frank and Paul reached the terminal, the Russian ship was already surrounded by a ten-man SWAT team and scores of local police, all equipped with bulletproof vests and high-powered rifles. Waiting for the order to shoot, the men were ready in their respective positions, each with a clear field of vision to his assigned target.

As he approached the *Arzamas,* Frank counted twelve men on the ship, spread out from bow to stern, their AK-47s trained on the people on the dock. It was a classic standoff, with no clue as to which side would blink first.

Standing beside Frank, Paul pointed toward a cruiser with all four doors open. A woman in a green raincoat stood behind one of them. "That's Marcie," he said. "Let's find out what's happened so far." On his way to the car, he picked up a couple of Kevlar vests from one of the officers, and tossed one to Frank. "Put this on."

As Frank slipped on the vest, he spotted Sam, standing beside another cruiser. "What are you doing here?" he asked.

"I came with Marcie. I was in her office when Paul called." He scanned the huge ship. "You think she's in there, Frank? Alive?"

"Let's hope so."

Marcie Hollander was everything Jenna had told him she was—attractive, in a no-nonsense way, and efficient. His first question to her after Paul made the introduction was, "Have you seen Jenna?"

Marcie's gaze returned to the ship, and the armed men. "Not yet." She pointed to her right. "A translator asked them if Jenna was onboard. They said there were no female on the ship, only the crew. I hope to God this isn't some kind of wild-goose chase. I'd have one hell of a time explaining it to the mayor."

She took her eyes off the ship long enough to glance at Paul. "How much faith do you have in this Doug Crowley?"

"I wouldn't trust that snake to take out my garbage, but he swore he heard two of the sailors talk about the woman who was brought onto the ship earlier this afternoon, and I believe him. He's got too much riding on this to play games with me."

As he spoke, two more men stepped out on the deck, in plain sight. One was Aleksei Chekhov. With an AK-47 pointed at them, he looked more like the ex-KGB he was than the sophisticated hotel mogul Frank had talked to a few days ago. The other man was Sergei. He didn't have a gun. He didn't need one. Held in front of him, like a shield, was the best weapon of all—Jenna.

The urge to go and yank her from that maniac was strong, but Frank fought it. He had been in enough similar situations to know how costly a wrong move could be. If ever he needed to stay calm and collected, it was now.

The older Chekhov took them all by surprise when he addressed Frank. "Renaldi, can you hear me?" He came to stand by the railing.

"I can hear you," Frank replied.

"Then listen to me. You let my brother and me go, unharmed. Ms. Meyerson will accompany us as far as Franklin Air Field where a plane will be waiting. As soon as we are safely aboard the plane, we will let her go. If I see one police car, or hear or see any kind of activity on the tarmac, or in the hangar, Ms. Meyerson will be shot. Is that clear?"

Why was he doing all the talking? Frank wondered. Why not Sergei? The man in charge? "It's not for me to make that kind of deal with you, Chekhov. I'm just a regular P.I. now, remember? I no longer have any clout."

"You are the one with whom I wish to negotiate. I suggest you convince them. Or the girl dies."

Suddenly, Marcie stepped out in the open. "Sergei!"

All eyes turned to her as she addressed the younger brother. "Sergei, let the girl go. Now!"

Frank was close enough to the ship to see the startled look on Sergei's face. Women of authority were not common in his world, and Marcie's intervention had caught him by surprise.

"I can't do that," he shouted. "She is our only way out. We go free, she goes free."

"Don't be a fool, Sergei. We'll never allow you to leave. It's all over. You know it and I know it. Let's end this without any bloodshed."

"Uchodi Otsuda! Ne vmeshivaisya!"

Frank gave Marcie a sharp look. "You understand Russian?"

"No." Her voice shook. "Of course not."

"You must. Sergei spoke directly to you. He told you to get out of here, not to get mixed up in this."

When she turned to look at him, there was a strange look on her face. "Let me handle this, Frank. I think I can convince him to give himself up." She started walking toward the ship, her empty hands where they could see them. "I'm unharmed, Sergei. And I'm coming for Jenna. Don't do anything stupid."

"Marcie!" Paul yelled. "For God's sake, come back here."

There was a quick exchange of words between the two brothers, angry words, spoken too low for Frank to hear. Behind him, someone chambered a round of ammunition.

Paul, too, heard the sound. "Hold your fire," he shouted.

On the deck, Aleksei Chekhov raised his gun. "Stop right there, Madam D.A. Don't take another step."

Marcie paid no attention to him.

"What the hell is she trying to do?" Paul muttered. "Take on the Russian mafia all by herself?"

Frank thought of Vinnie's warning a few days ago. *"There's a leak in the N.Y.P.D."* The leak wasn't in the NYPD. It was in the district attorney's office.

The leak was Marcie Hollander.

"She sold you out," he murmured. "She sold all of you—"

Gunfire erupted. Marcie's chest exploded, taking the full burst of fire from Aleksei's AK-47. She fell to her knees, stayed there for a short second, then hit the ground, face first.

"Marcie!" The sound that came out of Sergei's throat was like the wail of a wounded animal. Still holding Jenna, he turned to his brother, his face contorted with grief and rage. "You bastard!" he shouted in Russian. "You killed her!"

"She betrayed you," Aleksei shouted back. "She should have warned you they were coming."

With his free hand, Sergei reached inside his jacket, pulled out a Glock and shot Aleksei in the heart. Then, as though not giving a damn anymore, he threw his gun on the deck, shoved Jenna aside and ran down the gangway, toward Marcie, who lay on the ground, dead.

All hell broke loose. People on both sides started firing. One man on the deck of the *Arzamas* clasped his chest and fell on the dock. Within moments, the SWAT team had stormed the ship, taking down two more sailors before the rest of the crew surrendered.

Sergei never reached Marcie. No sooner had he left the gangway, that two officers grabbed him.

He fought them hard. "Let me see Marcie! She needs me! Let me see Marcie!"

They wrestled him to the ground and held him

there while a third man snapped his hands behind his back and handcuffed him.

Ignoring a cop's order to stand back, Frank took off at a dead run, taking the stairs two at a time. At the sound of the first gun shot, Jenna had run out of the line of fire, but where had she gone? "Jenna!" He ran between the containers, calling her name over and over.

"Here I am." She peeked from behind a container and glanced both ways before coming out and throwing herself in his arms.

"What took you so long?" she asked.

Forty-Seven

Although Detective Stavos had told Jenna her statement could wait until the following day, she had insisted on doing it while the events were still fresh in her mind. As calmly as possible, she had given him a moment by moment account of a day that had begun like no other and had just kept on getting worse.

While she and Frank were at the station, they had learned that the *Arzamas* belonged to a close friend of Aleksei's, a shipping magnate who had been transporting goods from the U.S. to Russia for the past decade.

As *Bratstvo's* operation in the United States came to a crashing halt and more arrests were expected, the acting district attorney had agreed with Detective Stavos and Lieutenant O'Dell that Raul and Slim would have to be let go, as per their agreement.

Roy Ballard was also released. When he heard of Jenna's efforts on his behalf, he had insisted on stopping by the homicide squad room to thank her personally.

By far the greatest shock to the financial community had been the news of J. B. Collins's duplicity. Following his arrest, Faxel's stock had plunged and all trading had stopped in an effort to prevent a total collapse.

After Jenna had given her statement and signed it, Frank had refused to let her go home, and had brought her to Vinnie's house instead. If his claim to never let her out of his sight again was true, they were in for a very interesting relationship.

Now, less than twenty-four hours after the ordeal that had devastated a family and shocked an entire city, Jenna sat in Vinnie's living room while Frank was in the kitchen making her tea. The house was quiet, but wouldn't be for long. Ricco and the Renaldis had left the Catskills at noon and would be arriving sometime this evening.

She didn't know where her father was. She had seen him on the ship, and for a moment, as he stood there, his eyes filled with tears of relief, she had wanted to run into his arms. Something had held her back. Maybe a lingering of pain and disappointment? The fear that nothing would ever be the same again? Before she could figure it out, he was gone.

Frank walked in carrying a cup of tea and a plate of pizzelle. Ever since they had returned from the police station, he had been waiting on her hand and foot, making sure she wasn't hungry, or thirsty, too cold or too hot.

"You're turning into your mother," she had told him.

At three o'clock, true to his promise, Detective Stavos arrived to give them the latest news. He declined a cup of tea but gladly said yes to a beer. There was no sign of the grumpiness that had become his trademark. On the contrary, he was quite pleasant, and happy to see how quickly Jenna had recovered.

Frank handed him a bottle of Heineken and set a

bowl of cashew nuts on the coffee table. "Is anyone talking yet?"

"J. B. Collins is keeping a tight lip, waiting for his attorney to return from a business trip. Sergei, on the other hand, is a broken man, and broken men talk."

"Was he in love with Marcie?" Jenna asked.

"And she with him, ever since they met at the Faxel party four years ago. She didn't know he was the head of *Bratstvo* then. Maybe if she had known, she wouldn't have allowed herself to do something so out of character. When she did find out, it was too late."

Jenna had always thought of Marcie as a happy, well-adjusted woman. How deceiving appearances could be.

Stavos looked down at his beer and his voice turned wistful. "For all that time, she was Sergei's eyes and ears. She told him everything that went on in the police department and warned him of any bit of information that filtered into the district attorney's office regarding *Bratstvo*."

"Why didn't she warn him the police were on their way yesterday?"

He shrugged. "I don't know. Maybe the fact that you, the daughter of a dear friend, had been kidnapped and would most surely be killed, finally jolted her out of that spell she was under. Or she knew that it was only a matter of time before the truth came out, and wanted to do one last good deed. She may also have been afraid that Sergei would be killed in the bloodshed and preferred to see him in prison than in a coffin." He gave a fatalistic shrug. "We'll never know."

"How did it all begin, Detective? How did Adam find out that Faxel was in bed with the Russians?"

"We're not sure of that either, but somehow, *Bratstvo* heard about his one-man campaign to bring Faxel down, and from that moment on, Adam Lear was a dead man."

He eyed the bowl of nuts before finally taking a small handful. "After Marcie showed Sergei the photos and he saw the tattoo, his number one priority was to find the other set of photographs, the one you had kept for yourself."

"How did he know I had another set?"

"He didn't. But you gave him every reason to believe that you had made finding Adam's killer your mission, so he assumed you had printed an extra set. Those photos saved your life, Jenna. As long as they couldn't find them, you were safe."

"But they tried to kill me!"

"That wasn't part of the plan. Pincho Figueras took that initiative all on his own. When he ran into you in the lobby of your apartment building, he knew you could identify him."

"Instead, it was his smell I identified."

Frank wrapped his arm around her shoulder. "Didn't I tell you she knew what she was talking about?"

"Yes, you did, and for the record, Jenna, I apologize."

But Jenna wanted to keep the conversation on Pincho, who, as of yesterday afternoon, hadn't yet been found. "So, he was part of the *Bratstvo* network, too?"

"Not really. Aleksei found him through word of mouth. Normally an organization of this size would choose a hit man from within, someone they had carefully groomed. However, occasionally, they look for outside talent. And Pincho was a man of many talents and many disguises, as we found out when we searched his apartment. One of those disguises, was a janitor's outfit, the one he probably wore when he killed Claire. That's why we couldn't find the second janitor one of the witnesses reported seeing."

"Where is he now?" Jenna prayed Stavos would say he was securely locked up and would never hurt anyone again.

"He's gone."

"Gone where?"

Paul shrugged. "No one knows. Maybe Aleksei knew, since he's the one who gave him his orders, but Aleksei is dead, so we might never find the man. All I'm sure of is that he brought you to the ship, per Aleksei's orders, and then vanished. I suspect he has enough money stashed somewhere to lead a long and happy life."

A long and happy life was not the fate Jenna had wished on Pincho Figueras.

Stavos continued to chew on his cashews. "You mentioned finding the names of two informants in your father's files?"

If he was aware of her father's brief indiscretion, he gave no indication of it. With any luck, that dirty little secret would remain just that—a secret. "I was hoping to find out who had ordered the attack on Frank," she said simply.

He smiled, as if the thought of a civilian undertaking such a task actually amused him. "You wouldn't have found them. Both men died after Marcie gave Sergei their names. Anton Plushenko

drowned during a fishing trip at the Jersey shore, and
Viktor Orloff fell in front of an oncoming train one
night while walking his dog.''

"Sergei had them killed?"

"No. Aleksei did.''

Jenna looked at Frank, who seemed as surprised
as she was.

"That was a clever ploy on the part of *Bratstvo*,"
Paul said. "Although Sergei was the head of the or-
ganization, the man behind the boy was Aleksei.
He's the one who really ran the show.''

"Then why wasn't he *Bratstvo's* chief?''

"Because the organization had been trying to re-
cruit more high-ranking military,'' Stavos explained.
"*Bratstvo* was changing its image, and aiming for a
more structured look. The brass figured that the only
way to do that was to appoint someone military men
and women admired. Sergei fit the bill perfectly. He
was brave, dedicated and charismatic. What he
lacked was the ruthlessness to head an organization
like *Bratstvo*, so they named Aleksei as deputy and
gave him all the power he needed.''

"So Sergei was just for show.''

"Something like that.''

"How did Faxel manage to get embroiled with the
Russian mafia?''

"According to Sergei, Faxel fell onto hard times
and *Bratstvo* saw that as a perfect opportunity to in-
filtrate yet another American company.''

"And J.B. just let it happen?''

"J.B. liked to live well. He owned expensive art
work, a private plane and several properties. When
he ran out of his own money, he started dipping into
company funds. That's when the trouble began. Al-

ways on the lookout for a good deal, *Bratstvo* found out about it and offered to bail him out in exchange for control of the company."

Jenna thought of the day J.B. had surprised her on her roof garden, and how she had believed him capable of anything. "Did he have Adam killed?"

"Aleksei did. He ordered all the hits and made sure they were executed."

"Claire, too?"

"Claire especially. The file she found in your ex-husband's office—which was bugged, by the way—could have unraveled the entire operation."

"But Adam didn't think he had enough proof to go to the authorities. That's why he wanted to see the photos."

"Adam didn't realize what he had. A list of what appeared to be phone numbers were actually scrambled numbers of various bank accounts throughout the world. The money has already been frozen. Al Quaeda will never see another penny of Faxel money."

Paul stood up. "I expect there will be more information trickling in, in the weeks and months to come, but for now, that's all I can tell you." He smiled. "Oh, I almost forgot. Detective Delano in Jersey City called me. Billy Ray cracked under Delano's pressure, just as I thought he would. Angie was right after all. Amber was driving the car that night, and Billy Ray, poor sap that he was, agreed to take the fall for her."

"Was he blackmailing her?"

"He was, but I doubt Delano will charge him with extortion. Angie would never speak to him again if he did."

Frank gave a shrug. "I can't say I feel sorry for Amber. The woman got exactly what she deserved. Where is she now?"

"In a Jersey City jail. *Sans* her inheritance."

Frank laughed. "Warren must be thrilled about that."

After he and Jenna had walked Paul to the door and seen him off, they went back inside. Just then, the phone rang and Frank went to answer it.

"Who was that?" Jenna asked when he returned from the kitchen.

"Your father. He wanted to know how you were doing, so I told him to come and see for himself."

She gave him a startled look. "You invited him here? Why?"

"Because he is your father, and he loves you, and this wall you've built between the two of you is killing him. I don't know what he did to make you so angry, and maybe that's none of my business, but your happiness is my business now, Jenna, and it's clear to me that this situation with your father is making you miserable. So when he gets here, the two of you are going to talk. Okay?"

"Do I have a choice in the matter?"

"No more than I had when you played Nurse Ratched."

"Is he coming over tonight?"

"He said he'd be here at about six. So will Beckie. She left a message earlier." He walked over to where Jenna was standing and wrapped his arms around her waist. "That's two whole hours to ourselves. We'll need to do something to pass the time. Any ideas?"

"I've got one." She leaned into him. "But I'm not sure you're up to the challenge."

He must have felt a lot stronger than she realized, because he lifted her off the floor and headed for the stairs. "Why don't we go and find out?"

She looked so beautiful, lying there with her eyes closed and her hair fanned out on his pillow, that for a moment, he was tempted to get back under the covers and make love to her again. Before he could talk himself in doing just that, he remembered that his family should be back any minute. Bending over Jenna, he kissed her lightly on the forehead, dressed quickly, then tiptoed out of the bedroom.

In the kitchen, he scribbled her a quick note. "Had to run to get some wine for dinner. If you feel like it, why don't you set the table? There will be seven of us, eight if your father stays. I hope he does."

In the liquor store's parking lot, he called Ricco. "Where are you now?" he asked.

"We just passed Hoboken, New Jersey. Here, your kid wants to talk to you."

"Hey, Dad!" Danny said when he came on the line. "Why don't you come and meet us so I can make the rest of the trip with you? Lydia and Oma are driving me crazy with their bickering."

Frank laughed. At last, life had returned to normal. "I guess I can do that, bud. Put Ricco back on."

When a meeting place had been designated, he called Jenna to let her know of the change of plans.

She was up. "Oh, that's fine," she said cheerfully. "Don't worry about me. I have everything under control."

Now what had she meant by that?

He found out an hour later when he and the rest

of the Renaldis walked into the house. His mother was the first to notice the smell.

"What's that smell?" she asked, twitching her nose.

Jenna came out to greet them. Vinnie's apron was wrapped around her waist and was splattered with tomato sauce and something else he couldn't recognize. Her face was also smudged with sauce, and a strand of her hair looked...burned? A closer look confirmed that it was indeed, burned.

"I hope you don't mind," she said, looking from Mia to Vinnie. "Frank is always accusing me of not being impulsive enough, so I did something impulsive."

"What did you do?" Mia's nose twitched again.

Jenna smiled brightly. "I knew you'd be tired from the trip, so I cooked us all dinner."